DESIGNING SAMANTHA'S LOVE

PJ FIALA

RT
ROLLING
THUNDER

DESIGNING SAMANTHA'S LOVE

by PJ Fiala
Third Edition February 2016
Second Edition February 2015
First Edition – Second Chances April 2013

Printed in the United States of America

First published 2014

Fiala, PJ

Designing Samantha's Love / PJ Fiala

p. cm.

1. Romance—Fiction. 2. Romance—Suspense. 3. Romance - General

I. Title – Designing Samantha's Love

eBook:

ISBN-10:1-942618-22-0

ISBN-13:978-1-942618-22-5

Paperback:

ISBN-10:1-942618-43-3

ISBN-13:978-1-942618-43-0

❀ Created with Vellum

DEDICATION

I've had so many wonderful people come into my life and I want you all to know how much I appreciate it. From each and every reader who takes the time out of their day to read my stories and leave reviews, thank you.

My family for the love and sacrifices they've made and continue to make to help me achieve this dream, especially my husband and best friend, Gene. Words can never express how much you mean to me. To our veterans and current serving members of our armed forces and police departments, thank you ladies and gentlemen for your hard work and sacrifices; it's with gratitude and thankfulness that I mention you in this forward.

BLURB

They both have so much to overcome to realize their second chance.

Nothing terrifies Samantha Powell more than starting over, but after devoting three decades to a troubled man and an unhappy marriage, Sam finds the courage to seek her own happiness. She imagines a nice quiet life filled with friends, family, and a career that leaves no room for relationship drama. Unfortunately, no one told the alluring Grayson Kinkaide.

After escaping a bad marriage of his own, Grayson realizes his soul mate is still out there and his heart is set on Sam. Their instant attraction begins a steamy affair, but the women of Grayson's past aren't ready to let him go. Grayson must convince Sam that she is the only one for him.

***

Let's stay in contact, join my newsletter so I can let you know about new releases, sales, promotions and more. https://www.subscribepage.com/pjfialafm

A YEAR AGO

"Hello?"

"Mrs. Powell, this is Officer Garrison. I'm calling to inform you that your husband has been in a car accident and is being transported to St. Mary's Hospital. Do you have someone who can drive you to meet him?"

"How is he? May I speak with him? Was anyone else hurt?" Samantha rubbed her forehead; she'd always feared this call would come.

"I'm sorry, ma'am; he's in the ambulance now and being transported."

"Can you tell me *any*thing, officer?"

"I'm sorry, Mrs. Powell, we are still processing the accident, and I am unable to comment further at this time. I'm sorry for being vague. Do you have a way to the hospital, ma'am? I don't want you driving if you're upset."

Sam glanced around her home, freshly cleaned this afternoon and unusually sparse of photographs and pictures since her husband, Tim, hated anything on the walls. It was only one of many arguments they'd had over the years.

"I'm home alone, but I'll be fine. I'll be careful." She pulled her phone from her ear to hang it up, then remembered the officer. "Ah, thank you, Officer Garrison. I appreciate the call."

Tapping the end call icon, Sam turned toward her desk. She snatched her purse from the the desk and pulled it open to grab her car keys from the side pouch as she made her way to the garage. The plethora of thoughts that ran through her mind were dizzying. Had Tim purposely hit someone to end it this time? He'd been so depressed again lately—refusing his medication and not seeing his psychologist again. This would be one more thing to send him deeper into his despair.

She tapped the button on her visor, and as the garage door opened, she tapped the Bluetooth icon on her dash.

"Call Josh."

She carefully navigated the steep hill which served as her driveway—another argument they'd had over the years. Tim claimed she wasn't careful when she pulled onto their road. Her jaw clamped tightly together as her stomach began a slow roll.

"Hey, Mom, what's up?"

Swallowing, she replied, "Josh, the police just called. Dad's been in an accident, and I'm on my way to the hospital. I'll call you when I know more, but can you call your brothers and let them know?"

"Shit! How bad this time?" The resolve in his voice clenched her stomach further.

Tears instantly sprang to her eyes. Her children had been down this road with her before, and she hated it. Even now, Josh didn't panic as much as he dreaded the fallout of this latest accident in a list of damaging behaviors Tim had exhibited over the years.

"I don't ..." She cleared her throat. "I'm not sure. Officer Garrison said he'd already been placed in the ambulance and that I should meet him at the hospital ... St. Mary's. So, I'm on my way there."

She fought the panic that threatened to rise in her throat as she listened to Josh exhale loudly. "I'll meet you there."

"Josh, don't worry until I call you back. The kids are probably just getting ready to go to bed; you should tuck them in and spend time with Tammy."

"It's okay, Mom. The kids are at a sleepover tonight at Tammy's sister's house. I'll be right there."

She listened as the call disconnected. Taking a deep breath and releasing it slowly, she navigated her car from her heavily-wooded, treelined road and onto the main road that would lead her quickly to the hospital. At eight o'clock-ish in the evening on a Monday, traffic would be light, and her trip would last a total of ten minutes.

Entering the emergency entrance of the hospital, her eyes darted around to locate a nurse or employee who could tell her where Tim was. She walked to the nurse's station and addressed the tired-looking nurse sitting in front of a computer. Her name badge boldly announced her name as Shari; the dark circles under her eyes said she'd put in a long day already.

"Hi. My name is Samantha Powell, and my husband Tim was just in a car accident and brought in or on his way in. Can you help me find him?"

Shari's light blue eyes held Sam's as her mouth turned down. "Let me see what I can find out for you." She stood and briefly glanced around. "Follow me, please."

Shari walked from behind the desk; her Crocs softly squeaked on the highly-polished floors. Sam silently followed as she fought the panic rising inside. She was lead to a darkened room which Shari illuminated by tapping a switch on the wall just inside the door. "Please take a seat in here, Mrs. Powell. I'll see if your husband has been brought in yet and come back right away."

Sam stepped into the softly-lit room, furnished only with a deep blue sofa and two red upholstered chairs with a table in between. Sighing heavily as Shari refused to meet her gaze further, Sam's fingers shook. The clock on the wall, one of the three wall decorations in this room, ticked off the seconds as her mind whirled.

Exactly five minutes and thirteen seconds later, Josh and Tammy entered the little room. Josh's handsome face was marred with worry, and Sam fought the tears that threatened once again. He was her spitting image in male form—green eyes and sandy blond hair. Though he was a foot taller, there was no denying his parentage. She jumped up and shivered when his strong arms squeezed her tight. "It'll be okay, Mom. Any word?"

She shook her head, embraced her daughter-in-law, Tammy, and motioned for them to sit with her. "Not a word, and I don't want to sound like an alarmist, but I don't have a good feeling about this. The nurse wouldn't look me in the eye."

Tammy leaned forward and folded her chilly hand in a soft embrace. "She could be tired. Or preoccupied with a million other things."

Sam scrunched her face and cleared her throat. "I'm sure you're right. I'll try not to borrow additional troubles."

Her sons, Gage and Jake, entered the room. They silently glanced around before immediately approaching her. "No word yet, boys." She hugged each one before they settled in to wait.

It was about thirty minutes before a doctor entered the now-cramped room. Noting no additional seating, he held up a finger and stated, "I'll be right back with another chair." He was back shortly, wheeling a flimsy looking desk chair into the room and promptly sat in it. He rested his forearms on his knees and folded his hands together. His eyes roved the room before landing on Sam.

She held her breath, waiting for the words she'd already assumed were coming. "Mrs. Powell, I'm your husband's attending physician, Doctor Sinclair. I'm very sorry to tell you that Mr. Powell didn't make it."

Choking back a sob, Sam glanced around at her sons watching carefully for their reactions. Gage teared up but sat stoically beside his brother on the sofa. Her eyes met his and held. Jake's raspy voice broke the silence in the room. "Can you tell us what happened?"

She swallowed as she sadly watched her sons processing the news that their father had died.

"I'm afraid all I can tell you is the medical side of things. The police will need to fill you in on the accident. In general terms, Mr. Powell died from a ruptured spleen. He was alive at the scene and rushed here, but he died in the ambulance. We tried to resuscitate once he arrived, but we were unable to. I'm very sorry."

1

"You should sign up for the same dating service I did. It's time you meet someone, Sam. It's been a year now," Jessie said.

Jessie was a perky little blonde with wavy hair and bright blue eyes. Her voluptuous body and her bubbly personality were hard to resist.

"I don't think a dating service is for me, Jess. I would hate having to start all over again—multiple times. I don't think I'm a kiss-as-many-frogs-as-you-can kind of girl," Samantha replied. "That being said, how was your date last night?"

Jessie's bright smile lit up the room. "Oh, it was great. He's funny and smart, and we talked all night. I don't think I got home until about three this morning. I'm seeing him again tonight—I can't wait!" She smoothed her blue blouse and tucked a blonde lock behind her ear.

Grinning, Sam replied, "I'm so happy for you, Jess. You deserve a great guy." Dropping her car keys into her purse, she continued, "Three in the morning, huh? Your day is going to drag."

Giggling, Jess responded, "It might, but totally worth it. I'll be thinking about him all day."

Sam grinned as she made her way back to her office. Jessie was a great person to see first thing in the morning. No matter what her mood, she could brighten your day. Hopefully, this boyfriend would work out for her. The last one had cheated on her and broke her heart, right after Tim had died. The women helped each other out in their respective grief. Jess, ten years younger than Sam, had been married at one time but had already been divorced when Sam began working at the law office five years ago. She now lived vicariously through Jessie and her boyfriends. Not that Jessie was a tramp—far from it—but she was always trying out dating services and dated a lot. She continuously tried to encourage Sam to sign up on one of those sites, but so far, she just couldn't bring herself to do it.

As her computer booted up, she mentally clicked over her day. It was Tuesday, meaning Mrs. Koeppel was coming in. The feisty little lady, in her mid-eighties, was full of spunk. Sam had some documents for the spritely woman to sign; then she was meeting with one of the attorneys for additional work to be done on her rentals.

****

Grayson Kinkaide woke early; he'd always been an early riser. He'd drink his cup or two of coffee in the morning while reading the paper and then another cup while heading to the office before anyone else arrived. He'd worked hard to build his architectural business. After spending years in a horrible marriage, he'd decided it was time to break free, not just from the sham of a marriage, but from his father-in-law's business as well.

Gray and Suzanne had been divorced for seven years, and Gray still worked hard to feel in control of his life. He fought the bitterness that crept in as he watched his best friend, Caleb; his brother, Jamie; and his sister, Dani, with a special someone in their lives. He was grateful they were happy and had found their other half, but he'd never found that special someone to complete him.

Of course, he'd felt guilty for his bitter thoughts, especially when five years ago, Jamie's wife died of cancer. He wondered why he'd ever begrudged Jamie any happiness at all. He still had to work on a lot of issues. By throwing himself into his work to build the business he'd always dreamed of, he was finally accomplishing just that.

Today, as a matter of fact, he and his son Jackson were meeting with his friend, Bill, an attorney in town, to discuss further business expansion. Jax was now home from serving in the Army, and Gray wanted to add an arm to the Kinkaide Architecture and Engineering firm—demolition.

Jax had been working as a demolition specialist for about a year, and the demolition jobs were bringing more work to the firm, so it seemed the time was right.

******

Around 9:50, Jess buzzed Sam's office. "Mrs. Koeppel is here for you, Sam."

Smoothing her soft gray top as she made her way down the hallway, Sam let out a shallow breath and rounded the corner. There sat Mrs. K, prim in her deep red suit and her black walking shoes, her ankles crossed. She was old-fashioned in some ways, very forward in others; if something was on her mind, you'd hear it.

Having been widowed herself, now eighty-four and married to her second husband, Albert, Mrs. K was someone to aspire to be like. She and Albert had what seemed like a nice relationship and proof that second chances exist.

"Good morning, Mrs. K. How are you today?"

"Oh, my dear, I'm doing very well. Nothing like having a man dote on a woman to put a smile on her face."

The smile spread across her wrinkled face and Sam couldn't help but grin back.

"It looks good on you, too. I assume Alfred is in the car waiting."

"Yes, dear. He says it's my money and I should do with it what I want."

"He's quite the catch." She kneeled in front of Mrs. K. to help her with her shoes. "Once again, I must compliment you on your outfit, Mrs. Koeppel. Your brooch is beautiful," she added as she pulled the side table forward and set the papers for her to sign in the middle.

Mrs. K smiled and murmured, as if it were a secret, "Tell me, my dear, have you met anyone special yet? I can tell you, having a good man in your life is very nice."

Why did everyone keep asking that question? The thought terrified Sam. Starting all over with someone—meeting family, kids, and grandkids, learning their likes and dislikes—was all so overwhelming.

She smirked. "Mrs. Koeppel, if God wants me to have a man in my life, He's going to have to have him walk right through that front door. I don't go anywhere but here and home, so those are my choices."

Mrs. K and Jessie both giggled as Sam clicked open a pen and handed it to Mrs. K.

"You'll find someone, I'm convinced. I even dreamed about it last night." Her sly smile appeared again as she looked through her bifocals at the papers in front of her. "Where do I sign, dear?"

"Oh, so now you're dreaming about me finding someone? Don't you have anything more interesting to think about before you drift off each evening?" Sam pointed to the line at the bottom of the page.

Laughing heartily, the older woman slapped her hand on her knee. "Oh, now and then. But, I can also be a bit psychic, you know."

Sam smiled softly as she watched her favorite client sign her name, though mostly illegible, across the bottom of the page. "You sure do know how to pair your shoes to your outfits, Mrs. K. We could learn a thing or two from you."

Jessie giggled. "Isn't that the truth?" She sat behind the reception desk watching the two women.

Mrs. K finished signing and handed the pen to Sam. She took the proffered pen, picked up the papers and started moving the table back to its spot, when Jessie waved her away, moving the table for her. "I'll let Mr. Patz know you're here, and I'll see you later to say goodbye, Mrs. K." The older woman nodded and picked up a magazine from the coffee table.

Walking back to her office, Sam's thoughts turned to Tim. They'd been married for almost twenty-nine years. When they met, they'd instantly connected, got along well, and she thought he had a great sense of humor. They liked many of the same things and enjoyed spending time with friends. A year after being married, they were overjoyed when she became pregnant with Josh.

Gage came next, and about four-and-a-half years later, they had Jake. Things seemed to be going along well, but Tim was especially passive where his mother was concerned. She constantly butted into their lives. Whenever Tim and Sam would make decisions as a couple—like married people do—about the kids or the house or vehicles, she would step in and decide something different. It didn't matter what it was; Tim would just roll over and agree with her. She and Tim fought about that the most. Her thoughts, feelings, and decisions were just second to Tim's mother's, and there was no getting around it. No matter how many times she cried, he would not— maybe could not—tell his mother to back off. Shaking her head of the morose thoughts, she poured over the documents she was proof-reading for one of the attorneys.

At ten forty-five, Jessie buzzed Sam. "Mrs. K is leaving soon."

"I'll be right up," she responded. Picking up her desk phone, Sam dialed Alfred's number. "Good morning, Alfred. Mrs. Koeppel is finished with her appointment ... Of course, I enjoy taking care of her. I'll see you in a few minutes." Sam hung up the phone and turned toward her office door and the reception area.

Mrs. K was already in a chair and chatting away with Jessie. When Sam rounded the corner, the front door opened, and Sam stopped in her tracks when she saw two men walking in. The first man was impossibly handsome—dark hair with a smattering of gray at the temples and threaded throughout, longer on top and shorter on the neck, but long enough that it brushed his collar and curled up just a bit. He had a perfect nose and full, kissable lips. He laughed at the man with him. Oh, my—that smile!

Her stomach spun. His warm, brown eyes—the kind she was sure she could gaze into all day—crinkled at the corners. *Dreamy.*

He stopped abruptly as his eyes landed on hers and held tight. The man walking in behind him bumped into him, pushing him forward.

Sam took that opportunity to quickly kneel in front of Mrs. K and tie the lace on her shoe.

Her face burned brightly. Stupid hormones. Mr. Gorgeous' voice —deep and sexy—floated over her as he spoke to Jessie. "Grayson Kinkaide and my son, Jackson, here to see William Chase."

"Please take a seat. I'll let Mr. Chase know you're here. May I get you something to drink?" Jess asked.

"No, thank you. We're fine," he replied.

Grayson sat in a chair across the coffee table from Mrs. K. Each time Sam lifted her gaze to look at him, he was watching her. Her hands shook slightly, and her body tingled with awareness.

Having a hard time concentrating on what she was doing, her shaking fingers made the simple task of tying a shoe overly difficult. Mrs. K chuckled slightly and cleared her throat. *Oh, my God!* Sam held her breath and jerked her head upward. When Mrs. K had something on her mind, she didn't hesitate to say it.

"Mr. Kinkaide, did you say? Are you married, Mr. Kinkaide?"

And ... there it was. Sam didn't think her face could flush more than it had already. The burn continued, and she held her breath. It seemed like time stood still as they waited for him to answer. She was afraid to look up and see the expression on his face.

Finally, after what felt like an eternity, he chuckled and said, "No, I'm not married."

Mrs. K quickly added, "Really? Are you seeing anyone?"

Not able to control herself, Sam whispered, "Mrs. Koeppel! What are you doing?"

She heard the two handsome men chuckle and Mrs. K tried

unsuccessfully to look embarrassed. Grayson replied, "No, I'm not seeing anyone. Did you want to ask me out?"

Sam was shocked to hear the humor in his voice, and her face reflected just that when she looked up at him. It only made everyone laugh.

Mrs. Koeppel was in prime form this morning. The gleam in her eye and the smile on her face said it all.

"Well, I can't wait to tell Alfred I was just asked out on a date; he's going to love that one. Well, maybe I wasn't asked out, but the innuendo was there," she giggled, giving Sam a wink. Grayson frowned, feigning disappointment.

"Alfred! Are you telling me you're already taken, Mrs. Koeppel?"

Oh, so handsome. Sam allowed herself to glance his way. His teasing smile and dark brown eyes held her gaze. He appeared to be having a good time with the charade. He glanced at Mrs. Koeppel and then at Sam. Jackson chuckled. He had the same half-grin as his dad as he watched the show playing out before him.

Mrs. Koeppel grinned. "Oh, thank you so much for making me feel so young and flirty today, Mr. Kinkaide. That feels good. Alfred is my husband, for about fifteen years now. I was asking you because just about an hour ago, Sam here, told me that if God wanted her to meet someone, he would have to walk right through that door, and here you are!"

Oh, no! She did *not* just say that. There wasn't a place close enough to crawl and hide from her embarrassment. Sam's face grew redder than it had ever been before if that was even possible; the heat caused dampness to form between her breasts and under her arms.

Horrified, Sam snapped her head up and looked at Mrs. Koeppel.

"What on earth are you doing? Please, Mrs. Koeppel, don't ..."

Mrs. K put her hand under Sam's chin, ensuring she was looking right at her, and said, "My dear girl, I've watched you this past year deal with your husband's death. You've grown, you've started making a different life for yourself, and you've continued through all the pain and sorrow. Now, it's time for you to have some fun, enjoy life again, and meet new people. I had the feeling you wouldn't have spoken a word to Mr. Kinkaide, and he would have walked out, not knowing you're available. I'm just trying to, at the very least, make an introduction. The rest is up to you and him."

Sam dropped her head onto Mrs. Koeppel's knees, mortified and afraid to look at anyone.

The front door opened again and Alfred walked in. He chuckled and said, "It looks like maybe I'm too late to keep Marjorie from embarrassing you. Sorry, Sam."

At least she had someone here to help change the subject—sort of. Jessie giggled and began relating the whole embarrassing event to Alfred. Sam continued with Mrs. Koeppel's shoe—the faster, the better—to get her out of there. She had teased Sam in the past, and everyone always laughed about it later, but this was just too much.

Alfred chuckled and shuffled closer to the two men and extended his hand. They both smiled and stood up for the handshake. Alfred glanced quickly to Mrs. Koeppel and back to Grayson.

"You know, she just thinks everyone should be happy and have someone to share their life with. We had both been widowed and alone for so long when we met that neither of us realized how lonely we had been. Now, she's determined to make sure that others living that same way are enlightened. When she can, she tries to do something about it. Besides, we both like Sam; she's a special person."

He said the last with a wink at Sam, to which she sweetly smirked. It was very nice to hear that they both liked her. Sam looked at Alfred and mouthed, "*Thank you.*"

Grayson and Jackson returned to their seats. Alfred shuffled over to Mrs. Koeppel and Sam. Still feeling self-conscious, she glanced at Grayson who still watched her. She saw Jackson lean over and whisper something to his dad, and Gray furrowed his brow and sat back quickly. His expression was thoughtful, but he continued watching Sam intently.

She cleared her throat. "Mrs. Koeppel, did you wear a jacket this morning?"

"Yes, dear, I did."

Mrs. K smiled and winked at Sam. Over time, Mrs. Koeppel and

Sam had many conversations about her desire to see Sam happy and about how happy she was when she'd met Alfred.

With a sigh, Sam said, "I'll go get your jacket."

Thinking that maybe a little humor would keep her body from spontaneously combusting, Sam turned to the group but looked at Mrs. Koeppel and said, "While I'm out of the room, try as hard as you can to not marry me off to the next person who walks through the door. Some decisions should be left to me."

The whole room laughed, and Sam felt a little better about having to return to that room with everyone staring at her.

The conversation started up again as Sam rounded the corner to the coat closet to retrieve Mrs. Koeppel's jacket. Grayson's voice was beautiful—deep and smooth—like fine silk winding its way around her. When she returned, the mood in the room seemed a bit lighter. Mrs. Koeppel struggled to stand up, and Sam leaned down to help her steady herself.

Sam held out her right arm, bent at a 45-degree angle so Mrs. K could use it as an anchor. Grayson jumped up. "May I help?"

Her heart beat faster and she blushed, but she smiled up at him and heard him suck in a breath.

"Thank you, but we have a routine here."

He continued to stand—a little closer than before—and Alfred shuffled over to close the distance between Mrs. Koeppel and himself.

As he walked, he said, "In our advanced years, there are certain things our bodies just don't want to do for us any longer, and helping each other stand is just one of those things. But we get by, don't we, Marge?"

Mrs. Koeppel beamed up at him and winked. Boy, she was a flirt, wasn't she? She hugged Sam and patted her back.

"See you soon, dear. David is working on some estate planning documents for me, and I'll be back in a week or two to sign them. I'll see you then."

Smiling, Sam returned Mrs. Koeppel's hug. "I'll make sure to watch for you." She held onto Sam's arm while Alfred walked to her other side and put his arm out for her to grab it. Sam stepped back and allowed them to walk toward the door. They were extremely cute together.

Grayson had stepped in front of them to open the door. "It was very nice meeting you both."

If one could call a man beautiful, this man was certainly that!

Mrs. Koeppel replied, "Mr. Kinkaide, she really is a wonderful person. Don't let this opportunity pass you by." She winked, and a smile spread across his face.

Sam couldn't imagine any woman could resist that smile. Grayson replied, "I promise you, I will make every effort not to let the opportunity pass me by." Sam's eyes grew wide, and her mouth was ajar as she gaped at the three of them. Jessie giggled, and Sam scowled.

Jessie smiled broadly and winked. "That Mrs. Koeppel sure knows how to make an exit."

Grayson turned to walk back into the room as Bill Chase entered the lobby from behind Sam. He watched the elderly couple leave and nodded. "I see you've met Mrs. Koeppel and Alfred. They're a cute couple, aren't they?"

Grayson smiled. *Oh, my God, that smile!* He nodded at Bill. His eyes were so beautiful—dark like black coffee, thick lashes and sexy crinkles at the edges. A sigh escaped Sam, and Bill gave her a sideways glance. She blushed again and said a mental *Crap.*

Bill walked forward and shook hands with Grayson and Jackson. Sam was rooted to the spot just watching them—him.

Bill greeted his guests. "Gray, it's about time I got you to come to me for legal assistance. I was beginning to wonder if I could ever talk you into it."

Grayson smiled as Jackson stood. "Well, Grandpa was insistent that we use his attorney over the years, but now that he's retiring, we felt we could make a move," Jackson offered.

Bill turned to lead the way to the conference room, which was her cue to stop gaping and go back to work. Glancing at Jessie—who still wore a grin on her face—she shook her head and turned to walk back to her office. Grayson spoke up, "Sam, may I have a word with you?"

She froze in her tracks, took a deep breath, and slowly turned around to face him. Bill looked first at Grayson and then at Sam with a furrow in his brow.

"Is there anything wrong, Gray?"

Jackson put his hand on Bill's shoulder and chuckled as he said, "I'll fill you in on our interesting visit so far."

Bill and Jackson continued to the conference room.

At a loss at what to say or do when Grayson spoke, she stared at him until he said, "Is there somewhere we can talk in private?"

She opened her mouth to speak, but nothing came out. Clearing her throat and smiling, she tried again. "Sure, we can go to the small conference room."

Leading the way, her heart raced, and her face continued to burn. She reached into the darkened room and flipped the light switch, illuminating the small sterile room. A picture of a landscape decorated one wall; two black floating shelves were on the other. The upper shelf held a red vase with nothing in it. The lower shelf held a tablet, a red pen, and a telephone. The round black table in the center of the room was barren of anything indicating no one ever used this room. For the first time since working here, Sam felt a bit embarrassed at the starkness present here. Clearly, a man like this one was used to more luxury.

He entered behind her and closed the door, and she turned to face him. In the enclosed room, the aroma of his cologne, which was clean and fresh and reminded her of the Old Spice her grandfather wore, filled her senses and goose bumps danced on her arms. She squared her shoulders and lifted her gaze to his.

His dark brown eyes held hers, the faint crinkles at the edges slightly pronounced in the overhead lighting. Standing this close to him, the broadness of his chest and height seemed to diminish the small room further, and if she hadn't been so turned on being this close to him, she'd almost be afraid of the way he looked into her eyes.

He smiled and swiped his hand through his hair, causing the

graying strands to sparkle in the light. Such a contrast to the darkened hair that hadn't turned yet.

Her nerves made it impossible to stand still; her heart hammered and the butterflies continued to flutter in her tummy. She blurted out, "I'm sorry about Mrs. Koeppel. I hope she didn't embarrass you or make you feel obligated to—"

He held his hand up and smiled. "I think you were the one who was embarrassed, and if you don't mind me pointing it out, I thought you were adorable."

Surprise rounded her eyes, and her throat grew incredibly dry. "Adorable?" she squeaked out.

He chuckled. "The reason I wanted to speak with you privately is that I noticed how embarrassed you were and I didn't want to embarrass you further. I would like to take you to dinner. Are you free this evening?"

Stunned and excited, she blurted out, "Please don't feel obligated to ask me out because of Mrs. Koeppel. It really isn't necessary."

He smiled. "I don't feel obligated at all. We both have to eat, and it would be nice to get to know you a little better. What do you say?"

She couldn't *say* anything. Her mouth flopped open and quickly closed, before opening again.

Gray's smiled widened. He raised a brow, cocked his head, and patiently waited for her to respond.

Taking a shaky breath, she responded, "I would like that very much."

"Excellent." He pulled his phone from his pocket, tapped a few times and said, "What's your number?"

She quickly responded, but her mind was whirling. She watched his fingers deftly add her to his contacts and was impressed at his speed. He glanced up briefly and asked, "Where's your phone?"

She lightly shook her head and blinked. "On my desk."

Reaching into his shirt pocket, he pulled out his business card and handed it to her. "Put my number in your phone as soon as you get back to your desk." One side of his mouth hitched up. "I'll pick you up at seven tonight. Once you have my phone number in your phone, please text me your address."

Recovering from her stupor, she nodded.

He turned, opened the door, and stood aside to let her precede him. Gathering her thoughts as she walked down the hall, she realized there would be a whole afternoon of questions and smirks from Jessie. She stopped in front of the conference room door and motioned with her hand that this was his stop.

He paused before turning the doorknob, and silkily said, "I'm looking forward to seeing you later."

Oh, my God, so sexy. Her lips trembled. "I'm looking forward to seeing you as well." Her heart hammered in her chest, and her knees slightly trembled. It had been more than thirty years since she'd been on a date—before life had beaten her up. This was a whole new game now.

"Don't forget to text me your address or I *will* come looking for you when my meeting is finished." He winked and disappeared into the conference room.

Holy crap! There was no way she'd make it through the whole date. She was so befuddled around this man, she found it difficult to speak—let alone form complete sentences.

2

After answering a million questions from Jessie, Sam returned to her office and put Gray's number into her phone. She tapped out his number to text him her address. Feeling a bit spunky, she added, *Don't be late or I'll need to come looking for you when my day is through.* Before she could change her mind, she hit *send* and was immediately nervous that perhaps she'd been too forward.

Is there a way to retrieve a text message once it's sent? She'd need to check on that. So far, it seemed like being around Grayson Kinkaide made her behave like a complete and total idiot, not to mention it made her a little queasy and hot. She felt the burn of embarrassment again as she thought about it. This probably wasn't a very good idea.

Around three, Jessie knocked on Sam's office door. "Do you have any errands?"

Sam smiled. "Nothing today, Jess."

She hesitated a moment before asking, "Are you excited about your date or are you nervous?"

Sam looked up from her paperwork and asked, "What do you think?"

Jessie grinned. "You seem nervous and look like you might run away."

Sam huffed out a breath. "I thought I could easily text Gray and tell him that I had a family issue that needed to be tended to. That would probably make him feel better since he was obviously only asking me out because Mrs. Koeppel made him feel like he should."

"Why would you think such a thing? My God, Sam, he couldn't keep his eyes off you. I thought he was immediately taken by you. When Mrs. Koeppel started in on dating and such, he had such humor in his eyes. He probably wanted to hug and kiss her for giving him an *in* to ask you out."

Sam frowned and whispered, "I suppose so."

But she didn't believe it.

Jessie soberly looked at Sam and asked, "You're going to go, aren't you?"

It took Sam a while to decide what to say, and Jessie spoke in a tone that brooked no argument. "You're the one who's been saying the dating pool is very shallow and you hadn't seen anyone anywhere that you would even consider dating. Now, this gorgeous man walks right into our office, which, by the way, you said had to happen for you to know that God wanted you to date, and you're considering not going?" She gratefully took a breath and shoved her blonde bangs from her forehead. "I'm so shocked that you would throw this opportunity away. I could shake you! Geez, Sam, haven't you learned anything from watching me wade through this dating pool? I've kissed more frogs than I ever dreamed a girl would have to do, all hoping to find love, and you have this chance here, and you might not take it?" She planted her hands on her hips. "Well, I'll tell you what, you WILL go. If I have to show up at your house, drag you into the shower, and get you dressed, you will go!"

Jessie turned and stomped out of the office. Sam's thoughts were all over the board; she must have walked through some time continuum or something last night. Today was certainly the weirdest day she'd ever had.

. . .

******

Gray worried the remainder of the day that Sam would change her mind. Funny, he never worried about a woman changing her mind before. If he wanted, he would just find another one. Since he'd been divorced, he didn't look for a relationship—just random sex when he needed it, and that was that.

He received a text and took a deep breath before looking at it. He breathed a sigh of relief when it was his brother, Jamie. There was *something* about Sam he couldn't put his finger on. She seemed different. His response to her was unlike anything else. He knew today his life was forever changed in that one moment, and he was clueless as to why or how it was. He was breathless and unable to look away from her, for fear if he did, she would disappear. That was one thing, but when she dropped to her knees in front of Mrs. Koeppel, Gray thought he would lose it right then and there. She looked submissive and eager to please. He had to concentrate to keep his breathing steady. When Jax leaned over and asked him if he was okay, Gray realized he wasn't doing a very good job of it. He couldn't help it. His body instantly responded to her.

He spent the rest of the day trying to concentrate, but he found it difficult to do so. He barely remembered his meeting with Bill and Jax. The remainder of the afternoon, Jax had unrelentingly teased him. Gray just shook his head. He didn't know what this was, but it was powerful, and it was new and exciting, and he couldn't wait to explore it.

******

Sam arrived home at five-thirty; her stomach rolled as she jumped into the shower. She took her time to make sure she was shaved and polished—not that anything would happen. She never did the casual sex thing—it seemed seedy and whorish. She needed an emotional connection with someone to have sex with them, but a girl feels better about herself when she's ready and clean, so she went through all the motions.

She sparingly applied her makeup. Since getting older, makeup seemed to accentuate rather than hide the small lines around her mouth and eyes. Contemplating calling her best friend, Pam, to tell her about her date, she ultimately decided she'd wait to see how it turned out.

Glancing at the clock, her stomach rolled again. Placing her hand over it to settle the rumble, she strolled to her closet to pick out something to wear. She'd forgotten to ask Gray where they were going, so she could dress appropriately, then remembered the little black dress rule, so little black dress it was. If Gray got here and was dressed in jeans, she could change.

She finished her outfit off with her usual—a gold bracelet and diamond stud earrings. Since she was as ready as she was going to be, she thought a glass of wine might help to alleviate some of her nervousness. She padded to the kitchen to pour herself a drink, but the doorbell rang before she got there. She took a couple deep breaths to calm herself, then another because the others didn't seem to be working. Before she hyperventilated, she thought she'd better just stop and answer the door. Here goes ...

Opening the door to the most beautiful sight she'd ever seen, she sighed. Gray stood in the doorway, wearing black dress pants and a nice white shirt—the top two buttons opened. He had his hands in his pockets and a beautiful smile on his face. Yikes! She was going to have to work hard to not make a complete fool of herself tonight. After several moments frozen in place staring at one another, Gray's smile widened, and he said, "I didn't want to be late and have you running around trying to find me."

The deep sexy tone of his voice floated over her and caused goose bumps to rise on her arms.

She sucked in a breath. It took a minute to realize he was teasing her about her comment earlier today. She giggled. He cleared his throat and lifted a brow.

"Come in. I'm glad I don't have to spend my evening hunting you down because, to be honest with you, I wouldn't have a clue where to look."

He walked in and glanced around the house.

She led him into the living room quickly darting her eyes around the room to make sure everything was in place. He said, "You have a beautiful home, Sam. I wondered all day what kind of home you had."

She turned to look at him, her brows knit together.

"Is that the architect in you talking?"

He looked amused. "Partly. I was wondering about you as well, of course. After all, if I'd have gotten here only to find that you lived in some dark, damp dungeon with no windows, I may have had to cancel—afraid to come in and all."

She laughed when she thought of him nervously walking up to a dark, damp dungeon with no windows. "Good point. I guess I never thought of that and how men probably wonder about that stuff when meeting someone at their home for the first time. I was just wondering if I had time for a glass of wine before you got here. Would you like a glass or should we get going?"

The smile on his face brought out slight dimples in his cheeks, and she had to steel herself from whimpering at the sight. "Do you always have a glass of wine before a date?"

"Well, I wouldn't know since I haven't been on a date in over thirty years. But I had hoped it would calm my nerves a bit."

His smile never wavered. "You're nervous to go out with me?"

Sam put her head down and looked at the floor. She twisted her fingers together and let out a long breath, wishing she were better at knowing what to say and when to say it. Some people were just gifted like that. He placed his hand under her chin, gently pulling her head up to face him. Her skin was hot where he touched her. It felt like an electrical current running down her body all the way down to her toes.

When their eyes met, the sensations that skittered down her spine made her shiver. "I'm nervous, too. Every time I got a text message today, I was afraid to look at it because I was worried you would cancel on me."

Sam opened her mouth to say something, but, once again, words didn't come easy. "I thought about doing that. I thought you might feel relieved not to have to take me out. Mrs. Koeppel did kind of make you feel obligated. You were kind enough not to say it, but she did push."

The light from the windows sparkled in the deep brown depths of his eyes, the dark lashes framing them a perfect complement. *She could only imagine what it might be like to wake up and see them first thing in the morning. Whoa!*

Sam held her breath as Gray ran the pad of his thumb over her bottom lip. Oh, my God, that made her pulse race and a tightness pull in her lower core. Still gazing at each other, she worried that if she didn't start breathing normally soon, she would pass out from oxygen deprivation. That would impress the hell out of him, wouldn't it? Although she was pretty sure he was used to having women swoon over him, *she* didn't want to be one of them.

*****

Gray's eyes swished over her lips. The need to kiss her was overwhelming. Jesus, but he was in way over his head here. He bent slowly and very gently placed a light kiss on her soft lips.

He stood up, backed up about a half a step, then offered, "I asked you out because I wanted to, not because I felt obligated, Sam. The second I walked in the door and saw you, I was stopped in my tracks. When you looked at me, your green eyes ran straight through me, and I lost my breath. Good thing Jax was behind me to run into me and make me breathe again."

He smiled at her as he watched the emotions play on her face. Surprise and nervousness seemed to be the primary ones. Her short hair perfectly complemented her oval face. Her lightly glossed lips trembled as they spoke. He underestimated her inexperience in the dating world, thinking earlier that she was playing coy. Now, however, he could see that she was the real deal.

"Maybe we should leave now and head to the restaurant. If I stay here alone with you and add alcohol to the mix, I may not be able to control myself," he offered softly.

He winked and stepped back, allowing her to lead the way. He couldn't help that his eyes landed on her backside, just briefly, before taking in her straight posture and sexy legs. He was a lucky man.

3

Walking to his SUV Sam silently worried about gracefully stepping up into it with a dress and heels. It sported twenty-two-inch rims which made the Escalade tall. At only five-three with heels on, she was no match. He quickly stepped around her and pressed the fob in his hand, unlocking the door, and much to her relief, releasing floor boards from their hiding places. He held his hand to offer his assistance, and she fluidly stepped up and sat in the vehicle. She watched as he walked around the front of the vehicle admiring the entire package. He appeared confident and smooth, and he oozed a sex appeal she'd thought only existed in the movies. *Damn*! She might need to pinch herself to make sure this was real.

He climbed into the driver's side and settled in his seat. As he turned the key in the ignition, he asked, "What kind of music do you like to listen to?"

She giggled, "I love rock and roll. Kid Rock is one of my favorites, but I like Bon Jovi, Aerosmith, Lynyrd Skynyrd, Bryan Adams, Ozzy Osbourne ... I also like some country and Josh Groban and Andrea Bocelli when I need some peaceful, quiet music. What do you like to listen to?"

Gray's smile spread across his face. "Would you believe that I love the same music as you? Not kidding, that's exactly what I listen to. I have my iPod plugged in, and you'll find all of that music and more on there. Would you like me to start with anything in particular?"

Sam chuckled and shook her head. "Anything you want to listen to is fine with me."

He picked up his iPod, tapped a couple of times and soon Kid Rock's "Born Free"—one of her personal favorites—floated from the sound system. Finding it hard to keep still but ever mindful of the fact that singing wasn't a strength of hers, she simply mouthed the words and nodded her head to the rhythm.

"We have something in common!" he chuckled as he put the SUV in reverse and backed from the driveway.

On the ride to the restaurant, she inquired, "Tell me about your business."

He smiled. "As you know, I own Kinkaide Architects and Engineering. I'm an architect and employ several others—my son, Ethan, being one of them. Caleb Locke, my best friend, was the engineer. He started the company with me; however, about a year and a half ago, Caleb had some health issues and asked me to buy him out. He had headed up the engineering division until then. Now my brother, Jamie, does. Jax heads up the demolition company, which is just in the first year of business. During his last deployment in the Army, Jax, Jamie, and I began talking about starting the demolition business, and it's already showing signs of becoming a huge success."

He navigated a corner and smoothly merged into traffic.

"Ethan, my youngest, was also military—the Army—and served in Afghanistan. He wanted to serve but didn't enjoy Army life. He served for seven years, then came home and completed his degree. He came into the family business, which, of course, I am extremely happy about.

"My daughter, Sarah, also works with us at the firm as an accountant. Sarah and her husband, Cole, have two children: Lily is six and Lincoln is three."

She enjoyed the pride in his voice and the serene look on his face as he talked about his children. "Cole is Caleb's son, so it truly is a family business."

"You're fortunate to be so close to them and share the business with them."

"I am indeed. It's beyond my wildest dreams."

Gray pulled into the parking lot of the restaurant. Walking in, he kept his hand on Sam's lower back. His heated touch did funny things to her body. After being seated, they each ordered a glass of wine, chuckling after the conversation at the house. The waitress left menus for each of them. Sam looked around and caught the eye of a few women glancing their way, who quickly looked away from her gaze. She glanced at Gray, who seemed oblivious to the secret looks, which she took as either he was used to it or he didn't care. She hoped it was the latter.

Not sure what she'd be able to eat, she searched the menu.

"The steak here is superb if you like meat. If not, they also have fabulous pasta dishes," Gray offered.

Looking into his eyes over the menu, she marveled at the earnestness in them. He made her feel like a silly schoolgirl and a sexy woman at the same time.

The waitress came back with their wine and took their orders, each settling on steak.

While they relaxed and waited for their meal, Gray asked, "Tell me, what do you do at the law office?"

"I manage the office, mostly keeping track of the HR functions and running interference with any issues that might come up. I'm also a paralegal, so I fill in during the busy times."

"What about your kids? Any of them work in the legal profession?"

Laughing, she answered, "No. I have three sons. Joshua and his wife, Tammy, live about thirty minutes away in the outskirts of Pulaski. They have eleven acres and play around with trucks and four-wheelers all the time. They have two children—Abby is six and Dodge is four." She giggled. "We both have grandsons named after cars."

Gray laughed. "We do. Another thing in common."

Sam continued. "Josh was in the Army and saw conflict in Iraq. Gage lives fairly close to me in Harmony and just started dating a girl recently, but he's still at the stage where he doesn't want to jinx anything. He won't tell me a thing, no matter how hard I try to get him to spill. Jake and his wife, Ali, are both recently home from the Army where Jake spent nine months in Afghanistan and was heavily involved in conflict. But he seems to be handling it well so far, and I hope that continues. They're both in school—Ali for business management and Jake for his general eds right now. He's trying to decide what he wants to do."

"It took my kids a little while to figure it out for themselves." He sat forward, placing his forearms on the table. "Mrs. Koeppel mentioned you're widowed. Was your marriage a happy one?"

Sam was surprised by the question, and it took her a minute to form an answer. Finally, with her thoughts together, she told him about Tim—all of it. Tilting her head to the side, she softly said, "I've never talked about all of that with anyone. It's too personal. Thank you for listening."

Her eyes searched his for condemnation, irritation, or revulsion. She found none of those. "What about your marriage. Were you happy?"

He took a deep breath. "I had an awful marriage. I was in the Army, which is where I learned about drafting and architecture. I came home and went to college. My last year in college, I met Suzanne. My friends and I were out at a club one evening when Suzanne and a group of her friends walked in. I thought she was very pretty and soon my friends and I and Suzanne and her friends were talking. She was in her first year of college as an art major. That night, I went home with her, and from that point on, we started dating. Things seemed fine—not great, but fine. We got along and enjoyed some of the same activities. My friends and some of her friends also hooked up, so we had mutual friends to go out with. Months later, I realized we only went out with groups of people and didn't spend any time alone together. She was insistent that her father introduce me to people who would help me develop a clientele when I finished college. I thought it was great that this was all happening, just at the right time. Caleb and I had always talked about starting our own firm, and these introductions could only help make that happen faster." He slid his hand through his hair and rubbed the back of his neck.

"Anyway, about four months into dating, Suzanne told me she was pregnant. I was stunned. She had been telling me all along that she was on birth control and I believed her. I found out that wasn't the truth. At first, she tried telling me that she must have forgotten to take her pill on time. Then, as time progressed, she confessed that she had never been on birth control. She told me a few years later that it was her intent right from the beginning to get into college and find someone to marry so she wouldn't have to work."

"Yadda yadda, throughout our marriage it was more of the same. I threw myself into my work and traveled more and became engrossed in the business. Caleb and I began talking in earnest about what we would need to open our own firm. I worked like a fiend; so did he. We made connections and put feelers out there. I learned everything I could about the business—what worked and what didn't—so when we made our move, we were ready. As soon as we were, I left Suzanne and her father's firm. Caleb and I started Kinkaide Locke, and it turned out, the contacts were ready for us to do things the way they should be done and we didn't lose as many people as Suzanne had wanted me to believe. The ones we did lose, we weren't sorry about.

"Suzanne was livid. All she ever wanted was to be the boss' wife or someone with some perceived power, and of course, she didn't want to have to work. She tried getting back together with me. She tried everything she could think of to make me think she had changed, but I'm never going back to that. Caleb and I have grown the business by leaps and bounds. My children are by my side, and I've been single ever since."

Sam reached across the table and held his hand.

She looked him in the eye and said, "I'm sorry, Gray... for all the terrible years you had to endure. A marriage is supposed to be two people loving each other, working together day after day for the common goal of building a good life together. You should look forward to waking up every morning and spending your day together, not biding your time until you can get out."

He squeezed her hand. "And it isn't all about feeling guilty and scared and going through the motions either. Aren't we a pair?"

They chuckled and decided to change the subject to other, less depressing topics. But Sam would always remember the sadness on his face when he talked about his marriage and how he wasn't loved.

They left the restaurant a while later. She had to admit, she'd greatly enjoyed being with him. He was smart, funny, and he was a loving man—she could tell by the way he talked about his children. The ride home was comfortable, and as they drove around the city, he drove past a couple of buildings he'd designed. She loved listening to him talk about his work. He had a true passion for it. After the tour of "Kinkaide" buildings was over—although not a full tour, he had designed many buildings over the years—they headed to Sam's house.

As they drove up the drive of her home, nerves took over, and she fidgeted with the strap of her purse. "Would you like to come in and have a drink?"

He put the Escalade in park and shut off the ignition. He turned his head toward her, and her breath caught as the soft light from the yard caressed his face. He was stunning, this man. Model handsome and nice to boot. "I'd like that very much," he responded.

Sam pulled her keys from her purse; Gray reached over and gently took them from her. Her lips trembled into a soft smile, and the butterflies set flight. She'd be hard-pressed to remember a day a gentleman opened the door for her.

Entering the dimly lit home she'd so lovingly decorated, she tapped the switch on the wall, and the soft lights on either side of the fireplace illuminated the living room; the outside lights shone from the window and lit up the heavily-wooded backyard.

"Red or white for you?" she asked.

Gray walked toward the windows and stared out at the trees

beyond. "What do you like?" He turned toward her, and she swallowed the lump forming in her throat.

"I usually like white wines, but I have a couple of great red after-dinner wines if you're interested."

"I'll have what you're having."

She set her clutch on the counter separating the kitchen from the living room. Tapping the lights on in the kitchen, she pulled two wine glasses from the rack above the counter. Pulling a bottle of red from the rack in the corner she quickly uncorked it with the help of her electric opener. She poured them each a glass and softly padded to the living room where the most handsome man she'd ever seen graced her living area and made it look more like a home than it had ever felt. The sensation that ran through her body at that notion nearly folded her in half.

Unable to look him in the eye for fear she'd say something stupid, she merely motioned with her hand toward the sofa and quickly seated herself before she fell.

He lightly tapped his glass to hers and watched as she sipped the deep red liquid. Once he'd taken a sip, he said, "I'd love a tour of your home if you don't mind."

Cocking her head to the side, she responded, "The architect needs to check it out?"

"That, and you seem nervous, so I thought it might put us both at ease."

She breathed deeply. "Yes, I'm busted. I'm not sure what's expected at this point."

He stood and held his hand out to her. "Nothing is expected. We're just friends getting to know each other. Tell me about your home."

Fair enough. She stood and began walking him through her home. "I've painted every room, some of them more than once. I enjoy it and decorating."

"You've done a beautiful job, Sam. You're very talented. I noticed you have a For Sale sign in the yard," he said.

"Yes ... this is just too much house for me. I have three acres and too much house to keep track of. I have enough to do each day without having to come home and be a slave to the house and yard. So, I waited six months after Tim died to list it and had a little sit-down with the kids and told them it was time for me to move on."

Gray nodded his head. "I get that, but it's still a shame. It's a beautiful home."

They continued talking, and when they'd finished their wine, Gray said, "I better get going ... work tomorrow."

He stood to leave, and Sam stood with him. She walked him to the door, and he turned to face her.

He reached down and put his hand on the side of her face and asked, "Will you have dinner with me again Thursday night? I have to finish a big project for a client this week, so I'll be burning the midnight oil until then. But I need to see you again."

He *needed* to see her again. Waiting two days was going to be torture. He wanted her in his bed right this damn minute. What an interesting turn of events today had been.

She smiled, and a thrill ran through him. She simply lit up the room—soft lips, perfect teeth, green eyes the color of spring grass. Stunning wouldn't come close to an accurate word to describe her. "I would love to have dinner with you again." Her soft voice wrapped itself around him and squeezed.

They gazed into each other's eyes for several long moments. He lifted his hand to caress her cheek with the back of his fingers. She closed her eyes and tilted her head into his hand. The rasp that entered his voice couldn't be helped, "I need to kiss you, Sam."

He slowly touched his lips to hers, and the instant they connected it felt as if he were home. A fire swept through him like he'd never known. He stepped into her, and the instant his body was against hers, he swore he saw stars. The softness of her curves against him caused an inferno to rage within him. His body responded by trembling, his breathing coming in spurts, the immediate thickening of his cock caused the blood to rush from his head to the bulging in his pants, and he felt light-headed. Pulling his lips from hers was discomforting but necessary. He pulled her close and wrapped his arms around her body and his heart beat rapidly when he felt her arms wrap around his waist. Her head tucked comfortably against his chest; he closed his eyes and willed himself to gain control.

He slowly pulled away from her, wanting more than anything to stay. "I need to go, Sam. But, I'll be waiting impatiently until Thursday, and thinking about you every moment until then."

She smiled. "I will as well."

He touched his forehead to hers and froze for a measure of time, letting his breathing regulate. Finally pulling away, he took her hand and kissed the back of it.

"I'll see you Thursday night at seven."

He stepped back and opened the door, and with a half-grin, he nodded and left.

Gray got into his vehicle and put the key in the ignition. His body still quivered, and his breathing staggered. He started his vehicle and slowly drove down the driveway. After he was a short distance from Sam's, he pulled over to the side of the road and took a few deep breaths.

******

Sam turned out the lights after placing their wine glasses in the dishwasher. She washed her face, brushed her teeth, and crawled into bed. Her phone chimed signaling a text. She grinned and pulled her phone to her, swiped the home screen and smiled when she saw a text from Gray.

Thank you for having dinner with me and the tour of your home. I'm looking forward to seeing you Thursday. Gray.

She hit reply and typed out a message.

Thank you for the lovely dinner and tour of Kinkaide designed buildings. I look forward to seeing more of your work in the future. Looking forward to seeing you Thursday as well. Sam

She tapped send and snuggled into bed. As she drifted off to sleep, all she had on her mind was her first date in more than thirty years and the second one she would have on Thursday night.

4

Wednesday morning, Sam woke to the television, set to turn on to gently wake her. She lay there thinking about her date last night. She'd been dreading that date, feeling awkward and foolish and had thought many times about canceling. She was so glad she hadn't backed out. He was easy to talk to, smart, accomplished, and he had a great sense of humor. She didn't sense any arrogance from him, but she *did* notice that more than one woman had taken a second look. He didn't seem to notice. She hadn't asked him about his dating life since he divorced, but she believed it had to be easy for him. Just looking at the man made her do silly things.

How would she feel if he had a very active sex life? It wasn't like he was hers, but the jealous response she felt in her stomach told her she had to get a grip. Anything he'd done before her was just that— before her—and you can't blame a person for their past. But her self-confidence was non-existent.

Fortunately, she did have confidence in herself on the job. She *knew* she did a good job, tried hard, applied herself, and was always looking for ways to improve things. She could give and take constructive criticism and wasn't offended if someone offered an idea different from one she had. She liked the networking part of making a change and coming up with a better mousetrap, so to speak.

But in a relationship, she had never achieved that feeling of confidence in who she was or who she was to the person she was with. Tim never fostered that self-confidence in her, either. Ironic that she was the one who grew up and had three boys while her brother, the "valuable" child, grew up and had two girls. Sam chuckled thinking that was God's little joke on her parents and she appreciated His sense of humor.

Sam rolled out of bed to start her morning ritual when she heard her phone chime announcing a text message. Feeling instantly giddy like an infatuated teenage girl, she grabbed her phone to see who it was. With a grin on her face, she swiped across her phone screen to read the text.

Good morning. I thought about you all night. Thursday seems like a decade away. If I didn't have a large project due, I would want to see you tonight. Gray.

Sam giggled; she had thought about him too. She smiled at the attentiveness from a man who had suffered through such a terrible marriage. He was not only attentive, but he was interested in seeking a relationship. After being single for so many years, maybe he was ready for that now. She agreed with him—Thursday *did* seem like a decade away. She tapped out a message and hit send.

Sorry, Gray who?

Within a couple of minutes, her phone chimed again.

I was the guy you had dinner with last night. You remember, the architect?

Ohh, the architect, sure. I think we saw some of your buildings, right?

Right, and when I took you home, I kissed you. I think you kissed me back.

Yes, yes, it's all coming back to me now. You were afraid I lived in a dungeon or something!

That's right. Glad you're starting to remember.

:) Yes, actually, you are quite unforgettable. Thursday does seem like a decade away!

Okay, I have to get to work so I can enjoy your company tomorrow. Gray.

Have a great day, Gray! Sam.

Well, that just made her day. Maybe texting and emailing with each other today and tomorrow will help them get to know each other a bit better. It seemed easier talking about certain things via correspondence rather than in person. She continued with her morning routine and got herself ready for work.

****

When Gray woke up—he wasn't sure he ever completely fell asleep—he was groggy, and his head ached. His mind raced at his good fortune in meeting Sam. She was beautiful, sexy, fun, had a great sense of humor, and that smile, those lips. He imagined doing many things with her. He wanted to slide his dick between those lips and watch them close around him. Just thinking about it made him hard and achy. He wanted to fuck her mouth, her pussy, and her ass —he wanted her on her knees, on her back, and over the sofa. As he looked around his house, he imagined fucking her everywhere. What the hell had she done to him?

He got up earlier than usual to get ready for work since he wasn't sleeping anyway. He'd get to work on his project and finish it. He snickered at the fact that when he'd first gotten this project, he was over the moon excited about it. It was a new bank building in Neenah, and the budget was enormous. Now all he wanted to do was get it done so he could explore whatever was going on between Sam and him. In just a few short hours, she had completely changed his train of thought. He was beginning to understand what had happened to his friends or his son when they met their women. He used to get angry at them for not thinking clearly and acting crazy and taking time off work. He thought they were completely whipped. But now, here he was with a project he'd coveted a few weeks ago, and all he wanted to do was finish it so he could spend more time with a woman. Not just *any* woman, mind you, but with Sam. He wanted to spend time with her, get to know her, and let her get to know him. And yes, he wanted sex. Now who's whipped?

He wanted her submissive to him. He had dreamed his whole life of having a woman *want* to please him, to be submissive to him. He wasn't talking extremes here—he didn't get into the collars and slave/master thing. But he wanted someone who would depend on him, allow him to make decisions, and let him take care of her. Something told him that Sam was the one, but he didn't want to scare her away. He also couldn't get the image of her on her knees in front of Mrs. Koeppel out of his mind. He mentally shook himself. *I need to get this project done so I can find out if this is what I've waited for all my life.*

5

SECOND CHANCES SERIES

J essie waited for Sam as she walked into work. She had hundreds of questions, of course, that Sam thought she'd slogged through. She gave vague answers and didn't tell her more than dinner was nice and he was easy to talk to and no they didn't have sex. She didn't even mention the hot kiss or two. Sam, however, had a question to ask Jessie, so she dove right in.

"Jess, can you tell me how it works before you have sex with someone? How do you bring up the sexual history questions?"

Jess's mouth opened, then closed. She cocked her head to the side but continued to stare.

Hmm, Sam chuckled, she'd never thought she or anyone for that matter, could ever make Jessie speechless.

"Wow, are you ... do you think ... are you planning ... what I am trying to say is, wow! Well, you just need to ask him if he is safe, has he been safe in the past. That is usually when I ask if he's been a whore; you know, a little levity, but you get the picture."

She flashed a smile that went all the way to her inquisitive eyes. Sam knew she wanted to ask more questions, but she turned and walked away before Jess could ask.

Stopping abruptly, she turned to Jess, who was staring in her direction. Before she could catch herself, Sam asked, "Well, is your new beau a whore?"

Jess burst into laughter. Good thing they were the only two in the office.

She shook her head. "No, not a whore. He's had a 'few' girlfriends, and I'm still trying to figure out what a 'few' is, but then again, I've had a 'few' boyfriends, so I'm not going to dwell on it much. We're both safe, so for right now, I'm happy with only knowing that much."

Sam nodded and headed back to her office. She hoped Gray hadn't been a whore.

Throughout her busy day, her mind wandered to Gray and how she could ask him about his past. Maybe she could ask by email? Maybe it was too soon to ask. That seemed pretty presumptuous, didn't it? She doubted she'd be able to ask him in person. Her stomach already did cartwheels when they were in the same room together, so it was safe to say she'd never be able to ask him that in person. She was curious, though, and she didn't want to get too emotionally involved if it was a situation she didn't think she'd be able to handle.

Sitting at her desk working on a document, she got an email from Gray. Again, her traitorous body did funny little flippy things in anticipation of what he'd written. She clicked on the message and read.

F*rom: Grayson Kinkaide*
To: Samantha Powell
Date: April 10, 10:46 a.m.
Subject: Concentration – Not as easy as you would think

I*'m having a very hard time concentrating; you keep popping into my head.*

· · ·

Grayson Kinkaide

Sam laughed. That was positive.

From: Samantha Powell
     To: Grayson Kinkaide
Date: April 10, 10:52 a.m.
Subject: Wandering mind is a sign of old age

You're not going to get your project done before tomorrow if you let your mind wander. We'll have to wait until Friday!

Samantha Powell

Getting back to work, she flipped her document to the next page when her email chimed.

From: Grayson Kinkaide
     To: Samantha Powell
Date: April 10, 10:55 a.m.
Subject: When you're right, you're right

You're right, of course, I can't help it.

. . .

G *rayson Kinkaide*

S he giggled. This was kind of nice.

F *rom: Samantha Powell*
To: Grayson Kinkaide
Date: April 10, 11:05 a.m.
Subject: I'm right?

W *ell, I'll remember that you said that. It may come in handy someday.*

S *amantha Powell*

H e didn't respond right away, so she figured he needed to get his work finished, and so did she. She couldn't help but look at the clock – often—and she couldn't help the smile that seemed to appear on her face at the slightest thought of him. Her email chimed.

F *rom: Grayson Kinkaide*
To: Samantha Powell
Date: April 10, 3:00 p.m.
Subject: Thursday is better than Friday

· · ·

I *made some great headway on my project. Dinner is on for TOMORROW night, not Friday.*

G*rayson Kinkaide*

S am leaned back in her chair trying to think of something to say when Jessie appeared in her doorway. "Any errands?" She looked at Sam, and a smile spread across her face. "What are you doing sitting here with that sappy look on your face? Did you hear from Gray?"

"Yes, I did. We've been emailing a little bit today. He has a great sense of humor, Jess. I'm just giddy thinking about seeing him tomorrow night."

"Well, finally, Sam has a boyfriend! Did you ask him about being a whore?"

"No, I didn't. It seems too presumptuous to bring it up now."

Before turning to leave, Jess said, "You know, there is no perfect time for that conversation. It seems unromantic if you discuss it just before you have sex; it seems presumptuous if you ask now. Bottom line, he's probably thinking about it, too, and wondering when the right time is to ask. One of you has to 'man up,' so to speak." Jess quietly left her with her thoughts.

It was driving her crazy thinking about this. If he was offended by the question, they could just call off their date, and that would be the end of it, right? She typed, deleted, typed, deleted, typed some more, and finally, she had her email ready to go.

F *rom: Samantha Powell*
       To: Grayson Kinkaide
    Date: April 10, 3:20 p.m.
    Subject: Presumptuous or inquisitive, you decide

. . .

I hope you don't think this is presumptuous or too personal, but will you tell me if you've been with a lot of women? I'm not sure how to go about this part of it, but while we were kissing last night, I got the impression that you were "interested" in more than just a kiss. But, when it comes to that part of your life, I really don't know a lot about you.

S amantha Powell

S he hit send, and her stomach immediately rolled. Well, it was out there now, so she guessed she needed to live with it. She was disappointed and nervous when she didn't hear from Gray for the rest of the day. She figured it meant he'd been offended. She knew she'd be great at this dating thing. Gah.

Leaving work around five-thirty and in no hurry to get home, she drove through town; her stomach was still doing somersaults over that stupid email. Why couldn't she have thought that one through a little more? *Mrs. Koeppel must be rubbing off on me.*

She pulled into her driveway at five fifty-five-ish, and Gray's SUV was there. Oh, my God, he was so pissed he came here to talk to her in person! Her thoughts rolled around in her head. Her stomach flipped so much she thought she would throw up. *Crap!* She pulled into the garage, turned off her car, and took a deep breath. Her hands shook and her face burned hot, her chest felt flushed. When she opened the door, Gray had walked up to the car. She stepped from her vehicle and took a deep breath; her breathing was ragged, and her heart was hammering.

*****

Gray stepped up to her and looked into her eyes. She was beautiful with her green eyes glassy and bright, her face flushed and her lips trembled, just a bit. He assumed she was nervous about what she thought was coming, but he needed to speak to her in person about this subject. Her tongue nervously swiped at her bottom lip, and his mind blanked for a moment. Shaking the carnal thoughts racing through his brain, he said, "I got your email and thought we should have this discussion in person."

She continued to stare, then swallowed. He lifted a brow to elicit a response.

Her head bowed, "I sent you the email because I didn't think I would be able to have that conversation in person."

Inwardly sighing, he put his fingers under her chin and forced her face up.

Smoothly, he responded, "Yes, I thought as much. But I want us to have this conversation in person. And, I didn't want your mind wandering and assuming the worst."

Her grin acknowledged that had been her thinking thus far. He took her hand and led them toward the house, entering from the garage. Halting just outside the door, he held it open for her and followed her inside.

She laid her purse on the little table in the hall and continued into the house. "Do I need wine for this conversation? Do you?"

Chuckling, he replied, "A glass of wine would be fantastic; I'll have whatever you're having."

He watched from the doorway to the kitchen as she pulled glasses from the rack, chose a bottle of white wine, and expertly opened it. Her fingers were sure, her posture rigid. She twisted to pull a wine stopper from the drawer, and he admired her backside, which looked perfect in the soft gray slacks she wore. Her petite frame belied her strength – no one could go through all she had and be weak. That was admirable.

She handed him his glass and swept her free hand toward the living room. "Why don't we sit where we can try to be more comfortable?"

He chuckled at her formal tone but followed her as he continued to admire the view. Sitting on opposite ends of the sofa, he began.

"You know I've been divorced for close to seven years. During my marriage, which I told you was awful, Suzanne and I didn't have sex very often. I would say in the better years, which were not very many, we had sex maybe once a month or once about every six weeks. Imagine being a young healthy male and not being able to have sex with your wife any more than that! I was frustrated and horny most of the time." Leaning forward, he set his wine glass on the coffee table and folded his hands together, resting his forearms on his knees. "I didn't cheat on her until that last four or five years of our marriage after I found out she had been cheating on me for years. I needed to connect with someone, and I needed a release—sexual release. Even then, I didn't cheat often, but three or four times each year and only with random women. I didn't want any emotional attachments."

She slowly set her glass on the table and nervously brushed her slacks of invisible lint.

"After our divorce, I felt free and sowed my wild oats as they say. About three years ago, I dated a nice woman named Cheryl. She was in the same boat I'd been in, had a cheating spouse and endured it for years. We dated for about a year. She broke it off with me when I couldn't emotionally engage with her. She kept telling me she loved me; I couldn't say it back. I didn't love her. I wanted to, but I just couldn't or didn't. I didn't blame her; I would have broken up with me, too, under the same circumstances. Since then, there have been a few here and there, but I was always safe."

He let out a sigh and watched the emotions play on her face. She took a deep breath and let it out slowly. Pasting on a smile, she responded, "I don't know what to say." She rubbed her hands together softly. "I do want you to know that I'm not interested in a random fling." She motioned in front of her with her hands. "I don't do that. Can't. I can't do that."

"NO, no you're not random." He scooted closer to her and rushed on, "Sam, that's just it. I walked into your office, and I was stopped dead in my tracks when I saw you round the corner. It was like an electric current running through me. I have never, NEVER, had a reaction like that to anyone ... ever. That's why I believe there's something here. I so badly want to explore it and see where it goes. I want to spend time with you, get to know you, and see if this is as special as I think it could be."

"We barely know each other. How can you know it's special?"

"I don't know. It's a feeling. I'm not lying to you when I tell you I've never had a reaction to anyone like I had – have—with you."

She swiped across her face, smoothing away the worry. "I have to tell you; it does worry me. I don't want to get involved with someone who can't become emotionally attached. I don't want to get my heart broken. I've had a lifetime of that. I want an honest-to-goodness all-out loving relationship with someone who wants to be with me as much as I want to be with him. The cheating worries me. The inability to connect worries me." She turned to watch two squirrels play in a tree just outside the window.

He watched her slightly rotate her shoulders to relieve tension. She sat back and looked into his eyes. "My biggest fear is that I won't be able to keep you interested in me for a prolonged period of time. You'll get bored and need other stimulation. I'm not very remarkable."

Gray sucked in a breath and leaned forward. "Did I just hear you correctly? You don't think you're remarkable?" He reached over and took her hand in his. Slowly caressing her fingers with his thumbs, he marveled at the softness of her skin, her small perfectly manicured fingers only adorned with a gold thumb ring on her left hand. She should have beautiful jewelry to complement the woman she is.

His voice was rough and foreign to him when he finally spoke. "You're the most remarkable woman I've ever met. I mean that, but if you tell my mother I said that, I'll deny it." He smiled and released a breath when she grinned.

She turned her hand in his, clasping his fingers with hers. "I wouldn't want you to judge me by my past; I know it can't be changed. I do want to explore this relationship as well if you honestly think you want to. But, until we can trust each other, we need to be open and honest. If you get to a point where you don't think you can emotionally connect with me, will you be honest with me? Can you do that?"

Gray leaned over and kissed her lightly on the mouth. She stood and twisted from side to side slightly. Stepping in front of him, she kneeled taking his hands in hers.

"My back is a bit knotted, and leaning wasn't helping anything."

His breathing hitched up, and his heart pounded in his chest. He took in her submissive position and nearly exploded. Her eyes looked so earnest, her lips soft and kissable, his dreams playing out right in front of him.

Afraid he'd scare her away, he leaned back into the sofa. "Your turn."

She furrowed her brow in confusion, and she began to stand. He put his hand on her shoulder, a silent command to stay where she was. Their eyes connected and held and what he saw there was his future.

"Well, I was married for twenty-nine years, and we dated about two years before marriage. I wasn't a virgin when we met. I had had two other boyfriends before meeting Tim. I was faithful to him during our marriage. I'm pretty sure he was faithful to me. Most of the time, he was so depressed that he wasn't interested in sex. The last two years of our marriage, we didn't have sex at all. So, counting this last year since Tim has been gone, I haven't had sex in three years."

He cleared his throat, "I suppose you think I'm a selfish person for not staying faithful during my marriage. Your marriage wasn't much better than mine, and you did. If I could change it, I would." He let out a long, ragged breath, a bit embarrassed at his lack of strength.

She stared into his eyes, her lips briefly formed a straight line, then lifted into a soft smile. "We all deal with our issues in our own ways. I shut down; you reached out. Neither one of us was right. We just did what we needed to do to get by."

Sam stretched up, and Gray leaned forward to meet her lips with his. He grinned at her initiation of a kiss. Progress. He reached under her arms and pulled her forward onto his lap. His heart swelled when she snaked her arms around his shoulders. He captured her mouth with his as his arms encircled her waist pulling her fully into him. Their tongues danced, their lips softly gliding together, soft, moist kisses he'd never forget.

Ending the kiss, he put his forehead on hers. His breathing was ragged.

"Sam, I remember just getting back into the dating scene, and I know it can be scary. Trust me; I don't expect anything from you. When I walked into your office and saw you with Mrs. Koeppel, I thought you were so sweet to take care of a little old lady and make her feel so special. I remember thinking, 'What a kind person she must be to be so thoughtful of others that way,' when you had not long ago suffered your own pain and sorrow. You didn't seem bitter and angry; you seemed happy and loving and kind. Do you understand how different and special that is to me? After living with a manipulative, condescending, selfish woman for so many years, to come across a woman who I think is sexy, smart, and kind to others, it seemed like God was finally answering my prayers. I knew then that I would do whatever I needed to do to get to know you, to see if this could be something special. I want to know you, Sam. I don't expect anything from you except a chance."

She inhaled and looked across the room into the cold, dark fireplace. He followed her line of vision then looked up at her alluring face. The dainty gold balls she wore in her ears caught a glint of light; a few gray hairs peeked through the blonde highlights at her temples. His lips lifted in a smile as he was reminded of their ages; he felt like a teenager again until he looked into a mirror or stood after sitting for a time.

"A chance is perfectly acceptable to me. It's more than I thought I'd ever get again—the chance to find someone to finish my days with."

He chuckled. "I'd rather not think of finishing my days but starting them if you don't mind." Her soft perfume floated over him, and he inhaled deeply, wanting even her smell imprinted upon him.

She giggled then, and the sound was like a special piece of music. "That does sound better – starting."

They sat for a time; he enjoyed holding her in his arms. After a while, she laid her head on top of his and sighed. His cock thickened of its own accord and he knew she'd feel it pressing into her backside as she sat on his lap. It became painful in its confinement, and he found it necessary to readjust or lose one of his favorite body parts.

He gently lifted her hips and set her beside him on the sofa. He turned to face her, pulling his knee up between them and took her hands in his.

"I don't want to jump the gun or seem too forward, but I do want to ask you if you've ever ... experimented? Sexually, I mean."

Her brows rose then furrowed. "Experimented? You mean like positions or something?"

He kissed her fingers then cleared his throat. "I mean like tying up, erotic positions, things like that."

She gently pulled her hands away and stood. She let out a deep breath and stepped to the large picture window. "Are you into some sort of dominance stuff?"

He chuckled, unable to not. "Well, not like I suspect you're thinking. But, more like sex play. Just between two people who are careful and loving with each other but trying something new."

She rubbed her hands over her arms as if she were warding off a chill. The soft pink silky blouse she wore tucked into her slacks accented her tiny waist, but in this light, showed off her figure beautifully and he found that he needed to sit and think of hairy balls or something to keep his erection at a minimum.

"No. I've never experimented." She ran a hand around the back of her neck then swiveled her head to ease tension. She softly continued, "I told you I'm not very remarkable. I'm not worldly in that way. Not like I suspect you are."

He stood and stepped up behind her. "I'm not worldly in that way either. I've always wanted to experiment with a few things but never had anyone I wanted to experiment with. This week, those thoughts have been running through my mind, and I just wanted to voice that.

No pressure, and if you can't bring yourself to try it, I'm just fine, Sam."

He massaged her shoulders to ease the tension he felt there and released a breath when he felt her relax. "I still think you're remarkable. Please don't think otherwise."

She chuckled and laid her head back against his chest.

"Don't overthink it, Sam. It is what it is, and we both have a strong attraction to each other. It doesn't need to be more than that right now if you aren't ready."

She nodded and turned toward him. "While we're 'exploring' this relationship or whether we have a relationship, does that mean we're not dating other people?"

Stunned was his first reaction, but when his words finally came, they were clipped and sharp. "I'm not interested in seeing anyone else. Are you?"

"No, I'm not interested in seeing anyone, either. I just wanted to make sure. I told you ... up-front and honest. I'm so green at this dating thing; I don't know what's what."

He exhaled loudly and walked with her to the kitchen where they placed their glasses in the dishwasher.

"Have you already eaten or can I make you something for supper?"

He grinned. "I need to get back to work. I'll grab something along the way. I wanted to finish up this project tonight and will probably be working late into the evening."

"I'm sorry you felt the need to come over here when you have so much work to do."

"Well, to be honest with you, I really wanted to see you again, anyway, and I guess I used it as an excuse to kiss you a few times."

Wrapping her in his arms, he pulled her close, breathing in her scent and willing his heart to slow down for fear of a heart attack.

"I better get going, or I won't be able to leave. Besides, if I don't finish up at work, we won't be able to go out tomorrow night."

He leaned down and claimed her lips once again. He wanted the passion he was feeling to seep into her, to keep her company when he wasn't there with her.

His voice cracked as he said, "I'll see you tomorrow, Sam. Think about me."

"Ha! Like I'll be able to get you out of my mind!"

He chuckled as he turned toward the front door. Sam walked with him and said "Goodnight." One light kiss later and he was out the door and climbing into his SUV.

6

S am poured herself a glass of wine and walked to her bathroom, where she turned the water on in the tub. A nice hot bath while thinking about a sexy man and their date tomorrow seemed to be a great way to spend the evening. After undressing, she settled into the tub as the warm, fragrant water sloshed around her. She closed her eyes and thoughts of her date with Gray formed in her mind. She hadn't asked where they were going and wondered if she should text him and ask so she could dress appropriately. She simply had a difficult time thinking clearly around the man.

******

Thursday morning started out just like every other morning. She had been so tired after her bath that she crawled right into bed and slept all through the night—first time in a long time. She reached for her phone and smiled when she saw she had texts to read.

Where would you like to go tomorrow night? Gray.

Oh crap, she'd fallen asleep and hadn't answered him; she hadn't even heard her phone chirp. That was at nine last night. Then another one about twenty minutes later.

You haven't changed your mind, have you? Gray.

After their conversation, his thoughts probably raced. Poor guy. If she'd caused him to worry, she certainly hadn't meant to. Another text at ten p.m.

Please don't change your mind. I can't change my past; all we can do is move forward. Give me a chance. We'll take it slow. Gray.

Oh no! She began texting Gray when her doorbell rang. *Crap!* She pulled on her robe and tried taming her crazy bed hair as she made her way to the door.

Peeking through the peephole, Gray stood with two cups of coffee in his hands. She groaned as she slowly opened the door.

"I didn't know what you like, so I got chocolate mint. Hope that's okay."

Sam gasped and pulled her palms over her face. *No makeup, hair a mess, and in a robe for goodness' sake. Well, he sure wouldn't want to go out now.* She heard him chuckle. He tapped her fingers with one of his, still holding a coffee in his hand.

"I think you look cute."

He even knew what she was thinking.

She let out an unladylike snort. "I doubt that 'cute' is what anyone would call me right now." She stood back allowing him to enter. "Well, now you've seen what I look like in the morning. Want to turn and run?"

He handed her a cup of coffee and walked into the house. His gray dress pants and crisp white dress shirt—sleeves rolled up a couple turns—was a pleasant sight first thing in the morning. His shirt had a slight shimmer to it and fit snuggly, just enough to show off his physique. He wasn't in body-builder shape, but he was fit and trim for a man in his fifties. And right now, watching him walk into her living room, she got a nice view of his great behind. Her face flushed. Gray spoke, breaking into her thoughts.

"Nope, I'm here because you didn't answer my texts last night and I was worried you had changed your mind. I knew I wouldn't be able to concentrate at work today if I didn't speak with you and know what you were thinking."

Sam followed him into the living room where he sat on the sofa making himself right at home. She followed him into the living room, trying to flatten the cowlick in her hair with one hand and holding her coffee in the other.

"I'm so sorry, Gray. I was just reading your texts. After you left last night, I soaked in a nice warm bath, and when I finished I realized how tired I was, so I went straight to bed. I didn't hear my phone chirp at all. I'm sorry—I didn't mean to worry you."

He exhaled and flashed a big, beautiful smile. "Great! I thought you'd decided not to see me anymore. I tossed and turned all night, worrying about it. I'm so relieved you haven't changed your mind."

He just took her breath away. She could feel herself being swept away by this man and it was scary as hell. She faintly smiled. She wasn't a morning person, but she was trying.

"If you still want to go out with me when you know what I look like without makeup and with my hair looking all crazy in the morning, I still want to go out with you. I'm sorry I made you worry. I didn't sleep much Tuesday night after our date, and I guess it caught up with me last night."

Gray's perfect lips formed a sly smile as he leaned forward. "Were you thinking about me?"

Pfft, he knew darn good and well that she was thinking about him. So now he just needed his ego stroked a little.

"Naw, I was thinking about time travel."

She smiled then sipped her coffee. He frowned and sat back which made her laugh. "Of course, I was thinking about you. You can't kiss a girl like you kissed me and believe she isn't going to think about you."

He grinned as he stood up and walked toward the door. Sam followed, enjoying the view of his fabulously toned behind. When he walked, his butt wiggled a little. He turned around suddenly and caught her staring at his butt. He tilted his head and raised an eyebrow in amusement. She turned beet red and shrugged her shoulders.

"You're the one who came over here dressed all sexy and everything. You can't blame a girl for noticing."

He got a hearty laugh out of that one. "So, now you think I'm sexy?"

She shook her head. "I doubt you don't already know that, Gray. I saw the way other women looked at you when we were out on Tuesday. I'm sure finding random women was very easy for you."

Gray's smile immediately faded.

"I'm sorry, I didn't mean for that to come out so sarcastic. I simply meant that you are a very attractive, sexy man. I would have to be blind to not think so. I apologize if it sounded insensitive. "

He nodded his head, but she could see some doubt there. They stood for a minute looking at each other, trying to gauge what the other was thinking when Sam reached up and touched his face.

"I'm sorry, really. That information is so fresh, and it was out of my mouth before I even thought how that was going to sound. I'm truly sorry, Gray."

He leaned down and kissed her softly. "I understand. I hate that I can't change that, Sam; I really do. If for one minute I ever thought I would meet you, I would change everything in my past to be different for you."

His regret for his past seemed so sincere, and it touched her heart.

"Gray, neither one of us can change what happened in the past. If we could, I doubt we'd be the people we are right now—for bad or good. Please don't dwell on that. I promise I'll try very hard to not dwell on it."

Gray smiled. "I'll see you at six o'clock then. And, since you didn't answer my question, how about I cook for you tonight? Besides, I'm excited for you to see my house."

Sam smiled and looked up at him. "Great, I'll be there at six. Can I bring something?"

"Nope, I've got this one. I'll email you my address and directions. See you then."

He was out the door and jumping into his SUV in a heartbeat. Looking back, he waved as he backed out of the driveway. She let out a long, heavy sigh. Not only had he seen her without makeup and with bed head, but she'd also offended him. She'd need to be careful to not let his past bother her, and she certainly didn't want to throw it in his face all the time. After all, he'd been honest with her. That took trust and courage on his part, and she needed to respect that. It bothered her in that even though she believed he had regrets, when a person can justify things, they tend to be repeat offenders.

Sam sipped on her delicious coffee as she got ready for work.

******

Gray chuckled as he drove to the office. She was cute with her hair all mussed up from sleeping. He only wished he'd been sleeping with her. He was going to change that tonight. He was happy she hadn't changed her mind about going out with him—something he laid awake thinking about last night.

Shit! This was crazy to be so hung up on a woman so fast. But the more time he spent with her, the more time he wanted to spend with her. She had already taken over every waking moment of his time since he met her. He had a hard time concentrating at work; he had a hard time concentrating at home. In a word, he was fucked! He felt restless and unsteady until he saw her. This morning he'd been awake at three a.m., just waiting for the clock to reach a reasonable time to go to her house so he wouldn't freak her out.

The second she opened the door, it took all he had not to grab her and haul her to the bedroom and fuck her. She probably didn't have anything on under that robe, either. He groaned at the thought. It made his dick throb and twitch. Tonight, he would have her in his bed. He was sure of that.

7

SECOND CHANCES SERIES

Arriving at the office early, Sam popped into Bill's office. "Morning. Just wanted to let you know we'll be cracking on the trial documents today and have them compiled and bound for you by noon. And, I'd like to leave at three today."

Bill, the firm's lead attorney—her boss of five years and Gray's friend—looked up from his paperwork and smiled. "Morning. Thanks, and of course you can leave early, you know that."

She smiled at this kind man; she enjoyed working for him—a couple of the other partners, not so much, but Bill was wonderful. "Thanks, I appreciate it."

She waved as she continued to her office. It was hard not to smile with the happiness surrounding her today.

"So, plans for tonight?" Jessie asked as she met her in the hall, making an air quote movement with her fingers.

The smile on Sam's face never faltered. She stepped into her office, Jessie on her heels. "I'm going to Gray's for dinner."

Sam only smiled, but Jess jumped right in.

"Ooh, his house for 'dinner,' of course." There were those damned air quotes again. "How exciting for you."

Jess turned to leave, then stopped at the door, and said, "I can't wait to hear all about it."

She shook her head as Jess walked away.

At three o'clock, Sam quietly left her office and slipped out the back door. She didn't want to answer any questions, and she was both nervous and excited to get home and freshen up for her date. Traffic was light, and the sun had come out today, even though it was still cool outside for April. They hadn't broken the fifty-degree mark in days; however, the sun was beautiful and lifted her spirits. Sam walked into her house and went straight to the bedroom. She started the shower and looked through her closet for something to wear.

She chose a nice pair of jeans, a darker blue color with some fading on the butt cheeks and upper legs. They had nice detailing on the back pockets—just a little bling. She found a long-sleeved, bright pink T-shirt that was slightly see-through but with mottling in it that camouflaged the transparency, while it still left something to the imagination. She finished off with her cool, black peep-toe shoe booties with rhinestones across the top and front. They gave her some height and made her legs look longer and leaner. It was amazing what clothes could do for a girl.

After dressing, she styled her short hair. It was an easy style to work with, but there were times she'd wake with it sticking up all over her head. She hoped Gray hadn't thought about that all day. Now for a little makeup and away we go. There was plenty of time. It was five-ish, and, according to the address and directions he'd sent, he lived only about ten minutes from Sam's house in the same part of Harmony Lake. Funny they lived this close to each other and had never met before.

Wanting to do something special for Gray, she zipped over to Cheesecake Haven and picked up dessert for tonight. Keeping it simple, since she didn't know what he liked or what he was making, she decided on a French Vanilla cheesecake with chocolate sauce and cherries, and of course, whipped cream for garnish.

When she pulled into Gray's driveway, her mouth fell open at the beautiful landscaping, abundant hardscapes, and winding walkways.

She could see perennials starting to pop up, even in the cold spring. She'd have to ask if he enjoyed working in the yard or if he had someone work with him. His brick driveway curved around the beautiful landscape up to the gorgeous house—a sprawling brick ranch with a great wraparound porch. Rocking chairs with a table between them added just the right amount of homey atmosphere.

She took a deep breath, then opened her car door. Gray stepped off the porch, and her heartbeat sped up. He wore jeans that fit him well—very well, in fact—and a black, long-sleeve T-shirt. It made her want to touch him—all over. She could see the full outline of his body revealing his great build. This was going to be a long dinner. When he smiled at her, her face flushed and her knees grew weak. She took a couple of steps toward him, and when they reached each other, he put his arms around her and picked her up off the ground in a big bear hug. She threw her arms around his neck, not only to hang on but because she wanted to get as close to him as she could. They lingered there for a bit, lost in each other's touch.

When he finally set her down, he leaned in and kissed her, immediately dipping his tongue into her mouth. He pulled her so close there wasn't a place their bodies weren't touching. He slanted his head to the side allowing their mouths to fit together perfectly. The skill he used to kiss her was intoxicating.

She slid her palms down and back up his arms, then cupped the back of his head and held him close. He left one hand on the small of her back, keeping her close to him, and slid his other hand up to the back of her head, holding her head in place while he continued exploring her mouth with his tongue. She kissed him back—stroke for stroke—her tongue following his lead. Perfect. Just kissing him made her tingle everywhere. The long, dormant feelings of desire he'd awakened in her were heady. They pulled away from each other and Gray rested his forehead against hers. Time to let her heart stop racing.

"Sam, I'm always amazed at what you do to me."

She laughed. "I feel the same about you. We're screwed, I guess!"

He stepped back and looked her over. It was a bit disconcerting the way he stared. She nervously shuffled on her feet until he finally spoke.

"Sam, you look beautiful."

She laughed. "Well, I wanted to erase your memory of me this morning. I am still mortified at the thought of it. Every time I thought about it today, I wanted to run and hide."

"I told you I thought you were cute and I meant it. Remember, we won't say anything we don't mean."

Impressive! He *had* listened to her.

"Right."

She sighed. Gray took her hand and started toward the front door when Sam stopped.

"Oh wait! I brought a cheesecake for dessert. Do you like cheesecake?"

"Yes, I like cheesecake, and you didn't have to do that. But good thing you did, I didn't think about dessert."

Laughing, she opened the back door of her car and pulled out the cheesecake and toppings. She explained what everything was and why she decided to do it that way when he leaned down and kissed her forehead.

"Forever thinking of others. Thank you, Sam."

She blushed as they turned to walked to the house. "Your home is gorgeous, Gray."

He chuckled. "When I built this house, I waited a couple of years before tackling the landscaping. Once I was finished building and had more time, I worked out here, more to keep the loneliness at bay than anything. My parents would come out and help me sometimes, but they are both in their seventies, and it's getting harder for them to do this bending and twisting. They like being outdoors and enjoyed helping me with this project, though. Wait till you see *their* gardens. Plus," he rubbed the back of his neck, "I think they were a little worried about me being alone, so they were here to keep me company. It was nice spending the time with them."

After all those years with that awful woman and then to be alone, they probably worried constantly about him.

Entering the house, she was stunned. The foyer boasted wide plank, rough-hewn hardwood floors stained in dark brown. From the foyer, straight ahead was the living room and a bank of windows looking out over the colorful yard and expansive deck. From here you could see a pond surrounded by lush landscaping. It was breathtaking! To the right of the windows was a floor-to-ceiling brick fireplace graced with a large mantel and a raised hearth. It was stunning, and the two together were very stimulating. She didn't know where to look first.

"Wow, this is just beautiful, Gray."

He smiled and took her hand. Walking farther into his home, the kitchen was to the left of the living room, decorated in tans and browns in the floor tiles, dark maple cabinets, and stainless-steel appliances. The countertops were a beautiful dark brown granite with copper flecks twinkling from the sunlight streaming in through the windows. There was a center island with seating on one side; the other side sat directly in front of the stove. Great for cooking and meal prep. Cut up vegetables on cutting boards sat on the counter waiting to be cooked. Something delicious-smelling was sizzling away on the stove. Another bank of windows in the kitchen on the same wall as the windows in the living room lightened the whole room. And there was a set of French doors leading out onto the deck.

Gray set the cheesecake in the refrigerator and turned to take the toppings from her hands.

"Wine?" he asked, his eyebrows raised.

"Absolutely."

She smiled when she saw him pull out a bottle of her favorite wine, Oktoberfest. He remembered! He peeled the foil from the top of the bottle and opened the wine as though he'd done it a few times. She smiled when he handed her a glass, and he leaned down and placed a light kiss on her lips.

"Your smile is breathtaking. I could look at it all day."

She slightly scrunched her face and stifled a chuckle.

"You're going to have to get used to me complimenting you. I'm afraid I'm unable to stop."

She giggled. "How much wine have you had?"

He shook his head and took her free hand.

"Let me show you the rest of the house; but first, did you notice anything ... familiar?" Then he tilted his head toward her, his brows raised.

She glanced around again, and her eyes grew wide in surprise as she looked into the living room. "Oh, my gosh! Your living room is painted the same color as mine. And the carpeting is the same color, too. Did you pick these colors out yourself?"

He laughed. "Yes, I did, and I can't tell you how hard it was to not say anything when I first walked into your house. It made quite an impact when I realized all we have in common, including our decorating and color schemes—the combination of which makes a house a home."

The aroma floating in from the kitchen caused her stomach to growl. She giggled and placed her hand on her tummy.

"That's my queue; I need to stir the chicken." He briskly walked into the kitchen, and she followed, watching him from the doorway. As he stirred the meat in the frying pan, she continued to look around. Upon further inspection, she noticed his granite countertop was the same as hers. She shook her head in dismay as she enjoyed the gentle sway of his ass while he stirred the meat on the stove.

Gray replaced the lid on the frying pan, turned the heat low, and took her hand leading her from the kitchen and through the living room. There was a hallway that led from the foyer and along the kitchen wall. The first room to the left was Gray's office. The serene room was graced with a wall of built-in, oak bookshelves and a large oak desk sat in front of the bookshelves—his closed laptop the only item on it. Across from the desk were two leather-upholstered chairs.

Two large windows faced the front of the house. Her car was visible from this room, the sun glinting off the windows. On the wall, directly across from the desk was a collage of family pictures, enclosed in frames of differing sizes and styles, all placed on the wall, so they fit like a puzzle. It was charming. She walked to the pictures, recognizing Jax from seeing him in the office. There were pictures of a younger man who looked like Gray, but he had bright blue eyes.

Gray followed her line of sight. "That's Ethan, my youngest."

In one of the pictures, there was a beautiful blonde woman with him. Pointing he said, "Ethan's girlfriend, Eva. They've been together for over two years."

He continued pointing out people in the pictures. "My parents, Harrison and Mary. My sister, Dani, Dani's husband, Nick, and their kids. My brother, Jamie, and his wife, Kathy, who died of cancer about five years ago." His strong hands moved as he spoke, lovingly touching each picture as he introduced her to his family "This is my daughter Sarah and her husband Cole on their wedding day. These little munchkins are my grandchildren, Lily and Lincoln."

They were a beautiful family, all of them similar in looks but still with their own unique features. Gray looked like his dad, Harry, with his dark hair and eyes. She could see that Jamie looked like Harry in height and build but he had his mother's coloring, sandy brown hair and blue eyes. Dani had the dark hair and blue eyes, a blending of the two senior Kinkaides. Gray's children were a mixture. Jax looked more like Jamie with sandy hair and blue eyes, and Sarah looked like Gray with the dark hair and dark eyes. Ethan had his dad's hair and his grandmother's blue eyes. Well, they could be Suzanne's; Sam hadn't seen a picture of her to know what she looked like.

They left the office and continued down the hall to the master bedroom. It was enormous. The four-poster, king-sized bed with decorative wrought iron slats running from post to post sat in the middle of the largest wall with the matching dresser and armoire to the right. A bump-out with large windows looked out to the back of the house and a portion of the backyard and its lush landscaping. It was stunning. Sam could see the view from the bed, and she imagined how peaceful it would be waking up here with this view greeting you each morning.

Leather chairs, similar to the ones in Gray's office, were placed in the bump-out, a small table in between and a large matching ottoman in front of them. She imagined curling up in a chair to read or listen to music as she watched the birds and squirrels play outside. To the left of the bedroom door was a massive bathroom that housed a large Jacuzzi tub built up two steps. Alongside the tub was a two-person, walk-in shower. The jets and sprayers were positioned so you could spray your whole body at once. There was a long granite counter and two sinks, each with an oval mirror directly in front of them. Directly across from that was a water closet.

The enormous walk-in closet had little cubbies for shoes and drawers for clothing, though it was only partially filled and Sam wrinkled her forehead, wondering why he would build this big massive room and closet for just himself. She didn't think Suzanne had ever lived here.

She turned to see Gray in the doorway watching her.

"When I built this house, I had every hope and dream that it would be my home with the love of my life. So far I have only lived here alone."

She pursed her lips and stared into his mesmerizing eyes. She already felt so much for this man—sadness at his life, his loneliness, his hopelessness, and his hopes and dreams for more. She truly understood; she'd had those same feelings for years. Closing the distance between them, she stood on her toes and kissed him gently, but firmly enough that he knew she meant it. Warm, soft lips met fully yielding lips. Her heart raced at this simple act of affection, and a shiver ran from head to toe as moisture gathered between her legs sending carnal emotions surging through her body.

He pecked her lips softly and took her hand leading her down the hall to the other side of the living room where there was another hallway with a bathroom and two bedrooms with their own en suites.

Taking a breath to gather her emotions, she once again said, "You have a lovely home, Gray."

"Thank you. It means a lot to me that you like it." He nodded toward the kitchen. "I have to finish dinner before it burns. Please join me."

They entered the bright, happy room, full of sunshine and

aromas of dinner. The wine she'd sipped warmed her belly and lifted her spirits.

"May I help you with something?"

"Yes. Sit right there at the counter and talk to me."

She smiled as she sat and began telling him about her day and the craziness that had ensued. She asked him about his project and how he felt about the end result. He told her about it and noted the client was very happy.

She enjoyed watching him move around his kitchen. He expertly managed dinner, efficiently filling pots and pans, moving and chatting with her at the same time. He picked up his wine glass and sipped, his eyes on hers, and the thrill that shot through her body was heady. It was probably him that made her feel giddy; the wine was just a beverage at this point.

He finished cooking dinner, and they moved to the table to eat. He'd made stir-fry chicken with snow peas, carrots, baby corn, and rice noodles.

She wanted to know this man. "Tell me about your childhood, Gray."

"I have great parents; we were well taken care of. My father worked in a paper mill his whole life until he retired ten years ago. My mom didn't work outside the home. We always had a hot meal on the table, a clean house to live in, and clean clothes to wear. We did things as a family when we could, and to this day, every Sunday is dinner at Mom and Dad's. My mother insists on it. She's worried we'll drift apart as a family, so we all go every Sunday to have a noon lunch at their place." He set his fork on his plate. "Come with me this Sunday."

She froze with her fork halfway to her mouth, "You want me to meet your family? So soon?"

He shook his head again. "Sam, why not? How are we going to get to know each other if we don't include each other in our respective lives? My parents are going to be over the moon to meet you. Besides, they already know about you." He resumed eating as her stomach knotted.

"They know about me? How do they know about me?" she squeaked.

He laughed. "Well, first of all, Jax has had a field day telling everyone how you stopped me in my tracks when I first saw you. I've heard it over and over again. Then, because everyone at the office has heard it and my dad stops in the office a couple of times a week to have coffee and catch up with all of us, he heard about it. I told him that I felt an immediate connection with you and about Mrs. Koeppel and how everything had worked out. I'm very close to my parents; I feel like I can tell them anything." He picked up his wine glass and took a sip.

She set her fork on her plate and folded her hands together in her lap. "Wow. I'm just a little overwhelmed, I guess. It's scary meeting a whole family at one time and knowing that they'll be judging me and comparing me to your other girlfriends."

"First of all, I have only taken two women to meet my family—Suzanne and Cheryl. They hated Suzanne, and after we had been married a couple of years, she refused to go over there, so I took the kids and went without her. Cheryl only came with me a few times; sometimes she worked and sometimes I just didn't invite her. I told you, I didn't feel that connection with her, so it really didn't matter to me one way or the other if she came along. But I would really like it if you'd come with me on Sunday. In fact, I insist."

He stared into her eyes, and the earnest, hopeful look she saw in the deep brown depths made it hard to resist. Swallowing, she nodded yes.

After cleaning up the dishes, they took another glass of wine into the living room. Gray started a fire as the sun set, and the coziness of the room felt like a warm blanket on a chilly day. He leaned over and kissed her lips. He tasted like wine, the citrusy scent of his shower soap combined with the warmth of his body filled her senses eliciting goose bumps on her arms and moisture between her legs. He pulled her onto his lap and quickly laid back on the sofa, his arms tightly wrapped around her. They lay side by side, their lips sliding together, soft and moist, their bodies pressed together from shoulder to toe. She could feel his cock grow between them, the thickness exciting her and causing her breathing to increase as her body pushed into his, seeking more. Gray pushed against her, and the moans escaped her throat of their own accord.

He took her hand and pulled it down between them covering his erection. She'd nearly forgotten the feeling of a hard man in her hands. She rubbed and squeezed relishing the pants of air escaping his lungs and the moan of desire as he captured her mouth, exploring with his tongue. Feelings flooded through her in waves—longing, happiness, and amazement at the level of sexual desire, all of it.

Sam reached up and slid her fingers through his hair and fisted it. He groaned in her mouth sending riotous vibrations running through her body. She could feel him quiver, and she felt so alive to still be able to excite a man. Gray deepened his kiss, pressing his lips firmly, but oh, so perfectly, against hers.

He stood and pulled her to her feet. Placing his hand on the small of her back he pulled her into his body. His engorged cock pressed into her lower belly, hastening the desire and need in her.

She slid her palms behind his back and tried pulling him into her harder so she could find release. He moved his palm from the small of her back up to her cheek, cupping her face between both of his hands, his voice ragged and jerky.

"Sam, if we keep doing this, I won't be able to stop; not sure if I can stop now. You need to stop me if you can't go any further."

She didn't hesitate. "I don't want to stop, Gray. I want to be with you."

Gray exhaled loudly. His mouth came down on hers, this time a little more insistent. Pressing firmly against her lips, he deepened his kiss while wrapping both of his arms around her. Her hands slid around his neck and back into his hair as she met his kiss with her own. She explored his mouth like he had explored hers earlier— tongue for tongue, stroke for stroke. They were both breathless. She felt her feet leave the floor and opened her eyes to see he was carrying her to the bedroom. She wrapped her arms tighter around his shoulders and slid her face along his, finding his ear with her tongue swirling it around the shell making him stumble.

He gruffed, "Be careful or we won't make it to the bedroom, woman, and I'll have you right here on the floor."

Sam mumbled, "I don't care where you have me."

He growled and quickened his pace. Gray laid her gently on his bed while keeping his left arm under her back. He hoisted himself on the bed, lifted her with his left arm, and slid her farther back, moving with her.

He laid down, half on top of her, and continued to kiss her. Long, slow, moist kisses that removed all thought from her mind. His right hand worked her shirt from her jeans. She did the same with his shirt. He unhooked her waistband and unzipped her jeans and slowly slid his hand into her pants and panties. As soon as he touched her, she sucked in her breath. He slid his fingers through her curls and into the fleshy folds. Then, he found that perfect little spot and slowly circled it with the pad of his finger.

Mind. Blown. His fingers were magic and instinctively knew where to touch her. She moved her hips to add pressure. Yes, she had missed being touched, being needed and worshiped. His breathing was ragged and deep. He laid his forehead on hers.

"God, Sam, you're so wet for me. You feel absolutely amazing."

He kissed her again as she unhooked his waistband. Reaching in, she felt his length—large, long, and thick. The satiny skin was such a contrast to his hardness. As soon as she touched him, his breath caught in his throat, and he groaned and pushed into her hand.

"Sam, I need to be in you."

She pulled her hand from Gray's pants and pushed them down his lean hips. He did the same with hers. He reached down and pulled off her shoes, followed by her pants, then his own. She had on her prettiest bra and panties, one of her splurges for herself. They felt good which, in turn, made her feel good. He turned to look at her, and she held her breath. Oh, my God, he would see her. Instinctively, she started to roll away so he couldn't see her. How could she have forgotten what she looked like? He grabbed her arm and stopped her from rolling away.

"No, Sam, don't turn away from me. Let me look at you."

"No, Gray, I can't ... I'm not ... I have ... You won't ..."

"Sam, I think you're beautiful. I want to see you, to look at you."

"You don't understand, Gray. I've had babies, big babies. I've had surgeries and, on top of that, Mother Nature isn't really all that kind to some people. You'll be disappointed."

"God, Sam, how can you think that? Do you think I'm perfect? Good Lord, I've had surgeries, and I'm not as fit as I once was. Mother Nature isn't kind to anyone. We all suffer life's journeys. We're in this together. I need to see you."

She swallowed the dryness away and slowly lay back down, keeping her arms across her stomach. A tear slid from her eye, down the side of her face and into her ear. Gray reached up and swiped at the tear and kissed her very softly. He put his hand over her arms and, while he slowly kissed her, he gently pulled her arms to her sides. He was careful not to look at her, but he slid his palms over her toned abdomen. He slowly caressed her tummy and slid his fingers into her panties, placing the pad of his finger over her sensitive flesh. She moaned as he circled her little nub of nerves. Sliding his fingers farther down, he gently pushed one finger inside her body. A loud breath escaped her; she groaned and pushed into his hand.

He left her mouth and slowly kissed his way down her body, stopping first at her left breast. Lifting her bra out of the way, he pulled her breast into his mouth and suckled. Her breasts felt heavy and achy with need. Circling her breast with his warm, wet tongue, her nipple puckered, her breathing hitched, and the heat climbed from her toes to her face. He sucked her breast in again and let it go to focus on the other, giving it the same treatment. Gray reached around her with his free hand and unclasped her bra, then gently pulled it away. Sam reached up to cover her breasts with her hands, but he stopped her.

"No ... no. Shh."

He then moved downward with his mouth, licking and sucking

along the way. She felt heavenly—warm, floating in pleasure. She tried not to think about how much experience he had; she needed to keep those thoughts at bay.

Gray continued kissing her as he slid her panties down. He licked over her sensitive flesh causing her to pant shallow breaths. First, he licked with the point of his tongue. When he flattened his tongue and licked with more pressure, his finger moved inside her in rhythm with his tongue. Ecstasy was the only word that came to mind.

Gray moved up her body and stopped to pull off his underwear, and her eyes were riveted on the beauty of this man. His eyes sought hers, and she moved to cover herself. He shook his head and slowly slid his palm up her body, along her heated skin causing gooseflesh to form in its path.

He sighed, "Sam, you're so beautiful. You take my breath away."

Covering her body with his, he captured her lips with his and commanded her mouth once again. She felt consumed in the most delicious way. The softness of his hair in her hands, the firmness of his body on hers, the scent of his skin and his tongue – well, hell.

When he spoke, his voice was raspy, deep and so damned sexy, "I'm about to make you mine, Sam. Do you understand me? You will be mine, only mine."

She opened her eyes to stare deeply into the dark brown orbs staring back and saw raw emotion looking back. Yes, she wanted to be his.

"Does that mean you'll be mine, only mine?"

"Yes, baby, that's exactly what it means."

She nodded and smiled, never taking her eyes from his. She felt the broad head of his penis pushing against her entrance, and she slightly lifted her hips to ease the way. Slowly, Gray slid into her—painfully slow, inch by inch, watching her the whole time. It was intense, surreal, and it felt oh-so-good. The crinkles at the corners of his eyes faded to perfection as he sank deeper into her. Her lips tingled from his kisses. Her muscles, taut from need, only enhanced the feel of him pulling out only to push back in farther than before. The sweet friction of their union ignited feelings she thought were long dead and the reawakening almost brought tears to her eyes.

"Ahh, Sam, I've thought about you so much and how good you would feel, but, my God, I didn't realize how good you would actually feel."

She closed her eyes and sighed.

"Open your eyes and look at me, Sam. Watch me while I make love to you. I want you to be with me."

He moved slowly in and out, creating a beautiful rhythm and she matched him stroke for stroke. She held his gaze as the self-conscious feelings fell away and her building orgasm began taking over. One by one, he moved her hands above her head and locked their fingers together. Sam's eyes started to close as she felt the tension build.

"Open your eyes and look at me. Keep your eyes on me the whole time, baby," he huffed out.

Opening her eyes to watch his face as he moved in and out was surreal. She wrapped her legs around his upper thighs and felt him push farther into her. He groaned and his breathing became more ragged, but he never took his eyes from hers.

He swirled his hips, putting pressure on her in just the right way. She mewled as a breath escaped her mouth. He continued moving, varying the sensations. It was maddening, bringing her close and then slowing.

He huffed out, "How close are you, Sam? I need you to be close."

"I'm close, so close, Gray ..." she managed to say.

She sucked in a deep breath as the waves of her orgasm rolled over her—bucking and shaking and watching his eyes turn a deeper shade of brown as his nostrils flared, thrusting his hips into her until his orgasm hit. He jerked two more times before falling onto his elbows, the magic of their connection floating around them like the warmth of a fresh fire.

She had never made love while watching her partner before. It was incredibly sexy. She saw all the emotions on his face, and he on hers; she watched him as her body gave him such pleasure.

He laid on her for a few moments, both of them catching their breath. His weight on her was comforting. She wrapped her arms around his middle and stroked his back, enjoying the feel of his damp skin on her fingers. Slowly relaxing her legs, they fell below his ass, her ankles still crossed. The feel of the coarse hair on his thighs against her freshly shaved skin was such a contrast but felt perfect. Likewise, the hair on his chest against hers complimented their differences.

Slowly, their breathing evened, and Gray lifted himself up—but first he stopped and looked into her eyes. He rubbed his nose on hers a few times, kissed the tip, and took a deep breath.

"Now, you're mine, Sam ... only mine." He softly pecked her lips. "That was more incredible than I ever dreamed it could be. I needed to watch you while I made love to you."

She swallowed the lump forming in her throat and watched his face soften in the afterglow. His hair had fallen forward over his forehead and stuck in places. The muscles in his shoulders bunched as he moved out of her and to the side. He reached up to the nightstand and pulled a couple of tissues from a box and moved to clean her up. He wiped himself off with the other tissue and threw the tissues in the wastebasket beside the bed. He pulled her into his side and wrapped his arms around her. Sam rested her head on his shoulder as they laid there quietly basking in the afterglow. She drifted off to sleep, his strong arms holding her, his fresh citrusy scent teasing her nose.

8

SECOND CHANCES SERIES

G ray slowly woke as the last rays of the sun set outside the windows of his home. A smile creased his face as the weight of the woman he was quickly falling for lay against his body, her soft, even breathing tickling the coarse hairs on his chest. He closed his eyes to fully savor this moment. He'd never gazed into a woman's eyes as he had sex with her; maybe this was the difference. He'd been compelled to watch the emotions play on Sam's face as he made love to her. Though only knowing each other for less than a week, he was somehow certain that is what had just happened.

She took a deep breath and moved her leg along his as he turned to look into her lovely green eyes. "How are you?"

She smiled sleepily and responded, "I've never been better."

He chuckled and leaned up to kiss her.

"Me either. I'm completely and utterly content. I've never felt content in my life. Do you need anything, maybe dessert?"

"Sure, let me get dressed, and I'll go and pull out the cheesecake and toppings."

"No, don't get dressed."

Gray kissed the top of her head, then pulled his arm from under her head. He rolled and stood on the floor, glancing over her body briefly so as not to make her shy again. Stunning was the word that came to mind. They were both in their fifties but had managed to maintain some semblance of fit physique despite life having its way. Her smooth skin, while loser in parts than probably had been in her youth, maintained a clear smoothness he found sexy.

He walked to his dresser and opened the top drawer, pulled a T-shirt out and turned to Sam. "Just wear this."

He smiled and winked. She giggled, and his heart beat faster at the sound.

She sat up and crossed her arms over her stomach and chest. He didn't make a move to walk toward her; he just stood at the dresser holding his shirt. He watched her eyes as they darted between his and the T-shirt he held in his hands, the indecision on her face clear. She bit her bottom lip, and he chuckled.

"Sam, we just made love to each other. I was inside of you, and I've already seen you. Don't be shy in front of me."

She closed her eyes and took another breath. She scooted to the edge of the bed and quickly walked toward him, reaching out for the shirt. He grabbed her around the waist and pulled her close, enjoying the feel of her flesh against his. Her supple body fit perfectly against his, her soft skin impossible to leave alone.

"Thank you." He breathed into her hair, the scent intoxicating.

He stepped back and handed her his shirt. She quickly slipped it over her head as he leaned over and pulled out a pair of pajama pants from another drawer. He slid those on and took her hand before leading them to the kitchen.

Gray pulled plates from the cupboard and forks from a drawer as Sam opened the refrigerator and pulled out the cheesecake, cherries, chocolate sauce, and whipped topping. He grabbed a knife from a block on the kitchen counter and cut the cheesecake into eight slices. She pulled two pieces from the whole and put each on a plate. They topped their respective slices with toppings of choice. His with cherries and whipped cream and Sam's with chocolate and whipped cream. She grabbed a couple of cherries and placed them on top as she slid him a sly smile. Gray smirked, and not to be outdone, he poured some chocolate sauce over his cherries and whipped cream, enjoying the sound of her giggle as she watched him.

He motioned to the living room, and she turned and led the way, giving him the opportunity to view her slim legs poking from his T-shirt which caused his cock to move around in his drawers. She sat on the sofa and pulled her legs up close to her body. He smiled. "Hold this, please?" he asked as he handed her his cheesecake. He reached over to the coffee table, which was a refurbished antique wooden travel case. He opened the top and pulled out a light blanket, covering her legs and tucked it in around her feet.

"Thank you."

"You're welcome." He winked and took his dessert back.

"Did you redo that travel case? It's beautiful."

Gray looked at it again and shook his head.

"No, I bought it that way. I found it at an estate sale I stopped at one day. I was working on a project not far away. The house was an old Victorian that looked like it had been well cared for. I had never gone to an estate sale before and I thought what the hell. This trunk was in the basement, with various items displayed on top. I liked it and asked if it was for sale. The woman running the sale told me it was, for a hundred dollars. Of course, I snatched it up right away. It seemed like a steal."

Her mouth dropped open. "One hundred dollars! Holy cow, a steal is right!"

Gray smiled. "Do you go to estate sales?"

Sam nodded. "I've been to a few. I love old things, and I can usually see when something can be repaired or restored to be something amazing. Recycling at its best, I guess. I usually look for pieces like this travel case or something that can be made into a furniture item or a useful piece within a home. But I love redoing the pieces myself. There's something about sanding, staining, working on something that someone thought was past its prime. The act of giving it love and attention and making it pretty again gives me great pleasure. You should see my office. I have several pieces there that I've refinished."

He nodded. "I would like to see it."

"I bet Jax finds some really great pieces in buildings before he tears them down. I would love to go in with him sometime and see if there are things that can be repurposed before he destroys them."

Gray laughed. "Jax doesn't look at things in buildings like that. When he goes in, he's looking at structure, walls, windows, and the best way to bring the building down. That's it. He's really good at his job and totally focused on the task at hand. But I'll let him know you would like to go into a building with him. I think he's going to look at a building tomorrow if you would like to go."

"I'd love that, and I don't work Fridays at the office so it would work out perfectly."

They finished their dessert and watched the fire for a while. Gray poured them each another glass of wine and picked up their plates to take them into the kitchen. When he came back into the living room, he placed their wine on the coffee table and sat in front of Sam on the sofa.

He looked into her eyes and asked, "Do you trust me?"

She pulled her eyebrows together but nodded. He put one of his hands behind her head and pulled her close to him and kissed her, very softly and very slowly. He tilted his head so his mouth fit over hers completely and continued to kiss her. His breathing became ragged. He reached up to her face with his other hand and ran the back of his fingers down her cheek, her jaw and down to her neck. He pulled away and looked into her eyes.

"Stand up."

He stood up and reached for her hand and helped her to her feet. He pulled her toward the kitchen but stopped at the end of the large soft leather sofa with oversized arms. He walked her in front of the large arm of the sofa and turned her to face it. His heart raced, and his fingers shook slightly from excitement. She looked up at him her brows raised in question. He leaned down and pecked her lips with his. He began to perspire, and his cock grew thick and full just thinking about this. He stepped behind her and reached forward and took one of her hands in his and slowly brought it behind her. With his other hand, he pulled the soft string from his pajama pants and tied it around her wrist. He heard her breath hitch and whispered, "I won't hurt you, I only want to experiment with you. We're together in this." He waited for her to nod and reached around and pulled her other hand behind her, securing it with the remaining tie.

With her hands tied behind her back, her breathing became shallow. He stood behind her and gently kneaded her shoulders, crooning soft words into her ears. "Look what you do to me, Samantha." He stepped into her body, her hands in the perfect position to touch his hardened length. He slowly pushed himself into her hands and let out a long breath when her fingers closed around him. He hissed as her hands moved slightly, stroking him with her soft hands. The heat rose in his body, the excitement almost too much to bear, and he stepped back and enjoyed the view.

He softly said, "At any time you feel you want me to stop, you just need to tell me. Do you understand me, Sam? Just tell me to stop."

She nodded, and he watched her swallow.

"Say it, Sam, don't nod. I need to hear you."

She took a deep breath. "If I want you to stop, I have to tell you."

With his hands still on her shoulders, he gently pushed her down so she was bent over the arm of the sofa. Her feet were still on the floor, though only her toes touched it. Her hands were behind her, and her bare bottom was exposed. He softly whistled, and her moist pussy came into view. Sexy.

He ran his hand over her heated skin very slowly, kneading and enjoying the feel of her bare bottom on his hands. Placing his other hand on her ass, he gently pulled her cheeks apart. He bent and slowly licked her opening, swirling his tongue around until he heard her gasp. She tightened her legs, and he groaned.

"Open your legs, Sam. Let me in."

He felt her relax then tighten again, so he licked her again and moaned, sending vibrations through her. He closed his mouth over one of her fingers and gently sucked a few times until he heard her whimper. He stood, unable to restrain himself much longer; the throbbing in his cock and the tightening of his balls were dangerously close to exploding. He leaned over and licked the shell of her ear, gently pushing himself against her sweet ass.

He whispered, "You're so beautiful, Sam. Looking at you like this —with your hands tied behind you, showing me so much trust, your sexy bottom showing itself to me—I can't tell you what this does to me, what it means to me."

He grasped her hands in his and began rubbing small circles with his thumbs. He lifted his hands from her, shoved his pants down his legs and kicked them to the side. He stepped in close to her, using his feet to spread her legs open for him. He huffed out a breath as he watched her pussy open to him. Moving his cock to her opening, her moisture easily allowing him to slide inside, he groaned as her warm, tight entrance gave way to his length.

"Oh, so wet for me, so ready for me," he huffed.

He heard her whimper, and it excited him beyond words. He pulled out and thrust in, almost fully seated inside her. She moaned and fisted her fingers, and he looked down to watch as his cock pulled out, glistening from her juices, and slid back into her warmth. His heartbeat increased, his fingers shook, and it was hard to pull a full breath into his lungs.

He quickened his pace, moving faster and pushing into her harder and harder, his balls slapping against her as he rapidly climbed the mountain of ecstasy.

"Let go, baby, let me hear you when you come, I need you there now." She tried to say something, but cried out and stiffened before words came, and he thrust in hard and fast three more times before spilling into her. He leaned over her, his heart thumping against her back. Her breathing was rapid and shallow.

"Sam, what you do to me," he managed when his breathing regulated. "Wow!" He slowly stood and pulled out of her, grabbing tissues to clean them up.

"I'm not as young as I used to be; you've worn me out. Shall we go to bed?"

She gathered her thoughts as he untied her hands. "You want me to spend the night?"

Gray chuckled. "Of course, I do. We're adults, Sam. We don't owe anyone an explanation. We've just made love, and I want to sleep with you beside me."

She slowly stood, stretching her back, and turned to face him. He patiently waited for her answer though she knew it was no use arguing about it. Besides, she wanted to stay. She nodded, and the smile that stretched across her face seemed to give him all he needed.

He grinned and took her hand. "Let's take a shower, shall we?"

Entering the massive bathroom, she pointed to the water closet and stepped into the smaller room, closing the door behind her. She heard the water run in the shower and felt a bit more comfortable that he couldn't hear her, which was silly, but still.

As she stepped out of the room, Gray was coming back into the bathroom with a fresh T-shirt and pajama pants. But he was completely naked. Her mouth went dry admiring his body, which was still toned for a man his age. He stepped up to her and took the hem of the T-shirt she was wearing in his hands pulling it up and over her head. He stood back to look at her and Sam turned away from him. He came up behind her and wrapped his arms around her body, pulling her tightly to him.

"I believe you were just looking at me. Fair is fair."

He chuckled and led her to the shower.

9

SECOND CHANCES SERIES

S am opened her eyes and saw the beautiful view of the flower
gardens outside. The colors had begun peeking from the buds
in the garden, and the variety was stunning. Birds sang out
morning songs, and the faint sound of a dog barking somewhere in
the distance made her smile. She stretched slightly, and Gray pulled
her into his chest.

He whispered in her ear, "Good morning. Did you sleep well?"

She sighed contentedly. "I sure did. How about you?"

He chuckled. "I feel amazing. Thank you for staying. I haven't
slept that well in such a long time. The last time I slept that well was
the first few weeks after leaving Suzanne and feeling free from her
manipulation and bullshit. Do you want coffee? I want to get up and
call Jax to find out what time he's going into the building if you still
want to go with him."

She nodded and yawned. "I would like that if neither of you
mind."

"Neither of us mind, Sam. I love that you're interested in what I
do. If you find something useful in the meantime, great; it serves
many purposes."

He scooted to the edge of the bed and stretched upon standing.

She rolled over and admired the muscles bunching and stretching in his back. And, of course, his ass, which filled out the pajama pants he wore nicely. She slid out of bed and padded into the bathroom to try and tame her stupid hair. She figured it looked awful, and it did. She ran water in the sink, put her hands under it and ran them through her hair to tame it in the wild places. It wasn't perfect, but it would do. She dressed in her clothes from yesterday and walked out to the kitchen following the aroma of freshly brewing coffee.

"Mmm smells amazing. I love the smell of coffee in the morning."

Gray looked over at her and frowned. "What's wrong?"

Gray shook his head and shrugged his shoulders. "I didn't think you would get dressed."

Sam looked at him and said, "Well, I can't walk around an old building naked—that's just wrong—and with your son, no less."

"I just wanted to enjoy looking at you a bit more. I'm selfish like that."

She giggled and sat at the counter as he slid a freshly poured cup of coffee toward her.

"I decided to play hooky with you. So, if you don't mind, I would like to go with you. I want to see what you see and what you think you can make beautiful again."

He walked around the counter and kissed her, wrapping his arms around her waist.

"That sounds like a great plan. I hope your boss isn't a jerk or you might get into trouble."

She giggled and picked up her cup of coffee. "Don't talk about my boss that way," he said as he winked. "Do you mind if I turn some music on?"

"Of course not. I love music, and besides, it's your house."

"Yes, but I want you to love being here with me," he said as he stepped into the living room and turned on the stereo.

Sam smiled and sipped her coffee while Gray called Jax and told him the plan.

Finishing his phone call, he told her about the building as they made breakfast together. She enjoyed watching him cook; and dang, he wasn't hard on the eyes either. She cut celery for their omelet as he whisked the eggs. The butterflies in her tummy took flight again as she marveled at this situation. She glanced his way, smiling at his hair, still slightly rumpled from sleeping, yet she liked the way he looked in the morning, especially knowing he'd slept alongside her last night.

They ate breakfast and cleaned up the dishes. Sam followed Gray to the bedroom so he could change clothes.

She sat on the edge of the bed, her feet hanging free as he pulled clean clothes from his drawers. He walked into the bathroom and turned on the water, and she turned to stare out the windows at the lush landscape.

Listening absently as the water splashed and changed its tune, the soft music piped through the house serenading her with a Josh Groban love song. She slid from the bed and walked to the leather chairs in the windows, and sat sideways in one of them, inhaling the smell of leather. It seemed the smile was permanently fixed on her face.

The water turned off, and the towel and clothing rustled as she watched two birds swooping and diving outside, then a gray squirrel skittered across the lawn and shot up a tree, his bushy tail swishing.

"You make me happy, Sam."

She turned to see Gray standing at his dresser, his arms at his sides, perfectly fitted jeans fit over his form nicely, a black, long-sleeved T-shirt stretched across his chest and tucked in, showing off his waistline. A shiver slid down her body as his fresh scent wafted to her nose. "You make me happy, too. Thank you."

He chuckled and stepped toward her, his eyes catching sight of the playing wildlife in his yard.

"Those two go at it every morning," he said watching the birds flitting around.

She smiled. "They seem perfectly choreographed." She stood and stepped toward him.

"I would like to run home and put on some makeup and change clothes. Do you mind?"

"Of course not. If you want to run now, I'll do a bit of work and be over in about an hour."

Sam smiled. "That'll be great, thank you. I'll leave the garage door open for you so you can let yourself in."

She kissed Gray and waved as she stepped out the door. Starting her car, the giggles erupted as the music played Kid Rock. She was looking forward to today.

She jumped in the shower as soon as she got home. She dressed casually in jeans and a long-sleeved T-shirt, just as Gray had and pulled a sweater from her closet before walking out to the living room. There he stood, admiring the pictures on her mantle.

She stepped up next to him and pointed out her children and grandchildren in the photographs. They chatted for a few moments before she stepped back and saw his boots.

"Those look like Harley-Davidson boots. Do you ride?"

The smile that curved his lips nearly took her breath away. "You look beautiful, Sam."

Then he stood back a step and smiled.

"Yes, I ride. Not as much as I used to, but I have a bike. I love getting out on the open road. Most recently I've been riding with the Rolling Thunder guys."

Sam had heard of the Rolling Thunder garage in town. The owner, known as Dog, ran a bike repair garage and they also built custom bikes. His bikes were high-end and caught a lot of attention. They looked like a hard-core group of bikers, but they were a great crowd of people.

She laughed and grabbed his hand. "I have something to show you."

She walked him back to the garage and hit a button on the wall to open the door to the second garage across the driveway. They had the second garage built when they moved in to store all the toys the boys began to collect as they grew up. They entered the second garage and skirted past the four-wheelers, lawn mower, and miscellaneous gardening tools. Sam uncovered a 110th Anniversary Harley-Davidson V-Rod in brushed aluminum.

"This is mine. I'll ride with you anytime you like. And, for the record, I also wouldn't mind riding on the back with you once in a while."

Gray laughed and shook his head. "I should have known." He walked around the bike and seemed to admire it. She was proud to show him this part of her life and so happy he had a fondness for it too.

"I've had other Harleys before, but as the motors got bigger, there were heat issues. My short legs got too close to the pipes and rear motor, and I got burned a couple of times. This one fits me."

"It's a beauty, Sam. Just like its owner." He kissed the tip of her nose. "We've got to get going baby; Jax will be waiting."

She closed the garage doors, and they jumped into Gray's SUV. The building was by the river just on the outskirts of Harmony's downtown area. It was a section that had seen better days, but developers were beginning to take a second look at it with the downtown revitalization project underway. The old mall downtown had already been demolished, and condos and office space were being built in its place. Along the river, new condos were being built. In addition to that, they were building a river walk boardwalk along the water downtown, so people could sit and watch the water, walk, or jog. It was beginning to take shape, and existing businesses were upgrading and adding decks and patios for employees and customers to sit and look out at the water.

When they pulled into the lot where the building was located, Jax's truck was already there. He sat in his truck, working on his computer. When they pulled up alongside him, he jumped out and met them in front of the vehicles. Gray hugged his son; Sam enjoyed watching the two men—so similar and yet different.

Jax looked at Sam and smiled. "So, you want to see what you can find in there?"

"Well, it never hurts to look, right? Besides, I'm interested in what you guys look at when you're getting ready to demolish a building."

He nodded and turned to walk into the building. Pulling a set of keys from his pocket, he approached the padlock on the entrance door and quickly unlocked it.

"The electricity is shut off, but I have flashlights," he said, pulling mini lights from his hoodie's pocket. Pulling open the large metal door, a moderate amount of light filtered into the entry room, allowing them to see some of the room.

Jax said, "Go ahead and take a look around. I need to look at a few things myself. We'll mark what you think you want when I'm finished."

Sam nodded. "Thank you." She looked at Gray. "If you need to go with Jax, go ahead. I'll be okay."

He smiled and nodded at Jax. "He knows what he's doing; I learned early on to stay out of his way. I want to see what *you* do."

She shrugged and walked forward. Gray followed her as Jax headed off toward the back of the building with a knowing smile on his face.

The main room was large and, for the most part, empty. But right away a large wall of shelving caught her eye. Sam walked over to the shelving and took a long look at it. It was all hardwood, beat up and dirty, but it had the potential for restoration, and she could still keep the distressed edge. Perhaps it could be cut into smaller sections if need be and made into smaller bookshelves. It boasted a large base which was still in decent shape—a little sanding, and it would be fine. What really caught her eye was how beautiful the top was with its scrollwork and raised wood designs. It was unique and very pretty.

"I wonder why they would have something like this here. If this was a factory, why would they have something so decorative?"

Gray looked up at it and shrugged his shoulders.

"I would like to try and work with this if I could. Do you think it's too big?"

He looked it over. "If you don't mind if it's cut up. We can mark where you would want it cut, and the guys can take it out in smaller pieces."

"Really? That would be great."

Gray pointed toward a back room, and they walked that way. Sam noticed right away that the door closing the back room off was an old barn-type door with the large hinges on the top. It was a plank style with large wrought iron hardware on the outside. The handle was one you lifted up out of the wrought iron latch on the wall. The hardware was rusty, but it could be sanded and painted black or whatever color you wanted. The planks were in tough shape, but they might be useful. She looked at Gray. "I would like the door and hardware."

"Really? What will you use that for?"

"Fixed up and given some love and attention, it will be a great piece in an office or studio, lending an eclectic feel. You'll be amazed at how beautiful that piece will be."

He shook his head as they continued through that room since there weren't many useful items found. This room had probably once held large pieces of equipment that had since been removed.

They moved on to other rooms where Sam found a few pieces still in good shape but needed refinishing—an old desk and three wooden chairs.

Gray said, "While you work on this stuff, I would love to help you. I want to see it from start to finish."

"It's a deal." She looked forward to working with him.

They walked around for about an hour and met back up with Jax. He had gone out and gotten his computer and was putting in some numbers and coordinates when they found him at the front of the building. He looked up when they approached and smiled.

"I'm almost finished here. Did you guys find some things you want?"

"Yes, we did. How would you like us to mark them?"

He cocked his head, "I have some masking tape here if it'll stick. We can put tape on what you want to keep and mark it with instructions."

As they marked the items, Jax shook his head. "I don't see how you're going to make anything out of some of this stuff. But I can't wait to see it."

Once they exited the building and walked to their vehicles, Gray asked, "Jax, would you like to join us for lunch?"

"Sure, yeah. Where do you want to go?"

"Let's go to the Fox Harbor." Looking at Sam, he asked, "Good?"

"Good," Sam replied.

She climbed into Gray's vehicle, her face flushed and smiling. "That was fun!"

He laughed at her and shook his head. "I don't know many people would think that was fun, but I'm glad you enjoyed yourself."

He leaned over and kissed her, touching the tip of her nose with his finger. He turned the key in the ignition and backed out of the parking area in front of the old factory. They drove to the Fox Harbor Pub & Grill, a nice little bar and restaurant on the riverfront in downtown Harmony. When the weather was warm, customers could eat outside, but today wasn't warm enough for that. They sat in the back of the bar area and ordered something to drink.

Gray smiled. "I told Sam you've been giving me a hard time about our first meeting and now everyone at the office *and* Mom and Dad are dying to meet her."

Her face turned bright red as her head snapped up to gape at Gray.

"What? Jax was there, Sam. He knows everything, and he's been teasing me relentlessly about it ever since."

Jax laughed. "My dad is usually fairly reserved, but I've never seen him completely speechless. All you had to do was walk into the room, and he was not only speechless, but he also couldn't move, either. While we were sitting there, I leaned over at one point and asked him if he was okay."

Her face burned, and she looked down at the table. She heard both men laugh and Gray's arm snaked around her shoulders as he kissed the side of her head.

"It's okay. I'm happy I met you, even if you did render me speechless."

She peeked up at him. "I'm happy I met you, too, and I hate to say it, but right now would be a good time to be speechless."

Laughing, Gray told Jax about Sam's bike, and they started talking about places they've been and places they wanted to see. Jax and

Ethan also rode. Sarah's husband just bought a bike, and this would be their first year with it, so they were all hoping to get out and ride a bit. She told them that her boys all had bikes as well and hoped they could all ride together sometime. Their lunch came, and they chatted and enjoyed the remainder of their time together.

After lunch, Jax headed back to the office.

Gray asked, "What would you like to do now?"

"I had no idea you'd be spending the day with me. I would love to see your office or more of your buildings if you want to show me."

Gray drove her to his office building. It was a fabulous old building on the lake in downtown Harmony—more on the west side of the downtown area than where they'd been that morning. The building was an old storage building back in the day, and to date, they had only converted the first floor, with plans to eventually convert the entire building. The first floor was clean and nice, but she'd expected to see more personality for an architectural firm. It seemed sterile and cold.

As they walked through, Gray introduced her to some of the employees. He explained that many times the architects were out looking at building sites or checking on work sites, so most days, there were only a few people in the office. Gray's office was at the back. It was a little more comfortable but still felt industrial.

He looked at her expression. "I get the feeling you were expecting something else."

Her eyes grew wide. "I'm so sorry, I don't mean to be negative, but I thought it would have more personality, I guess."

He smiled and shrugged his shoulders. "We've been meaning to make changes, but we're so busy with work and no one takes the time to work on this." He turned in a circle, then faced her. "Do you want to help with that?"

"Really? You would let me help you with this?"

He laughed at her excitement. "Yes. I think it would be fun to see how well we work together. Do you want to try?"

Oh boy, *did* she! She was already thinking of the items they'd found at the old sewing mill this morning. Once the pieces were cleaned up and repaired, she thought they'd look great in this building

"Absolutely, I want to try. This'll be a fun project."

He walked her through the other floors of the building. "I'd envisioned the architectural firm would eventually be on the second floor leaving the first floor available for rental space. The third floor is going to be for the demolition company. As we grow, they will need more than the little offices they currently have on the first floor. The fourth and fifth floors are up for grabs."

There was an old service elevator in the building that could still be used. He wouldn't want his clients using that, so an elevator would have to be installed, as well as better hand railings in compliance with ADA requirements. The spaces were large; it could be fun working with Gray on this.

"Well, you and your people can handle the zoning requirements, ADA, and inspections. I just get to do the fun stuff. I already have some ideas. How do we get this rolling? Do you want to hear my ideas or do you want to give me a list of requirements or no-no's first?"

He laughed. And the first thoughts flitting through her mind were that she wanted to make him laugh all the time. As they continued walking around the second floor, Sam shared some of her ideas for the items they found today.

"Where do you intend to refinish those items, Sam?"

She thought for a moment. "Do you think those bookcases will fit in my garage? They *are* quite large."

"Follow me." They went back up to the fourth floor. "How about right here? There's plenty of room. You can use the service elevator to bring the pieces up and then to take them back down when they're finished. You'll have people here to help you if you need to move something around or out of the way. And, the bonus is, I can come up here and see you when I want to."

"Oh, ulterior motives!" She giggled. "It does seem like a good idea. Nothing is finished up here, so I won't be messing anything up. When do you think they'll start moving the pieces out of the old building? I'll need to get up here and clean a little before they bring them in."

"Why don't we go down and see if Jax is still here and we can ask him," Gray said.

They spoke with Jax for a while. He thought it would be about three or four weeks before they'd start bringing things in. Permits had to be applied for, and it took that long to get the ball rolling. Sam had refinishing supplies at home that she would bring with her, and of course, Gray insisted on buying anything that she needed. By the time they were finished at the office, it was almost time for supper. They left with a wave to Jax and the remaining employees and climbed into Gray's SUV. Once they were on the road, he reached over and grabbed her hand and pulled it up to his lips for a kiss. Sam smiled.

Gray said, "I really enjoyed today with you, Sam. Thank you for making my day great."

"Thank you for allowing me to tag along. I enjoyed it immensely." She was getting the feeling no one had ever treated Gray like he mattered.

Back at Gray's house, they settled on the sofa with a glass of wine. Neither of them was hungry so they thought a little downtime and relaxing would be nice. Gray turned on the stereo system. Sam leaned back into the sofa with her feet up on the coffee table, and Gray did the same right next to her. He reached over and held her hand, and they sat listening to music for a few more songs. It was nice, peaceful, and comfortable.

After a while, Gray sat up and turned to look at Sam.

"Would you like to go riding tomorrow? The weather is supposed to be warm, might even get into the seventies. We can dress warm and stop as often as we need to."

Sam smiled. "That sounds great."

"You said you didn't mind, so I hoped you would ride with me. I want to be able to touch you and talk to you a little while we ride."

"Perfect. I'll need to go home and get warmer clothes and my boots and jacket, though."

Gray leaned forward, took her wineglass from her hand, and set it on the table. He grabbed her up and put her in his lap and kissed her.

His full lips on hers felt so perfect. She slid her arms around his shoulders and up into his hair. When they needed air, Gray pulled away from her mouth to her cheek, her jaw, and down her neck. When he got to her ear, he nibbled and licked the outer shell before he lightly licked inside.

"Are you hungry, Sam? I can make us something to eat."

"You're hungry?"

He chuckled a little. "No, I just thought I would ask, so I wasn't being rude."

"Good, because after that kiss I wondered why you were thinking about food."

Gray picked her up and carried her to the bedroom where he laid her on the bed.

He rasped, "Get undressed completely and kneel in the center of the bed. I'll be right back."

He walked into his closet, and she could hear drawers opening and closing. She undressed, still embarrassed about being naked in front of him. She thought about climbing under the covers and waiting for him to come back. He returned before she could do anything, and he frowned at her.

"You're supposed to be kneeling in the center of the bed."

She swallowed before taking a deep breath and slowly climbed on the bed and kneeled in the center. Her cheeks burned, and she could feel the heat on her chest as her heart hammered.

Softly he said, "Now, come over here and kneel in front of me."

She crawled over to kneel in front of him, and he leaned down and kissed her.

"You're so beautiful."

He kissed her again, more insistently this time, spreading a different warmth throughout her body. He placed his hands on her shoulders and turned her away from him placing a blindfold snugly over her eyes and securing it in the back. He leaned down and whispered in her ear.

"Anytime you want to stop; you just need to tell me. Do you understand?"

She nodded, but Gray interrupted her.

"No, say it."

Her voice was weak and shook, nerves and excitement taking over. "I understand."

Her heartbeat increased and felt like it rocked her whole body, the blindfold heightening her senses. "Good. Now I want you to stay here for a minute."

She put her arms around her stomach, and Gray took her hands and pulled them down.

"No, you are not to cover yourself up. Sit here, hands and arms down."

Her lips quivered, and her breathing grew unsteady. A few seconds later she felt something soft around her wrist. But then he lifted her up and laid her on the bed and positioned her in the middle. The hand that he had just tied the scarf around was slowly pulled up and tied to one of the posts of the bed. He efficiently tied her other hand to the opposite post. Before she knew it, he was on the bed and straddling her. It felt like he still had his clothes on. He softly kissed her lips, licking in between warm wet smooches, exploring her mouth with his tongue before he began to slowly work his way down her body, all the while whispering sweet words of adoration between soft pecks from his eager lips.

When he reached her most tender spot and licked, she moaned and wriggled. Gray held her hips in place.

"Not yet, baby," he whispered between lavishing her clit with kisses and swipes from his talented tongue.

Changing the pressure from his tongue, flat to firm, swirling to suckling on her he had her worked up to a frenzy in a hurry. Unable to control her movements, her hips bucked and thrust, seeking the ultimate release but never quite getting there.

Very slowly, he slid his finger inside of her, sliding in and out. Then he inserted two fingers and she whimpered. As her orgasm was building, her breasts felt full and warm, her skin tingled, and she could feel her whole body flush. Her breathing was stilted, and she imagined what he looked like with his face between her legs, his salt and pepper hair, his deep brown eyes. Just then as he swiped along her clit and sucked it into his mouth, she exploded. Her chest rose and fell as the sparks behind her eyelids continued to flash. Gray climbed up her body, gently kissing along the way.

Reaching her lips, he softly kissed her once. "That was absolutely beautiful."

He slowly guided his cock to her entrance and slid inside of her, the pace relaxed and patient. He pulled out and pushed back in. "You feel just perfect, Gray."

He drew in a raspy breath. "No, baby, we're perfect together."

His pace was steady and even, in and out, his weight just above her, his arms alongside her body. He held her shoulders with his strong fingers cupped over them; his breathing increased as his hips followed suit. She wrapped her legs around him as high as she could and hung on for the ride. He kissed her passionately, thoroughly— their tongues blending and dancing and tasting each other. His scent surrounded her, the fresh clean fragrance he used seemed to grow bolder as his skin heated. She felt surrounded by him, and it was intoxicating.

He rolled his hips, and she moaned, "Gray, I'm going to come."

"No, Sam, don't come until I tell you to. Hold on."

She panted as his pace increased with each thrust into her—his breathing ragged. She whimpered and heard him groan.

"Now, baby, come now."

Her body jerked as her orgasm flowed through her. Two strokes later, Gray came with a groan. His body spasmed and his weight slightly pressed into her.

"You make me have the strongest orgasms, Sam."

She laughed softly. "Gray, it isn't me. It's you."

She felt him exhale, his full weight on her. She didn't care; she could lie like this forever. She loved this feeling right after—no barriers, no pretenses, just pure feeling. He reached up and untied her right hand and rubbed it to get the circulation going, then did the same with her left hand. Finally, he reached up and removed the blindfold from her eyes. When her eyes met his, he was smiling.

"You don't mind that I like to tie you up or blindfold you?"

Her lips formed a soft smile. "It's a little scary. But it's also hot, and if you like it, I'd do it anyway to make you happy."

He raised his brows. "Sam, I don't want you to pretend anything for me. It has to be what we both want, or it won't work. Promise me. Remember, you're the one who keeps saying 'open and honest.'"

She nodded. "I promise."

He kissed her again and sighed heavily. "You make me feel so good. I never dreamed I could feel content. But I do with you. I never have before, Sam. Never."

She put her arms around his shoulders and slid her hands into his hair staring into his eyes. "I'm so sorry you've never felt content, Gray. That's very sad, but I'm so glad that I can make you feel that way. As long as you don't get bored with feeling content."

She smiled, and he chuckled. "I'll never get bored with this feeling. I've longed for it my whole life."

She hugged him close for a long time. He moved to slide off her and grabbed tissues to clean them up. She couldn't wait to snuggle back up to him.

Gray pulled her close, and she eagerly snuggled into him. She closed her eyes as both of his arms wrapped around her, but then her stomach growled and spoiled the moment.

She giggled. "I'm sorry. My tummy is being a pest."

He laughed and said, "I'm getting hungry, too."

They got up, and Sam bent over to grab her clothes.

Gray said, "No, no, wear one of my T-shirts. They're in the top drawer. I like the way you look in them."

She giggled. "I doubt it's that you like the way I look and more the convenience of it, but I like wearing them, so I won't fuss."

He shrugged his shoulders and pulled on a pair of pajama pants.

They found roast beef from the night before last in the refrigerator and made sandwiches, then sat at the table and talked about the things they wanted to do at the office and on the fourth floor and put together a plan of attack.

"Go ahead and come up with ideas, then we can discuss them. I'll check and see what can and can't be done per code and ADA restrictions. We'll go from there."

"What's my budget?"

"As long as you don't go overboard, we should be fine. Besides, if you intend to use a lot of reclaimed pieces, it shouldn't break the bank."

"But there must be some limits. Gray, I've never worked without a budget. What if I do something wrong?"

"Sam, please don't worry. I'll be right here all the time. I'll be helping you with the refinishing. If something looks out of place or it seems as though it's getting expensive, we'll talk."

All in all, she was looking forward to it, but it was going to be a lot of work. She'd work at the law office during the day and have to spend evenings refinishing pieces and working out plans with Gray for the second and third floors. But they would be doing it together, and that would be fun, too.

10

SECOND CHANCES SERIES

T he sunlight filtered into the bedroom and draped itself across Gray's chest, warming it and waking him. He cracked open his eyes and inhaled deeply, immediately recognizing Sam's perfume. The musky scent was now imprinted on his brain and would forever make him think of her. Best smell ever. That was something, wasn't it? Throughout the night last night, he'd woken up and wrapped his arms around her, pulling her close to him so he could drift off to sleep once more. His heart was full right now; it seemed like life was finally working in his favor. 'Bout damned time.

Sam lifted her head to glance at the clock on the dresser, then nestled into her pillow once more with a sigh.

It was nearly impossible not to smile as he watched her. "I'll go get us coffee if you want to sit in bed and drink it while you relax."

Sam sighed. "That sounds great. I hope you plan on joining me."

Gray chuckled. She hadn't even opened her eyes. "I wouldn't be able to concentrate on anything else knowing you were in my bed ... naked."

She hummed and let out a deep breath. He pulled on his favorite pajama pants, the black ones with light gray pinstripes, and sauntered down the hallway to the kitchen. The timer had gone off on the coffeepot, and the aroma of freshly brewed coffee filled his lungs and made him groan in delight. Best smell ever. No, wait, second best smell ever.

He enjoyed pouring two cups of coffee, each with a splash of creamer added. They even drank their coffee the same. Carrying the cups back to the bedroom, he envisioned this being every morning and he liked the way that looked.

He set her cup on the bedside table, setting a napkin and two cookies next to her cup. Unable to stop himself, he kissed her soft lips before saying, "Rise and shine baby. We need to decide what to do today."

She sat back, the sheet tucked under her arms, her hair adorably mussed and standing up in places it normally didn't. He smirked and sipped his coffee, wanting to give her the time she needed to wake up, but he was just so excited to start the day.

After breakfast, they drove to her place for warmer clothes and her boots, then headed to the fourth floor at Kinkaide & Associates. It was only nine, so they had a couple of hours to do a few things. They talked about how the floor should be laid out and started moving some things around.

Gray stopped sweeping and looked at the back corner of the floor. Sam stopped and watched him, deep in thought.

Gray turned and smiled. "You *know* ... with a glass wall around the front, it would be a nice second studio for me to do some drawing. That way, I can work when I need to and still be with you, so you won't be alone."

"That sounds like a great idea," Sam said, clapping her hands together.

"I have some catalogs for the glass walls downstairs. Let's grab them before we head out today and we can look at them tonight."

"That sounds awesome. I can already see it in my mind."

They took a motorcycle ride along the lakeshore, only about a hundred miles, but the feeling of her sitting on the back of his bike, her arms around his waist, was also imprinted on his brain.

Once they returned to his house, they made a nice dinner together, then relaxed on the sofa afterward.

"Tomorrow is dinner at my parents' house."

She softly replied, "I know." Inhaling deeply, she continued, "I'm so nervous about that. Are you sure there isn't a better time for me to meet everyone?"

"Nope. Don't worry, you're going to love them, and they're going to love you."

About one in the morning, Gray woke up thinking about Sam. This little woman had completely turned him inside out. Not in a bad way, but his whole thought process seemed to be consumed with just her—the way she looked, the way she moved, and the way her eyes crinkled when she smiled. And that smile. When she smiled at him, his heart raced, and he became weak in the knees. She wrapped around him so perfectly when he hugged her, kissed her, and made love to her. He'd never thought an orgasm could be any different at any given time in his life. They were simply that finale from the act of sex. But something was different with Sam, something profound and wonderful. That was the most confusing thing of all. Gray had *always* enjoyed sex. What man didn't? But sex with Sam was a whole new experience.

He pulled her into his arms and kissed the top of her head as he inhaled her scent and drifted off to sleep.

11

Arriving home just before ten in the morning, Sam entered the house and felt like a foreigner there. It had been a few days since she'd been here and already it felt like she didn't live here anymore. She'd lived here for so many years, through some of the hardest times in her life, and yet, it didn't feel like she'd ever lived here now. She looked around and sighed. She changed clothes, gathered mail and made sure everything was in order before leaving for Gray's parents'. Her stomach rolled, and she placed a hand over it waiting for the queasiness to pass.

They arrived at the Kinkaide house at eleven-forty—a little early, but Sam didn't want to be late. Arriving late would only draw more attention to her. Being there first meant she'd be able to meet Gray's parents first and then each family member as they arrived—not everyone at once. Gray said everyone was supposed to be there around noon, but usually, no one was on time and dinner wasn't served until after twelve-thirty, so that gave them time.

Harry and Mary lived on the outskirts of Harmony Lake, on a small farm. They had twenty acres and a couple of outbuildings. Gray's mom loved to garden and had the most beautiful perennials, which were starting to show themselves from the earth.

"Ready?" He chuckled.

She nodded and exhaled. Gray got out of the vehicle, and as she watched him walk around to open her door, she took a deep breath. He reached in, took her hand, and helped her from the SUV. He held her hand all the way to his parents' door.

When Gray and Sam walked in, Harry and Mary both smiled. Gray pulled Sam to his mom first and gave her a big hug; then he stepped aside for introductions. Harry sat at the counter with a cup of coffee and Mary worked on the other side on a vegetable dish. It smelled delicious, and it looked like Mary had been cooking for a while.

"Mom, this is Sam. Sam this is my mom, the best cook in the county!"

She chuckled and grabbed Sam in a big bear hug. "We are so excited to meet you, Sam. Welcome."

"Thank you for inviting me, and it's very nice to meet you."

She patted Sam's shoulder and nodded her head.

Gray pulled Sam around the counter to meet his dad. He gave his dad a big hug while she enjoyed the similarities in them. Gray looked like his dad, even more so than in the pictures she'd seen at his house. Harry was a couple of inches shorter, but their shoulders were the same size, and their facial features were similar. This is what Gray would look like when he was in his seventies—very nice. Harry still had those deep brown eyes that he'd passed onto his son, and his hair, while gray, still had quite a bit of dark in it as well.

As soon as Gray pulled away, he grabbed Sam's hand and pulled her forward.

"Dad, this is Sam. Sam, my dad, Harry."

Harry pulled her in for a hug, though thankfully not as hard as he and Gray had thumped on each other. She hugged him back, and he whispered in her ear.

"We've been dying to meet you, Sam. Jax and Gray have told us so much about you."

Sam looked back at him, her eyes big and her brows a little furrowed.

"Really? Then I probably won't have much to add. But, I'm happy to meet you both."

Harry laughed and winked at his son. Mary said, "Sam, dear, what can I get you to drink?" She glanced at Gray. "I assume you'll have a beer?"

"Yes, I'll get it." He winked at Sam and smiled. "Sam likes wine, Mom, what do you have here?"

She started to protest, but Mary shushed her off with a wave and a tsk. "I've stocked up a bit. Gray told us you like the Von Stiehl Winery. I have the Oktoberfest, Cranberry, or a Late Harvest Riesling. What's your pleasure?"

Sam's face flushed. "That's very nice of you, but really, you didn't need to do that. Thank you." She giggled, "Will you be joining me?"

Mary laughed and said, "Well, why not!"

She turned and looked at the bottles, not sure which one, causing her to giggle again.

"The Oktoberfest is very good, one of my favorites. Light and crisp. The Cranberry tastes just like cranberry sauce with a little punch, and the Riesling is a sweeter wine and a little fruity, but not too."

Mary thought just a moment and grabbed the Cranberry wine.

"Perfect." Sam nodded.

Mary giggled as Harry lifted an eyebrow in question.

Gray leaned down and whispered, "My mom likes you. She doesn't drink with just anyone."

Then he kissed her on the cheek, and her face flushed a nice bright red to match the wine. Perfect!

Mary struggled with the bottle and Gray walked around the counter and offered to help. She happily let him. He opened the bottle and poured them each a glass. He handed Mary her glass and walked around the counter to hand Sam hers, but before he handed it to her, he held it back with a snarky grin on his face.

"Pay for it!"

She knew he was teasing her, but she wasn't quite sure what he meant. Then she heard Mary giggle and look at Harry. Okay, so he wanted to play, she grabbed his face in her hands and stood up on her toes to reach him. She kissed him, licked his lips, then kissed him again full on the lips. When she stepped back, she had a big grin on her face.

He raised his brows. "Well played."

From the doorway, they heard, "You're letting them make out in the kitchen?" They turned and Sam recognized the man from the pictures at Gray's house—his brother, Jamie. He laughed as Gray shook his brother's hand and gave him a hearty shoulder slap.

"Jamie, I would like you to meet Sam. Sam, this is my brother, Jamie."

Jamie walked over to Sam, and as soon as he was standing in front of her, he said, "My turn!"

Her mouth dropped open in surprise, her face turned bright red, and she looked over at Gray, who very quickly walked up behind Jamie and shoved him away.

"Find your own girl, Jamie."

Laughing, he shrugged his shoulders just as Gray had done moments before.

"Can't blame a guy for trying! Nice to meet you, Sam."

"Nice to meet you, too, Jamie," Sam said, her face bright red.

Jamie helped himself to a beer from the fridge and looked over at his mom.

"You're having wine?"

Jamie looked at his dad, and Harry raised his eyebrows and nodded toward Sam. She shrugged.

"I like this wine, too, Sam. You're right; it *does* taste like cranberry sauce."

Sam nodded in agreement. The door opened again and in came Dani and Nick. More introductions were made, more raised eyebrows at Mary drinking and more hugging. This family liked to hug. Sam felt comfortable—as much as she could—in a room full of people she had just met. Gray stayed close, making sure she was introduced to everyone. They genuinely liked to spend time with each other. Sam wasn't sure what to think when Gray said his mother demanded Sunday dinner. If people hated coming, it could be awful.

They grabbed plates of food and carried them into the dining room. As soon as all the food was on the table, they found places to sit. Gray grabbed Sam's hand and walked her around the far side of the table from the kitchen, and they sat at the end, next to his dad. Sam sat next to Harry, who was on the end, and Gray on the other side of her. It was nice to sit at a big family table and enjoy each other's company. She didn't grow up in a family like this and never had anything even close to this growing up. So, she spent a great deal of time watching the way the siblings all acted with each other. It was nice.

Jamie sat directly across from Sam, and after they were finished eating, he looked at her with a mischievous grin on his face and leaned in.

"So, Sam, do you want to hear some stories about Gray while we were growing up?"

She smiled. "I would *love* to hear some stories about Gray!"

She looked up at Gray only to see a grimace on his handsome face.

Jamie began telling a story about when they were younger, about nine or ten, and they snuck out of the house one night to go throw stones at a crabby neighbor's house. The story grew long, and Sam got the feeling by some of the snorts and eye rolling that the story had been embellished some. Gray chimed in occasionally, but he seemed to be enjoying this.

After a while, he leaned down and said in Sam's ear, "When I meet your parents, I'm going to ask for stories about you growing up. It's only fair."

She immediately looked down at her hands and froze. She hadn't told Gray about her parents or her family yet. It was hard to talk about. Even her best friend, Pam, didn't know everything; she just didn't talk about it.

"Is everything all right?"

Sam looked at him and nodded. "Can we talk about it later?"

He furrowed his brows, but he nodded and kissed the side of her head. Conversation resumed to normal.

She cleared her throat. "I do have a question to ask. I noticed that many of you wear similar tattoos on your left forearms. What's the significance of that?"

Harry answered. "My grandfather started this tradition. When he met my grandmother, he knew she was the one for him. He didn't have enough money to buy her a ring. He promised her he would one day; but, in the meantime, he wanted everyone to know she was his. I guess he was a little possessive."

Harry smiled, and everyone giggled—apparently, that was a Kinkaide trait as well.

"He asked her to wear his mark. He designed the tattoo with his initials and told her he wanted her to wear it on her left forearm. That way, every time she looked at it, she would remember she belonged to him. She agreed, but she had a stipulation—if everyone was going to know she was his, she wanted everyone to know he was hers, so he would need to wear her mark as well. He wasn't the *only* one who was possessive."

Everyone laughed again.

"My father and his siblings followed suit, I and my siblings and their children, and my children have followed the tradition. There are a few exceptions, but, for the most part, it has been a tradition in my family for five generations now."

Harry laid his arm on the table so Sam could see. Mary laid her arm on the table as well. Sam admired the beautiful tradition. Dani and Nick laid their arms on the table as did Sarah and Cole, Sean and Leila.

"I see you all have the same font. Is that part of the tradition as well?"

"Yes. The original tattoo that my grandfather drew was taken to an artist when my father and mother got married. The artist was asked to use those few letters to draw the whole alphabet for our family. We all use it."

"I think it's a wonderful tradition."

Sam hadn't seen a tattoo on Gray's arm, so she wondered if he'd had his removed.

Dishes were cleared, and the family moved to the living room to visit. Gray and Sam chatted about the ride yesterday and some of the sites they'd seen and the pieces she found at the old sewing mill. They talked in general terms about everything and nothing. Sam said something to cause Gray to laugh; then he said something that made her laugh. Wholly enjoyable.

As soon as Sam put her cake plate down, Lily came over and climbed in her lap. She was a beautiful little girl, long dark hair and those dark eyes like Grandpa. She faced Sam and looked at her and then at Gray.

She kept looking at them for a minute and blurted out, "Are you my new grandma?"

Sam felt a hot flush creep across her face and was certain she'd catch on fire at any moment. Thankfully, Gray spoke up before Sam had to.

"We've only known each other for a short while, let's not scare Sam off, okay?"

Lily smiled and nodded and threw her arms around Sam hugging her tightly.

When she finished hugging Sam, Lily asked, "Do you want to read a book with me?"

Sam smiled. "Of course, I would."

Lily ran off to grab a book, and they moved to a corner of the room so they wouldn't be disturbed or disturb anyone else. In all, they read three books.

Sarah walked over after the third book. "Lily that's enough now, go put your book away and start saying your goodbyes." She grumbled a bit but did as her mom bid.

"Sorry she commandeered you, Sam."

"No problem, I liked it. My granddaughter is her same age. I hope they can meet soon."

Sarah smiled. "That would be nice. You know, my mom doesn't

spend a lot of time with the kids, so she is excited Dad has a new grandma for her. I hope she didn't embarrass you too bad before."

Sam laughed. "I wasn't sure what to say, what she knew or thought. More than anything, I didn't want to say the wrong thing."

They chatted a bit more, but soon, Sarah and Cole began packing up the kids and getting ready to leave.

Gray wrapped his arm around Sam's shoulders. "Are you ready to go?"

She nodded. "I guess I'm a little exhausted from meeting everyone." Mary took Sam's face in both of her hands and kissed her on the cheek.

"It was very nice meeting you, Sam. I'll see you next week, okay?"

"If you're sure, I'd love to join you. May I bring something?"

"No dear, this is my gig. We enjoy having our family over, and I enjoy fussing and cooking. Just join us."

Harry hugged Sam, then he and Gray hugged and shoulder patted, and they were off. Gray took her hand and walked her to the SUV, opened her door, and as she was starting to step up, he grabbed her waist and held her for a minute. He gave her one of his toe-curling kisses that she loved so much.

"Thank you."

Sam looked at him and said, "For what?"

He smiled. "For coming into my life. Thank you."

Her eyes teared up. Wow, he was thanking her for coming into his life? She should be thanking him!

12

On the drive home from Gray's parents', Sam asked, "I haven't seen a tattoo on you or a scar where one might have been removed. Didn't you get marked when you got married?"

Gray took a deep breath. "No. Suzanne wasn't my soul mate. She wasn't someone I wanted to mark myself with."

"But you were together for so long; you had children together," she remarked.

He glanced toward her and then out the windshield. "I've always wanted that—to be marked and to have someone to wear my mark. In my family, it's very important; it means you belong to someone and someone belongs to you. Not in a slave-master way, but in a loving way that means someone loves you enough to wear your initials on their body forever. But I didn't want that with Suzanne."

Sam nodded and squeezed his hand again.

"I'm sorry you haven't had that in your life, Gray."

Gray pulled into the garage and turned the ignition in the truck. They silently walked into the kitchen, and he promptly poured them a glass of wine. They plopped down on the sofa next to each other. Gray flipped through the channels and found nothing of interest. He stopped on the news and turned the volume down and looked over at Sam.

With a bit of a pained expression on his face, he asked, "Can we talk?"

"Of course. Is something wrong?"

He took a deep breath, and as he exhaled, he turned toward her.

"Are you ashamed of me?"

"No, I'm not ashamed of you. What on earth would make you think that?"

"Sam, when we were at my parents and I mentioned meeting your parents and getting some stories about you, you looked away from me and froze. I got the impression you didn't want me to meet your parents."

Sam took a deep breath, set her wineglass on the coffee table, and turned to face him head on. His heart hammered in his chest. Her face scrunched up, and her posture grew rigid.

"It's embarrassing and heartbreaking at the same time."

She took another big breath. "First of all, my father passed away three years ago. So, you won't be able to meet him. My mother is still alive, but I never want you to meet her. Gray, I didn't come from a family like yours. My family didn't want me. They didn't want female children; they only wanted boys. All my life I was told I wasn't good enough, smart enough, pretty enough, or anything enough to be something, to be successful, to be happy, to be anything. My mother repeatedly told me I would be lucky if I ever found anyone who would marry me. And, if I did, I should thank my lucky stars and stick with that person forever, because that would be a miracle."

She swiped at the tears in her eyes. He ground his teeth together at this heartbreaking revelation.

She took another breath and continued.

"My parents were both raging alcoholics, drinking every day and every night. I grew up cooking, cleaning, farming, and basically running the house because they were usually too drunk to do it. By the time I was twelve, I was running the barn, keeping track of the breeding records of our cows, milking morning and night, and coming in to make supper for my brother and me. Then, if I had homework, I would stay awake until late at night, trying to catch up. Usually, I had to hide that I was doing homework. If my mother knew about it, she'd come into my room and scream at me that it was useless. She said I wasn't going to amount to anything anyway and I could be using that time doing laundry or a hundred other things around the house that needed to be done.

"I learned very early to be invisible and not call attention to myself, and above all else, never get in any kind of trouble in school so my parents wouldn't be called. I was there to make sure there was food on the table, the cows were milked and bred when they were due, and keep track of the household bills. I needed to tell them when something was due and I had better not be late. My brother didn't need to do anything; he was a boy. After all, he was going to carry on the family name. I wasn't."

Gray couldn't say anything. He continued to stare at her as she wiped her eyes. He slowly reached forward and pulled her into his arms. Kissing the top of her head, his heart broke for the little girl who never got to be little. His breathing came in ragged breaths; his eyes grew glassy from unshed tears.

The silence stretched on for lack of knowing what to say.

"Do you think less of me now?"

Gray straightened his back. "Why would you think that?" He pulled away and turned her to face him. "Why would I think less of you?"

Sam's voice quivered, "Well, I didn't come from a good family like you did. That's important to some people."

"Oh God, Sam."

He pulled her onto his lap, pulled her head down on his shoulder, and wrapped his arms around her.

"I think more of you. Look at you. You're beautiful, smart, funny, happy, loving, and you did it all on your own. You educated yourself, raised a family, and you aren't bitter or resentful in any way. Now when I think of how you were with Mrs. Koeppel, it amazes me even more that you could be so compassionate in light of your past. No, Sam, I don't think less of you, I think more of you."

Gray held her for a long time. He rocked her back and forth, and it felt good to soothe her and comfort her.

After a while, he cleared his throat. "Do your kids know about them?"

Sam sighed. "A little. I didn't tell them everything because I didn't want them to have hate toward my parents. But they've only seen my mother about three times in their lives, so they don't know her. They saw my father a bit more, but he never talked to anyone, so they didn't know him either.

"My parents divorced after I graduated from high school. So, that's why they saw my father a little more. I still felt responsible, like I owed it to my parents to make sure they had Christmas and birthdays. I know in my head it wasn't my responsibility, but I had such guilt if I didn't try. When Jake was seven, my brother and I had to have our mother committed. She had gotten so bad with her drinking, she didn't have a job. She had charged groceries and liquor all over town and wasn't able to pay her rent, so her landlord had served her with eviction papers.

"Finally, her neighbor got my brother's number from my mom and called him and told him what was going on. He called me and said we had to have her committed.

"My brother had straightened out her finances, so when she got out, he'd found her an apartment close to his house. She found a job and was working to supplement her social security. My brother checks on her unannounced and rummages through her garbage and cupboards to make sure she is staying sober. She stayed clean—for a number of years actually—but she wouldn't have anything to do with me. I had invited her to Jake's birthday party, and she said she would come and never showed up. I stopped trying with her after that. She has since fallen back off the wagon, and now she's worse than ever. She won't even have anything to do with my brother now. He has paid her bills, helped her out over and over, but she won't speak to him because the last time she was at his house, he refused to give her any alcohol."

Sam sat up a bit and looked at Gray. "I'm sorry I didn't tell you sooner, open and honest and all. It's hard for me to talk about, and to tell you the truth, the only other person I ever said anything to was Tim. Even my best friend, Pam, doesn't know everything."

Gray squeezed her tight, swallowing his anger and resentment. "I'm so sorry, Sam. I had no idea you had a childhood like that. No child should ever feel like they don't matter, especially not you. You're good, do you know that?"

She swallowed a few times, and finally, she nodded.

"I try to remember that, but I struggle with it. It's where my self-esteem issues come from; after all these years, it still lives inside of me. My head knows better sometimes, but my heart and my subconscious forget. But I *do* try to work on it. Every day is a struggle."

He pulled her up to look at him. "I'll help you, Sam. You need to know just how special you are."

"Gray, it can be very trying dealing with someone like me. I apologize ahead of time."

Smiling at her, he looked deep into her eyes and ran the back of his fingers along her cheek and her jaw. He reached up and ran his thumb along her bottom lip. She opened her mouth and sucked his thumb into her mouth. His pupils dilated, his nostrils flared, and he watched her mouth suck on his thumb. She sucked it in and out a few times, and he began pushing his hips up and grinding his erection against her body. Her eyes never left his as she took his hand in hers and sucked on each of his fingers, very slowly, licking the ends of each one a few times. He slid his arm under her legs and kept his other arm behind her back, and stood up, carrying her with him to the bedroom.

They made slow, sweet love and fell asleep with Gray still inside of and on top of her. They slept entwined in each other's arms for a couple of hours, both sated, happy, and so completely into each other.

13

S am sat at her desk pouring over a contract in the early afternoon a couple of weeks after her first dinner with Gray's family. Things had been going along rather nicely. He was easy to talk to, attentive, a great lover, he loved his family, and they genuinely loved him. There was a warm love there that you couldn't fake. She was blissfully happy and hoping she wasn't jumping into the deep end of the pool too soon. Jessie winked and giggled like a schoolgirl throughout the day. Her new beau, Joe, was keeping her happy and content as well. Both women were walking on cloud nine.

Gray and Sam had spent every night together since the first night they'd made love. Usually, they stayed at his place, but sometimes at Sam's. She told him she wanted people to see activity so there were no shenanigans. They would stay at her place, maybe two nights a week, but she always ran over on her lunch hour to make sure everything was okay.

Today was Friday, and the following day her boys and their families were coming over for dinner to meet Gray, and she wanted to meet Gage's new girlfriend as well. They decided on an afternoon lunch to keep it casual. She hadn't said much about Gray, other than they had been dating a few weeks and that she liked him and they got along well.

Two Mondays ago had been the one-year anniversary of Tim's death. Sam and the kids met at the cemetery and put flowers on Tim's grave and told stories about him. Afterward, they went to lunch, and that's when she told them about Gray. She apologized for the timing, but they were supportive and said it wouldn't bring dad back anyway, so she should move forward with her life. She had great kids.

She finished up her contract and some miscellaneous things on her desk and decided to quickly check her personal email. There was a Facebook message announcing Gray had been tagged in a photo. Naturally, she had to look, but as soon as it opened, her stomach flopped and her heart raced. There was a picture of Gray with Suzanne and Lily looking like the happy family. The date on the picture was today, and the caption read, "Gray and I at school with Lily for Grandparents Day!!! We had such fun."

Gray hadn't told her he was going to school with Suzanne for Grandparents Day. They had talked about her doubts and concerns and that they needed to be open and honest with each other all the time. As a matter of fact, just this morning she had asked him if he had a busy day ahead and he said, "No, just the usual."

He lied to her!

The tears streamed down her cheeks. She jumped up and closed her office door so no one would see. She had been *so* worried something like this would happen. Of course, they were Lily's grandparents, but how was she supposed to be able to trust him when he lied to her? She hated jumping to conclusions, but pictures don't lie, do they? She just needed a minute to get herself under control.

She sat for a few minutes and waited for the tears to stop. She cleaned her face up the best she could, shut her computer down, grabbed her things, and quietly left her office. When she got to her car, her knees shook so badly that she sat for a few minutes to collect herself. She texted Jessie and told her she needed to leave early, and she'd explain later. They were supposed to stay at Gray's tonight, but she didn't know if she could see him right now. She would fall apart for sure. Shit!

She put the car in drive and headed to her place. Maybe she would go down in the basement and work out hard and get some of this aggression out of her system before she saw him. Her mind numb and reeling from that stupid picture, she navigated the roads carefully. Of course, Suzanne would have posted that; she knew Gray and Sam were Facebook friends along with Sarah and Dani.

Entering her house, she threw her purse on the bed and dressed in her workout clothes. She marched downstairs and turned on her *Body Combat* DVD and started punching and kicking like she never had before. She sweated hard after only twenty minutes but made herself continue the full hour. When she was done, she dropped to the floor, closed her eyes and let out a deep sigh. Dammit!

She was about to collect herself when she heard someone upstairs. Shit! She didn't bring her phone down and didn't have a clock down here, either. She sat and listened to see if it was friend or foe. She could hear walking around and the footsteps on the basement stairs. She pushed herself quietly up the wall until she stood as Gray came around the corner. His face was full of concern and worry.

"What are you doing down here? I thought we were meeting at my place for dinner. I've been calling you, and you didn't answer."

She stared at him and wiped her eyes, which she was sure were all black from her mascara running into her tears.

"My God, Sam, what's wrong?"

"Nothing, I needed to work out, that's all."

Gray took a couple of steps toward her, but she moved away. He bunched up his forehead.

"Hey, what's wrong?"

Sam turned the TV and DVD player off and headed toward the stairs. Gray jumped in front of her and grabbed her arm.

"What. Is. Wrong?"

Sam took a deep breath. "Did you have a nice day?" Her voice strained as she feigned calm.

His brow furrowed further. "I guess."

She jerked her arm out of his grasp and walked up the stairs.

"Great! Glad to hear it."

He followed her. Once upstairs she walked to her desk in the far corner of the living room and flipped open her laptop. She opened Facebook and pulled up the picture. She turned her computer around and showed Gray. She walked off to the bathroom to take a shower. She heard him suck in a breath.

"Shit! Sam, please let me explain."

"How in the hell do you explain that you lied? I cannot think of any way to EXPLAIN that. You. Lied. To. Me. To be with Suzanne."

She walked into her bathroom and turned the shower on to warm the water up. He came into the bedroom and sat on the edge of the bed. His head hung down. She wasn't sure if he felt bad about lying or about getting caught. Either way, it didn't matter to her right now.

Sam walked past him to get to her closet, and he reached out to grab her, but she sidestepped quickly.

"Sam, please sit and talk to me."

She grabbed some clean clothes from the closet.

She stopped directly in front of him. "The last thing in the world I want to do right now is talk to you. I have this nasty little temper that luckily doesn't come out very often, but when it does come out, it's ugly, and that's right now. I need a shower and several more cries before I can speak with you."

She walked into the bathroom and slammed the door. For good measure, she locked it. She stepped into the shower and sobbed.

Her fingers and toes were pruny—her whole body was when she finally felt like she could come out. She dried off, buttered up, got dressed, and dried her hair. She didn't put any makeup on because she wasn't sure if she was finished crying yet. She never should have let herself believe this relationship would work.

When she opened the door, Gray wasn't there. She took a deep breath *Okay,* so she could collect herself. She slowly walked down the hall to get a glass of wine from the refrigerator. Gray sat on the sofa, waiting for her. She could tell he felt bad, but she didn't give a shit right now. She couldn't be in a relationship like this. She *wouldn't* be in a relationship like this. She walked into the kitchen and grabbed a wineglass from the cupboard and a bottle of wine from the refrigerator and poured. She leaned against the counter and took a sip and let herself feel it flow all the way down her throat. She closed her eyes and took a deep breath and exhaled very slowly.

When she opened her eyes, Gray stood at the kitchen door watching her. They stared at each other for a long time. She didn't have anything to say. She took another sip of wine and waited.

Gray took a deep breath. "Can you talk to me yet? I really do want to explain."

She could see the pain on his face, in his eyes. She supposed he could see it in hers as well. She shrugged her shoulders and pushed herself away from the counter.

"You want a glass of wine?"

He nodded. She turned to grab a glass from the cupboard and poured him a glass. Handing it to him she made sure her fingers didn't touch his. She saw the pain flash across his face and her heart hurt.

Sam walked from the kitchen to the living room and sat on the sofa. Gray followed behind her and sat at the opposite end. He faced her and rubbed his face in his hands.

"I'm so sorry, Sam. I shouldn't have lied to you. I didn't know how you would handle the fact that I was going to be there with Suzanne. I know we've talked about being open and honest and I am so, so, sorry. I swear to you; I'll never do it again, ever. And for the record, that picture is not what it looks like. We did not spend a happy day together. I got there at the very end of the Grandparents Day gathering, and Suzanne told Lily to come and ask me to have her picture taken with me. We were posing for our picture and Suzanne jumped in the picture at the last minute. I swear to you that's what happened."

Sam turned her head and looked out the window, trying desperately to find a critter to watch as it played to lift her heavy mood.

She took a deep breath and let it out slowly. "I can't be in a relationship like this. I want better—no lies, no manipulation. We've talked about this. I can't do it."

Gray gasped like she'd knocked the wind out of him. "Sam, please forgive me. I swear to you; I'll never lie to you again, I swear it. I didn't want this scene, that's why I didn't say anything."

Sam jumped up off the sofa, pissed. "This scene is happening because YOU LIED, you son of a bitch! I know that both you and Suzanne are Lily and Lincoln's grandparents. I'm not an idiot. I asked you this morning if you had anything special going on today and you said it was a regular day. YOU LIED! Did you know yesterday that you were going? For that matter, how long have you known you were going to Lily's school for Grandparents Day?"

Gray looked up at her. His eyes glistened. "I knew Wednesday."

She was stunned; he had been lying for three days.

"You fucking jerk! You make me fall in love with you, and you lie to me. You son of a bitch!"

She turned to walk away, but Gray jumped up and grabbed her. She tried squirming, but he wouldn't let her go.

"Please calm down and talk to me. Don't run away. *Please*, Sam."

She fought to get away, but he held her tight. She finally quit fighting him and stood there, tears running down her face.

"Bastard."

"You can call me all the names you want. I deserve it."

His breathing was ragged, and he was sucking in deep breaths, trying to calm himself down. He wrapped his arms tightly around her.

"Sam, you said you love me. Is that true? Do you love me?"

Oh, my God, she did say that! Crap, she said it, and she *does* love him, but right now was not when she felt like saying it to him again. He tightened his arms around her; they stood that way for a long time. After a while, he began rocking them back and forth , slowly, back and forth. She heard him sniff and she could hear his heartbeat, strong and solid. He put his hand on her head and pulled her head to his chest. He put his arm back around her and held her tight. He smelled good, too, dammit. They rocked back and forth for a long time—no talking, just soothing, sensual motion.

When he sensed that she had calmed down, he pulled his arms away slowly, reached down and put his fingers under her chin. He tilted her face up, so she was looking him in the eyes. She saw that he'd been crying, too.

"I love you, Sam. I think I've loved you from the first moment I saw you. One thing I know for sure, though, is I love you now. Please don't leave me. Let's try and work it out. I swear I will never lie to you again. I swear it."

She whispered, "Tell me why you did it."

She stepped back and looked into his eyes; she needed him to look at her and tell her the truth.

He shook his head back and forth. "Sam, I really didn't know how you would handle it. I meant to tell you. I tried a couple of times, but I just couldn't get the words out. I didn't want to hurt your feelings; I would never try to hurt your feelings. I didn't know if I should invite you to come with me. I knew that Suzanne would be there, although she spends no time with the kids, but I'm sure she was there because she wanted to do just what she did—manipulate the situation to make it look like something it wasn't.

"After a little while, it seemed like too much time had passed. I had already lied to you on Wednesday when I told you there was nothing special going on this week, and I was scared. I swear it's the truth."

Sam took a deep breath and turned to sit on the sofa. She put her head in her hands and looked down. Staring into his eyes was not helping her think this through.

Gathering her thoughts, she softly stated, "Gray, you still allow her to manipulate you. You know this is something I can't deal with. I hate the lying, and if you ever lie to me again, there will be no more chances. I mean that. But, if you're still letting her manipulate you, we need to end this right now. I won't be in a relationship again with a man who is constantly manipulated by someone else. I never want to be in that situation again."

She had enough of that to last a lifetime; but no more. She took a deep breath and exhaled. Her breath was shaky. *Everyone deserves a second chance.*

"I don't want to end this, Sam. We … we're just getting to know each other." He swept his hand through his hair and sat on the sofa next to her. He took her hand in his. "There will be bumps in the road, but I can promise you this, I will never lie to you again."

She exhaled the breath she'd been holding. She'd laid down the ultimatum, and he met it with a promise. "Okay." Lame, but she felt bruised and exhausted right now.

Gray apologized over and over for the remainder of the evening. When they went to bed that night, they didn't make love; they just held each other. She tossed and turned all evening; her mind wasn't convinced that Gray would be able to stop himself from being manipulated by Suzanne. Only time would tell, but how much of a price would her heart pay in the meantime?

14

Gray woke the next morning and glanced at Sam. Her eyes were puffy and red from crying. He knew she hadn't slept well last night; he'd felt her tossing and turning, and the guilt that came along with that kept him awake. He'd come so close to losing her, and it scared the shit out of him. He didn't like liars, and if the shoe were on the other foot, he'd be so pissed and hurt, it would be hard for him to forgive her. He would because he loved her so much, but it would be hard. The fact that she was willing to give him another chance made his heart swell for her. Disappointment in himself was an understatement. What a dumbass!

The sun dusted across her cheeks; her jaw relaxed in sleep, her arm lay across her belly. She inhaled and rubbed the bridge of her nose, then her temples.

"I'm sorry, Sam. I know you didn't sleep well last night."

Her eyes slid in his direction, held for a moment, and then closed. He lay on his side with his head resting on his hand studying her.

Sleepily, she replied, "I think we should call the kids and cancel; I don't feel like doing this today."

He breathed in sharply, reached over and touched her face, running the back of his fingers along her cheek.

"Please don't cancel. I know yesterday was awful, but I don't want to take a step backward. Can we try to keep moving forward, please?"

A tear slipped from the corner of her eye and along the side of her face. He reached it before it slid into her ear and wiped it away with the back of his finger.

"I hate that I caused all of those tears last night and this one this morning."

Then he kissed the damp trail softly.

"When Cheryl broke up with me the first thing I did was go and talk to my parents. It wasn't that I was heartbroken about her breaking up with me, it was more that I wasn't. I was terrified that I was incapable of loving anyone. I realized I'd never loved Suzanne, not like you should love a wife, and after a few years of her crap, I didn't love her at all. I asked my parents if some people just aren't able to love and be loved."

He took a deep breath and gently turned her face toward his. "I grew up watching my parents love each other through thick and thin. I watched my brother and sister marry people they loved and build happy lives together. I've watched my aunts and uncles and cousins all find people they love, marry and be happy. Sarah and Cole are happy, but I've never had that. I thought maybe I wasn't capable of it." His eyes sought hers and stubbornly stayed fixed.

"They reminded me that I love them, and my siblings, my children, grandchildren and that if I were a person who couldn't love, I wouldn't be able to love them. They told me that I just hadn't met the right person yet. I needed to be patient and that God would bring that person to me when He felt I was ready to accept love. So, I prayed in earnest for God to bring someone into my life who I would love and who would love me in return.

"And then, I met you. You're that person, Sam. Unfortunately, I'm not perfect. I make mistakes and I probably will again, but I *do* love you."

Another tear slid from her eye and then another. She turned onto her side to face him and touched his face with her fingers. He stared deeply into her eyes; then she kissed him very lightly.

"I make mistakes too, Gray, and I'll probably make them with us, but I love you, too."

A sob escaped his throat, as he reached over and pulled her tight to him.

He held her for several long moments, inhaling her scent, enjoying her skin against his. When he spoke, his voice was raw, "I was so afraid you wouldn't tell me again, that I'd ruined it. I love you, Sam; I love you."

He claimed her lips with all the passion he could muster at that moment.

"I really need to make love to you."

She giggled. "Yes, please."

He rolled onto her, his body instantly ready, her scent in the early morning filled him. The soft smile she wore as he gazed into her eyes made his heart race, the green of her eyes rivaling the fresh grass peeking from its winter haze. He reached between them and pumped himself a couple of times, the anticipation of entering her heady. Her lips lifted on one side; her fingers splayed on either side of his face, "Don't take away my fun," she whispered.

He guided himself to her entrance and her legs raised to wrap around his hips. He swiped her moist entrance with his finger, exhaling when he encountered her wetness. "I love your wet pussy. Makes this so much more enjoyable."

He rocked his hips forward nesting his cock inside, pulled out and pushed in again, seating himself completely in her. He watched her pupils dilate as her eyes drifted closed, her hips raised up to meet his. He slowly pulled out. "Open those beautiful green eyes and watch me while I'm in you," he huffed out.

Her lids popped open, and he immediately thrust into her again and again. The warming of their skin and the aroma of their mating filled the air around them. The soft puff of scented air the sheets produced threatened to send him into a frenzy, much like the pheromones released when a buck is in rut.

His pace increased urged on by her moans and whimpers. Her hips meeting his with each thrust excited him further. Everything about her excited him. He searched her face, committing to memory the way her mouth shaped a perfect "o" during their passion-filled forays. And he committed to memory that moment when she realized her orgasm was about to roll over her—her body stiffening and her legs tightening around him. He raced to catch up to her, pounding furiously into her. As she cried out her orgasm, he continued his pace to reach the crest and then let himself spill into her. The release sent shivers through him, the spasms of his muscles releasing the energy forcing his breathing to stutter.

All energy sapped for a few moments, and he laid on her, enjoying the way her body accommodated his in every way—even now a comfortable softness to cradle his exhausted body, his cock loath to leave the warm snugness of her pussy.

*****

The kids began arriving around eleven-forty—the first being Josh, Tammy, and their kids, Abby and Dodge.

Her beloved grandchildren ran through the door first yelling, "Grandma!"

Sam ran and knelt on the floor and hugged them both, getting and giving kisses at the same time. Abby had long, curly blonde hair and Dodge's hair was short and sandy blond. Both kids had beautiful blue eyes and sweet little smiles. They giggled and talked at the same time, each one trying to be the first to tell Sam something. She looked back at Gray who stood close by watching, a sexy grin on his face. She stood and walked over to grab Gray's hand.

"I want you to meet Gray."

Gray kneeled and held out his hand like he would to shake hands with an adult. Dodge was first to walk forward and take his hand.

"My dad said you have to squeeze real hard when you shake hands, so you don't look wimpy!"

Gray laughed and shook Dodge's hand.

"Wow, you have a great handshake, Dodge. You're certainly not wimpy!"

Dodge smiled and looked at Sam and giggled. Abby wasn't sure she wanted to shake hands, but she shyly stepped forward and put her hand in Gray's and shook it up and down a couple of times. Then giggling she ran away with Dodge on her heels toward Josh's old bedroom to find the toys.

Josh and Tammy had come into the house and watched the hand-shaking with smiles on their faces. They all stood in the kitchen when Gage and his new girlfriend, Tracie, walked in. Introductions were made all around, drink orders filled, and finally Jake and Ali entered. The introductions were repeated, and the family moved to the living room. The kitchen was just not big enough for everyone.

Gray chatted with the boys about everything from sports to cars to life in the military. After all, he'd been there and so had his sons, so it was an easy conversation.

The girls helped Sam pull food from the refrigerator to set on the dining room table. Gray was grilling burgers; they wanted it light and casual. With the grill just off the dining room and the dining room being open to the living room, it was easy for everyone to participate in conversation. As soon as the burgers were ready, they all refilled their drinks and sat at the table to eat.

Lunch conversation flowed well, and Sam was relieved and happy to see that the kids all seemed to like Gray and he seemed to like them. The conversation never felt stiff or forced. Tracie seemed nice, and Sam thought she began relaxing through lunch. It helped that the kids had just met Gray, so she wasn't the only 'newbie.'"

The kids told stories on each other, starting with, "Mom, did you ever know about ..." and ending with Sam usually telling them that she *did* know. When they looked shocked that she knew all their terrible secrets, she shrugged.

"I'm a mom. I know things. It comes with the baby when you have it."

She smiled as her children rolled their eyes. Tammy nodded and said, "It's true," then winked at Sam. The truth was, Sam didn't know all their secrets, but her plan was to not overreact and act like she knew so they'd continue to tell her things. She would get all their secrets eventually.

"So, Gray's mom has Sunday dinner for the whole family – I've gone the past three weeks. Mary, his mom, would love it if you all could join us one Sunday. You could meet Gray's family, and Abby and Dodge, you could meet Lily and Lincoln."

"Yeah." The grandkids said in unison. "Can we play with them now?" Dodge excitedly asked.

"No honey, they aren't here now. How about next Sunday?"

When they'd finished eating, Jake stood up, "I have an announcement." He smiled at Ali. "Ali and I are going to need one of those baby manuals. We're having a baby!"

Sam jumped up and hugged Ali first, then Jake. "Congratulations, you two. I couldn't be happier."

"I hope it's going to be a girl," Abby remarked.

"No way, Abby." Dodge scrunched up his adorable little face. "A boy and we have to name him after a car." He pointed to himself, "Dodge." Smiling up at Gray he pointed to him, "Lincoln." Then giving it some thought he said, "Ford" as he pointed to Jake and Ali.

Ali laughed. "We'll have to see Dodge."

A short while later, the kids packed up, leaving Sam and Gray a bit exhausted but certainly feeling better than this time yesterday.

They sat on the sofa and Gray pulled her into his arms. "I see why you were so tired on that first Sunday at my parents'. It's exhausting trying to remember everyone's name and occupation and keep the conversation rolling. Whew!"

She laughed. "Yep."

15

SECOND CHANCES SERIES

Gray and Sam fell back into their routine, dividing their time between their two homes; setting hurts aside was hard.

Thursday at work, Sam found herself needing to see, or at least talk to, Gray. This happened often, and she giggled as she thought about how much her life revolved around him in such a short amount of time. She called him around eleven-fifteen. "Hey there, how would you like it if I bought you lunch today?"

He responded, his voice clipped, "Oh. Um. Well, would you mind if a guest joined us?"

"Are you okay? Did I interrupt something?"

She listened as he drew in a deep breath, hesitated, then he blurted, "Cheryl stopped by to see if I would have lunch with her. Would you like to join us?"

"So, that means you're having lunch with her. How long have you had these lunch plans?" The edge to her voice was front and center. Closing her eyes, she tried to control herself and not jump to conclusions, but she wasn't succeeding very well.

"She just stopped in; I told you that. As in, just about ten minutes ago, and asked me to lunch. I was just about to pick up the phone and call you to join us when you called." She heard him heave out a deep breath.

Sam slowly inhaled then released the air in her lungs. "I don't know what to say, Gray. I'm kind of shocked here and a little hurt I guess."

She sat in her desk chair before her legs gave out from under her.

"Come with us. You'll see there's nothing more to it."

Sam snapped, "I should have lunch with the woman you used to have sex with?"

She closed her eyes, bit her bottom lip, and stared at the picture of an Easter flower on her wall that Abby had drawn for her in school. "Sorry, I'm just reeling here. I don't think I should go. I don't even know her, and I doubt she would be comfortable with me there, anyway. I'll talk to you later."

She quietly hung up her phone and stood quickly to make a trip to the kitchen for the lunch she had brought. Feeling sheepish about taking this so hard, she wondered if she was ready for a relationship. Hopefully, it was just too soon after the whole lying about Suzanne and Grandparents' Day and they hadn't fully healed from that yet. Now his second ex is showing up. Today sucks!

Closing her office door to spend her lunch alone and thinking some retail therapy might help, she checked some Internet sites on some things for the fourth floor.

A knock on her office door brought her out of her shopping stupor around 50 minutes later.

"Come in." She absently called, one-clicking on a lamp for Gray's desk.

She turned in her chair to face the door when Gray walked in. Frozen in place, she stared at him, then glanced at the clock; it was around noon. It's so easy to lose time while surfing the Internet.

"Are you okay? I know you were thrown when I spoke to you on the phone. I was, too. I didn't know she was in town or stopping at the office. I know that's probably hard for you to believe, but it's the truth, Sam."

She nodded. "Yes, I was thrown, and I can't believe the timing.

Just when I thought God brought us together because we were meant to be, suddenly these obstacles keep popping up and making me doubt everything. I told you it wasn't easy being with someone like me."

Gray locked his eyes with hers. He was simply gorgeous, in his black dress slacks, soft yellow shirt with the top button undone, and the sleeves rolled up to show off his perfect wrists. Well, everything was perfect about him, including his wrists. No wonder Cheryl couldn't stay away. He walked over and knelt in front of her, took her hands in his, and kissed the back of each.

"Sam, we *are* meant to be together; I knew it right away. Every relationship has tests. We'll probably have more as time goes on. I don't want Cheryl; I didn't when I was with her. I'll never want anyone but you. I love you, Sam."

She leaned down and kissed him tenderly on the lips.

"I guess I can't blame her for wanting you back ... you *are* kind of incredible."

Gray furrowed his brows. "What makes you think she wants me back?"

Sam shrugged her shoulders. "Why else would she ask you to lunch unannounced? You said she had married someone else a short while after she broke up with you. If you were just friends, she would have emailed and said, 'Hey, I'm coming to town; want to get together for lunch?' But she just stopped in, so she could catch you off guard. Am I wrong?"

Gray shook his head in disbelief. "That brain of yours is incredible."

He took a deep breath.

"Yes, she wanted to know if I was seeing anyone, and I told her I was. She asked if I ever thought about her, and I was honest and told her no, I didn't. She took that kind of hard, but I didn't want her to get the wrong idea. She asked me if I thought you were the one, and I told her we haven't been dating very long, but yes, I knew you were very special from the minute I laid eyes on you and that I love you very much."

Sam kissed him again, longer and deeper this time. Gray reached his hand up and wrapped it around the nape of her neck and held her there. When she started to end the kiss, he deepened it. She slid her hands into his hair and held his head. They kissed until they were breathless. Needing air, Gray laid his forehead against hers.

"I'm sorry you were thrown, Sam. I was about to call you when you called me. She was sitting in my office, and I told her you and I had talked about having lunch today. When I saw it was you on my phone, I asked her if I could have a minute to speak with you and she got up and waited outside. I wouldn't have lied to you—I need you to know that."

Sam pulled back to look into his eyes; he looked sincere, and she believed him. Nodding, she asked, "Are we going to have trouble with her?"

Gray smirked. "I don't think so. Her husband was killed in a car accident about a year ago, and she's just feeling lonely. But she knows there's nothing between us. I made it very clear that I love *you*."

He stood with a slight groan. "I have to get back to the office, but I'll see you at home around five-fifteen, okay?"

"Yes, I'll be there."

He kissed her again and walked out the door. She decided to finish her shopping therapy and get back to work. About an hour later, she got an email.

F*rom: Grayson Kinkaide*
     To: Samantha Powell
  Date: May 2, 1:33 p.m.
  Subject: Tests aren't just for school kids

I *hope you aren't letting this eat you up this afternoon. I have some fun things planned for later. I love you.*

. . .

Grayson Kinkaide

From: Samantha Powell
    To: Grayson Kinkaide
Date: May 2, 1:39 p.m.
Subject: "Fun things" can be construed in many ways!

I wasn't getting eaten up until I got your email; now I'm not sure. I usually like your "fun" things. I love you, too.

Samantha Powell

Apparently, her wit had taken a nap. She'd been teetering between being pissed and scared that Cheryl could come and win him back. He said he wasn't interested in her, but what if absence *did* make the heart grow fonder?

From: Grayson Kinkaide
    To: Samantha Powell
Date: May 2, 1:52 p.m.
Subject: Terrible testers usually have to stay after school

I didn't mean to bring it up. Don't be late.
    Grayson Kinkaide

. . .

From: Samantha Powell
    To: Grayson Kinkaide
Date: May 2, 2:01 p.m.
Subject: Please, please tell me you're sure

Gray, are you absolutely positive you don't have feelings for her? If there is even a little bit there, please tell me now rather than later.

Samantha Powell

She didn't want to drive him crazy, but seriously, he did go to lunch with her. He didn't have to. So, he must have wanted to see her too.

From: Grayson Kinkaide
    To: Samantha Powell
Date: May 2, 2:02 p.m.
Subject: Never been more sure in my life

Don't be scared, and I'm so sure. Actually, seeing her made it even clearer in my head, not that it wasn't before. She doesn't hold a candle to you, in any way. I wasn't lying when I told you I don't have feelings for her. But I do have feelings for you. Have I told you today that I love you?

Grayson Kinkaide

.   .   .

From: *Samantha Powell*
       To: Grayson Kinkaide
Date: May 2, 2:15 p.m.
Subject: Glad you're sure

O kay. *I won't be late.*
       Samantha Powell

S he decided to stop playing games and start cracking at her work. So, she turned away from her computer and dove in to get this day over with.

Pulling into the driveway around five-seventeen, she opened the garage door and parked alongside Gray's SUV. She could smell something delicious all the way out in the garage. He must have been home for a while. When she stepped into the kitchen, he was at the stove stirring something that smelled heavenly. He looked at her as she walked in.

"Hi, glad you're home. Glass of wine?"

She nodded and walked over to the stove to see what he was cooking. He put his arm around her and kissed the top of her head.

"I've wanted to make this for a while now. I saw the recipe one day on the Internet and thought tonight would be a perfect time to try it out. Parmesan chicken breast, carrots and Brussel sprouts fried in garlic olive oil and double chocolate cake for dessert. I bought the cake. Baking is something I haven't tried my hand at."

Sam looked up at him. "It smells delicious."

Gray turned from the stove and poured her a glass of Late Harvest Riesling from the Von Stiehl Winery. He poured himself one, too. They clinked glasses, and each of them took a drink. Delicious.

She walked to the bedroom to put her purse in the closet and take off her shoes. Dressing in yoga pants and a tank top she walked over to look out the windows in the bump-out. The flowers were starting to peek their heads out and she could see the view was going to be breathtaking when everything was in bloom. She was watching a cardinal playing around in the trees when strong arms came around her and hugged her from behind.

He squeezed her to him and hunched over to rest his chin on the top of her head—without heels on, she was quite a bit shorter than he.

"It's going to be beautiful when everything is in bloom."

Gray stared out the window with her for a while.

"Yes, I believe this year it will be the prettiest I've ever seen it."

He hugged her tighter. "Because you'll be here to share it with me."

She let out a breath. Sometimes he just crushed her. She felt a tear slip down her cheek, but she couldn't stop it before it hit Gray's arm. He turned her around to look at him. He used his thumb to wipe the tears away.

"Please don't cry, baby. We have to stay strong for each other. We have to stick together."

She knew that, but it was hard.

"I'm sorry. I've been in this funk all afternoon, and I'm having a hard time shaking it. Don't worry; I'll be fine."

Gray took a deep breath. "What should I have done?"

She shook her head. "I don't know, Gray. If it was the other way around, and a week ago I lied to you and this week an ex popped in and wanted to have lunch with me, and I had accepted before speaking with you, what would you want *me* to do? That's what I keep asking myself."

He sucked in a deep breath. "Well, shit, when you put it that way, I would have come over and hit the guy. You're mine, and I'm keeping you."

She nodded her head. "That's how I feel about you. I thought if I went to lunch with you, I would look jealous and insecure—which I am—but I didn't want to be and didn't think it would be right to go out to lunch with her. At the same time, you say it was harmless, so I guess I'm just overreacting. I'm sorry."

He wrapped her in his arms and held her close. The scent of his cologne drifted into her nostrils and instantly calmed her. Something about his strong arms and his scent—the man she loved—swirling around her was reassuring.

"I didn't think about it the other way around. I would hate it if you went to lunch with an ex after what we've been through. I'm the one who's sorry, baby."

Sam hugged him tight and let his warmth seep into her. His strong heartbeat under her ear, his deep raspy voice when he called her baby created gooseflesh and shivers.

"Dinner will be a little while. I want you to take a nice hot bath and relax. Then, I want you to come into the living room, with no clothes on. Do you understand me?"

She tilted her head back to examine his expression.

"Gray, I ... you know .... Why would you want me to do that?"

Gray kissed her forehead.

"I told you I had some fun things planned. Be a good girl and do as I say. Remember, you said you were willing to let me have some control."

He turned around, walked into the bathroom, and started running a bath for her. Unable to move, she stared after him and tried to wrap her head around what he wanted her to do. She still had issues with the way she looked naked and walking around the house naked was a big deal to her. She turned to look out the window again and take a moment or two.

"It's all ready for you; come on in."

Softly stepping into the bathroom, Gray walked toward her and lay his hands on her shoulders.

"Do you need me to help you, Sam?"

She shook her head no. He nodded and started to walk out of the bathroom.

"Dinner will be ready in half an hour. Don't be late. I want you in the living room in thirty minutes."

She looked up at him and he at her, determination on his face. Sam slowly nodded and began removing her clothing. He left the room as she dipped her toe in the water; it was warm, but it felt good. The last couple of months had been a roller coaster. She wondered if she was getting too old for all this emotional upheaval. She just wanted a nice, quiet life, with an amazing man, without all this bull-shit. How does a person get that? It was all just a little too much for her—especially tonight.

Settling into the bathtub and laying her head against the back, she let the warm, fragrant water flow over her. She would have to ask Gray what he put in the water; it smelled amazing, like spice and musk and something else like the homemade soaps you smell in specialty stores. She closed her eyes and willed herself to relax. There were so many thoughts running through her mind that it was a diffi-cult task. She kept her thoughts away from Cheryl and Suzanne. She didn't need to give either of them any more of her attention than she already had.

Stepping from the tub, she dried with the fluffy towel he'd laid out for her, inhaling deeply of the fragrant scent of the laundry soap she'd recently switched to. Applying lotion to her warm skin, she mused over the naked foray through the house and worried about this new 'fun' he wanted to have. She stared at the door, took a deep breath, and the door opened. She jumped back as Gray entered the room, brows raised in the air.

"I was just trying to work up the courage to walk out."

She heard his intake of breath. "I don't understand why you need to work up courage at all. I expect you in the living room in two minutes."

With that, he turned and left. Well, she didn't like to be ordered around. She had no idea what he had planned, but if he thought he was going to start bossing her around, he had another thing coming. She didn't care how perfect he was!

She took a deep breath and walked out of the bathroom and toward the bedroom door leading out to the hallway. She inhaled and walked down the hall. It was a little cold without any clothes on, and her skin was still damp. Reaching the living room, she sighed when she saw the fire in the fireplace. It seemed to be calling to her as her skin instantly warmed, and the aroma of burning wood, reminding her of campfires, and lazy days. Gray joined her, a small smile on his face.

"I'm proud of you. I wasn't sure you were going to be able to do it."

Hmm.

"I wasn't sure I would be able to either, but you sort of pissed me off by ordering me around back there. My emotions are all over the board right now, so I guess it didn't take much."

Gray chuckled. "That's why I did it. Now come over here and sit back on the sofa."

He took her hand and led her to the sofa where he had a blanket laying out. She sat on the blanket, and he pulled her feet up and placed them on the sofa, then covered her up with the other end of the blanket. He tucked it into the sofa and sat on the edge of it facing her. He kissed her deeply and oh so well. She struggled to pull her hands from the blanket, but he stopped her by holding them in place. He continued to kiss her, and while doing so, pushed her slowly into the back of the sofa, so her head was resting on the back of the corner. As he nipped and licked her lips, she felt something soft and silky slowly slide over her eyes.

"Now, I want you to lay just like this, and I'll be back in just a minute. No moving, do you understand me?"

She nodded her head.

"Say it, Sam."

She sighed. "I understand."

She felt him stand and heard him walk back into the kitchen. She could hear the music playing from the stereo—of course, her favorite, rock'n'roll—and silverware touching a plate and the lids being pulled from the pots and pans on the stove. Soon, she felt Gray sit down beside her on the edge of the sofa.

"Open your mouth, Sam."

She did as she was told and he slid a fork in her mouth. "Mmm, that's good."

She heard Gray chuckle. "Glad you like it. I know you love Italian food, so I wanted to make you a special dinner. Parmesan chicken. Open up."

He put another forkful of chicken in her mouth.

"Mmm, so good."

Gray kissed her lightly on the lips.

"Do you need something to drink?"

"Yes, please."

She heard him chuckle again. He even made a chuckle sound sexy. She felt a glass touch her lips and the liquid. Mmm, wine. Her hearing honed in and she could hear him taking bites in between hers, but she got the feeling he was also watching her very closely. It felt strange not being able to see his face and wonder what he was thinking. Sometimes she could tell by looking into his eyes, but without the visual, it was hard to tell. She felt the wineglass touch her lips again and she drank some more wine. Gray kissed her sometimes in between bites. She was never sure what was coming next— chicken, veggie, wine, or kiss. There was no particular order.

"Gray, I'm full. I can't take another bite. Thank you ... it was very delicious. You're a fantastic cook."

She heard him set the plate down on the coffee table and his lips were on hers again. She moaned—he felt so good and tasted even better. He touched her face, her hair, and her neck. She felt the blanket lift and his hands were on her. He slid his mouth down her neck and to her breasts. He suckled on each one, making her nipples pucker and ache for more. He kissed his way down her stomach to the part of her body that eagerly waited for his mouth. She sighed as he lightly licked over and around her clit.

She moved her hands to his hair, but he grabbed her fingers again and held them together with one of his hands. She felt his head lift from her body.

"Keep your hands at your sides, Sam, or I'll tie them."

She scrunched her face and heard him chuckle.

"When you touch me, I lose control, and I want this to last. Tonight, is about you."

Oh, well, okay then. He released her hands but not before gently pushing them down to her sides. Then his tongue was back on her. One of his hands slowly parted her legs, and she felt his finger slowly enter her. Ohh, she moaned again. His wet soft lips sucked her clit while his finger worked its way slowly in and out of her. She felt the vibrations run through her when he moaned and inserted two fingers.

"God, Sam, you're so wet for me. It drives me wild," he mumbled against her.

Her hips raised of their own accord urging him deeper into her.

His tongue was magic. There were times she was ready to come at his slightest touch. He knew the perfect amount of pressure to apply and exactly where to lick her. His hands touched her in the way she needed to be touched. And his fingers—goodness, his fingers were their own form of wizardry—long and graceful, nimble and sure at finding all her sexually sensitive places.

"Gray, please, I need more, just a little more."

He pushed his fingers in farther and used his tongue to apply more pressure on her clit. A soft cry escaped her lips as her body heated and her breathing became labored.

"Yesss. Gray, I need to come," she whimpered.

Gray smiled against her clit and increased his pressure and pace. She moved her hips. He slid his tongue from her entrance up to her clit, the sensation so pleasurable gooseflesh formed on her skin and her orgasm rolled over her causing her to stiffen and let go with a throaty moan.

He kissed his way up her body, swirling his tongue around her navel and up to her breasts laving attention on her nipples, her neck, her jaw and finally her lips. His kiss deepened, running his tongue inside her mouth, around her teeth, over her tongue. When he was finished fully assaulting her mouth, he licked her lips. He lifted his head, and she felt his hands move behind her head and remove the blindfold. As she felt the soft cloth slip away, he gently kissed each of her eyelids.

"Okay, Sam, you can move your hands now."

Finally! Slowly her palms moved to Gray's face, and her fingers roamed his cheeks. She looked deep into the beautiful, deep brown eyes that held her prisoner. She wanted to see his thoughts and his feelings to know what he needed from her. She kept her hands on the side of his head and leaned up to kiss him. Unbuttoning his shirt, she pulled it from his pants, then unbuttoned the last two buttons.

She slowly unhooked his slacks and inched the zipper down, reached in and caressed his erection. He moaned and leaned forward to lay his forehead on hers, his breathing raspy as she manipulated his cock. The satiny skin stretched tautly felt fabulous in her hands. The intensity in his breathing and the sexy sounds he made as she moved to pleasure him made her feel powerful. His hips pushed forward into her hand. She swiped her thumb over the head, smearing the precum over it, sliding easily over his heated skin.

"Sam ... God, it feels good when you touch me."

He swiftly twisted to remove his pants and let them fall to the floor. His opened shirt showed a large expanse of his broad chest, dusted in dark and silver hairs, his nipples taut disks. "Boxers, too," she managed to whisper.

He quickly divested himself of the constricting shorts and lay between her legs, thrusting his hips forward and back, grinding his hardened cock on her sensitive tissues, still tingling from her orgasm just moments ago. She was ready for another round—enjoying his excitement, smelling his heated flesh, and hearing his gasps and pants as she lovingly explored his body.

Gray smiled at her, the intensity in his eyes intoxicating.

She managed to get him to roll over, giving her the advantage of touching, gazing, and controlling the pace. Powerful indeed. She kissed his chest and his stomach and all the way down to his beautiful cock, closing her mouth around him. She moaned sending the vibrations through his body. He gasped, and his hands sought her head and threaded his fingers into her hair.

With her hand at the base of his penis, she pumped and simultaneously sucked him wrapping her tongue around his cock and adding pressure. He gasped as the air rushed from his lungs, his hips thrust upward into her mouth.

"Sam," he ground out. "I'm going to come." It was almost a growl.

He groaned once more as she felt the first warm spurt hit the back of her throat. She swallowed and continued to work him up and down, eventually slowing the pace. She continued to swallow as he continued to release. Her eyes watered and she needed air, but she wanted him to fully enjoy this, so she swallowed and softened her sucking, then finished with softly licking him as she felt him relax.

Sam lightly kissed her way up to Gray's lips, before lying down next to him, grabbing the blanket with her. They lay there for a while alternately napping and watching the fire, neither of them saying a thing.

A long while later, Gray cleared his throat. "I wanted tonight to be about you; I didn't mean for you to take care of me."

She sighed. "Gray, we both had a stressful day, and if we're going to stay a couple, it can never be all about one of us, it has to be about both of us."

His arms tightened around her, and he kissed the top of her head. "Sometimes, it needs to be a little uneven. That's the way it works, Sam. I wanted to show you how much I want you, how much I love you, without you needing to give me anything in return. But, you need to know that I'm not complaining, I just wanted you to feel special, wanted, and much loved."

Sam nodded. "I did feel special and wanted and loved. Thank you for everything. Dinner was amazing. You must have left work early to get home and make that fantastic meal."

Gray shrugged a little. "I did leave a bit early. I couldn't concentrate knowing you were feeling bad."

16

They only had a couple of days left before Jax and the guys began bringing the pieces from the old sewing mill to the fourth floor. They'd made a lot of headway: they'd moved out the junk that was on the floor and cleaned the windows, sills, and floors. The space had been painted a light tan, and where there was exposed brick on the outside walls, she'd sealed it with an egg shell sealer to give it a slight sheen. It made the brick come alive. The wooden floors, although not the nicest wood, were probably going to get scratched and gouged anyway, so they cleaned, sanded, and put a few coats of varnish on the floors to seal them for ease in sweeping and cleaning.

Once they had an open space, they sectioned it off for separate areas. First was Gray's office. He needed enough room for a drafting table and a larger table to roll plat maps and blueprints out and a desk area for his computer and printers.

Sam wanted a receiving area where new items would come in and a sanding/construction area where the actual work would take place. In addition, a finishing area would be needed, but it must be dust free so as not to disturb freshly painted or varnished pieces. Gray thought the area right next to his office—back in the far corner and completely across the room from the sanding area—would work nicely. They bought glass walls and doors for that space as well as for Gray's office.

Today, the glass doors and walls were being installed, and Sam couldn't wait to see them. She intended to go over on her lunch hour and see how things had progressed. Her morning dragged because she was so excited to see it. She must have looked at the clock every fifteen minutes. She kept emailing Gray to see how things were going. He was patient with her and told her how things looked; he even took pictures and sent them to her every so often, but she wanted to be there. At eleven-thirty she couldn't take it anymore and left for an early, long lunch.

Arriving on the fourth floor, the first thing she noticed was the flurry of activity. There were contractors and some of the office staff looking around to see what was going on, and of course, Gray was overseeing everything. When she walked into the room, he was talking with a contractor about something, but when he looked up and saw her, he instantly walked toward her. She met him in the middle where he bent and embraced her, then spun her around. She giggled and held him tight.

When he set her down, he gave her a big kiss and took her hand. "Come and see what's been completed so far."

She happily walked over to where his second office would be. The walls had been installed, and contractors were working on the doors. The glass walls were in six sections, with each section containing sixty smaller panes of glass framed in oak and stained a medium color. They looked so rich and fit the feel of the room. She squealed and raised her hands to her face.

"So, I guess that means you like them."

She looked up at him, smiling. "Of course, I like them. What's not to like? They're beautiful."

The French doors matched the walls, and they would open wide enough to allow for the larger table to be brought in. The finishing area walls were the same, except they would be on tracks to open all the way allowing larger pieces to be brought in. Then, when working on a piece, she could open the walls so it wouldn't get stuffy and close the walls when she was painting or staining. They also installed ceiling fans throughout the space to keep air circulating and venting to suck dirty air out. She couldn't wait to start working up here.

A blonde woman stood across the room watching them closely. "Gray, who is that woman across the room?"

He glanced up at the woman, then into her eyes, "That's Amanda. She's Ethan and my administrative assistant."

"She doesn't look very happy. What's that all about?" Sam asked, looking at Amanda, who seemed to be glaring. Slightly plump, her hair cut into a sharp bob, heavy dark eyeliner, gave her the appearance of being unapproachable.

Gray looked back down at her. "I don't know what her issue is. This week she started complaining about what was going on up here, first to Ethan then to me. I don't see how it affects her, but she's been asking a lot of questions and rolling her eyes a lot. Today, she's come up here several times, looking around and then leaving again."

Watching her leave, Sam asked, "Have you ever dated her?"

"Good God, no. I would never date someone who worked for me. Why would you even ask that question?"

She shrugged. "Well, the looks she was shooting at me tell me she is focusing at least some of her irritation on me specifically. I can't imagine where that comes from, so I wondered."

Gray looked at where Amanda had been standing and shrugged; then he turned Sam to look at the plans for more lighting. She saw him furrow his forehead and thought he was wondering the same. Another woman they could add to the mix of exes and troubles was not what she'd hoped for today.

They finalized the lighting plans and looked once more at their progress.

"I can't wait to start working up here with you, Sam. Did you eat lunch? Should we go somewhere?"

"I can't wait to start working with you here, either. Yes, please, let's go have lunch."

They took the stairs down, and Sam noticed the new railing had been put in as well.

"Wow, you didn't tell me these had been installed. They look great!"

They were wrought iron, painted a deep rust, which Sam thought went well with the old building. They didn't have a lot of detail to them—straight, squared spindles with every fourth spindle having a circle and a K in the middle of the circle. Sam liked the way it looked simple, old world, and yet customized.

Gray laughed. "I wanted to surprise you. The guys put them in yesterday. I wasn't sure they would get them all installed. I like the way they look. You have great taste, Sam."

She giggled at his praise and squeezed his hand.

"So do you, Gray. We make a great team."

He kissed her lightly again, and they continued walking down to the first floor. Once there, they walked to Gray's office, to make sure he didn't have any voicemails waiting for his immediate attention. Before they got to his office, Sam noticed Amanda's workstation. She hadn't noticed it before. Amanda sat at her computer, but she was watching Gray and Sam. She squeezed Gray's hand when she noticed Amanda; Gray glanced in her direction, too. Her expression was dark.

"Amanda, have you met Sam? Sam, this is Amanda, our administrative assistant."

Sam walked over to shake Amanda's hand, but Amanda crossed her arms. "Hello. I've been hearing a lot about you."

"It's nice to meet you. How long have you worked here, Amanda?" Trying civility.

Amanda shrugged her shoulders. "I guess about a year. Oh, Gray, you have some messages on your desk. Should I order you some lunch, your favorite?"

Interesting. Gray leaned down and kissed the side of Sam's head.

"No, Sam and I are going out to lunch. I'll grab my messages and return calls later, maybe while I'm upstairs. If anything important happens, call my cell. See you later."

Gray turned them toward his office, grabbed his messages from the desk and they began leaving. When they were a few steps away, he let go of her hand and put his arm around her waist and squeezed her.

Then he leaned down and whispered, "I think you might be onto something."

She looked up at him, and he grinned. They climbed into Gray's SUV and before he turned the key in the ignition, he turned to look at Sam.

"I've never had any interest in her and I never will. To be honest with you, I had no idea she had any interest in me. And maybe she doesn't. Maybe she's feeling jealous for another reason, but I don't want you to worry about it, okay? I'll talk to Ethan about her behavior and see if he's noticed anything."

Sam leaned over the console and kissed him on the lips, a little peck at first. That little peck didn't seem enough, so she kissed him more thoroughly, and then she licked and lightly sucked on his bottom lip. Gray groaned. Part of the fun of a new relationship was figuring out what the other person liked. It was also the worst part of a new relationship.

Then she sat back. "Wow, I'm starving."

He shook his head. "Tease."

She winked, and they pulled out of the parking lot and turned toward the restaurant.

Over lunch, they talked about the fourth floor and what else needed to be done that week. Jax and his team were going to start bringing up the pieces from the sewing mill in a few days. They discussed which ones Sam would work on first, second, et cetera and how they should be brought in. Sam told Gray about her ideas for almost all the pieces to be installed downstairs on the second floor. The old wooden bookcases would look great against the brick walls of the conference room. She thought his clients would find them impressive.

There was an old chest that she thought would look great in Gray's office and the chairs would work in the reception area. Sam continued through all the pieces, including the old barn doors they'd found.

Lunch passed quickly, and Sam groaned. "I hate to go back to work. I want to see what's happening and watch the progress. But I'll be there as soon as I can get out of work."

"Play hooky with me. We can work on the fourth floor."

"I hate to waste a day playing hooky when I can't do anything. I don't want to be in the way," she responded.

He laughed and the richness of his voice and the beauty of his being threatened to steal her breath. "I thought that was going to be the case with me today, too, but there are a hundred questions from the contractors, and actually, I could use your help with them. Play hooky with me," he said with a wink and clasped hands as if in prayer. It was hard to refuse him.

Shrugging, she countered, "Why not?!"

Laughing they gathered their things to leave the restaurant. Sam called Jessie and told her she was playing hooky, and if anyone needed anything, they could call her cell.

When they arrived at the office, they observed the progress that'd been made. The tracks for her walls had been installed, and the guys were working on installing the first wall panel. The walls were heavy, but once on the tracks, they would glide smoothly across with little effort. She was thrilled to be able to watch them.

Gray was right. There were tons of questions to answer: Do you like this? What about that? Where will this light go? There seemed to be a never-ending barrage of questions. But it was also fun. The contractors finished with her walls, and she was terribly excited to play with them and watch them work.

Gray stood in his new office, without furniture, but it was quieter, and he could still watch what was going on. She enjoyed watching him in action. Sexy!

Toward the end of the day, Jax, Ethan, and Sarah came up to see what had transpired. They had stopped in a couple of times throughout the day, so before they headed home, they wanted to see how far along they'd gotten. They played with the walls of the finishing room and were complimentary of the design.

Gray and Ethan went into his office to talk. Sam assumed they were discussing business and maybe Amanda's attitude toward her, but she wasn't sure.

17

F ive weeks into dating things seemed to click.

"Sam, the firm purchased a table at a fundraising event for Downtown Harmony Lake. It's black tie a week from this Saturday. Will you join us? Ethan and Eva, Jax, Dani and Nick, and Jamie will be going. We'll all be guests at the Kinkaide & Associates table."

"That sounds fantastic, Gray. I'd love to go. Do you sponsor a table every year?"

"Yes. It brings in quite a bit of business. We'll be meeting other downtown business people, including the board members of Downtown Harmony Lake. Plus, we enjoy dressing up and going out on the town. Actually, the girls enjoy that part; the guys aren't all that interested in it."

Dani and Sam went dress shopping one afternoon after work. Dani was excited too; after all, it isn't often they get to dress up in pretty dresses and spend a night on the town, so to speak.

On the Saturday of the Downtown Harmony Lake event, Gray and Sam spent a relaxing day at Gray's house. She had her own drawers for makeup and necessities now in the bathroom and space in the closet for clothes. Gray had a couple of drawers at her place, but they didn't spend much time there, especially knowing the house was for sale and not a permanent part of their future in any way. Gray sat on the sofa answering emails on his laptop and Sam was reading a book when her phone rang. She looked at the display, and it was Shelia, her realtor.

"Hey, Shelia, how are you doing?"

"Hey, Sam, I'm good. I have a couple moving in from out of the area, and they're interested in your house. May I bring them by tomorrow? They're prequalified buyers, and I think they could be the buyers we've been waiting for. I've spoken to them at length; it's exactly what they're looking for."

"Fabulous, Shelia. Yes, let's not let this opportunity pass us by."

She tapped her phone to end the call. "Shelia has a potential buyer for my house; I'm going to run over and make sure everything looks presentable. If it's a late night, I won't feel like it tomorrow."

"Do you need help?"

"No, it's not bad I'm sure. I'll just vacuum and dust and make sure everything is ready. I won't be gone long."

She stood and grabbed her purse from the floor, leaned over to kiss Gray on the lips and with a wave, she sauntered out the door.

After sprucing up the house, she pulled into Gray's driveway around four and saw another car there that she didn't recognize.

Walking into the kitchen from the garage, she heard Harry and Mary's voices. Gray's parents had come to visit. When Sam entered the living room, they were talking about the flowers outside and when they would like to start working on them. In Wisconsin, Memorial Day was usually the beginning of the gardening season. By then, the fear of frost killing everything had normally passed.

Sam rounded the corner and was met with three big smiles.

"Hello, everyone." She grinned. Gray held out his arm for her to come and sit with him at the end of the sofa. She snuggled in against him, and he leaned down and kissed her.

"Everything look good?"

"I think so. The house should show well. We'll see if these are the right people or not tomorrow."

Mary changed her position on the love seat.

"What will do you then, Sam?"

"I was thinking about a nice little condo or smaller home that's easier for me to take care of."

Harry and Mary looked at Gray. Sam shrugged and said, "Do you all mind excusing me? I need to get ready for tonight."

"Oh, no, you go, dear. We won't be long. We were driving in the area and thought we'd stop in. You have fun tonight," Mary said as she stood to hug Sam.

"I'm excited. I've never been to this event. It was nice seeing you both."

After hugging each of them, she turned and walked down the hall to the master bedroom.

She was excited to wear her dress. Truly, she was excited just to get dressed up and feel pretty. She undressed in the bathroom and stepped into the shower. Gray joined her in the shower soon after she climbed in and they enjoyed soaping each other up and playing little shower games.

Gray dressed and went to his office. It wasn't fair that it didn't take him as long as it took Sam to look fabulous. She finished dressing, taking her time with her hair and makeup. She wanted to look great for him. Her evening dress was champagne in color, strapless with a split front, and covered in crystals. Brushing the floor and swishing as she walked, the crystals twinkled and glimmered while the rest of the dress hugged her body like a glove.

Gray sat on the sofa watching the news when she entered the room. The appreciation on his face as he examined her was evident.

"Sam, you look simply beautiful."

He stood and sauntered toward her. He stopped directly in front of her and stared.

"I'm a very lucky man. I'll be the envy of the entire room tonight."

He leaned down and kissed her. The smile she bestowed on him was a combination of hunger for his touch and happiness in his attentiveness.

"I think I'm the lucky one. You look gorgeous, Gray. I don't even have the words to tell you how handsome you are."

Someone knocked on the door, and the spell was broken.

"That will be the car. We thought it would be nice if we could all have a couple of drinks, so we ordered a limo to pick us all up. We're first, so we can enjoy some champagne while we pick up the others. Are you ready to go?"

Sam nodded. He held his arm out for her, and she slid hers through, and he escorted her out to the car. Sam slid in first as the driver opened a bottle of champagne, poured them each a glass, and set the champagne in the chiller in the side of the limo.

Gray held his glass up. "To us, to a great evening, and a great life. I love you, Sam."

"I love you too, Gray."

They clinked glasses and sipped their champagne as each member of the family joined them.

When they arrived at the event, Gray held out his arm for Sam, and they walked in with everyone following behind them. They were greeted at the door, given their table assignment and told that dinner would be in an hour and a half. They stood chatting as a group after getting drinks, and she was introduced to many of his business acquaintances and clients.

Suddenly, Jamie muttered, "What the *fuck* is she doing here?"

They turned to see it was none other than Suzanne. Fuck is right! Both Ethan and Jax shrugged—then took that moment to excuse themselves saying they saw someone they knew. Ethan dragged Eva with him. How convenient!

Suzanne was a beautiful woman—about five-foot-nine and slender with shoulder-length blonde hair and light blue eyes. She wore a floor-length red gown and bright red pumps. As soon as she arrived at their group, she was overly friendly. She said hello to everyone then looked at Sam.

Gray introduced them, and Sam shook her hand.

"Oh Sam, did you see the picture of Gray and me with Lily?"

Sam smiled. "I sure did; it's a nice picture."

Suzanne looked up at Gray and beamed.

She wrapped her arms around Gray's arm and said, "Sam, you don't mind if I introduce Gray to a couple of potential clients here, do you?"

Sam started to open her mouth when Gray spoke up first.

"Don't start your crap, Suzanne."

She grinned widely at Gray. "What crap? It could be big business. If you prefer, we could catch Sam up on the Grandparents Day recital or did you already tell her all about it?"

"Sam!"

Everyone turned to see who was yelling Sam's name.

She smiled and responded. "Oh, my God! Nate, how are you?"

Nate was a hulk of a man, about six-foot-one and carried three hundred pounds or so. He didn't have a neck—just a large head, and he wore his sandy blond hair short cropped and gelled up on top. His sparkly blue eyes with long, dark lashes gave the impression of happiness, and he wore a large smile on his face. He busted right between Suzanne and Dani and grabbed Sam in a bear hug and spun her around.

"Woo-wee, girl, you look stunning! You clean up good!"

Sam laughed and tried catching her balance as he set her on her feet. Gray reached out to steady her so she wouldn't fall.

"Nate, I didn't expect to see you here. You look amazing! Wow, who knew YOU could clean up so good!"

Laughing, she looked at Gray and introduced him.

"Gray, this is Nate—Nathan Johns. Nate, this is Grayson Kinkaide, my boyfriend."

Nate and Gray shook hands.

"Nate, let me introduce you to everyone else here. This is Dani and Nick Harper, Gray's sister and brother-in-law. Jamie Kinkaide is Gray's brother. And Suzanne, Gray's ex-wife."

Nate shook hands with everyone, and his eyes narrowed at Suzanne who kept trying to wrap her arms around Gray's arm. He would pull away, but she went right back at him. Nate looked back at Sam and raised his eyebrows in question. She shrugged and frowned.

"Nate and I used to work together. Then he got too big for his britches and decided to move on. He now runs a small airline here in Harmony."

Sam turned to Nate. "Still like it?"

His large infectious smile displayed white straight teeth, the front tooth slightly chipped in the corner. "I love it! You know, my offer still stands. I would love it if you would come and work with me. We're a great team!"

She smiled. "I'll keep that in mind. I'm good for now, but you know how attorneys can get under your skin. I may just take you up on it one day."

"Little Bit, I would hire you anytime you decide it's time to come on over, seriously."

Suzanne snorted, "Little Bit?"

Nate looked at Suzanne, narrowed his eyes, and sidled closer to Sam.

He put his beefy arm around her and said, "She is just a little thing next to me. I started calling her Little Bit the first day I met her."

He looked down at Sam with a warm smile on his face.

Suzanne took that moment to make her move.

"Gray, I want to introduce you to a couple of potential clients for Kinkaide & Associates."

Gray took a deep breath and glanced at Sam.

"Come on, Gray; it won't take that long."

She pulled him, and he looked at Sam and shrugged, then walked away with her. Sam could *not* believe her eyes. Suzanne had manipulated him right in front of her, and he went with it. She took a deep breath and let it out very slowly.

"That woman is a grade-A, number one bitch," Dani muttered, as she watched Gray and Suzanne walk over to a group of people.

Jamie and Nick agreed, then turned to Sam and nervously made small talk. Sam took out her phone and looked at the time. He had a few minutes and then she was leaving.

Nate looked at her. "Sam, why would you let him just walk away with that bitch?"

She cocked her head to the side. "What, I'm supposed to make a scene and give her the satisfaction? He needed to tell her to take a hike, but he didn't."

Nate nodded, and the small talk continued. "I'll see you later, Little Bit. I've got some hands to shake." She watched him amble over to a group of people, then her eyes sought out Gray and Suzanne for the tenth time in ten minutes.

At one point Gray glanced her way. She could tell he was uncomfortable, but he wasn't exactly walking away either. She decided to keep her back to him and not watch this. She made small talk with the others and a few other people she knew as well and did her best to make conversation and not think about Gray and Suzanne.

It had been some time when she looked at her phone again and noticed it had been almost an hour. Taking a deep breath, she set her drink down, and Dani put her hand on Sam's.

"Don't go, Sam. He's been watching you the whole time. I can tell he's nervous about this; he's trying to keep Suzanne from making a scene. He's put up with her antics for so long that he knows when they're coming."

"You know, Dani, we've had this conversation about her manipulating him. I lived for close to thirty years with a man who was constantly controlled by his mother. I have told Gray repeatedly that I would not be in a relationship like that again. She might be manipulative, but *he's* allowing it, and *he's* the only one who can stop it. It doesn't look like he's trying to stop it now. I'm not going to make a scene; I'm just leaving."

Nate came back over just as Sam set her drink down.

Nate said, "Hey, are you leaving?

"Yes."

"How are you getting home, Sam?"

She straightened and sighed. "I'll call a cab."

"Hell no! I'll take you."

She shook her head. "No, Nate, I'm fine really. I'm just finished with this bullshit. Gray needs to man up and tell Suzanne to pack it, and clearly, he isn't doing it tonight. I'll be damned if I am going to stand here and be ignored. Besides, it won't look right if I leave with you."

"Bullshit! What doesn't look right is him parading that bitch around while you're standing here. If he gives you any grief about leaving with me, I'll take care of it."

Sam smiled and touched Nate's arm.

"I really just want to leave without any big scene, and I just want to be alone right now. I appreciate the offer, but no thank you."

Sam stood on her toes and kissed his cheek. She went over to Dani, hugged her and said goodbye to Nick and Jamie. Then she turned and walked toward the front doors, her head held high, her back rigid.

When she stepped outside, she hailed a waiting cab and got in quickly. She didn't want anyone to see her cry. She took a deep breath. Where was she going to go? There were people coming to look at her house in the morning, and she didn't want to see Gray right now. She told the cab driver to take her to her house. She would change clothes and have him take her to Gray's to pick up her car. She was in a hurry. She didn't know if Gray would follow her or not, but she didn't want to be around if he did.

When they pulled into her driveway, she leaned forward, "Please wait for me, I'll be right out." She ran in, changed clothes very quickly, and grabbed a few items she needed for an overnight stay and fresh clothes for tomorrow. She always kept some toiletries packed in a bag for a quick trip on the motorcycle. She hung her dress in the closet and made sure she didn't leave anything lying around so the house would show well. She was out the door in no time.

Asking the driver to drop her off at Gray's house, she pulled money with tip and her keys from her purse before they pulled into the driveway. She dropped the money on the front seat, jumped out of the cab, and ran around the side of the house to the side of the garage. She opened the door, threw her things in her car, got in and started the car hitting the garage door button at the same time. As soon as she had clearance, she pulled out of the garage and sped out of the driveway.

She drove to a hotel, out of Harmony Lake in Green Bay, asked if they had a room, and was relieved when she was told they did. She got to her room, jumped in the shower, and cried her eyes out. When she couldn't take the water any longer, she got out and dried herself off. Her phone was chirping, and she quickly glanced at the plethora of messages and missed calls. Not interested in the drama anymore tonight, she shut her phone off and crawled into bed and cried herself to sleep.

18

SECOND CHANCES SERIES

As expected, Sam didn't sleep well. She tossed and turned through the night and cried in between. By eight in the morning, she rolled out of bed, went to the bathroom and looked at herself in the mirror. That. Is. Hideous. Her eyes were puffy and red, her hair looked like hell, and the lines around her mouth were prominent. She used the toilet and turned the shower on to heat up the water, brushed her teeth, stepped into the warm running water and let the water flow over her. The shiver that ran the length of her body and the gooseflesh that rose soon washed down the drain as the temperature of the water warmed her.

Today, she had a twenty-first birthday party at her brother Adam's house for her niece, Julie. They lived only thirty miles away, so she'd drive in that direction until it was time to go over to their house. Dusting a bit of powder on her face, it was soon apparent the damage done during the night wasn't to be concealed, so she packed away her makeup to call Shelia and see if the showing was still happening this morning. Turning her phone on she saw thirty-two text messages and almost as many missed calls.

Taking a deep breath, she dialed Shelia's number and felt relief that she answered her phone on the second ring.

"Sam, are you okay? I just got to your house a few minutes ago, and there was a man here looking for you. He came out as I was coming in, and he asked if I had spoken to you. I told him I hadn't spoken to you since yesterday and he asked me to call him if I spoke to you. His name is Grayson Kinkaide. Is everything okay, Sam?"

Sam sighed, closed her eyes, and rubbed the bridge of her nose. "Yes, I'm fine. Gray is my boyfriend, and we had a fight last night. Don't worry and please don't call him. When I'm ready, I'll touch base with him."

"Okay. I'll give you a showing report when we're finished. Take care of yourself."

Sam drove toward her brother's house and decided to hang out at the mall for a while. After a little mall walking, she felt like she could make it through the day, so she turned her phone on and called her brother.

"Hey, I'm in town a little early. I stopped at the mall and thought I would call and see if you needed anything before I head over."

"We have everything we need. Just come on over."

She arrived at Adam and Janie's house, hugged them each, then her brother asked, "Are you feeling okay? You look tired."

"It was a late night ... big event."

"Where's Gray? I wanted to meet him."

"He had a family thing to take care of, so I'm solo today."

There were quite a few people there already, many she didn't know—Julie's friends and their parents mostly—but she knew her sister-in-law's siblings and spent the afternoon visiting with them. Of course, Sam's kids came for a while, too. The day was warm and sunny, so she sat outside in the courtyard and enjoyed their company in the warmth of the afternoon sun. When her kids asked her about Gray, she simply repeated her small fib from earlier.

Sam met Adam and Janie's neighbor, Dr. Eric Anderson. He was nice looking, Nordic, blond hair and blue eyes, and handsome. She guessed him to be in his late forties. He was recently divorced and had moved in across the back lawn from her brother. Adam had been spending time with Eric fixing up old cars. Sam sat with Eric, and they chatted most of the afternoon about many different things. He was a heart surgeon and fairly new to Wisconsin, originally from Chicago. Of course, they debated the Packers/Bears rivalry, and in Wisconsin, the Packers are always the better of the two.

Around eight p.m., Adam built a fire in the pit, and they moved their chairs out to sit around the blaze. After about an hour, Adam's phone rang. He sat across the fire from Eric and Sam. He seemed upset and stood to walk toward her. As he neared, his foot hit a hole in the yard and he began to fall. The drink in his hand spilled, and he squeezed the glass during his fall, causing it to shatter. On the way down, one of the shards swiped across Sam's right arm, slicing the back of her arm open.

Several people jumped up to help Adam stand. He had turned his ankle, and Sam was bleeding badly from the cut. Eric grabbed her hand and ripped his shirt to make a tourniquet to stop the bleeding.

"We better get in the house so I can see how bad this is."

They stood to walk to the house. Sam felt woozy and stumbled. Eric picked her up and carried her the rest of the way. Someone behind them helped Adam. When they got into the kitchen, Eric began cleaning up Sam's cut. Janie ran around gathering what medical supplies she had. Eric rewrapped Sam's arm and told Janie to hold her hand over it, applying pressure. He ran back to his house to get his medical kit.

Adam hobbled over and sat next to Sam.

"I'm so sorry, Sam. I never meant to hurt you."

"I know you didn't, Adam. Please don't worry about it; I'm fine." Tears sprung to her eyes, probably more from the nerves and emotions she had bottled inside. Adam leaned over and hugged her.

"Then why are you crying?"

"It's just been a stressful couple of days. No worries."

Eric stepped into the kitchen carrying his medical bag. He began pulling the ripped shirt gently from Sam's arm, and she quickly turned her head.

Adam took a deep breath. "Sam, that call I got was from the hospital. Mom died a few hours ago."

Sam turned and caught Adam's gaze with hers. Unable to speak, she simply stared.

"She had a heart attack today and died before they ever got her to the hospital."

Sam nodded her understanding and noticed Eric watching them. "Okay," she replied. Eric furrowed his brow and looked at both of them again, waiting for a reaction.

Adam told Eric about their mother. He was always more open about their family dynamics. He would get angry with their parents, and that's how he dealt with it. Sam, on the other hand, kept her feelings bottled up inside. She didn't want anyone to know about their family.

He cleared his throat. "I'm very sorry ... for all of it."

They both shrugged. They'd both been numb to her for so long that they didn't have any emotion over the news of her death. It was almost a relief.

Sam cleared her throat. "I suppose we're going to have to clean out her apartment and talk to her landlord, right?"

Adam nodded, and they both sat quietly, lost in their thoughts.

Eric said, "I'm going to give you a shot to numb your arm so I can clean it and stitch it up. Okay?"

Sam sat quietly, staring into space.

"Sam, did you hear me? I need to make sure you don't have any glass in your wound."

Sam looked at Eric and nodded. He handed her a rolled-up rag and told her to squeeze it. She did as he asked and when he stuck her with the needle close to the wound, she jumped.

"Ouch! Shit, Eric, that hurt!"

"Sorry, you'll be numb in a minute. Breathe through it, Sam."

She took a couple more breaths and soon her arm was numb. How could a person's life be so completely turned around in a day and a half?

A couple of hours later, Sam had twenty-three stitches. Eric said he put a lot of little stitches in to try and minimize the scarring. Adam had his ankle wrapped up, and they sat in the living room, deep in thought. Finally, Sam took another deep breath.

"I'll go tomorrow and speak with her landlord. Do you have keys to her place? I suppose we should take a look at how much stuff she has. Then what? Do we need to contact the hospital? What do we do now? I guess I'll call the office in the morning and speak with our probate attorney, Jane, and see what she thinks we should do."

She rambled out her thoughts as they came to her, unable to organize them.

Adam nodded. "I have keys, and I'll go with you. Why don't you stay here tonight and we'll go in the morning and figure everything out?"

"Well, I'm going to go home then. You all look like you need some sleep." Eric stood to leave. Everyone else had left when all the medical attention started taking place. Way to kill a party!

Sam nodded. "Thank you, Eric, for all of your medical attention. It was a pleasure meeting you though I wish it would have ended differently." A small smile creased her face. She stood and followed him into the kitchen.

"It was a pleasure meeting you as well, Sam. I'll check on you in the morning."

"What do I owe you for making a house call?"

He turned and looked at her. "Would you have dinner with me?"

Really? Another great looking, nice man wanted to have dinner with her. This last one had her on the roller coaster ride of her life.

She smiled weakly. "I'm just getting out of a relationship. I'm sorry. I'm just not ready right now. I hope you understand."

He nodded. "I do, but I'll be asking again. I called in an antibiotic for you. You'll need to stop off at the pharmacy and pick up your prescription first thing in the morning. I want to see you in a day or two to make sure there's no infection in your stitches."

"I promise. I'll call and set up an appointment." He handed her a business card.

She waved as he left through the garage by way of the kitchen door and walked across the lawn to his house.

Adam and Janie started making their way to bed. Sam had stayed here before and knew how to help herself.

"Do you guys need anything?" she asked, as she watched Janie help Adam up the stairs.

"No, we'll see you in the morning. Make yourself at home, Sam."

She crawled into her bed without turning on her phone. She didn't even want to know how many messages she had now.

19

SECOND CHANCES SERIES

The next morning Sam woke to her arm throbbing like a beast. She'd forgotten to ask Eric if she could get the stitches wet. The smell of the campfire from last night hung in her hair, and she and Adam had a full day ahead of them. She carefully rolled out of bed and padded to the bathroom to turn on the shower. She decided she'd take a quick shower and wash the stitches off a little. Then she'd check to see what medical supplies Janie had to cover them up. She showered quickly and did the best she could with her hair. Luckily, Adam and Janie had company often, and the bathroom was fully appointed with a blow dryer and curling iron.

She didn't spend any time with the curling iron, but she used the blow dryer, attempting to make her hair behave. She put her dirty clothes on from yesterday, though they were sticky where Adam's drink had spilled. At least *she* was clean. When she made her way upstairs, Janie and Julie were in the kitchen. Julie was sitting at the breakfast counter, and Janie was making breakfast.

"Hey there, kiddo; you really know how to throw a party." Sam smiled at her niece and gave her a little hug before sitting next to her at the counter.

Janie looked at Sam. "How are you feeling?"

"My arm hurts like a bitch, and my clothes are stiff and sticky, but otherwise I'm great."

Janie chuckled at Sam's feigned positive attitude. She walked over to the table where Janie had set out a pair of sweat pants and a T-shirt, along with medical supplies and pain reliever.

"I don't really have any clothes that will fit you, but I thought if you wanted to wear clean clothes, you could pull these on and Julie can help you doctor up your stitches. I have something that might take the edge off the pain too."

Sam smiled at her. "Thank you, Janie. I really appreciate it."

She clutched the clothes to her chest and strolled to the downstairs bathroom to change. When she came out of the bathroom, she could hear Adam grunting and groaning as he was making his way down the stairs. She ambled to the end of the staircase and looked up at him, a nonchalant smile on her face.

"Party too hard last night?"

Adam looked down at her. "You're not funny."

She shrugged. She thought she was damn clever.

"Do you need help?"

Adam shook his head and continued to slowly make his way down the last few steps.

"My ankle is swollen like a bitch, and I have a headache."

Sam shook her head and held up her arm with the stitches. "Throbs like a bitch."

They grinned at the other as they made their way into the kitchen. Julie stood and motioned for Sam to sit at the table so she could apply some antibiotic ointment to her stitches and wrap her arm in fresh gauze.

Sam looked at their medical kit and noticed it had everything in it. "Quite the medical kit you have here."

Julie smiled. "Dr. Anderson left it last night in case we needed anything. He said he would stop over before he heads to the hospital today to see if our patients are okay."

"What time is it anyway?"

Janie looked at the clock. "Six-thirty. Do you two need me to go with you today to your mom's place?"

Sam glanced at Adam. He shook his head no. If he didn't think so, Sam didn't care. Janie had a very level head on her shoulders and would be very helpful to have with them, but she didn't need to deal with their mother's crap, too, so Sam shook her head no. They would take care of their mother's things themselves, as they always had.

Breakfast was served, and while it smelled fantastic, she simply wasn't hungry and only nibbled on a piece of fruit. The last time she ate something was on Saturday at lunch with Gray. It was now Monday, and she hadn't seen Gray since Saturday evening. So much had happened since then. She supposed she *should* listen to her voicemails, but her stomach lurched at the thought. She didn't want to hear his apologies right now. In her mind, three people in a relationship was one too many. He was still allowing Suzanne to manipulate him and she didn't want any part of it. But it hurt like hell.

Adam looked over at Sam. "You okay?"

She nodded. "What time do you want to leave?"

"We can get rolling anytime. If the office isn't open when we get there, we can go to Mom's apartment and see what we're dealing with first."

"That sounds good." She stood up to go downstairs and get her purse when there was a knock on the door.

Julie left to answer the door, and Sam heard her say, "Morning, Dr. Anderson. How are you?"

"I'm fine, Julie. How are you?"

She listened to them make small talk as she and Adam walked back to the kitchen. When Eric rounded the corner, he looked fabulous. Sam didn't realize how handsome he was. Those blue eyes found hers and held them captive. Feeling uncomfortable, she looked at her toes.

"How are the patients today?"

Adam looked over at Eric. "Well, my ankle hurts like a bitch and Sam said her arm is the same. I think we're both dreading this morning. On a scale of one to ten, we're at about a three!"

What a drama king!

"Speak for yourself; I'm at least a four," Sam said with a smirk. She looked up at Eric, and he smiled at her.

"I would say at least a ten."

A flush crept across her face. Adam snorted. "Laying it on a little thick, aren't you?"

Eric shrugged.

"Sam, can I look at your stitches? I want to make sure they don't look infected. I was pretty confident that I got all the glass out, but I'd like to make sure."

Nodding, she sat at the table again. Eric unwrapped the bandage and complimented Julie on her nursing skills. He looked and thought things looked good, but her arm was feverish and was slightly pink, so he wanted to keep checking. He reminded her to fill the prescription that he'd called in and stood to leave. Sam thanked Eric again and started to head to the basement stairs when Eric's phone rang. He answered it, and she heard him say he would be right there.

"Sorry, emergency. A patient had a heart attack. Gotta run."

He was out the door quickly, and Sam finally made her way downstairs to retrieve her purse. With a heavy sigh, she turned on her phone knowing what she'd probably see. Yep, more messages. She peeked at a couple of the texts:

Sam, please call me and let me know you are okay. I'm so sorry.

Sam, please, please call me or text me, just let me know you're okay.

Sam, I love you, please talk to me.

Where the fuck are you?

God dammit Sam, at least let me know you're okay.

That was enough; she couldn't look at them any longer. She thought it *was* selfish of her to not at least let him know she was fine. Of course, he'd be worried. She tapped her phone and texted, *I'm fine.*

She tapped send, then dialed the office number and got the voicemail. Leaving a message for Jessie, she called Bill on his cell and told him her mother had passed, and she needed to deal with things today. He was concerned and told her if she needed anything she should let him know. When the call ended, she turned her phone off and went upstairs.

Sam drove because Adam struggled so much with his ankle. While they drove, she called Josh and told him what was going on. When they spoke, she was relieved that he didn't mention Gray other than to say that Gray had called looking for her Sunday evening. He'd told Gray that she was at Adam's. Okay, so Gray knew where she was and didn't come bursting through the door, so that was good. Josh *did* ask if everything was okay with them. She couldn't get into it; she didn't think she could talk about it yet without bawling her eyes out. She asked Josh to call Gage and Jake and let them know about her mom; then she ended the call.

When they got to the apartment complex, Sam was stunned at how run-down it was. Rusting cars, garage doors either hanging from their hinges or dented and rusting, and many apartment windows were covered with blankets tossed across the curtain rods haphazardly rather than curtains. The office wasn't open, so Adam pointed in the direction of their mom's apartment.

He said, "You know, we could really make this easy on ourselves."

Sam looked over at him, her brows furrowed.

"Look at this place, Sam. I bet the people who live here would love to pick through this stuff. Why don't we go in and see if there's anything we want first. Then, in a week or so we can put up signs with 'first come, first served' and be done with it. We're probably going to throw most of it out anyway. She smoked like a chimney, so all her stuff is going to reek. What do you think?"

She nodded. "Actually, that sounds great. The only thing I want is to see if she had any pictures. Do you know I don't have a single picture of myself as a baby or small child? They never took pictures of me ... only you. I would like to know what I looked like as a kid."

Adam furrowed his brow. "Really?"

"Really. Not a single one," Sam answered.

He didn't say anything as he struggled to get out of the car. He had an old pair of crutches retrieved from his basement that he was using to get around. Eric told him it would be better if he kept weight off his ankle for a few days. The problem was, their mother's apartment was on the second floor, and there wasn't an elevator. He groaned when he realized what faced him and turned around to sit on the bottom step.

"I better not hear one word from you on this," he warned.

She smirked as he started backing up the steps one at a time on his butt, using his good foot to push him up the next one.

"Should I stay below you in case you fall or can I go ahead of you?"

"What don't you get about 'not one word'?"

Laughing, she passed him on the stairs and waited at the top. His face was pinched in a scowl when he finally reached the landing. They walked down the hall to their mom's apartment. Adam opened the door, and they were greeted with the pungent odor of smoke. She'd always hated that smell.

She scrunched her face as they walked through the apartment looking for anything salvageable or of any worth. The furniture was old and of no value; the stench alone would turn off anyone remotely interested. Her clothing was nothing more than sweatshirts and sweat pants. Sam didn't want to sound like a snob, but it looked like she shopped thrift stores for her clothes. When you spent all your money on booze, there wasn't anything left for luxuries.

Locating a storage closet, she began rummaging around in it, finding a box, about the size of two shoeboxes put together, containing pictures and papers. She took it out of the closet and told Adam she would look through it later. They walked around a little more, and Adam found a couple of rings and a bracelet in the top drawer of her dresser.

"Do you want these?" he asked.

She shook her head no. "I don't want anything of hers—just a few pictures," she replied, nodding toward the box she held.

They checked the refrigerator and found it mostly empty except for a twelve pack of beer. Adam opened a pantry door to find alcohol —a couple cases of beer and two bottles of vodka. There were a couple bags of noodles and some dust-covered canned goods. Nothing else.

The office had opened, so they went in and asked to speak with the manager. She walked them to her office where they chatted for a bit. She told them that their mom's neighbor kind of looked out for her, and she was the one who found their mother lying on the living room floor. She called the ambulance, but their mom had died before the ambulance arrived. They thanked her for her time and information, wrote out the required Notice to Vacate, and left the office.

Once in the car, they talked about what they needed to do next. Sam called Jane at the law office to speak with her and to get a plan of action to focus on.

Next, they headed for the hospital to see what, if anything, needed to be done. A member of the hospital staff told them their mother had been taken to the funeral home that Adam had directed them to call when he spoke to them the night before. That was the next stop.

Leaving the funeral home at about two-fifteen in the afternoon, Sam was exhausted, and her arm throbbed. She drove Adam home and then went to get her prescription filled. Now all she wanted to do was go home and take a nap.

She walked into her peaceful, quiet house, took her pill with a glass of water and lay on the sofa. She turned on the television and flipped through the channels, finally stopping on a show she'd seen before, but she was tired and didn't care. She covered herself with a blanket and closed her eyes.

20

Gray knew he shouldn't walk away with Suzanne, but he could tell by her mood that she was going to dig at Sam and him all night. He thought if he appeased her by meeting a couple of people with her she would behave. He tried walking away a couple times, and she always found a reason why he should stay there. When Sam turned her back to them, he knew she was pissed. This was supposed to be a fun night for them. When he looked her way and saw Sam walking out the door at the Downtown Harmony Lake event, he jerked away from Suzanne and strode through the building to catch up with her. When he got to the front door, he saw her riding away in the back of a cab. By the time he got a cab, she was too far ahead of him. He'd screwed up again. Fucking Suzanne!

He slid in the back of a cab and told the driver to take him to his house. He hoped he could catch her. When he got there, her car was there, but she wasn't. Thinking she'd probably gone to her house, he jumped in his car and drove over there, but when he got there he saw her dress hanging in the closet; he must have just missed her. She wasn't anywhere to be found. The sinking feeling that hit his stomach when he realized she'd probably gone to his place to get her car almost brought him to his knees.

Jerking his phone from his pocket, he continued calling and texting her, but she wasn't answering. He had a friend who ran a security company, so Gray called David.

"Is there a way to track a cell phone?"

"Gray, are you sure you want to do this?" David sighed, then releasing a long breath, he continued. "There's a way to trace a cell phone, provided it's turned on."

"Check. Please. Will you check and see if hers is turned on?" His stomach lurched and threatened to empty itself.

"Sorry Gray, it isn't. No signal right now, but I can keep checking. Do you think she's in trouble?"

He rubbed the bridge of his nose as he sat with his elbows on his knees, perched on the edge of his sofa.

"I don't know, David. I just need to make sure she's not in trouble."

They ended their call, and he scraped his hands through his hair, bent his head, and locked his fingers behind his neck. The throbbing in his head rivaled the roiling of his stomach, and he wasn't sure if he was going to throw up or have an aneurysm. What he did know was sitting here was getting him nowhere, and yet, he didn't know where to go.

He called Sam's friends, Pam and Jessie and a couple others he could remember her mentioning. No one had seen or heard from her. He didn't want to call her kids and get them worked up—yet. After a few hours, he called his parents and told them what happened. They asked him to come over and talk to them. Dani had already called—she was worried.

Gray arrived at his parents' house, and Dani and Nick had been there for about an hour. They, too, were trying to figure out where Sam would have gone. Dani lit into Gray, reciting all of his transgressions and reminding him how stupid he was to let that bitch, Suzanne, once again ruin his life. When would he learn? How many times would he let her do this to him? What would it finally take for him to tell her to fuck off? On and on Dani went, until finally, Mary asked her to stop.

After Dani had calmed, she told Gray what Sam had said about him allowing Suzanne to manipulate him. Then she asserted, "If you get her to talk to you again—which is doubtful because if it were me, I wouldn't *ever* talk to you again—you better know what you're dealing with. You're the *only* person who can stop Suzanne from manipulating you, and being afraid she might make a scene is chump change compared to what you'll lose."

Gray took a deep breath. He didn't want to blast his sister, but she was scaring the crap out of him. There was no way he was going to let that happen. He needed to find her.

"I wasn't afraid of Suzanne creating a scene, Dani. I don't give a shit. I was afraid she would make Sam feel bad. Sam has self-esteem and self-worth issues. Suzanne was getting ready to pounce, and I didn't want Sam to have to deal with that."

Dani snorted. "You think watching you walk away with your bitch of an ex-wife helped her self-esteem and self-worth issues? You made her feel like Suzanne was more important, Gray!"

Gray dropped his head and covered his face with his hands. The cold dread crawling through his stomach threatened to steal the very breath from him. His back stiffened so that he felt one wrong move would break him. He sat hunched over in the kitchen chair in his parents' kitchen and a hopelessness settled in over him. Tears sprung to his eyes at the thought that he'd made Sam feel unimportant, just like her parents. No, he was worse than them because he told her he'd never do that to her.

Mary spoke up. "That's enough. We need to find Sam. Gray, you need to grovel, beg, or do whatever you need to do to get her to talk to you. It isn't going to be easy."

Harry added, "It's getting late. Gray, why don't you stay here tonight?"

"Thanks, Dad. I want to be home in case Sam comes home during the night."

Dani reminded Gray, "Your house isn't her home, and I doubt that she'll show up there."

He stood abruptly and stalked to the kitchen door, letting it slam behind him. He drove home and sat on the sofa continuing his efforts to get her to answer his calls or texts. He stopped being angry that she wasn't responding to him and became scared thinking he'd never see her again.

The little sleep he got was while sitting up on the sofa. He rotated his head hoping to relieve his stiff neck muscles. Standing, he stretched his sore muscles. He'd been so stiff and tense that his muscles now protested. He slowly made his way to the master bathroom, turned the water on its hottest setting and took two aspirin while waiting for the water to steam up the room.

He drove to Sam's house and found Shelia there showing the house. She said she hadn't spoken to Sam, but if she did, she'd let Sam know he was looking for her. Gray thought he would go to the mall and see if she was there. She liked going to Starbucks, so he'd start there. He'd drive around all fucking day if he needed to.

Around ten o'clock Gray's phone rang, and he instantly answered without looking, "Sam?"

"It's Dad, Gray. Any luck?"

Closing his eyes, he leaned his head back against the headrest in his SUV. He'd been watching the plethora of people coming and going from the mall. He was simply at a loss as to where she'd be.

"No," he responded softly.

"Well, come on over and have some lunch. Your mom is worried you haven't been eating and you need to be with family right now."

"Dad …" He let out a breath. "I just can't. I won't be able to handle it if everyone starts in on me. I'm barely hanging on as it is."

He heard his father mutter, "Fuck." Which caused his head to pop off the seat. Harry never swore. "Gray, don't make me come and find you. We're worried about you and Sam. When your mother worries, I worry. When we're both worried, your sister worries and, dammit, we need to see you and know you're okay. So, get your ass over here now!"

Taking a deep breath and rubbing his tired eyes, he said, "Okay. I'll be there in a little while."

Pulling into the driveway, he exhaled in relief to see he was the first one there. He walked in and sat at the counter with Harry while Mary cooked. The sad looks on his parents' faces made the tears flow, and for the second time in two days, he cried. If he could just talk to her and tell her how sorry he was.

"Mom, I love her so damn much. I never dreamed I'd find her. She's the one; she is, I knew it the first moment I saw her. I've been trying not to scare her by moving too fast, but dammit, as soon as I find her, I'm going to marry her. I'll do anything to get her back, *anything.*"

His mother came around the counter and hugged him to her. She laid her cheek on the top of his head and smoothed the tired muscles in his back. She cooed soft words to him and reassured him Sam would come home when she'd been able to lick her wounds.

"I made her feel just as bad as they have all her life. I *have* to make it right. I broke a promise to her that I'd never treat her like she didn't matter."

Lunch passed agonizingly slow. Gray pushed the food around on his plate, but each time he thought about taking a bite, his stomach revolted. He was the first to leave, wanting to finally call Josh.

Josh told him that Sam was at Adam's for Julie's birthday party. Then Gray remembered that she'd told him about it. He felt better knowing she was okay, but he knew if he went there, it would cause a scene, and he didn't want that. So, he decided to wait for her to come home.

He called Sam's phone a few more times and still no answer. Her voicemail was full, so he couldn't leave another message; it wasn't helping him anyway. He went home and tried to sleep, but when he could fall asleep, he couldn't stay asleep. By three a.m., he got up and went into his office to go through emails and see if he could get anything done.

On Monday morning, Gray's phone rang. Popping his head up

from his desk, he grabbed the phone, hoping to God it was Sam and was disappointed to hear Dani on the other end.

"Sorry to disappoint you, brother, but I wanted you to know that I went to Sam's office to see if she was there and Jessie told me she called in sick today. Jessie didn't know where she was, just that she wasn't coming in."

Gray closed his eyes. He couldn't go another day without finding her.

"Gray, did you hear me?"

Gray sighed. "Yes, thanks for checking, Dani, I appreciate it."

"We all love her Gray, and we love you too. I'm sorry I bitched at you; I'm sure you feel awful."

He took a deep breath. Shit, he felt like crying again.

"Thanks, Dani. I love you, too. I *have* to find her."

"I know, Gray; you will. Let me know if there's anything I can do."

He closed his eyes and pinched the bridge of his nose. Shit! "I will. Thanks again, Dani."

After hanging up, he felt lost and hopeless. He was exhausted, frustrated, and worried. Finally, his phone chirped a text, and he grabbed it so fast he almost dropped it.

A text from Sam. *I'm fine.* That was it; just she's fine. He tried calling her right away, and it went straight to voicemail.

He needed to get his head on straight, and he needed to work the words around in his head that he would say to her. For some reason, he didn't think "sorry" was going to cut it. He was going to have to beg, grovel, beg some more, then beg some more after that. He just needed to be face-to-face with her to do that. His phone rang, and without even looking at it, he answered.

"Sam?"

"No Gray, it's Cheryl. Is this a bad time?"

The air left his lungs, and he blankly stared out the window of his office.

"Actually, Cheryl, it *is* a bad time. I'm waiting for a call."

"Gray, I'm sorry to bother you. I just wondered if I could see you again. I know you're involved with someone else, but I can't stop thinking about you. I'm having a hard time. I still love you, Gray. Can I see you?"

Honestly? He had no intention of seeing her again. Especially not now.

"Cheryl, that's not a good idea. I'm sorry you're having a hard time, but I never led you on, and I never gave you any indication there would ever be more between us. I love Sam. I love her with my whole heart."

He could hear soft crying on the other end of the phone. He sucked in a long breath and swallowed the litany of profanity he wanted to spew. He had no patience for this stuff right now.

"Please Gray, just for a little while. I can come over to your place. You don't have to go anywhere."

"NO! Cheryl, there's nothing that needs to be said that I haven't said already. I'm not interested, and as I told you earlier, this is a bad time. I need to go. Goodbye."

He tapped the end call icon and shoved his phone into his back pocket. Standing abruptly, he grimaced at the sharp pain shooting through his back. His hands flew to the spot as his fingers began rubbing away the pain. He paced his office a few times; then it occurred to him that Cheryl may just decide to come to the house anyway. He sure as hell didn't need that, and if Sam did come home and Cheryl was here, it sure as shit wouldn't look good. Exhaling sharply, he grabbed his keys from the hall table and climbed into his SUV. This was bullshit!

It was close to four-thirty in the afternoon. He decided to go back to Sam's house and see if she was there. When he opened the garage door, her car was there, and he almost cried from relief. His hands shook as the magnitude of feelings rushed through him; this was the moment that could make or break them. Opening the door, he stepped lightly into the back of the house into the dining area and softly walked around the fireplace to the living room to see Sam sleeping on the sofa. He had to fight back a sob from escaping his lips when he saw her lying there. Tears had already formed in his eyes. He carefully sat on the sofa by her head and watched her sleep. Even while she slept, he could tell she looked tired. Her eyes were red and puffy and dark smudges marred the skin under her eyes where her lashes rested.

He could hold back no longer. Softly, his fingers smoothed her hair then gently massaged her scalp. She lightly sighed and his lips curved into a smile. Her hands peeked out from the blanket covering her body and gently rested under her chin, her fingers curled around her thumbs. He enjoyed the feel of her hair, the soft silky strands gliding through his fingers. No hairspray or gel impeding his soft strokes. She brusquely shot up, her eyes wild as her brain caught up to the fact that it was him here with her and not a stranger. He silently stared at her, unsure of what his first words should be.

She closed her eyes, then opened them again, lightly rubbing under them. She pulled her knees up to her chest and looked out the window behind him.

"Go away, Gray. I can't deal with this right now."

"NO!" He said louder than he meant. Softening his voice, he continued, "No, Sam, I will not go away until you talk to me."

"Well, apparently, you *can* say no—only to me, though, not Suzanne. Perfect. Go away."

"Sam, please talk to me."

She shook her head. He inched closer, and she moved back quickly and almost fell off the sofa. He jumped forward to catch her, but she pulled away like she'd been stung by his touch. He sat down next to her, closer than before and turned to look directly into her eyes.

"Sam, I'm so sorry. I could see she was going to be bitchy and start making things hard on you. She would have dredged up past events and made it sound like we were one happy family and try to make you feel uncomfortable and hurt your feelings. I didn't want that. Once Nate walked over, I thought you had someone to talk to as well as Dani, Nick, and Jamie. I thought if I walked away for a couple of minutes, it would satisfy Suzanne and you would be okay."

"One hour! One fucking hour, Gray! And please tell me what you think she could have said that would have been more hurtful than you walking away, parading her around like she's still your wife with her arms wrapped around yours. Tell me what could have been said that would have been worse than that!"

He took a deep breath and raked both of his hands down his face. Sam got up to walk away, but he jumped up and grabbed her.

"You're going to stay here and talk to me."

She tried to pull away, but he held her tightly and wrapped both of his arms around her. She continued to struggle until she hit her arm on his arm.

"Ouch! Fuck, that hurt!" she whimpered

She stopped moving and held her arm against her tummy.

He watched the pain flash across her face and the way she cradled her arm. Tears began pouring like rain down her cheeks. He walked them to the sofa and sat down with her, his arm still firmly wrapped around her shoulders. She pulled her knees up, so her feet rested on the sofa and continued hugging her arm to her. He sat quietly as she cried. His own tears fell here and there, but he managed to get himself under control. Once her crying stopped, she reached forward for a tissue on the coffee table, wiped her eyes, blew her nose, then let out a long shaky breath.

"Can you talk now?"

Sam closed her eyes.

"What more is there to say, Gray? Haven't you put me through enough?"

"I never, never meant to put you through anything. I would rather die than hurt you. I thought I was saving you from Suzanne, not hurting you. I didn't think about it the way you did. Now that I see how you feel about it, I would do anything to turn back time." He ran his hands down his face if only there were a way to wipe away the worry and stress from the past few days. "For the record, you've put me through quite a bit these past few days. Your disappearing act was bullshit."

She turned her head and looked him in the eyes for the first time. She opened her mouth to speak, then promptly closed it. He held her gaze, now that she was back, he fought the anger that threatened to creep in.

"In my mind, I wasn't hiding; I was finished. I've told you from the beginning I wasn't ever going to be in a relationship where my partner allowed himself to be manipulated. In a matter of just two or three weeks now, Suzanne has manipulated you twice, and you blindly go along with it."

He took in a deep cleansing breath and slowly blew it out. He swallowed the lump that formed, cleared his throat and softly asked, "Where do we go from here? And before you answer, let me just say this; Dani told me what you said. She told me what Nate said, too. I get it, Sam, I do. I was wrong, and I'll never—ever—do anything like that to you again. I swear it."

She took a deep breath and looked out the window, but she wasn't kicking him out, and she wasn't running away. There was hope.

When she spoke, her voice was soft. "Three people in a relation-ship doesn't work; I want more."

"You deserve more. I'm going to give it to you."

Her eyebrows raised into the little blonde whisps of hair on her fore-head. The dark smudges under her eyes were prominent, the creases at the corners seemed to have deepened this weekend. He imagined his eyes looked much the same. He slowly reached over and pulled the arm she favored toward him, careful not to tug or harm it further. He held her hand in his and glanced down at her arm. She wore a long-sleeved blue T-shirt, which hung loosely on her small frame, but he sucked in a breath when he saw a splotch of fresh blood oozing into the fabric.

"What happened to you, Sam?"

She took a deep, shaky breath. "Well, Adam fell and cut me with a glass, and my mom died. That's the short version, of course."

Gray's brows furrowed. "My God, Sam, are you okay?"

She retold the story, and he sat quietly and listened until she mentioned Dr. Eric Anderson and that he'd taken care of her and asked her on a date. That's when his heart hammered in his chest and his throat burned from the dryness. When he felt he could speak without sounding like a jealous lover, he was proud of himself when he simply said, "We each have a promise to make – You don't run anymore, and I won't allow Suzanne to manipulate me anymore. We stand together. Deal?"

She softly smiled, "Deal."

21

SECOND CHANCES SERIES

Around four-thirty in the morning, Gray's phone rang. They had fallen asleep last night, both exhausted and spent. The gentle music that signified his mom's ring seeped into his sleep-fogged brain until it registered what the music was.

Gray was already reaching for the side table where his phone lay, "Hi, Mom, what's up?"

"When?"

"Is he going to be okay?"

"Where is he?"

"When is that?"

"Do you need anything?"

"We'll be there in a little while."

"Yes, she's with me."

"Okay, I love you, too."

He rolled over to face Sam, the worry creasing his forehead. "My dad had a heart attack and is at the hospital. He's having heart surgery in a couple hours. Mom would like us all to be there. She's happy you're with me. She loves you, you know."

"I love her, too. Is your dad going to be okay? How bad was the heart attack?"

Gray shook his head. "We didn't get into all of that. I'm sorry, Sam, but we need to go."

Sam scrambled out of bed and threw on clean jeans and a soft sweater. She did her best to tame her hair, brush her teeth and she did her makeup in the car. After all they'd been through, she didn't want to arrive looking like something the cat dragged in.

They arrived at the hospital, and Gray asked the receptionist which room his father was in. They were directed to the fifth floor and found his room. When they entered, Mary, Jamie, Dani, and Ethan were there. Harry was awake and communicating, but not talking much. Jamie and Dani stepped aside to allow Gray and Sam to say hello to Harry.

Mary hugged Sam and kissed her cheek. "I'm so happy you're here, Sam." Sam hugged her back. "I am too, but sorry we have to be here."

She looked at Harry, and he smiled at her. "Great to see you, Sam. I thought Gray really screwed up this time."

His voice was weak. "Well, it looks like you've gone overboard in looking for attention, don't you think?" She smiled at him and was greeted with a grin.

He nodded yes. She took his hand in hers and held it. Gray placed his hand on Harry's shoulder and kept it there for a long time. Harry looked at Gray and smiled weakly. "I love you, Gray. You hang onto her, okay?"

Gray's eyes welled with tears, but he nodded. "I love you too, Dad."

Sam stood next to Gray and put her arm around his waist. He wrapped his free arm around her shoulders never letting his hand slip from Harry's shoulder.

Someone walked into the room behind them, and Sam heard a familiar voice.

"Sam?"

She looked up to see Eric Anderson.

She smiled. "Eric, I didn't realize you worked at this hospital. Small world."

They hadn't talked about his career much at Adam and Janie's, mostly about things to do in the area and neutral things. Gray's arm tightened around Sam.

"So, can you fix him?" Sam asked with a smile, pointing to Harry. Eric looked at Gray for a few moments, then back at her.

"Yes, I have every confidence that Mr. Kinkaide will be fine."

Mary cleared her throat and Sam looked over at her. "Have you all met Dr. Anderson?"

Introductions were made. Eric studied Sam for a moment, then asked about her stitches. She wrinkled her face. "They're pink and feverish, but I'm taking my antibiotic."

"I'll have someone look at them while I'm in surgery."

She nodded, and Eric began talking to Harry and Mary mostly, but each person in the room listened to him explain about the surgery, how long it would take, and what to expect afterward. When he was finished, he asked if there were questions. Everyone shook their heads, and he turned to leave, saying he would come into the waiting room and speak with them all after surgery. He looked at Sam and nodded before walking out the door.

The room was quiet for a moment, and Mary looked at Sam.

"How do you know Dr. Anderson, Sam? And what did he mean about stitches?"

Sam squeezed Gray's waist. "I met him over the weekend. He's my brother's neighbor and was at my niece Julie's birthday party. There was a little accident, and my arm was cut and Eric—Dr. Anderson—stitched me up."

She held out her arm and pulled her sleeve up to her bandage.

Soon a team of nurses came into the room to prep Harry, so they said their goodbyes and told him they would see him in a few hours and left Mary and Harry to say what they needed to say to each other before he went into surgery.

They waited in the hall for Mary so they could walk down to the waiting area together. Dani was the first one to speak.

"So, hunky Dr. Anderson stitched you up? What kind of accident?"

Sam told them the story about her brother and her mother passing, although not how she died, and the commotion that took place afterward. Dani walked to Sam and gave her a hug.

"I'm sorry to hear about your mother passing, Sam. My condolences."

Mary walked out just then, and they walked to the waiting area.

After entering the brightly lit room, everyone helped themselves to coffee and tea and looked for places to sit for the four or five hours they would be waiting. Unable to forget the last time she'd sat in a room like this, she pushed the morose thoughts away. She had to believe the outcome would be different this time. Gray sat in a recliner and pulled her down on his lap. He put his finger under her chin and pulled her face around to look at him.

"Do I have to worry about Dr. Anderson, Sam?"

Sam let out a quick breath. "No, Gray, you have nothing to worry about. I like him, and he's a nice person. He helped Adam and me when we needed it. He asked me out. I declined. That's it. Nothing else."

Gray let out a breath, nodded his head, and kissed her lightly.

A nurse walked in a few minutes later and called her name. She held her hand up as everyone else pointed to her and the nurse walked toward Sam. She had a rolling tray with her, and as she approached, she smiled. "Dr. Anderson asked that I come in and take a look at your stitches. He's concerned about infection. Is this a good time?"

"Sure," she said as she pulled her sleeve up and noted the nurse's name badge—Nancy. Nancy asked if she wanted to sit somewhere else and Gray cleared his throat.

"No, she can stay here."

He tightened his arm around her waist. Nancy nodded and opened pouches with ointments and bandages and a syringe. Nancy then turned and removed the gauze covering Sam's stitches.

When they were uncovered, Gray sucked in a breath. "Geez Sam, you really downplayed the stitches. Shit!"

Sam looked at them. They were red and swollen, and the cut was crooked, but she thought overall, Eric did a great job of making it not look so bad. Nancy held Sam's arm in her hand as she took a good look at it, gently touching it to see how feverish it was.

"Well, all in all, it might be a little infected, and I'll give you a stronger antibiotic in a shot which will kick-start the healing process. It doesn't look too bad though, and Dr. Anderson did a nice job with the stitches. Your scar will be minimal in a year or so."

Nancy cleaned the stitches with alcohol and put on fresh antibiotic ointment and new gauze. She said she needed to give Sam the shot and thought the other arm would be better. Sam switched herself around on Gray's lap and slightly winced as the needle poked her arm.

"Continue to keep these clean, keep this antibiotic ointment on them." She pulled a few packets of ointment from a box on her tray. "Try and get some rest, that helps more than anything. Nice meeting you." Nancy turned and quietly left the room.

Gray pulled Sam back to him, and they reclined in the chair, her freshly bandaged arm resting over his heart. The family softly chattered and kept Mary occupied. Sam fell asleep. Occasionally, Sam would hear voices, soft and murmuring, then drift back off. She wasn't sure how much time passed, but something woke her up, although she was having a hard time waking up completely.

She heard Gray's voice and felt the vibration through his chest, which is what initially woke her. She felt a palm on her head feeling for fever.

"She feels a little warm. Has she been sleeping the whole time?"

"Most of it," Gray said.

Then there was silence for a long moment, and she heard Gray say, "Is there anything else you need?"

What made Sam come around was his tone.

"She snuck up on me, you know." It was Eric. Opening her eyes, she turned to his hand over his heart.

"She does that, but she's mine!"

The two men silently stared at each other.

"How long has surgery been over? Is Harry okay?"

Eric stood back. He turned to find Mary, pulled a chair close to her, and began explaining the surgery and Harry's condition.

The surgery had gone well, and Harry was expected to make a full recovery. Eric answered questions and told everyone they could see Harry in about an hour. They were relieved and happy about the news. The conversation was livelier after the news, and it seemed like time passed quickly. Before they knew it, a nurse came in and informed them they could see Harry.

Of course, he was sleeping when they entered his room. Monitors beeped and blipped and IV lines ran from their respective bag of potion to his arm. She watched the heart monitor for a long time, loving the fact that it never wavered, his heart was steady and strong. They whispered as they spoke, not wanting to wake Harry up. Mary sat next to the bed, holding his hand. Sam couldn't imagine what was going through her mind all day. She was wrecked herself and Harry wasn't her husband.

Gray called Sarah and Cole and checked in at the office, and Sam needed to go through her voicemails and clean them out. That was going to be hard. They chatted quietly with Mary, telling her they would be back later in the evening. She and Gray left after hugs and goodbyes. The ride home was quiet. When they arrived home, Gray went straight to his office, and Sam sat on the sofa to listen to her voicemail.

She had forty-one messages from Gray and one from Shelia, simply asking Sam to give her a call whenever she could.

Tears streamed down her face by the time she finished listening to all her messages. The pain in his voice was awful. And she finally got it, she'd been selfish in her behavior, and that was inexcusable. She was old enough to know better. She'd keep her promise and never run away again. Gray walked into the room and saw her crying. He came over, sat next to her, and pulled her to him.

"Are you okay, baby?"

She nodded.

"I just listened to my voicemails. I'm so sorry Gray; I was very selfish for not at least letting you know I was okay. Please forgive me."

Gray sighed. "We hurt each other badly, Sam. I'll do everything in my power to never hurt you again."

Sam hugged him tightly. "Me too. I do love you."

"I love you, too, Sam."

They sat quietly, holding hands and staring ahead.

Finally, Gray broke the silence.

"You were wrong about Dr. Anderson, you know. He has feelings for you."

Sam sighed. "I've only known him for about four days, and in that four days, I've only spent about eight hours total with him. Most of that time was him stitching me up and working on Adam. I highly doubt that he has feelings for me."

Gray pulled away from her to look into her eyes. "I fell in love with you the moment I saw you."

Sam leaned in and kissed him.

"I fell in love with you in that same moment, and I'm still in love with you and only you."

22

T he following week Gray and Sam spent most of their time at his house, talking and working through things.

Gray admitted, "I've always caved into Suzanne because it was easier to let her manipulate me than it was to watch her hurt the people I care about."

"That's so sad." She kissed his lips, and the flutter his heart made gave him a thrill.

"So, my uncle's granddaughter is getting married in two weeks, but I have a sneaking suspicion that Suzanne will be in attendance. The bride's mother is friendly with her. I think we can do this, don't you? Be in the same room with her?"

"Yes, I think we can do this, Gray. Absolutely; it'll be a second chance."

Later he worked on the business side of things at Kinkaide & Associates; he was behind after their botched night out on the town. Sam was off shopping for the wedding with the Kinkaide women. He poured over a form he'd found online after he and Ethan had chatted about needing more structure at the firm.

"Aww, that looks very interesting. I'm sorry to interrupt your reading." Sam's sweet voice floated over him.

He looked up and smiled warmly.

"Please, please interrupt me."

He chuckled as he stood and walked toward her. He pulled her into the office and Amanda appeared at the door.

"Gray, I'm so sorry, she just walked right in."

He glanced at her and sighed. "Amanda, Sam never has to be announced, and she can always walk right in. I don't care if I have a room full of people, this woman is welcome anytime."

He hugged the little woman who'd stolen his heart and ignored Amanda who now had a scowl on her face.

"To what do I owe this wonderful pleasure?"

Eventually, Amanda left the office though neither he nor Sam noticed her.

Sam told him about the shopping, lunch, and the manis and pedis. She sat on the edge of his desk and showed him her toes peeking from her sandals. She had them painted in a French mani-cure to match her fingernails. The nail tech painted tiny little sage colored flowers on her big toes and a couple on her fingernails to set off her dress. She excitedly told him about the dress she'd found, and he had a hard time looking away from her happy face.

"Sam, I have no doubt you'll look stunning for the wedding in *any* dress; I can't wait to see you in it. But don't be offended if I can't wait to take it off of you!"

She laughed. "What were you reading that looked like it pained you?"

He grabbed the document he'd been reading and handed it to her. "We're trying to do employee reviews, and someone found this review form online, which I don't think is relevant to what we need here. I just hate dealing with this stuff."

She moved from the edge of the desk and sat in his chair in front of his computer and patted the desk next to her with a grin on her face. "Let me help you. My bachelor's degree is in HR management. This is easy."

"You tell me what you want to evaluate your employees on, and

I'll help you create a new review form. But I need you to sit next to me to keep me motivated."

She smiled and winked, and he thought he was the luckiest man on earth. He sat on the desk next to her. Watching her tap away on the keys, he leaned down close to her and licked the shell of her ear, then kissed the side of her face before he started down her neck.

"I don't think this is what I need to be motivated in, but I love your train of thought."

He laughed. "Okay, I'll behave for about ten minutes."

They worked for about an hour getting the form to look like something he was happy with.

"Sam, I'm so happy you came when you did. I never would have been able to get this done on my own. You should come and work here with me. You could help me run the business, so I can concentrate on being the creative geek."

"The thought sounds good, but if we broke up again, I would not only lose my boyfriend, I would lose my job."

"Ouch. I thought we'd gotten past the bad stuff."

She stood and wrapped her arms around his neck. "I love you, but let's give it a little more time. We've moved so fast—I don't want to jump from the frying pan into the fire."

Reluctantly, he agreed to let it rest—for a while. He kissed her in earnest this time; losing himself in her was his new favorite thing.

**

Getting ready for the wedding, he walked into the bathroom to see if she was almost ready and stopped in his tracks in the doorway.

"Wow, Sam. You continue to take my breath away. You look beautiful."

She grinned at him. "Thanks, baby. You look very sexy."

He smirked. "Turn around and let me see the back."

She turned, and he whistled. The sage green sheath dress had an underskirt that extended beyond the short sequined portion of the dress to about an inch above her knee. The underskirt had a smattering of sequins on it here and there, just for effect. The top of the dress fit right below her neck—no cleavage showed—and at the shoulders, the dress was about an inch and a half wide. The back was bare to the bottom portion of her back and from shoulder to shoulder was a thin drape of the sequined material that plunged down to the top of her butt and swayed when she moved. She paired the dress with a pair of strappy, high-heeled sandals in the same color as the dress. When she moved, she shimmered and sparkled.

He walked over to her and wrapped his arms around her. "You're so beautiful. Do you know what I like best about this dress?"

She kissed him lightly and smiled. "What do you like best?"

He rubbed his hands up and down her bare back. "I can touch your skin anytime I want to—which will be all night."

Sam laughed. "That might be my favorite thing, too."

They arrived at the church around four-thirty for the evening wedding. Candles flickered all over the church, and the altar was stunning in the twinkling glow. His sister and her husband, Dani and Nick, were already there. Since his dad still tired easily and wasn't up to outings, his mom came with Dani.

They were sitting in a pew when he and Sam walked in. His mom had saved them a seat, so before sitting down, they were greeted with hugs. They sat at the far side of the pew on the outside. He wrapped his arm around the back of the pew and Sam's shoulders. They chatted with his family when Ethan, Eva, and Jax walked in. Jamie and his kids came in next and sat behind Gray and Sam. Finally, Dani and Nick's kids came in and sat behind them in the pew with Jamie and his family. The music quieted, and the ushers walked the mothers to the front of the church. The bridesmaids were next.

When the wedding march began, the bride held her father's arm as he walked her down the aisle. She was a petite beauty with long, blonde hair and bright blue eyes. He remembered her as a little girl and had only seen her a few times in the past few years. She'd gone away to college, and as happens, life had been busy for them both. She reached her future husband, who shook hands with her father and then held his arm out to her to walk the final three steps to the altar.

He sat there in church watching his uncle's granddaughter get married, and he was restless. He wanted to be up there with Sam. He knew he wanted to marry her—he was sure of that fact. It was cemented in his mind after the whole Downtown Harmony Lake fiasco. While she was gone, all he could think about was how he wanted her to be his wife. He looked down at her now, admiring this beautiful woman he loved. She was amazing to be around. His family loved her, and she loved them. Her kids were great, and he enjoyed spending time with them. She glanced up at him and smiled.

"What?" she whispered.

He shook his head, whispering back, "Nothing. I love looking at you."

She chuckled lightly.

He leaned down and whispered in her ear. "Sam, I want that to be us. I want to stand up in church in front of our family and friends and make you my wife. I want them to listen to me say my vows to you and watch me slide my ring on your finger. I want them to see you wear my mark. I want to marry you, Sam."

She whispered, "You don't think it's too soon? What are you saying, you mean now? Soon?"

He looked at her for a long time. "Yes, I want to get married. Soon!"

Their whispered conversation was interrupted when everyone stood up to pray.

After the wedding, they walked across the street to the wedding hall. His part of the family walked together and ordered drinks at the bar, as the other wedding guests began to arrive. Relatives were excited to hear how Harry was doing and to meet Gray's girl. His hand seldom left her back. Usually, his thumb traced small circles over her skin. But mostly he wanted to stay close, so she knew how important she was to him.

Dinner was announced, and they walked in to find seats. They sat at the back of the hall, letting the more immediate family members sit closer to the head table. It appeared that the other side of the family wasn't as close as the Kinkaides were. After dinner, everyone got up to go to the bar and wait for the tables to be removed to allow dancing. And there she was! Suzanne walked toward them. Truth or dare time!

As soon as she joined their group, she greeted her children first, giving each of them tiny little hugs and air kisses so she wouldn't ruin her makeup. She nodded at Mary, Jamie, Dani and Nick and all the kids, and then she looked right at Gray.

"Hello, darling. How are you doing?"

Darling? He simply nodded.

"You remember Sam, don't you Suzanne?" His jaw tightened as he reminded Suzanne that Sam was here.

Suzanne gave Sam the once-over.

"Yes, of course. Sam, I thought you would wear the same dress you wore to the Downtown Harmony Lake event. After all, you didn't wear it very long."

Sam simply smiled at her.

"Oh well, too bad you had to leave early that night. We had a great time, didn't we, Gray?"

He huffed out a breath. "As I recall, I had a miserable time. It didn't get great until I left."

He tightened his arm around Sam.

"Hmm, well I guess you can remember it any way you wish. Anyway, I came over here because Janice was asking about you and I wanted you to come over and say hello to her. She broke her leg and isn't getting around very well."

Suzanne took a step forward to grab his other arm, but he stepped back. "Suzanne, I'm not here to spend any time with you. I'm with my family, which you are no longer a part of. *If* Sam and I get around to where Janice is sitting, we'll say hi."

Nicely done! He spoke to Sam, "Should we go visit with Uncle Frank, baby? I promised him I would bring you over. He's very excited to meet you."

Suzanne snorted. "Baby? What on earth kind of moniker is baby? Seriously, Gray, aren't you pouring it on a little thick?"

He looked Suzanne right in the eye. "Suzanne, what I call anyone is none of your business. My life is none of your business. But mostly, my life with Sam is none of your fucking business. Your little attempt here to once again try and manipulate me is over. Now, you'll need to excuse us. Uncle Frank is dying to meet Sam, and I'm dying to introduce them."

They turned and walked away to talk to Uncle Frank. His hand never left Sam's back, and he felt marvelous. That was positively liberating!

After chatting for some time, Sam stood on her toes to speak in his ear. "Are you okay?" she whispered.

He turned to her, put both arms around her and kissed her. "I've never felt better in my entire life. I mean that. You were right; that felt wonderful!"

She hugged him tightly. "I'm so happy for you, Gray. And, thank you so much for fighting for us." She winked, and his mind instantly went to undressing her, but then again, he thought that often.

A slow song came on, and he thought it was the perfect time to hold her close. "Dance with me?"

The look she gave him made his cock twitch. Yes, he was going to undress her soon. They walked out to the dance floor and put their arms around each other. They mostly just swayed back and forth holding each other. He enjoyed being able to touch her bare back and whispered in her ear.

"I can touch your whole back in public, and it isn't indecent. I'm going to insist you keep this dress."

She chuckled. Then quickly turned.

"I'm cutting in." Suzanne's grating voice interrupted the soft spell they'd woven.

Sam shook her head. "No, you're not. He's mine, and I don't share."

She turned back to him, and he couldn't help but smile. She was holding her own. Suzanne spoke a little louder than necessary.

"He was mine first. I want to dance with him."

People looked their way. He stood straight, about to say something, but Sam responded, "You were stupid enough to cheat on him and push him away, so you lost him. I've found him, and now he's mine—forever. Go make someone else's life a living hell. You won't be making Gray's life hellish ever again."

Suzanne looked like she'd sucked on a bowl of lemons. He had a hard time not laughing at that look, and he knew he'd never miss seeing it. It usually preceded an awful outburst. "Suzanne, all you're doing is embarrassing yourself. I never loved you. You never loved me. Let's not play any games here. You'll never manipulate me again. Now gather up what little bit of dignity you still have and leave us alone."

She stormed off. He pulled Sam back into his arms and held her close, continuing to sway to the music, he whispered in her ear. "You didn't answer me earlier, Sam. What do you think about getting married?"

She pulled her head back and looked into his eyes.

"You didn't exactly ask me; you made a statement then asked me what I thought. I want the whole ball of wax, Gray. I want the proposal. Possibly even a knee and everything."

Then she winked at him. He pulled her close to him as tight as he could and squeezed her.

"I love you, Sam."

She giggled. "I love you too, Gray ... very much."

When they got home, they were giddy and happy and felt elated. She grabbed Gray's hand and hauled him into the bedroom.

"You said something about wanting to take this dress off me. Now would be the time to do so."

He laughed and began removing her dress, kissing her everywhere her dress needed to be pulled, unzipped, or unhooked. He removed her shoes, kissing each toe, her heels, and the balls of her feet. Her pantyhose were next, and he kissed down her legs and back up again. Finally, her panties were removed and delicious kisses placed wherever they touched.

He kissed and lapped at the warmth between her legs. Once she was completely nude, he stood back and stared at her body, so lithe and supple. And the best part was, she let him.

He grinned. "You're so beautiful, Sam. And, look at you being so brave and letting me admire you."

She smiled. "You make me feel beautiful, Gray. I'm only beautiful with you."

She undid the buttons on his shirt and pulled it from his shoulders. She kissed his chest, his shoulders, and his arms, all the way to the waistband of his pants, unbuttoning his pants and slid the zipper down.

"Shoes first." He groaned. "Tease."

She pushed him down onto the bed, knelt and removed each of his shoes, kissing his toes, heels, and the balls of his feet the same as he had her. She slowly started to slide up his body, dragging her hands along his legs and stopping at his waistband. He watched her intently. He slid his hands into her hair.

"I love you so much, Sam."

She smiled and winked. She slowly pulled his pants down, kissing along the way, avoiding his private area which made him groan. She kissed his legs all the way down and all the way back up again. He made a low noise in his throat when her fingers slid under the waistband of his boxer briefs. Sam chuckled.

Slowly she started sliding his boxer briefs down, kissing and licking as she uncovered skin. When she uncovered his hard cock, she covered it with her mouth, sucking him into her warmth. He moaned loudly, unable to control the raw emotions running through his body.

"Oh, God, that feels so good," he panted.

She licked and sucked him, touching him and cupping his balls in her other hand. He groaned again which urged her on. She gently rubbed his testicles as she worked her mouth up and down in rhythm. Each time she reached the top of his penis, she'd roll her tongue over the head, causing his breath to shudder in his chest.

Soon, his hands reached down and pulled her up onto the bed with him. She climbed on top of him and ran her hands over his body.

"I love you beyond reason, Grayson Kinkaide," she said, breathlessly.

She kissed him very slowly, running her tongue around his mouth and licking his lips. She lifted herself up and reached between her legs, held his velvety erection and slowly slid herself down onto him.

He moaned loudly as she lowered herself, feeling every inch of movement. He closed his eyes enjoying the moment.

"Open your eyes and look at me, Gray. Let me watch you come."

He opened his eyes and grinned at her. He put his hands around her waist and moved her move up and down, keeping it slow at first, but she urged him to go faster.

He chuckled at her. "Easy, baby. Take it slow, or it'll be over too soon."

She groaned, and the sound coming from her made his cock throb. They studied each other intently, lost in their pleasure, then he picked up the speed.

Her breathing was labored, and her voice was ragged. "I can't wait anymore—you feel too good."

He saw the look on her face—the strain of holding back as well as the pleasure seeping through. Her skin was flushed and dewy, and he enjoyed the feeling of bringing her to the edge.

"Let's go, baby," he whispered.

And together they rode out their orgasms, sliding together in a burst of pleasure as one. Exhausted, Sam laid herself on his chest, and he wrapped his arms around her. They fell asleep wrapped up in each other with him still inside of her.

23

Two weeks later on a Sunday, Harry felt better and moved around more. His movements were still slow, but he was certainly improving. More than that, his mood was great. "I have a whole new outlook on life, and I'm going to make the most of the time I have left." It seemed to cheer up the whole family.

As the Kinkaides ate dessert in the family room, Sam's phone rang. She tapped her answer icon.

"Hi, Shelia."

She stood and walked into the kitchen. Dani and Sarah were pouring drinks when she walked in, so she went to the far corner to speak with Shelia so she could hear her.

"I'm sorry I didn't get back to you, it's been a crazy couple of weeks. How did the people like the house?"

"They liked it Sam; they liked it a lot. I brought them back last night. They had out-of-town family in who wanted to see it. It was last minute, and you weren't around, so I just went in. I'm sorry I didn't try harder to get in touch with you. I left a message, but I didn't hear back."

"I'm sorry, Shelia, I should have called you. Anyway, did they like it, again?"

Shelia chuckled. "They wrote an offer Sam, and it's a good one. They're offering you full price. There are some items in the house they would like to purchase from you, and they're clean buyers; they have nothing to sell. When can we get together and discuss their offer?"

"How about a couple of hours? Will that work for you? Can you come to Gray's or do you need me to go to the house?"

"Gray's house is fine. In the meantime, should I pull some spec sheets on condos that are for sale right now?"

"Yes, please. I would like to take a look at those. I'll see you in a couple of hours or three-ish. Thank you, Sheila."

She walked back into the living room, and Dani spoke first. "Did you sell your house?"

She nodded. "Well, I have an offer—a good one—I'll be meeting with Shelia in a couple of hours to review it with her. Is it okay with you, Gray, if we meet at your house?"

He nodded. "Of course, Sam. You know that."

Sarah spoke next. "Now what?"

She looked at Sarah. "Shelia's going to pull some spec sheets for me on some available condos and will bring them with her when she comes over to Gray's."

He took a deep breath and said, "Dammit. What the hell, Sam?"

He stood and stalked into the kitchen. She followed him, her brows furrowed. "What do you mean by that?" she pleaded.

He turned around to face her. "I assumed you would move in with me. Why won't you do that?"

She shrugged. "We haven't talked about it. I didn't want to assume."

He took a couple of steps away from her. "How can you not know? What the fuck, Sam? We talked about getting married."

"Hey!" she yelled. "Just a damn minute!"

He stopped his eyes round in surprise. He stepped toward her and she pointed to one of the upholstered kitchen chairs. He sat down, a frown marring his handsome face. She kneeled in front of him and took his hands in hers. Looking into his sad brown eyes, she took a deep breath.

"Hey, I didn't say I wouldn't move in with you. I said I didn't want to assume. I had no idea that you wanted that, Gray. We haven't had that conversation. You said you wanted to get married, but that was a couple of weeks ago, and we haven't discussed it since. I thought you were just caught up in the moment of the wedding." Thoughts fleeted through her mind, the house sold, marriage, condos, moving, and now this.

He leaned forward and put his elbows on his knees, cupping her face. "Sam, I've thought of you living in my house since the day I met you. You belong there with me; it feels natural with you there. I thought you felt the same way."

He smiled, and she thought he'd melt her panties right off the way he looked at her. "I want you to live with me, Sam. Move in with me."

Her eyes welled with tears. "Yes, I'll move in with you. I had no idea where you were at, Gray. You haven't said anything more after the wedding, and I thought maybe you regretted bringing it up."

He kissed her and whispered, "I just assumed you felt the same way. I didn't think we needed to have a conversation about moving in. As far as discussing getting married, I wanted to surprise you and make it perfect!"

She laughed. "Well, we're getting better at communicating, but I guess we still have a little work to do. For the record, it does feel natural being at your house, and I *do* feel the same way. I was just afraid to assume."

Mary spoke first from behind them. Gray's family had all crowded around the kitchen door to listen. "It looks like we have something to celebrate. Let's all get a refill on our drinks and make a toast."

As she realized the whole family had heard everything, her face flamed a nice bright red and Gray chuckled. He softly brushed her cheeks with his fingers, then kissed her gently.

"They know how I feel about you already, Sam. No need to be embarrassed."

Once all the drinks were refilled, Harry made a toast to Gray and Sam moving in together. They didn't discuss marriage.

Sam spoke first. "I hope you all know we're going to need a lot of help moving things out of my house, so everyone better be ready, willing, and able."

Jax spoke up. "Well, I think I'm kind of busy that day."

A few chuckles were heard, and Ethan laughed. "You don't even know what day, so don't even start, Jax. Besides, I have to be on the road for a while, so I can't be around."

Sarah smacked both on the shoulders. "You'll both be available, and you'll both help out."

"Sam, let's have your kids over next Sunday so everyone can meet, shall we?" Mary asked.

She nodded. "I think that sounds fabulous."

A couple hours later Sheila was at Gray's, and they sat at the kitchen table discussing the offer to buy Sam's house. Sam signed the offer, and Sheila congratulated her and said she would be in touch to set up the inspection.

Gray hugged her tight. "I'm so happy for you, Sam, and for me as well. This is what I've been waiting for all my life. To share my life with someone I love. I can't wait to have you officially here with me for good."

She hugged him back. "I'm excited as well. You know we have a lot of work to do before that can happen, right? Like what am I going to do with all of my furniture and what are we keeping and throwing away and my garage is full!"

She took a deep breath; she didn't want to overwhelm herself thinking about it all, but four weeks wasn't far away and the time would fly by. They'd learned *that* working on the fourth floor.

Gray held her tight. "Don't stress, babe. We'll work it all out. We should start by getting all of your clothes and necessities moved into *our* house first. Then, you should go through and decide what you want to keep. We'll decide together where to put it and what we need to get rid of from here to make room. Call your kids and ask them if there are things they want. There must be some of Tim's things you still have that they may want. Then we'll deal with everything else."

He made it sound easy broken down into smaller pieces.

Gray kissed her deeply, exploring her mouth, nibbling her lips. She'd never get tired of his kisses. His hand slid down her back and pulled her into him. Their bodies pressed tightly together; she felt whole. Her hands glided up his back and rubbed his shoulders. She was a bit shorter than he was, so she couldn't reach his hair with her arms under his arms, but she ran her hands up and down his back, touching him everywhere she could. His heat seeped into her—the firm planes and valleys his muscles created were sexy.

He kissed her softly, but her lips tingled when his lips sought her neck. He reached into her shirt and gently pulled out a breast, licked it and sucked it until her nipple became a hard peak. He lifted his head again and kissed his way back up her jaw to her lips.

He took a deep breath. "I want you to go to the bedroom, *our bedroom*, and get undressed. When you're completely naked, I want you to lay across the ottoman on your back and wait for me."

Sam looked at him, trying to gauge his mood and nodded. He kissed her quickly.

"Don't keep me waiting, Sam."

She turned and walked down the hall to the bedroom, both excited and nervous, not sure what to expect. When she got into the bedroom, she needed to quickly use the bathroom. So she wouldn't keep him waiting, she undressed while she used the toilet, threw her clothes in the hamper and washed her hands. She peeked out of the bathroom, he wasn't in the bedroom yet, so she hurried over to the ottoman and lay across it as he'd asked.

Before her thoughts took over again to things less romantic, he entered the room and stood next to her taking in her whole body with his smoldering gaze. He'd taken his shirt off and unsnapped and unzipped his jeans, which she thought was to relieve the bulge held back by the zipper. He rubbed his erection, very slowly. That. Is. Sexy.

When she looked into his eyes, he smiled at her.

"You look so gorgeous, Sam. You take my breath away."

He kneeled by her head and kissed her lightly.

"You especially take my breath away when you're lying there naked, waiting for me and not ashamed of yourself. I love that you're feeling more confident and not afraid to show yourself to me. That. Is. So. Sexy." He punctuated each word with a kiss.

His hand smoothed over her breasts and down the center of her abdomen until he touched her curls, then back up again.

"Push yourself back until your head is hanging over the edge of the ottoman. Remember, anytime you don't like something, you just need to tell me to stop. Do you understand me?"

"I promise I'll tell you to stop."

He grinned again and leaned down and kissed her. He nodded his head, and she moved back, so her head hung over the ottoman. He slowly removed the remainder of his clothing. She loved watching his muscles bunch and stretch as he moved. His olive complexion kept his skin from being pasty white, and the dark hairs on his chest, sprinkled with silver, were enticing. His strong legs were a sight to behold, especially with the erection he sported, then his strong fingers wrapped around his cock and he slowly pleasured himself as her eyes were transfixed. She licked the dryness from her lips, and he chuckled. He leaned over and touched her right palm, kissing each finger, slowly drawing them in and out of his mouth once, then he circled her wrist with a soft cloth he had laying alongside the ottoman—she hadn't even noticed. He tightened it and moved her hand down to the leg of the ottoman and tied it there.

He slowly moved to the other side and repeated his actions with her left hand, securing it to the leg of the ottoman. When her hands were secure, he kissed her very exposed neck and breasts—each one getting equal attention—making her nipples harden into little peaks. He kneeled in front of her face and told her to open her mouth.

"I want you to suck my cock with that sweet mouth of yours."

She felt the head of his cock touch her lips, and she opened her mouth as he slowly slid his throbbing erection into it. He began with small strokes, making sure she was okay. He groaned as her lips tightly encircled him. As he slowly pushed into her, he rubbed and pinched her nipples, bringing them to sharp points. She moaned as he pumped his hardness in her mouth. This was another new experience for her, and she loved exploring with him.

He ran his fingers through her hair and rubbed her scalp with one hand while he continued to play with her breasts with his other. His attentiveness was a turn on, knowing he wanted to pleasure her as she pleasured him. Soon he began pumping faster and a bit harder. Her eyes watered as she tried to settle her gag reflex. She opened her throat as much as she could.

He slowed down and said, "I'm going to slide into you, Sam, and when I do, I want you to swallow, do you understand?"

Sam nodded the best she could, and Gray slowly slid into her. When he was in as far as he thought he could go, she swallowed. The grunt that escaped his throat made her wet, so damned exciting.

He managed to huff out, "Oh God, that feels incredible, Sam."

Slowly he slid in and out of her a few more times, and she swallowed each time. His pleasured groans made her pussy wet. She squeezed her legs together to ease the sensations she felt.

"I'm going to come, Sam, can you take it? I want you to swallow all of me, do you understand?"

She groaned and nodded. He pumped only a few times.

"I'm coming, Sam. Hold on, baby, and swallow for me."

She felt the first spurt hit the back of her throat and she continued swallowing so she wouldn't miss anything. He pumped a few more times and began to soften in her mouth.

"Lick me clean, Sam."

She continued to suck him, her tongue less rigid as he softened. He wore a fine sheen of sweat, and his breathing was ragged. Slowly, he pulled himself out of her mouth.

He lifted her head and pushed her back onto the ottoman as far as he could with her hands tied, so her head was supported. He leaned down and kissed her softly.

"Sam, you completely drain me, and it feels so damn good. I swear to you, I've never felt like this before."

Running his hands through her hair, he asked, "Are you okay?"

"Yes."

He smiled and said, "Good. Now it's your turn."

He moved to the other end of the ottoman and pulled her legs open, sunk onto his knees in front of her. He licked first at her opening, dipping his tongue inside her, just enough to tease her. He slowly licked his way up to her clit. She huffed out short breaths, coming completely undone with need. Her hands were still tied so she couldn't grab his hair, but she needed pressure right there. Right. Where. His. Mouth. Was. He lifted her legs and bent them at the knees and put her feet on the edge of the ottoman. He began licking her clit in soft, smooth circles, licking and sucking and swirling his tongue. She'd nearly had her own orgasm when he'd reached his peak. Just watching and listening to him in the heat of the moment was so sensual.

She felt a finger slide into her, and oh, that felt so good. She sucked in a breath and moaned. He slid his finger in and out of her delicate softness while simultaneously licking her sensitive bud. She heard him chuckle a little.

"Sam, I'm going to insert a butt plug. Do you understand?"

She heard him squeeze lube onto the butt plug; then she felt the coolness of something at her anus. He applied a little pressure and slowly slid the plug into her anal opening. It felt strange—not bad—just different. He moved the plug slowly in and out a few times.

"Does that feel good, Sam?"

She nodded but remembered he wanted to hear her say it.

"Yes, it feels good."

"Good girl."

He chuckled. "It looks sexy. *You're* sexy."

She heard the lube again and very slowly the plug was inserted. Oh, it was tighter, bigger feeling. Still not uncomfortable, but it felt tight. She heard a click, and it began to vibrate. OH, that felt *very* good.

She felt Gray lick her again. All those sensations at once had her bucking and wiggling, so close to the brink of orgasm that she found it hard to control herself.

"Gray," she panted, "I can't hold it anymore. I'm going to come."

Gray groaned. "Let go."

She yelled his name as her orgasm rolled over her. She stiffened and pushed her hips forward into his face. He sucked hard on her clit as she came, the tightness completely gratifying. Best. Orgasm. Ever.

He chuckled. "Now we're going to finish, baby. Are you ready?"

He untied her hands and massaged each arm. He had turned the butt plug off, but it was still in her. He pulled her arms down to her sides and slid her down toward him at the end of the ottoman. He leaned up over her and kissed her long and slow like he always did so well.

Then he slid his mouth next to her ear and whispered, "I am going to slide myself into your sweet little ass, Sam." He lifted his head and looked at her.

"I want to come in your ass, can you let me do that?"

Sam looked into his hopeful eyes, his lips still moist from pleasuring her, and nodded yes. He raised his eyebrow.

"Yes, Gray."

He inhaled deeply then kissed her again. He helped her roll over and slid her down, so her knees rested on the carpeting. He pulled the butt plug out of her and massaged more lube around her anal opening before sliding his finger in and back out again. She let out a long breath, getting used to the feeling. She tried relaxing, which made it much more pleasurable. She felt the broad head of his penis applying pressure at her opening. He leaned over her, so he was almost lying on top of her, with his mouth by her ear.

"If you feel any pain, you let me know. Do you hear me?"

"Yes, I will," Sam breathed.

Then he slowly pushed himself inside of her. She had no words for how good it felt. He moved in and out slowly, and she heard him groan.

"Sam ... oh God, Sam. So tight. I never dreamed ..."

He leaned up and put his hands on her shoulder and pumped into her harder.

"Can you come like this, Sam?"

She thought she could, but her nerve endings were so fired up, she couldn't form any words. He reached down around her hips and applied pressure to her clit with his fingers.

"Ohh, Gray, yes." Her breathing was jerky and came in short bursts.

He pumped harder and her orgasm built, her body heated, and she fisted her hands as the sensations assaulted her. She heard his groaning and stilted breathing and sensed his orgasm nearing. She couldn't hold out any longer. She hissed out a breath and stiffened as waves of pleasure rolled over her. She heard Gray groan and push himself all the way into her as his cock pulsed deep inside. She dropped her head onto the ottoman and Gray lay his head next to hers. They laid there until their labored breathing steadied.

After a few moments, he stirred. "Stay here. I'll be right back."

He pulled completely out of her, stood, and walked to the bathroom. She heard water running but did as he asked and stayed where she was. She was too weak to do anything else anyway. Soon Gray was back and wiped her up gently. When he finished, he lifted her up, carried her to the bed, laid her down and gently kissed her.

"I love you so much, Sam." His voice was raspy and clogged with emotion.

She opened her eyes and watched him walk away to clean up. When he rejoined her, he wrapped her in his arms, and she sleepily snuggled close, happy and sated.

"I love you so much, Gray."

He chuckled. "I never dreamed I would have this. I thought about it ... hoped for it ... but ..."

They drifted off to sleep.

24

SECOND CHANCES SERIES

The next week flew by. They'd moved her clothes and bathroom supplies into his house—their house—on Monday. It was easy to make room for her stuff—the closet and the bathroom had plenty of room. Gray was so happy she was moving in that he simply didn't care if he had to throw everything he owned away to make room for her. He just wanted her there.

Once all her clothing and bathroom supplies were moved, they walked through her house, and Sam told him what she wanted to keep and what didn't matter to her. She asked, "Is there was anything you think will work at your place?"

"Our place, and yes, this desk will work, and the spare bedroom sets are better than the ones I have."

The kids came and looked at the remaining furniture, taking what they wanted.

Next came the garage. They went through the tools and things she had. She would take most of them to use on the fourth floor. Gray had what tools he needed at home already, so they had the kids come and look at what remained of Tim's tools to see if they wanted any.

Sam had to run to Appleton a couple of times to help Adam take care of their mother's things. They had gotten rid of everything, cleaned out her apartment, and returned the keys to the landlord. That was finally wrapped up. Gray didn't want Sam going to Appleton without him, but he had meetings both days that she went. He didn't say anything, but he'd been worried that she would see Eric. She made sure to reassure him that she hadn't, and he had to chuckle that she was so concerned about his feelings.

Sam got a call from Shelia that the inspection had gone well and everything was on track for the closing in two weeks. So, all in all, they were doing well.

***

Sam was at the house working one evening by herself. Gray had to work late and would join her when he was finished. About five-thirty, she walked to the mailbox. She'd miss this location, it was more wooded than Gray's place, but he had the sunlight and flowers which she didn't get through the thick trees, so it was a good trade. She pulled mail from the box, and slowly flipped through the letters. A typed letter caught her attention—it looked like it was actually typed on a typewriter. No return address—weird. She opened the envelope to find a single sheet of white paper, which seemed to be typed with the same typewriter. As she began reading, her stomach twisted and her hands shook.

You're making a mistake with Kinkaide. He's making a mistake with you.

She read and reread the words again, turning the paper over to see if there was anything else. She heard the vehicle approaching, but she was completely engrossed in this letter. She looked through the stack of mail to see if there was another letter or something of a clue. She looked at the envelope again, and that's when it hit her—no stamp. No postmark. Someone had been here. She turned her head to glance down the road and saw the truck approaching quickly. Her brain found it difficult to catch up with what was happening; as the dark colored vehicle was almost to her, she turned to run the few steps to her driveway.

****

Sam wanted to wake up and answer the questions being asked of her, but she couldn't open her eyes. She floated in and out of consciousness, occasionally hearing a snippet of conversation. She heard several different voices and couldn't grasp why these people were at her house. *Oh, my God, was it moving day already?* Sam panicked, her heart raced, then she heard beeping like she'd heard in Harry's room when he had heart surgery. *Did I have heart surgery? I don't remember.* Ouch! Her head hurt ... a lot of commotion ... then she was floating again.

She felt as though she was feeling better and she heard Gray talking softly to someone.

"I can't leave her until she wakes up and I can talk to her."

He's leaving me! Why? What did I do? She opened her eyes and saw Gray sitting in a chair bent over with his elbows on his knees, looking over at Mary and Harry. *They wanted him to leave me? Her heart raced.*

The beeping started again. Gray stood up and walked toward her.

"You're leaving me? Why? What did I do? Why are you leaving me?" She began crying, the tears spilling down her cheeks. Her head hurt, and her brain was foggy.

"No, no baby, settle down, it's not good for you. I would never leave you," he cooed softly.

She put her hands on her head to stop the pain. Gray climbed into bed with her and wrapped his arms around her.

"Shh ... shh ... easy baby. Please breathe ... easy ... don't hurt yourself. Slow breaths, in ... then ... out." he lovingly whispered in her ear. "I'm not leaving you, I swear ... I would never leave you. My mom thinks I need a shower." He kissed the top of her head and whispered, "She thinks I'm starting to smell."

He laid his head on hers, his arms wrapped around her tightly, his silky voice crooning soft words of encouragement and slow easy breathing.

Her heart slowly settled and her breathing returned to normal. She took comfort in the strong, loving arms that held her. She felt safe wrapped up in him. He pulled back and looked at her.

"Are you okay? How do you feel now?"

She looked into his eyes. The lines at the corners seemed deeper and more pronounced, and the shine usually in his eyes seemed to have dulled. He looked tired.

He kissed her tenderly. "I love you, and I'll never leave you. Do you understand me?"

She nodded then and took a deep breath. The nurses had come running in to check on her and observed Gray comforting her. One of the nurses walked over to check the monitor readings, her pulse, and to ask her if she was okay. She nodded and laid her head against Gray's shoulder. He laid his head against the top of hers, and they laid there for a few moments until she was calm.

He kissed the top of her head. "All better?"

She nodded. "I'm sorry. I guess I overreacted ... I thought you were leaving me," she whispered, wiping her eyes.

Mary and Harry both stood and walked to the opposite side of the bed from Gray. Mary leaned down and kissed her cheek.

"I'm sorry, Sam. I didn't realize you were waking up. I should have been a little more careful with my words." She spoke softly and patted Sam's hand.

"Please don't blame yourself. Thank you for being here."

Harry leaned forward and grabbed her hand. "Going a little overboard for attention, aren't you?"

Sam smiled. Her voice shallow, "I learned this trick just recently."

He laughed and patted her hand. A police officer entered the room.

"Ms. Powell, do you feel up to answering a couple of questions?"

She nodded, and Gray moved to get out of bed. "Can you stay with me for a little while?" she asked.

He squeezed her. "Of course, anything you want."

The officer introduced himself.

"Ms. Powell, my name is Tom Williams. I need to ask you a few questions about what happened to you. Do you remember anything?"

Nodding slowly, then closing her eyes to the throbbing, she softly replied, "I went to get the mail. I opened a letter that seemed ... off. I remember turning it over to see if there was more information on it."

She rubbed her forehead, then began smoothing her hair. She froze as her hand bumped into a bandage and a tender spot on her head. Patting the bandage lightly, she swallowed. "I remember hearing a truck coming down the road. But I didn't comprehend it; the letter confused me. Then I looked at the envelope again and realized there was no stamp on it. Someone put it there. I looked up, and the truck was coming at me, so I ran to the driveway. That's all I remember."

Ethan entered her room and silently stood alongside his father. Officer Williams continued, "Do either of you know who could have put this letter in Ms. Powell's mailbox? It could be someone you've just met. Someone who has a personal vendetta."

"I work in a law office, but we haven't had any contentious cases lately," she tiredly offered.

Officer Williams jotted on his tablet. "Have you recently met anyone new?"

A snort escaped, and she picked at the blanket covering her. "Many." She glanced into Gray's weary but handsome face. The movement sent pain shooting down her neck, and she winced. "Gray's ex-wife." She watched his lips thin, but he didn't look away. Ethan, however, did speak up. "Sam, I know my mother is a pill, and she's selfish and condescending, but she wouldn't try to harm you physically. That isn't her style – she'll focus on the head games."

A soft smile creased her lips as she took in Ethan's appearance. He stood casually at his father's side, but the weight of the past few ... oh, how long had she been here?

Slowly, so as not to send shooting pains anywhere, she turned to Gray. "How long have I been here?"

He ran the back of his fingers down her cheek. "Baby, you've been here since yesterday."

"Have you been here the whole time?"

"Of course." He kissed the tip of her nose. "Do you think I would leave you here and take the chance that you would wake up and me not be here?" His voice cracked with emotion.

Her head suddenly felt too heavy to hold up. She lay back and closed her eyes. "How did I get here?"

He took a deep breath and swallowed hard. "I found you just before six o'clock; you were lying at the edge of your driveway, your head was bleeding. I couldn't get you to wake up." His voice cracked, "I was sick with worry that I was too late."

Taking his hand in hers, she squeezed. "I'm so sorry you had to stay here so long. I didn't mean to worry you."

He snorted. "I know you didn't mean to worry me or any one of us. We just want you better and to find the son of a bitch who did this to you."

A voice from the doorway broke the moment. "Can't you leave her alone for a minute? Geez, Gray, she's in the hospital for God's sake."

Jessie walked in with a smirk on her face.

Sam smiled at her. "Jess, you don't understand. I thought he was leaving me and I panicked."

The look she leveled at Gray was scathing, her eyes narrowed. "Why are you making her think that in her state? What the hell, Gray?"

Sam held her hand out to Jessie. She quickly came forward, and took her hand, squeezing, tears shone brightly in her crisp blue eyes.

"Jess, it was a misunderstanding and no one's fault. Please don't lay any blame on Gray. He's been worried about me too."

Jess looked at Gray, her face softened. "Okay, but he better not hurt you."

A small giggle escaped, and Sam introduced Jessie to everyone in the room, including Jamie, who had just arrived, and Officer Williams. The officer took the opportunity to ask Jessie a couple of questions.

"Ms ..."

"Johnson," Jess supplied.

"Ms. Johnson, has anyone been around the office asking for Ms. Powell or acting suspicious in any way?"

"Yes, yesterday a man came into the office looking for her. I told him she was off."

"Did he ask anything specific?"

"He asked if she was in and I told him she had the day off. He asked where he might be able to find her and I told him I didn't know, a day off meant she didn't have to check in with anyone. He left."

"Can you describe him?"

She scrunched up her face. "He had really blue, cold eyes, and short dark hair. He was dressed well enough, but he looked smarmy."

25

S am was released from the hospital the following day with orders to take it easy and take the pain medication as needed. The stitches in the side of her head would come out in a week, and until then, she was to keep them clean and moist with an antibiotic ointment. She only had three stitches, so after her whole arm incident, this was nothing. They only had a week left before the closing on her house, and she had to have everything out.

The police were still looking for the man who had inquired about Sam and the truck that had hit her. In the meantime, Gray took Sam to work in the morning and picked her up afterward. She wasn't supposed to go anywhere for lunch, which was fine with her—she was still a bit weak and tired and usually spent her lunch hour turning the lights off in her office and closing her eyes for a few minutes. Sometimes, Jessie would come in and chat. The boyfriend that Jessie had met at the same time Sam met Gray hadn't worked out. She wasn't deterred, though. She was still going to find Mr. Right.

On the day of the house closing, Sam asked Shelia to come to the office so she could sign the papers there. She didn't want Gray to have to take off work to drive her anywhere. After the documents were signed, she handed over the keys with a sigh. That chapter of her life was officially in the past. All the memories were just that—memories. She still had her children and grandchildren and now Gray and his family, to make new, and hopefully better, memories. Shelia handed her a large check by way of payment. Onward.

She walked Shelia to the front door and said goodbye. Turning, she said, "Jessie, I'm going to walk to the bank and deposit the proceeds check. I won't be gone long, and I have my phone with me."

"No, Sam. You aren't supposed to go out by yourself."

"Jess, it's a beautiful day, and nothing has happened since the incident at my house, and to be honest, I'm a bit stir crazy. It's only a block away. What could happen?"

"Sam, tell Gray or I will. We are all on strict orders. A block away may as well be miles if no one is around to help you. I'm serious." The vivacious woman stood with her hands firmly planted on her hips.

With a sigh, Sam pulled her phone from her pocket and dialed Gray's number. He answered on the second ring.

"Hey baby, how are you?"

Smiling, she replied, "Hey there, yourself. I'm fine, how about you?"

His sexy voice floated over her, creating gooseflesh; she loved this feeling. "I was just sitting here thinking about this sexy little gal I'm in love with and what I want to do to her when I get her home tonight. Hmm, I can't wait to get her home."

Wow! The butterflies came alive in her tummy. "Ooh, I can't wait to get home. That sounds simply fabulous," she purred. "I just came into some money and am going to the bank to make a deposit. I thought I would call and let you know what I was doing."

Taking a deep breath, he responded, "Sam, please don't do that. Let someone else go to the bank or let me come and take you. Please don't go alone."

Sam was quiet for a moment. She turned to look out the big window at the front of the office. The sun shined brightly outside; people were walking on the sidewalks, shopping bags in their hands, dressed in summer fashion all with carefree looks on their faces. She wanted to go outside and play again.

"Sam, let me come and take you to the bank then we can go home early. How about that?"

"I don't want to disrupt your day, Gray. I just thought I would give you a call and let you know I wanted to walk to the bank. Actually, Jessie made me call you."

She heard a chuckle. "I'll be there in five minutes. Don't leave that building. I'll take you to the bank, and then I'd like to take you to Mom and Dad's. Don't leave. Do you understand me?"

"Yes, I understand. I'll wait for you." Sam sighed.

Ending the call, she looked at Jessie, "Happy now?"

"Yes." Jessie leaned forward placing her arms on the top of the upper counter of the reception desk. "I have a date tonight. It's our fourth. I'm so excited."

"Well, I hope this is the one. You haven't said anything about him. What's going on with you?"

"This one is different. I never would have dreamed of him. But, I just don't want to jinx it, so I'm waiting a bit to talk about him."

Sam chuckled. "Okay. Fair enough."

Gray entered the office and seeing him walk through the door where she'd first met him made her tummy flip. The smile she bestowed on him was genuine.

"Hello, sexy, what do you say we blow this place and go have some fun?"

Sam laughed. "You got it."

Jessie rolled her eyes and ordered, "Get out of my reception area. You two kill me."

With a chuckle, Sam said, "Have fun tonight, Jess." Gray took her hand and led her out to his SUV.

They drove through the bank auto-bank, and Sam deposited the proceeds from the house. Gray stated, "Buckle up, we're headed to Mom and Dad's."

"I thought you were making other plans when I called?"

He leveled her with a panty-melting grin. "I've made plans for you, and we'll get to those in a little while. Mom has something to show you first."

She furrowed her brows. "Okay."

He chuckled and drove out of town.

They walked into Gray's parents' house a few minutes later. Harry and Mary sat at the kitchen counter drinking lemonade. They'd been outside working in the flower gardens and were taking a break. Mary jumped up and offered Gray and Sam a glass of lemonade, and they sat making small talk.

Harry asked, "Has there been any word on the man who hit Sam?"

"No, nothing yet. But I keep in touch with the police department. I don't want that to keep us from moving forward, though. We aren't putting our lives on hold because of some jackass out there who can't even speak to me face-to-face and attacks my girlfriend instead."

"What makes you think it's about you?" she asked.

He turned in his chair and stared at her. "Because you didn't have any enemies until I came along. Now you've been mowed down in the street and been treated poorly. It must be because of me."

She sat back and raised her brows. "Not everything is about you, Gray."

"I didn't say ..." He paused and stared. He huffed out a breath, "Well, it makes sense to me that it's someone you've just recently met and that may just be because of me."

Chuckling, she patted his arm and added, "Don't take on guilt you don't need. The police will find out what's going on soon enough."

Mary excitedly changed the subject. "Jamie has a girlfriend. Did he say anything to you, Gray? He's tight-lipped about her, and I'm dying to know who she is, and well, everything about her."

He rubbed the back of his neck. "No, he only said he met someone, and they were taking things slow. I asked if we could have dinner together—just the four of us. He said maybe later; he wasn't ready yet."

"Hmm, well love is in the air. First you and Sam and now Jamie. I hope she treats him well."

"He won't stick with anyone who won't treat him right, Mom," Gray said. "Are you ready to show Sam your special flowers?"

Mary beamed. "Right now?"

Gray smiled. "Right now. I just said I didn't want to put our lives on hold."

Sam looked at one then the other. She didn't know what the unspoken message was but figured she'd find out soon enough. Mary and Harry shared a look and grinned. They stood and walked to the back door. Gray took Sam's hand and followed. They walked through the flower gardens.

My goodness, they were so beautiful! She had never seen so many beautiful varieties of flowers. Winding paths through the colorful, fragrant gardens stimulated her; she'd been cooped up too long. The paths lead them in different directions; one ended with a bench tucked away at the end so you could sit among the flowers and relax. Some of the paths had little overhangs where you could escape the sun. Another path had a little wrought iron table and two chairs.

Mary pointed. "That's where Harry and I sometimes sit and have lunch when it isn't too hot outside."

She led them on a path alongside a Koi pond. The croaking of frogs followed by the ripples in the water from their movement and the water flowing from the small fountain was serene. The colorful fuchsia and purple water flowers floating along the top was a sight to behold.

They walked along yet another pathway, and there were beautiful flowers in colors she had never seen before.

"These are wandflowers that Harry and I blended for Dani's family." Mary beamed.

They were the most unusual deep shade of orange. "Dani's favorite color," Mary said as she smiled proudly. "These are Nick's flowers. The rugged globe thistle seems to fit him. I liked this shade of purple, which blends well with the orange of Dani's flowers." The older woman proudly gestured with her hands as she pointed out the color variations and differences. "These are also wandflowers, germinated to produce the deep red with a burgundy center for Sean and a light pink with a deep red center for Leila. Zach's wandflowers are a cross between gold and yellow."

She continued along another path, and beautiful daylilies in a myriad of colors appeared.

"This is Jamie's family." She radiated pride.

"The deep burgundy is Jamie's. The lighter pinks were for Kathy, Jamie's wife." She longingly gazed at the soft pink flowers. "When she passed away, we cut the daylilies right from this garden and laid them on her casket." Swallowing, she smiled and allowed the grief she still held to float away. "The deep purple is for Shae, and her husband, Brian's, is the lavender. Mori's color is the orange."

Toward the end of the last path was an old barn door leaning against a wrought iron arbor with gorgeous flowers climbing the arbor and along the door. Colorful pots with a variety of succulents graced the ground alongside. Beautiful decorations were situated around and in some of the pots. Little glass jars and decorative birds were located here and there catching the light, chrome wings spinning in the slight breeze. A wooden bench sat in front of the barn door topped with a cushion in varying shades of purple, ivory, and grays. Mary took her hand and led her to beautiful rose beds nestled alongside the bench.

"These are Gray's family. Gray loved roses from the time he was very little. He would walk out in these gardens with me and gravitate to the roses. His interest is what first encouraged me to try and blend different colors and varieties for my family.

"Gray's are the deep purple roses. He was mesmerized by that color as a child, drawing his pictures of buildings and houses, always with purple in the picture somewhere. I remember asking him if he would like it if I could make a rose that color. He was so excited, I worked and worked until I got it right." She smiled and looked at her son. The soft smile he bestowed on his mom was deeply moving. "Jax's roses are the bright blue ones, actually a shade of the purple but in the flower world, they're considered blue. The bright pink roses for Sarah and the burgundy for Cole. Dusty pink for Lily. Lincoln's are the lighter blues. Finally, the bright red roses are for Ethan. We've been working on a color for Eva."

Sam looked around at the beauty of the garden spread out before her. It could be the Green Bay Botanical Gardens; it was so perfect.

"Didn't you make a color for Suzanne?" Sam had to ask.

Mary, Harry, and Gray laughed. "We grew a red rose bush for Suzanne just because we felt like we should. It was full of thorns and not very pretty. It was our little joke. As soon as we realized what kind of person she was and Gray told us Suzanne had cheated, we dug them all up. My garden has never been prettier than it is now, though." Mary turned them around.

On the other side of Gray's purple roses were the most beautiful champagne-colored roses Sam had ever seen. They were long-stemmed roses with perfect petals, and the color was one she had never seen in a rose or any flower before. They were perfect.

"Oh, my word, these are amazing. I hope you plan to show these off somewhere, Mary. I've never seen a more perfect rose in my life. The color is so beautiful."

Mary smiled at her. "We've been playing with flowers for years. We've been blending flowers and coming up with new varieties for the past thirty years or more. Sometimes we show them, sometimes we're stingy with them, and we keep them to ourselves. I didn't have the time to blend these, but I found them with a grower I occasionally use out on the West Coast. As soon as Gray told me about how much he loved that color on you, I started looking for them."

She couldn't stop looking at them. Then what Mary had said sunk in and Sam turned to look at Gray. "You liked that color on me?"

Gray stepped forward. He took her hand and walked her over to the bench and motioned for her to sit down. He kneeled in front of her and took both of her hands in his.

"Sam, I've loved you from the moment I first saw you. You took my breath away, and I'm still trying to catch it. The night of the Downtown Harmony Lake event, even though I would change how that night ended a thousand times over when you walked into the living room in that champagne-colored dress, I thought you were the most beautiful woman in the world—I still do. I saw my bride. I told my mom how beautiful I thought you looked in that color. It was perfect on you. I told Mom and Dad that weekend, I was going to fix what I had done, and I was going to marry you, and I wanted you to wear that color when I did. That was weeks ago. Last week Mom told me what she had been able to do with the roses and I came out and saw them on my lunch hour. I wanted to bring you here today to show you these roses. Mom and Dad have planted these roses for you, Sam."

She looked at Mary and Harry in astonishment. They planted these for her? Oh, my God, they were absolutely the most beautiful flowers she'd ever seen.

"Sam, will you marry me? Will you share my life, share my children? Will you be my wife and let me love you forever?"

She was stunned speechless. Looking deep into the dark brown eyes that had first stopped her in her tracks, what she saw was love, and she hoped she radiated that back to him.

"Gray, we haven't known each other very long. Are you sure?"

"We know enough about each other, Sam. We've been through so much, and we've made it through, and I meant it, I knew the moment I saw you that God made you for me. I don't want to wait any longer. At our age, why do we have to wait if we know for sure?"

She continued to gaze into his eyes. She loved this man more than she could have ever imagined loving anyone. Her eyes watered and she knew it wouldn't be long, and the tears would flow.

Softly, she responded, "Yes, I'll marry you, love you, share your life, and be your wife."

Gray stood and picked her up with him and held her tight as he spun her around.

"God Sam, I love you so much. I swear to you, I'll do everything in my power to make you happy, I promise you."

Sam laughed. "I'll do everything in my power to make you happy, too, Gray, I promise you."

"Oh, wait, we have to make it official."

He set her down and dropped to one knee, pulled a ring from his pocket. He slid the ring on her left hand. Sam was stunned at how beautiful it was. She stared at it for a long time.

It was the most beautiful ring she had ever seen. A two-carat princess cut diamond in the center. The band had smaller diamonds running up each side shank, which split in two and crisscrossed each other, then came to rest as the prongs for the center diamond. Just under the center diamond on the front and back was a small X in diamonds that looked like it was holding the center diamond up in the air. It was breathtaking.

"Do you like it, Sam?"

A loud sob escaped as she started to speak. "Gray, it's the most beautiful ring I've ever seen. Thank you."

He stood again, and Sam threw her arms around his neck squeezing him tight. He wanted to marry her; he wanted her to be his wife! All the emotions from today caught up to her.

Cupping her face in his hands, he asked, "Sam, will you wear my mark?"

His mark? The tattoo they each wore. "Really?"

He chuckled. "Don't you believe me when I tell you? I believe you are, without a doubt, my soul mate."

She cried. The tears rolled so fast she could hardly stop them. He put his fingers under her chin and pulled her face up to look at him.

"Sam?"

She nodded, swallowing and blinking furiously to stem the flow of tears. "Yes," she croaked. "Yes, Gray, yes."

Mary and Harry had been silently watching them, and she'd forgotten they were there until Mary came up behind her and patted her back. She was wiping tears from her cheeks. Gray hugged his dad while Mary hugged Sam.

"I know I've told you this before, but thank you for making my son so happy. He deserves to be happy after all he's been through. You saved him, Sam. Thank you."

She spoke between sobs, "He saved me, too. Thank you for everything, Mary, and thank you for the beautiful roses. They're stunning."

Mary looked at her ring and beamed. "He did well." She giggled as Harry pulled her into a big hug.

"Welcome to our family, Sam. Even though you've felt like family right from the beginning, I officially welcome you."

"Harry, thank you for welcoming me and my children into your amazing family. I love you," she whispered.

Harry patted her back and squeezed her again, unable to speak. Gray joined and picked her up and squeezed her.

"I love you, Sam—so much it scares me."

She laughed. "I love you ... so much. I need to ask, though, why now? We've had so much going on and so little time to deal with everything. Why now?"

"I intended to ask you to marry me today because your house closed and that chapter of your life was over. I wanted to start this new one immediately. I want to wake up every day with you; I want to go to sleep every night with you. I never want to be without you in my life. Why *not* now?"

They walked along a different path and Mary and Harry showed them flowers they'd blended for their parents and siblings. The love and care shown with each color pairing and the meaning behind made her speechless.

They meandered back to the house and Mary suggested they stay for supper.

26

SECOND CHANCES SERIES

Aﬀter a wonderful dinner with his mom and dad, he was more than ready to take Sam home and celebrate in private. He rubbed the back of his neck and rotated his head.

"Having second thoughts, Gray?" she smirked.

"No. I just have a funny feeling. It's probably nothing, but it hit me when we got into the SUV. It'll pass."

Sam looked around, craning her neck to see anything suspicious. Everything seemed normal. Reaching over, she rubbed his arm while admiring the sparkling ring on her finger.

"I get that sometimes, too. Just in case, you'd tell me if you were having second thoughts, right?"

He glanced at her, a grin on his face, "No second thoughts about us, baby. And, I would tell you if I did have them. So, no worries about that, okay?" He twisted to check the left lane before moving over, then smoothly navigated the ramp merging them onto the highway.

"Okay. It's just—"

BAM! They were hit from behind—not hard—enough to make

the SUV swerve. He yelled, "Hang on!" He righted the vehicle and turned on his right-turn signal to move to the side of the road.

"Shit, that wasn't an accident! Hang on, baby!"

He tapped the Bluetooth button on the dash. The operator responded. "Nine-one-one, what's your emergency?"

He watched in his mirrors and sped up, switching lanes.

Sam yelled, "My name is Samantha Powell and my fiancé and I are driving a black Cadillac Escalade on Highway 41 heading north. We've been hit from behind twice by a vehicle that seems to want us off the road."

"Okay, Ms. Powell, can you see the car that's hitting you?"

She turned to look behind them. Bam! They were hit again. "Yes." She craned around to peer behind them.

Gray gripped the steering wheel as he continued to watch his mirrors. The dark SUV pulled into the lane behind them. "Hang on!" he yelled. BAM.

The operator responded, "Can you tell me the make and model of the vehicle hitting you?"

"It looks like a Chevy Tahoe," he informed the dispatcher. "Dark blue or black."

"What's your current location?"

He switched lanes, pulling in front of a car and then slid into the far-right left lane, passing a semi. "We just passed the Mason Street exit, and we're still heading north."

The Tahoe pulled alongside them in the middle lane of the three-lane highway, leaving the semi he'd passed behind it. Glancing into his rearview mirror, he had no one behind him, so he slowed his vehicle to let the semi pass. As he scooted behind the semi, he saw the Tahoe move into the far-right lane he'd just vacated. He stepped on the gas and moved alongside the semi, quickly gaining speed.

The dispatcher offered support. "Take the Shawano Avenue exit, Mr.—"

"Kinkaide."

"Mr. Kinkaide, take the Shawano Avenue exit. Pull into the

grocery store parking lot at the bottom of the ramp. A police unit will meet you there."

"Got it." He navigated in front of the semi once more, the driver slowing to let him in. He pulled into the far-right lane to enter the exit ramp; the semi then sped up keeping the Tahoe on its left and unable to pull over in time to make the ramp.

Sam yelled, "I hear sirens! Is that for us?"

"Yes, Ms. Powell, they have the Tahoe in their sights, one unit will stay with it, and one will meet you. Stay on the line with me until you are with the officers in the parking lot."

Gray pulled off onto the Shawano Avenue exit, eased the SUV onto the roundabout and slowed to turn into the parking lot. A police car pulled in from the opposite entrance and drove directly toward them. He found a clear spot at the edge of the parking lot and stopped. His hands shook, his heart pounded, and his senses were on hyper-alert. Each slight movement in the parking lot from shoppers coming and going had him twisting his head to and fro. He took in a deep breath and slowly let it out, turning his head to watch Sam. She sat stone still, watching the road they'd just left for any signs of the Tahoe.

The officers motioned for them to get out of the vehicle. The dispatcher broke the silence. "Officers confirm sighting of you in the parking lot. Do you see them?"

He answered her. "Yes, ma'am and thank you." He wrapped his hand around hers. The chill in her fingers worried him; the temperature was in the high seventies today. She turned to lock eyes with him, and the fear in hers pissed him off.

"Are you okay?" She slowly nodded. "You?"

"I'm fine. Pissed. Scared. But fine." He raised their locked fingers and kissed the back of her hand. "Let's go give the officers a statement."

She nodded. He opened his door, stepped down on shaky legs and glanced over to see Sam slowly making her way around the vehicle toward him. The police cruiser had come to a stop next to them.

He heard the dispatcher through his speakers. "Officers, you have them with you now?"

"Yes, we'll take it from here," one of them acknowledged.

He wrapped his arm around Sam's shoulders and pulled her tight to his side. The officers exited their car and approached. "Mr. Kinkaide. Ms. Powell. Tell us from the beginning what happened."

When they'd finished talking to the police, he called David Haggerty, a friend of his who owned a security company. "David, I need some help, can you meet me at my parents' house in about an hour?"

He walked around his vehicle in the parking lot. A police investigation team had come and taken paint chips from his vehicle for samples and took pictures of the damage. His shaking had long ago subsided, but his anger now bubbled to the surface in full force. Sam now sat in the front seat of his truck; she'd wanted to call her kids, so they didn't hear anything from a third-hand source. News crews had followed one of the police cars, and the reporters now stood at the edge of the parking lot filming their stories.

His cell rang. "Kinkaide."

"Mr. Kinkaide, this is Officer Williams. We've found the Tahoe abandoned in a parking lot just out of town to the north. We're going through it to see if we can find anything that will give us an identity of the occupants and where they were headed."

He ended his call and jumped into his SUV. He related the information he'd just received to Sam. "Let's go back to Mom and Dad's to tell them what happened before the news hits the airwaves. With Dad's recent heart attack, I don't want him unnecessarily upset."

David Haggerty arrived at the Kinkaides', and he spent the better part of two hours discussing the recent events. Then he methodically went over every aspect of their safety with David, including security cameras on their house. David called in one of his men, who would be assigned to him and Sam for the time being. Probably a little overboard, but this was twice now, and it would be stupid to ignore the signs presenting themselves.

Their new security detail arrived at the house, and he watched as

Sam stifled a giggle when they were introduced to Tank. It suited him; he looked like a tank—no neck, broad shoulders and thick middle and thighs. He sported a buzz cut hair style and gave off the air of no-nonsense—ever. David ran through all the events of what had happened, and they sat through a litany of question from both men.

27

SECOND CHANCES SERIES

Once David Haggerty and his team put everything in place at Harry and Mary's, he was exhausted and ready to tuck Sam in somewhere safe. Their private engagement celebration would have to wait. Since it would be a day or two before the security system was installed at the house, he wanted to go to a hotel. His vehicle had been taken to the dealership for repairs by one of David's men, and Tank was now their driver. Fine by him; that experience had been more than he'd ever imagined he'd encounter.

They went to the house to quickly pack an overnight bag. Tank had cleared the house first, giving them the okay to go in, but with firm instructions to make it quick and pack light. They checked into a hotel, and Tank took the room next to them. They synced their phones with his so they could call with the touch of a button. Tank reviewed all the security precautions and told them they were not to leave their room—for anything—without calling him first. They weren't planning on leaving anyway, so no problem there. He got them some ice and made sure they were comfortable, and they bid him goodnight It was now close to midnight. It had been a very long and full day, and they were exhausted.

Once they closed the door on Tank, he turned to Sam and

winked. He went to his bag and pulled out a bottle of champagne he'd taken while they packed.

"I had it at home for our celebration," he whispered conspiratorially.

Sam grinned, went to her bag and pulled out a bottle of wine.

She winked. "Great minds."

He met her halfway across the room and hugged her close.

"I can't wait until you're Samantha Kinkaide."

She giggled. "I hadn't even had the time to run my new name through my head." She pulled away and set her bottle of wine on the desk. "I can't wait, either."

Gray walked into the bathroom and turned on the shower. He sauntered back into the room and held out his hand. "Come and take a shower with me?"

She took his hand. "Absolutely."

After showering and loving each other, they climbed into bed with a glass of champagne. "Not exactly the celebration I had in mind, but we'll get to it when we're able to go home." He tapped his glass to hers and winked. "Here's to a long and happy life together as Mr. and Mrs. Kinkaide."

"Cheers to that."

Reclining against the headboard with pillows propped behind them, he let out a long breath. The quiet felt nice.

Sam twisted toward him, "Gray, I just want to throw this out here. You don't think there's any way Suzanne would be involved in this, do you?"

He held her gaze for a moment. "Her behavior since I met you has certainly become more aggressive. She seems to enjoy keeping me on edge. It doesn't hurt to check into it, but Ethan's right, it's not her style. As you've witnessed, she usually just manipulates and causes trouble."

He wrapped his hand around her nape and kissed the tip of her nose. "We'll figure this out, Sam. I promise you that."

She sighed. "I have no doubt, Gray, and I'm not second-guessing you. I just wondered if she would be capable of something like this and I wanted to get it off my chest."

He kissed the side of her head, set his glass down on the table. "Not sure how much I'll sleep, but I'm going to try. Might be a long day tomorrow."

He turned off the light on the bedside table and snuggled down under the covers pulling her toward him.

She giggled, and the sound was like the finest music. "Congratulations, Gray. You're about to get married."

He tightened his arms around her. She nestled into his side, wrapping her legs around and through his, and they drifted off to sleep.

The next morning, he woke early and stared at the ceiling for a long time. Finding no answers there, he turned his head and smiled at the sight of Sam, sleeping peacefully, hands tucked sweetly under her chin. He slowly turned onto his side and propped his head up with his hand, lovingly feasting his eyes on her partially covered body. She'd kicked the blankets off during the night, her legs on top of them now, lying on her side, the graceful slope of her hip dipping into her waist caused his cock to stir. He'd been fortunate to find her, no doubt about it.

She brushed her fingers across her cheek and snuggled back in. The sparkle shooting from the diamonds he'd excitedly placed on her finger yesterday brought to the forefront that she'd said 'yes.' His dreams were coming true. She opened her eyes, the green orbs focusing in on his. It gave him a thrill and was his new favorite color, though he wouldn't tell his mom. She'd so painstakingly grown the purple roses for him over all these years; it would just be his secret.

"Good morning," she sleepily smiled.

"Good morning. Did you sleep well?"

She rolled onto her back and stretched. "Yes, though not long enough. You were watching me sleep again. Isn't that boring?"

His phone rang, and he looked at the readout. "Tank."

"Good morning. What does today bring?"

He listened to Tank explaining that they were needed at the office to go over some things with David. He glanced at Sam, watching her sit up and rake her hands through her hair. She leaned forward to glance in the mirror across from the bed and scoffed as she pushed down on the hair standing up on the top of her head.

A grin spread across his face as she grimaced. He held the phone to his chest. "We have to get going soon, what would you like for breakfast?"

She looked back at him, a slight frown on her beautiful face. "It's Wednesday—I need to get to work by eight o'clock."

"No, you can't go to work until this is all taken care of. We don't know who's after us or even which one of us is the target, so until further notice, we're on the lam, so to speak. I can't go to work, either."

He spoke into his phone. "I'll call you in a minute."

He ended his call and turned to Sam. "I would like you to give notice at work and come to work with me at Kinkaide & Associates. You're perfect for the position. You can help me run the business side of things so I can draw pictures all day," he grinned.

"Wow! With an offer like that, how can I refuse?" she sarcastically replied. "Gray, you don't know that I can even run a business like yours. It's a lot of responsibility and what if I screw it up?"

He smiled. "Look, if I can do it, you can do it. I've been basically only doing the bare minimum because I really don't care about that part of the business. I want to design buildings. I need you. You're smart, you've worked in the legal world for a while now, and you have the HR experience behind you. You also have excellent connections at the law office for advice. Besides, I'll be there for you to ask questions whenever you feel you need to run something by me. And, once we're married, it'll be half yours anyway, so you should spend time running half of your business."

She promptly responded, "Gray, you can't mean that. You'll want a prenup, right? What will the kids say about that? I don't want anyone to be upset with me."

"No, I don't want a prenup. I'm not entering this marriage thinking about how either one of us is going to get out of it. Period.

End of conversation. As far as the kids go, they're taken care of, and I have a will, and we can write up something to protect them in the future if something would happen to me." He stepped from the bed and walked around to her side, pulled her to the edge by her legs and leaned down, so they were nose to nose. "Work with me, Sam. Be my life partner *and* my business partner. I need you, and I want you. Besides, I pay well!"

She laughed, and the brightness lit the room and made his heart expand. "I'm very, very expensive, Mr. Kinkaide, and we haven't even discussed salary!"

He leaned in and kissed her firmly on the lips. "Don't I know that! The ring on your finger is just the beginning, but I would give you everything I own to keep you happy."

"I'll never ask that of you, Gray. Never."

She stood and pulled a T-shirt over her head. Sliding her arms through the sleeves, she glanced at him.

"Are you going to answer me?" he asked a bit impatiently.

"You know I've been frustrated with things at the office lately. And, I think I'd enjoy working with you. It sounds like a great idea, Gray; I'd like that."

The joy that just filled his heart threatened to burst it. "We're going to be a great team, you'll see! Now, call Bill and give your notice."

She scrunched her face. "I should do that in person, don't you think? Over the phone seems disrespectful."

"Fine, then we'll have Tank take us to your office this morning right after breakfast, and you can tell him in person. You're not going to the office without Tank and me."

Her lips tightened, but she nodded her head.

28

They showered and dressed for the day. Gray called Tank while she finished applying her makeup and decided to have breakfast brought to the room. Tank would join them so they could discuss what transpired overnight and what the game plan was for today. Gray hung up with him when Sam walked out of the bathroom.

He looked at her and smiled. "You look beautiful, as usual."

She walked to him and bent down to kiss him. "So, what's the game plan?"

"Until Tank gets here with breakfast ..." He grabbed her hips and pulled her onto his lap. "We can make out."

He cupped her breast making her laugh. "You're insatiable. I don't know if I'm going to make it."

Leaning back to look at her, he responded. "Okay, so let's talk about your new job. We're going to need to set up an office for you. How do you want that to work? Any ideas?"

She pursed her lips. "To be honest with you, I'm not sure. Do you think we can go to the office with Tank after I talk to Bill and take a look around? The plan before was to move your offices to the second floor. Do you still want to do that? And what will I be doing?"

He chuckled. "Yes, we need to move the offices. The demolition company is bursting at the seams. If we're on the second floor, the first floor can be rented out for retail space or other offices like you'd mentioned. So, why don't we look at how fast we can make that work? As far as what you'll be doing, we'll start with you learning about the business and becoming familiar with our clients. Then, once you're comfortable with that, you can take on more of the business responsibilities."

"Okay. Now my head is spinning with all that needs to be done, so what do you think about being able to go to the fourth floor today to work on some of the pieces that we'll use in the second-floor offices?"

"We'll talk to Tank about it when he gets here."

They heard a knock on the door. "Speaking of ..." Gray walked to the door—nice view as far as she was concerned. He looked through the peephole, opened the door, and let Tank in.

Tank carried in breakfast, and it smelled great. There were warm croissants, a variety of jams, bacon, fresh fruit cups, blueberry muffins, cream cheese coffee cake and butter, coffee, water, and tea.

"I wasn't sure what you liked, so I got a variety. Hope it'll be okay."

She grinned. "It looks great, Tank. Thank you."

Gray nodded. "This will be great. Thanks."

They spread the food out on the table in the room, and her stomach growled. Gray grinned, and she grabbed a piece of the coffee cake and took a large bite.

Gray told Tank, "We want to go to Sam's office first and then over to my office. We have a fourth floor we're using to refinish old furniture, and some of that will need to be used for the new offices on the second floor. Do you think we can go there and work if we stay on one floor?"

Tank thought for a moment. "Those are viable options for today. The security system will be installed in your house by this afternoon, so the timing would be great."

"Wow, I thought David said two days." Sam replied.

"He called in some part-timers to help out with other tasks so we could get it installed sooner. You must be important."

Gray laughed and oh the sight. He was a handsome man on any given day, but when he was happy, he was downright sexy.

"No, not any more important than anyone else. David and I have just been friends for a long time." He winked at her, and her heart fluttered. He still did that to her.

"How about you Tank, how long have you worked for David?" she questioned.

He set his muffin on his plate and swiped the napkin over his lips. "For about five years. I was the first employee hired on. A friend who knew David said he was looking for a security agent. I'd been in the army for twenty years before retiring, and the timing was right. I'd just gotten divorced."

After finishing breakfast, they checked out of the hotel and arrived at Sam's office around seven fifty-five. Bill was in his office, and Sam peeked her head around his door. "May I come in and speak with you?"

He smiled at her. "Of course, Sam. Come on in."

She smiled back. "I'm not alone; Gray is with me. Do you mind?"

Bill furrowed his brows, but shook his head and walked around his desk to greet Gray.

They shook hands, and Gray said, "Thank you for seeing us, Bill. This is important."

Bill cleared his throat. "I'm afraid I'm not going to like what you have to say, but please go ahead."

Sitting in one of the chairs in front of Bill's desk, Gray in the other, she leaned forward and cleared her throat. "Gray and I are getting married."

Bill grinned. "Well congratulations, you two!"

"Anyway, since I'll be Gray's wife, I'm going to work with Gray at Kinkaide & Associates, so I'm giving you my two-week notice. Of course, I'm sure you know this already, but I'll be available if there's anything you need while you transition someone into my position."

Bill nodded his head. "Sam, I'm very happy for you and Gray; really, I am. I'm very sad for us, though. You're valuable. Under any other circumstances, I would offer you more money, a bigger office, or anything I thought would persuade you to stay. But the competition here is insurmountable, so I'll wish you all the best and let you know that anything you need, either of you ever need, I hope you'll come to me."

She breathed a sigh of relief. "Thank you, Bill. Thank you so much."

The two men stood to shake hands, and Gray said, "Thank you, Bill. That means a lot to both of us."

She was glad that was over. Her stomach had been in knots. "There's something else. I'm not able to work today. We were involved in an accident yesterday, someone tried to run us off the road, and we have a security detail with us right now." She leaned forward and dropped her voice. "His name is Tank." She grinned.

Bill smiled. "Tank?"

"I know, right? Anyway, this building isn't secure enough with all the people coming and going, so at least for today, I can't stay. Moving forward, I may have to log in from home and work that way until the police can find this guy."

Bill leaned back in his chair. "Sam, anything you need. Do the police know anything about this guy and why he's targeting you?"

Gray joined the conversation. "We don't know who the target is, Sam or myself. That's why we have to be careful. But, after she was hit and then last night, I can't take any chances."

"Of course not." They made small talk then said their goodbyes.

She looked up at Gray. "I would like to say hi to Jessie. Do you think that will be okay?"

Gray nodded and looked at Tank, who'd been standing outside the door. "Tank, Sam would like to visit a little with Jessie. We'll go to Sam's office and ask Jessie to come back there."

Tank nodded his head. "That should work."

They walked back to Sam's office and closed the door behind them.

Gray asked. "Are you okay?"

"Yeah, I was nervous. I hated doing that."

He grinned. "I know you did, but you did well, baby."

She winked then turned to her desk and picked up the phone.

"Jessie, can you come back to my office? There's a big man with no neck at the door. His name is Tank. Just tell him who you are."

"Tank? Really? Tank?"

"Yes. Come on back, and I'll explain."

She noticed the message light flashing on her phone, picked up the receiver and hit the message button. She listened for only a second or two before her face turned pale and she began shaking. Gray grabbed the phone to listen to the message. "Fuck this! Tank!"

Tank opened the door just as Jessie got there.

Jessie looked at Sam. "Are you okay, Sam? What's wrong?"

She plopped down into her desk chair as she stared at Jessie. She nodded her head once and waved her in to come in and take a seat. Tank also walked into the office, and Gray took a deep breath. "Listen to this message Sam had on her phone."

He motioned for Sam to push the message button and she hit the speaker button at the same time. An altered voice warned, "You think you're so smart turning off the highway so we couldn't catch you? Well, you won't be safe next time, bitch. You're a dead woman!"

Gray's jaw clenched, his hands fisted at his sides. Tank looked at the office phone at the same time he pulled his phone from his pocket.

He hit a number on his phone. "Hey... Sam got a threatening message at her office. Listen to this."

"Play the message again, please," Tank said. He held his phone close to the office phone, so the person on the other end of the line could hear it. After the message played, he put his phone back to his ear and walked out into the hall to talk in private.

Gray walked over and wrapped his arms tightly around her. "We're going to find them, Sam, I promise you."

She nodded. "I know. It's just scary. They want to kill me." She fought the tremble in her lips. She'd not be weak; she'd face this and be strong. But, it was getting scarier by the day.

Gray filled Jessie in on what was going on and the news that they were getting married. Jessie squealed when she heard the marriage news and grabbed Sam's hand to look at her ring.

"Oh. My. God. Sam. That is the most beautiful ring I've ever seen! Huge, holy crap, huge." She turned to Gray. "Nice job, Gray!"

She nudged him then walked around the side of Sam's desk and gave her a hug.

"Congratulations, Sam. I'm so happy for you." She turned to face Gray. "Congratulations, Gray. You're a lucky man."

He winked at Sam. "I know I am, but thank you for confirming."

They talked a little more before Jessie had to get back to work, promising they'd talk again soon.

As soon as she left, Tank entered the office. He needed additional information; for instance, if there was a number of origination, what time the call came in, et cetera. He wrote the number down and recorded the call. They saved it on Sam's phone and her computer, then she forwarded it to her home email, as well as to Gray's, Tank's, and David's. When they were finished, they headed back to Gray's office, wondering if he had any messages waiting for him. As soon as they walked into his office, he checked his phone. He hit the message and speaker buttons so Tank and Sam could listen.

The same robotic voice warned, "You won't get away next time. That bitch of yours is dead."

"Dammit!" he scowled.

He paced back and forth, nervously running his hand through his hair. She never took her eyes off him while Tank retrieved the information from *this* call and emailed the message to all he'd sent the first message to. The voices in both messages were synthesized, so they couldn't be recognized. It seemed female, but Tank said they would have it analyzed to know for sure. In the meantime, he called David to fill him in on this new development. He asked about the Tahoe and if they had been able to get anything out of it. He also asked about the security system at Gray's house, asking David if he felt it would be adequate.

They talked for a while, and Sam's mind wandered. She'd never done anything so bad to anyone that she thought deserved this kind of reaction. She thought about the law office and decided she hadn't been directly involved with a case so nasty to prompt this kind of reaction. When Tank finished his call to David, he looked over at her, sitting quietly and lost in thought. "We're doing everything we can to keep you both safe."

She smiled. "I have no doubt. I was just thinking; do you think the attorneys and employees of the law office should be interviewed? I don't recall any nasty cases where someone was pissed at the outcome of their claim or felt the firm had treated them unfairly, but I did want to mention it."

Gray stopped his pacing and looked at Sam. He came over and knelt in front of her. "Sam, that's a great thought, but it wouldn't explain the letter, '*You're making a mistake with Kinkaide. He's making a mistake with you.*'"

She nodded. She'd forgotten about that.

Gray had his hands on her knees and was looking directly at her. "I won't let anything happen to you. Do you understand?"

She stared into his eyes. "I know you won't; I trust you completely."

He squeezed her knees and stood. His cell phone rang, and he frowned when he looked at the screen to see who it was. He sent the call to voicemail. She looked at him with a question on her face her brows raised.

Gray took a deep breath. "Cheryl."

She winced.

"I haven't spoken to her in a couple of weeks. I told you when she called. I honestly don't know why she keeps calling."

Tank asked. "Who's Cheryl?"

Gray looked at Tank. "She's a former girlfriend. We dated about four years ago. She broke up with me when she saw the relationship wasn't going anywhere. She got married and moved away. About two months ago, she stopped in the office to see me and told me that she was widowed and she wanted to know if I was seeing anyone. I told her I was and she didn't take it very well. She keeps calling me, and she's stopped in the office again to ask if I'd see her, but I haven't."

Tank thought on it a minute, then picked up his phone and punched in a number.

"What's her last name?"

"It was Hanson, not sure what her married name is."

Tank relayed that information to someone on the other end of the line.

They went up to the fourth floor with Tank. He went up the stairwell first, with Gray and Sam on his heels. He held his hand up to them to let them know to be quiet and stay on the landing until he searched the room. That wouldn't take long; it was all open space with only the furniture pieces lined up on the far wall by the elevator. He was back in no time, telling them to come in. Once inside the room, he locked the door. He asked Gray if there was a way to lock the elevator and Gray showed him how to do that. No one would be able to come in either way without Tank hearing them. He took up a position by the door, and Gray and Sam looked at each other and shrugged.

"What do you want to start on, baby?"

"Well, I was thinking the bookcases. They're the biggest of the pieces, and once they're finished and out of here, there will be more room to work on the other pieces. Besides, I can't wait to see what they'll look like when they're finished," she said, smiling. Despite everything else that was going on, Sam was excited to forget things for a while and work on the furniture and start making some changes here.

Gray looked over at the bookcases and nodded. "Okay, I think the best way to do that is to lay them down. They're too tall, and without a wall to support them, they're too narrow to walk on. And, while we're talking about that, you are never to walk on anything that is taller than you. I don't want you hurt. We'll lay it down or figure out how to build a catwalk around it or something that's less dangerous. Do you understand me?"

She saluted. "Yes, Sir."

Gray looked at her for a moment and walked over to her.

"Baby, your safety is everything to me. I never want to come up here and find you lying on the ground—it would kill me. I need you safe and alive."

He hugged her hard, and she hugged him right back.

"Sorry, I was snippy. I appreciate that you want me safe. I want you safe, too. I promise I'll be careful and not take risks."

They began wrenching the bookcases down from the ceiling-mounted winches. They had two of them laid down and were working on the third one. They took up a lot of space when laying out flat. Sam explained the process of first looking for any part that may need to be replaced or filled in with putty. Then they would sand and sand and sand. Once the sanding was complete, they would wipe them down to make sure the dust was gone, and then they'd start staining.

There wasn't going to be a lot of sanding on these pieces—they were in good shape, except the kickboards at the bottom. But she thought they would sand them to see how it looked. A little "distressing" would look good on them.

Once they had the last one on the floor, they rolled up their sleeves and started sanding. Music played softly in the room—Tank needed to hear if anyone was coming so they kept the volume low. They worked quietly, talking now and again about different things. It was awkward talking about personal things with someone else in the room.

After a couple of hours of sanding, Gray stood up and stretched to release the tightness in his back. She did the same and glanced at Gray. He watched her stretch, his eyes raking over her body. "Have you thought about when we should get married?"

"Ooh, you're a mind reader; I'll need to remember that. Did you have a date in mind?"

He tossed his sandpaper down and walked around to her. "Yes, two weeks."

"Two weeks! Are you kidding? We can't pull everything together in two weeks! Why two weeks?"

He took her shoulders in his hands and held her in front of him.

"I don't want to wait, Sam. We've waited a lifetime already. I want you to be my wife; I want it now. I think two weeks is generous. Besides, between my mother and all the kids, we can pull this off."

She was speechless. Apparently, he didn't realize all that went into planning a wedding. Sam was almost consumed with panic.

"Did you want a big wedding, Sam? I didn't even ask, but if you do, I understand. We'll make it happen."

Dresses, shoes, hall, food, family, invitations, flowers—her head spun with all that had to be accomplished.

"Earth to Sam!" She blinked and saw his eyebrows drawn together in worry.

She smiled weakly, staring into his beautiful brown eyes. "I just ... you just ... I don't know what to do first. There's so much to do. Do *you* want a big wedding?"

"Sam, I couldn't care less. As far as I am concerned, you and I can go to the courthouse right this minute and get married. I would be thrilled as long as you're my wife; that's all that matters to me." She hugged and held him for a few minutes. He smelled good, he felt good, and she fit him perfectly. They were two halves of a whole.

"Okay, let's be blunt. Are you sure you don't want a prenup? It's for your own good."

"No, Sam, I don't want that! I don't want to enter a marriage with the steps to get out of it written on a piece of paper. No."

She sighed. "They aren't the steps to get out of the marriage; they simply outline our respective assets and keeping them separate in case it doesn't work out. It keeps things from being messy if things go wrong."

Gray groaned and raked his hands through his hair. "If you think that I'll just let you out of our marriage, you need to know it'll be messy—messy as hell! I'm not letting you go without one hell of a fight. Do you understand me?"

His voice rose, and he spoke quickly, the worry marring his face. He held onto her shoulders again, keeping her in place. She looked into his eyes and smiled, reaching up to cup his handsome face in her hands. Softly she brushed his cheek with her thumbs.

"I'm not looking to get out of our marriage, messy or not. I wouldn't have said yes if I had any doubt at all. But you have this company and your children to worry about, I just thought you would want to make sure they were taken care of. I love you, Gray... so much it hurts. I would be devastated if you wanted to leave our marriage. I just know that it can be a hard subject to bring up and wanted you to know that if you wanted a prenup, I understand."

She stood on her toes to kiss his perfect mouth. His arms circled her waist and he pulled her close. She tightened her arms around his neck and held onto him with all her strength.

"Two weeks, huh? Yikes."

"You didn't answer my question, Sam. Do you want a big wedding?"

She nestled her face into his neck. "All I want is for the kids and your parents and siblings and my brother and his family to be there. I'd like some friends to come if they can make it, but the important thing to me is at the end of the day you'll be my husband!"

"I'm not waiting until the end of the day to be your husband. Two weeks from now I'll be fit to be tied that we aren't married already. It should happen in the morning—early morning."

She laughed and shook her head. "Early morning? You know I'm not a morning person. You're going to have to compromise on that one, Mr. Kinkaide."

He called his mom. "Mom, we're getting married in two weeks, and we need your help. We'll discuss some basics and give you a call at the end of the day. Then we'll need to call all the kids and fill them in."

"Why don't you come here for supper tonight? I'll call everyone together, and we can assign duties."

"That sounds like a great idea, Mom. Sam and I will call the kids and invite them over and tell them we're planning a wedding."

Once he hung up, they each grabbed their phones and started calling kids. After some hesitation and questions on why so soon, they each got their kids to agree to come to Mary and Harry's for dinner to discuss wedding plans.

Gray sighed. "I think it would be easier to elope and come back and tell them we're married and just plan a party."

She smiled at him and shook her head. "You're the one who wants a quickie wedding. Suck it up, buttercup!"

He wrinkled his face. "I didn't say I wanted a 'quickie' wedding. I said I didn't want to wait very long."

She kissed him and patted his awesome ass a couple of times. "Get a move on, Mr. Kinkaide. We have work to do."

29

SECOND CHANCES SERIES

Gray grabbed Sam's hand as they headed down the steps from the fourth floor. He knew he could make her happy, but he worried like hell he couldn't keep her safe.

When they arrived home, Tank told Gray and Sam to stay in the car with the doors locked until he gave them the all clear. They were in the garage with the door closed, but he didn't want them in the house if someone was there. His guys told him they'd installed a top-of-the-line security system with all the bells and whistles. They cleared the house before they left and turned the system on and had been monitoring it from the office. They would continue to do so 24/7. Tank just wanted to be sure it was still clear, and the security equipment was working the way it was supposed to.

He entered the house and the alarms starting ringing and his phone rang immediately.

After a few moments, Tank came out to the car and opened the door for Sam.

"We have the all clear, and in case you didn't hear, the alarms work."

Gray nodded. "I thought Sam was going to go through the roof."

She just nodded. They went inside and walked around as Tank showed them the alarm system and showed them on his laptop how to check systems and run through everything. It was impressive, to say the least—night vision cameras, still cams that were motion activated, infrared detection wires, and of course, the alarms. But, at any time, either of them could log onto their respective computers and check what was going on at the house and David's company would be monitoring all the time. They were open for business 24/7.

Tank informed him and Sam that he would be staying with them until it was safe enough for them to return to their normal lives. His work partner, Shane, would be relieving him. They would meet with Shane later in the evening. Once all was good, Tank set up in Gray's office to install the security software on Gray's computer.

They walked into Harry and Mary's house a little before five-thirty to find Mary bustling around in the kitchen. Harry was in the living room resting in the recliner. His strength still wasn't where it used to be, and he often took little catnaps.

"He thought he would need a nap to endure everyone's excitement tonight. He's been excited all day about your news and didn't take a nap earlier, but it finally caught up with him," Mary said, looking toward the living room.

"Gray, get yourselves something to drink and sit here with me while I finish up supper."

Gray walked to the refrigerator and pulled out a bottle of wine and looked at Sam. She nodded, and he pulled two wineglasses from the cupboard and poured.

"Mary, is there anything I can help with? I hate to have you both going to so much trouble on the spur of the moment."

Mary reached across the counter and grabbed Sam's hand. "I'm almost finished with everything. We're having a light meal with sliced roast beef and turkey sandwiches, potato salad, and chips. Nothing too fussy. Just sit, you'll have plenty to do in a short while."

He handed Sam a glass of wine, tapping his to hers before he sat next to her and opposite of the counter from his mom. Harry ambled in a few minutes later and patted Gray on the back as he walked past him. He leaned in and kissed Sam on the cheek and sat on her other side.

"Are you two ready for this?" He chuckled.

"I've been ready for this my whole life," Gray said, leaning forward to look his dad in the eye.

Sam turned her head to look at him and grinned.

He watched her expression for signs of panic, but only saw love shining back. It seemed too good to be true. "You know, we haven't talked about who will be standing up for us. Do you know who you'd like to stand up with you?"

She shrugged. "Well, it depends on how big you want it to be. If you want everyone included, then I would want all the girls: Tammy, Ali, Sarah, and Eva. So, if you wanted the boys to stand up with you, it leaves a boy without a partner. If we decide on friends, then I'd like Pam as my matron of honor and Jessie as a bridesmaid." He leaned forward and kissed her on the forehead.

"I would like Jamie and Caleb to stand up with me. They've been with me through thick and thin. The kids will always be our children and a big part of us. Jamie and Caleb will too, but they were there through all the bullshit with Suzanne and afterward when I was pulling the business together and moving on. Jamie and I have always been close, but after Kathy had died, Jamie and I were inseparable. We needed each other, and we were there for each other all the time. I want Jamie to be my best man."

When he first divorced Suzanne, he'd felt lost. It wasn't because he missed her, but for the first time in a long time he could do what he wanted to do when he wanted to do it. Ethan was with him, but Ethan was more interested in going out and doing things with his own friends. He simply didn't know what to do with himself. Jamie and Kathy and Caleb were with him through it all.

"Yes, that seems perfect, Gray. I'll have Pam as my matron of honor and Jessie as a bridesmaid. I'm going to call them right now."

She got up to walk into the living room, but he grabbed her around the waist and kissed her. "I love you, beautiful."

"I *know* you do and *I* love you!" She tapped on her phone as she walked into the living room. He listened as she chatted with her friends on the phone—her giggles and happy voice made him so proud. He glanced at his mom and smiled when she winked at him.

Sam walked back to the kitchen as the back door opened and Ethan and Eva walked in. Right behind them came Gage and Tracie. As the others drifted in, they joined everyone else in the hugging and the offerings of congratulations to Gray and Sam. After they'd settled in and had a drink in their hand, Jamie opened the back door and walked in holding hands with Jessie!

The room went silent. Jamie and Jessie stood silently for a few beats, and finally, Jamie said, "I'd like you all to meet Jessie." Sam ran over to Jessie and wrapped her in a hug. Jessie giggled like a schoolgirl.

"So, *he's* the mystery man?" Sam motioned her hand toward Jamie.

Jamie's smile spread across his face. "I met Jessie when you were in the hospital, Sam. I think we owe you a thank you for getting hit by a truck. It caused us to meet each other."

Jessie excitedly filled her in, "It was the day you finally woke up, and I walked in and yelled at Gray for making you scared that he was leaving. Jamie was there too. We visited with you for a while, and he left. A while later I left, and Jamie was waiting for me in the hall. He asked me out, and we've been seeing each other since then. When you called me a few minutes ago, I thought you had figured it out somehow, and that's why you asked me to stand up with you."

"No, I asked you to be my bridesmaid because you're one of my best friends, and I want you with me when I become Gray's wife."

Jessie hugged Sam again and turned to the room. Mary walked up to her and hugged her, as did Dani and Sarah. The guys all waved and said hello. Jamie and Jessie got drinks and Mary announced that they should all grab something and head to the dining room. Everyone did as they were told and sat down to eat.

The mood was light and jovial, and just as they were finishing up, Gray looked at Jessie. "Do you want to hear some stories about Jamie when we were growing up?"

Jessie snickered, "Absolutely."

Gray glanced at Jamie, a sly smile on his face and Jamie said, "Touché."

Gray proceeded to tell Jessie stories about him and Jamie, mostly Jamie being naughty. Everyone had a good laugh at Jamie's expense.

As soon as they were finished eating, each person took their dirty dishes and leftover food into the kitchen.

Mary said as loud as could be heard over the merriment, "Refill your drinks and head into the living room—we have a lot of work to do."

They did as Mary asked and as soon as they were each seated, Mary began.

"Okay, so Gray and Sam, you need to tell us what you want for a wedding, and we'll figure out who has the connections or expertise to get each task accomplished."

He nodded. "We already have our wedding party. Jamie is my best man, and Pam is Sam's matron of honor. Caleb is my groomsman, and Jessie is Sam's bridesmaid. After that, we don't have a long list of what we want."

Holding Sam's hand and rubbing circles on the back of it with his thumb, his heart damn near burst. He was planning a wedding—for real this time—and he was over the moon in love. They sat together in his favorite leather chair. Sam was turned with her back to the arm of the chair with her legs crossing over his. He caught her gaze with his. "Do you have anything else specific you want, Sam?"

She looked into his eyes and said, "I just want to look beautiful for you. And, I want to carry my roses and your roses."

He smiled at her and lifted her hand to his lips.

"You always look beautiful to me, Sam."

A few people in the room voiced a loud "Aww." Sam blushed and looked down. Gray lifted her head by placing his fingers under her chin.

"Don't be bashful about how I feel about you."

He kissed her softly on the lips and looked back at the room. She cleared her throat, her face bright red. "We'll need a place to hold the reception. Also, we'll need food, music, and drinks, of course. We'll also want a photographer and wedding programs, someone to sing at the wedding and decorations at the church and hall. Any ideas?"

Jessie spoke first. "My brother has a band, and they're pretty good. Sam, you've heard them. I'll ask them to practice up some Kid Rock in your honor!" Her face split wide with a smile.

"Are they available in two weeks?"

Jessie nodded. "I called him today when we knew we were coming here to plan, just in case you needed music. He said they were going to take that weekend off, but for you they would make an exception."

Mary spoke up. "I called Pastor Jay today, and he'll make the church available and marry you on the thirteenth. He already has a wedding scheduled at noon, so you'll need to get married at ten a.m. or two p.m., or later if neither of those times appeals to you."

"Ten o'clock!" Gray stated. "I don't even want to wait the two weeks, so I won't wait until later in the day!"

Sam looked at him and whispered, "Gray, it'll be a long day for people to wait until dinner is served following the ceremony. We could get our marks earlier in the day and have the wedding at two. Would you just consider it?"

He studied her face for a moment, then took a deep breath and reluctantly nodded in agreement. It was settled—they would get married on the thirteenth at two in the afternoon. Sarah knew the manager for the atrium at the lake and said she would give him a call and see if it was available. If it wasn't, she would call in a couple of favors for the Remington, a large hall in the area, which was another great place to have a wedding—with the hotel attached, people wouldn't have to drive.

Eva and Tammy said they would take care of the cake. Ali and Tracie would hire a photographer. Decorations would be taken care of by Mary and Dani. The men would help their girls with their tasks and take care of the beer and alcohol. Lastly, since it was too late for invitations, everyone would need to start calling and emailing relatives and friends. They started making a list of those who should be invited.

Gage offered to design an invitation on the computer to be emailed to invitees. He would have it ready tomorrow or the next day. The girls wanted to plan a shopping date, and he reminded everyone they would still need to take security with them.

"No one goes shopping with Sam without Tank or Shane. Sam, you don't go anywhere without protection. Do you hear me?"

"Yes, Gray, I promise you I'll be safe and always take protection with me."

He kissed her softly. "Good."

Talking resumed to various other topics, and they decided to meet up again in a couple days to see how the planning had progressed. Once they knew where they would have the reception, decorating could be decided, and family and friends could be notified. By nine-thirty family members began leaving the Kinkaides. It had been productive and fun, but he was tired. They'd been put through so many trials in the past few days, and he was beginning to feel his age.

The girls carried dishes into the kitchen and cleaned up the food that was still out. Jessie walked over to Sam and gave her a big hug.

"I can't wait to sit and have a conversation with you. I've wanted to talk to you about Jamie for so long, but we wanted to keep it quiet so no one would feel weird if it didn't work out—especially you. I'm sorry I kept the news from you, Sam."

Sam smiled at her. "Jess, that's your business, and I'm not upset with you at all. You were smart to keep it quiet for a while and test the waters. Jamie is great—this whole family is great. I'm so happy for you. So, you really like him?"

Jess laughed. "Oh, my God, I can't believe how much. You're right, he *is* great. I never would have dreamed it. I get why you fell so hard for Gray."

Sam nodded and hugged her back.

Eva squealed, "We have to have a bachelorette party, too! How about this Saturday?"

The girls squealed and started talking all at once. The guys drifted in to see what the commotion was all about. Jamie asked, "What's up?"

Eva told him about the party. Jamie glanced at Gray, his eyebrows raised. The girls quieted and waited for him to say something.

With hands on her hips, Jessie looked to him and said, "Gray, you have to let us throw her a bachelorette party. It must be done. Since you're pushing her down the aisle as fast as you can, we have limited time, so we *have* to do it this Saturday! You're getting married on the following Saturday."

He shook his head. "It isn't that I don't want you all to have fun with Sam or Sam not to have fun. It isn't safe, Jess. I can't risk Sam getting hurt. I can't." His voice cracked, and he swallowed rapidly to clear away the fear that threatened to clog his throat.

Sam walked over to him and wrapped her arms around his waist.

"It's okay, Gray, maybe we can just have a sleepover or something."

Sam looked at the other girls, and they all began squealing again.

"Sleepover, sleepover, sleepover," they chanted.

He looked down at Sam and whispered in her ear, "What on earth have you done?"

"Dad, a sleepover certainly can't be bad." Sarah had her hands on her hips, getting ready for battle.

He held his hand up. "Easy girls. Yes, if you're at our house where we have security and Tank or Shane, you can have a sleepover there. I can stay with Jamie," he said looking at Jamie. Jamie nodded.

The girls continued giggling and making plans.

Dani spoke up. "Don't forget, tomorrow is July fourth. Nick and I put on a picnic and fireworks every year, and we expect to see you all there. Four o'clock!"

Gray and Sam said their goodbyes with the promise they would all get together for lunch at Kinkaide & Associates in two days to discuss the wedding. They would have sandwiches catered in so no one had to do any cooking and cleaning. The conference room would be perfect for that, and they'd have security there.

Shane drove them tonight, so they climbed into the back of the SUV owned by Haggerty Security. It was a big, black Chevy Suburban with all the bells and whistles. The computers alone were staggering. There were weapons and tracking devices stashed all over, bulletproof windows, and of course, it was wired to the max with Bluetooth, an excellent sound system, and the dashboard looked like the cockpit of an airplane. Shane knew where everything was, though—he mastered the controls like he was born to do it.

He had his arm around Sam's shoulders and leaned in to kiss her temple, taking the opportunity to breath in deep. He loved her smell.

"What's going through that head of yours?" he whispered against her neck.

She shrugged. "Nothing."

"It looks like something. As soon as I said I would stay with Jamie, your expression changed. I thought you liked Jamie. Did Jess say something to make you think differently?"

She shook her head. "No. It's just my insecurities rearing their ugly heads. I'll be fine."

She sure didn't sound fine. "Hey, what insecurities?"

She took a deep breath and blew it back out.

"When you said you were staying with Jamie I had this ugly thought that you two would go out and look for women together like you used to. I wondered if you missed that time with him and would revert to old behaviors. Sorry."

He wrapped both of his arms around her and squeezed her tight.

"Oh baby, don't you get it? I love you. I only want you. The thought of being with another woman never enters my mind. Jamie and I went out together because it was something to do. We enjoyed spending time together. Yes, sometimes we met women. It filled a need, a release, but nothing else. Besides, I think Jamie is pretty hung up on Jessie. And we won't be going out; we'll be at his house with the other guys. I'm not sure if it's safe for me to be out either, so we'll just sit around and play poker and watch movies or drink and shoot the breeze."

A tear trickled down Sam's cheek. He reached over and wiped the tear tracks from her cheek.

"I'm sorry I'm pushing you so hard, Sam. I just love you so much; I can't wait to call you my wife. I want it now. I know it seems silly because I know you're mine, but I've waited so long to find you that I just want you to be mine—legally, emotionally, and physically—in every way."

She laid her head on his shoulder and wrapped her arm around his waist.

"I know, Gray. I appreciate that you love me. I love you, too. I'm sorry for being so ridiculous."

"You're not ridiculous; you're human."

They entered the house and looked around, waiting for something to happen. Shane chuckled and went to the office with a nod. He walked to the kitchen and flipped on the lights. "Go relax on the sofa, and I'll bring you a glass of wine."

He pulled the glasses from the cupboard and the wine bottle from the rack, pouring two glasses. He padded into the living room and followed Sam's line of sight out the window behind the fireplace. "Everything okay?"

She smiled a half smile as she lifted her glass from his hand. Tapping her glass to his, she chuckled. "I thought I saw something move out there." She looked him in the eye, "I guess my imagination is running wild these days." He glanced out the window, but all he saw was darkness.

He motioned for her to sit and he quickly joined her. The quiet felt nice, but it was soon interrupted when his phone rang. He pulled it from his pocket, glanced at the screen and scrunched up his face as he looked at Sam.

"Cheryl," he whispered.

He hit the button on his phone that sent it to voicemail. He looked at Sam and shrugged. "I haven't spoken to her in more than four weeks. I told her then that I loved you with my whole heart and there was nothing for us to talk about. I honestly don't know why she keeps calling."

Sam sighed a small sigh. "I would have a hard time losing you, Gray. I get that she would want you. What I don't get is that she broke up with you and married someone else. Now, all of a sudden, she's back and won't stop calling you. It's so weird, after four years. You haven't heard from her in all these years?"

He shook his head no. He didn't understand it either.

30

Two days later, Sam was working from home, trying to write down dates and deadlines for some of the specific things she was responsible for at the office. She had logged on in the morning and had a conference call with all the attorneys to go over job responsibilities and organize how they were going to divvy up her job until they found someone. She was pulling together the information they had asked for and writing down the things she could think of, but she was starting to suffer from brain drain. She looked at the clock—ten-thirty. She called in their lunch order to a friend's store in town which was ironically named, The Sandwich Shoppe. Today was the day they were eating lunch at Kinkaide & Associates and finalizing wedding plans. She ordered drinks, chips, and cookies to be delivered, as well as a few bowls of a couple different soups to go with their sandwiches. The food was to be delivered at twelve o'clock sharp.

She thought about the great evening they'd had the night before at Dani and Nick's house, which was beautifully situated on Harmony Lake, for the Fourth of July. The potluck meal was red-white-and-blue themed. They had a few drinks, and when darkness shrouded the trees, the lawn chairs came out, and the fireworks over the lake began. Gray sat in a chaise lounge and pulled her down between his legs to lean back against him and watch the show. Fabulous fireworks surrounded by family with all the kids—Gray's and hers—joined them. The grandkids loved the fireworks and had some of their own to light off beforehand.

Ready to shower and primp before heading to the Kinkaide office, she softly padded down the hall, so she didn't disturb Gray, but unable to keep herself from peeking in to look at her handsome future husband, she stopped in her tracks. He sat at his desk staring straight ahead.

She watched him for a moment, admiring his strong jaw and full head of hair—dark yet, but threaded with silver. As he continued to sit motionless, she couldn't stop herself. "A penny for your thoughts."

He blinked and turned his head toward her. Smiling he pushed himself back from his desk and patted his lap. She sat and lovingly wrapped her arms around his neck.

"What's up, babe?"

He sighed heavily. "I just can't figure out who on earth is trying to hurt you. I had hoped we would have figured this out by now. It's worrying the shit out of me. The more time they have to learn our security and patterns, the more of a disadvantage we're at. I'm stumped."

She squeezed his neck and kissed him softly. "It's not our place to figure it out. We're supposed to do as we're told and not test our security system," she admonished. "You don't have to save the world, Gray."

He sat back and pulled her back with him. "The only world I'm trying to save is mine. Call me selfish, but I want to spend years with you, and we can't do that if one of us isn't here."

She laid her head against his and sat quietly for a few moments. "This is nice, though, just being here with you."

He sighed, "In a couple of weeks, we'll be working together every day, and you can sit on my lap any time you want to."

She sat back and captured his eyes with hers. "I can't sit on your lap at the office!"

His voice grew husky, "Like hell, you can't. I plan on spending a lot of time with you. I dream of laying you on my desk and licking you until you come and having sex with you on every surface in my office. I've thought of all kinds of fun activities for us there."

"You know I have a brain, right? I am not just a body for you to slake your lust on." She smiled.

He laughed at her and squeezed her tight. "I love your brain, but I love your body, too."

He kissed her, moving his soft lips around her mouth, licking and sucking. He swirled his tongue in her mouth as he rubbed his thumb over her nipple. She moaned. He leaned forward and slid his arm under her legs and stood up with her in his arms.

Gray walked toward the door when she looked up at him. "What about Tank? He'll know we're having sex."

"I don't care. I am not going to stop making love to you because he's around."

Her face flashed a bright red.

"God, Sam, you're so sweet. I love you."

He kissed her again and continued walking down the hall toward the bedroom.

A couple of hours later, they were sitting in the conference room at Kinkaide Architects with the whole family. Jessie, Pam, and Caleb were there, too. The plans had come together nicely. The Remington was booked, the band was booked, and Eva and Ali had ordered a beautiful cake. They showed everyone pictures of the three-tier champagne colored cake with champagne and purple roses decorating the surface.

The photographer was a friend of Tammy's, and the girls were going shopping tomorrow and would spend the night at Gray and Sam's house. They told her not to do anything. They'd do it all—food, drinks, movies, et cetera. The plan was mani-pedis and maybe even facials. Excitement and giggling had already begun.

It seemed like everything was in place for the wedding and the bachelor and bachelorette parties. Jamie told Gray the guys were planning a night of poker, drinking, and bullshit. Jessie made Jamie promise no strippers and no women—period. Jamie agreed and told her he wasn't interested in strippers and women which made her feel better. She glanced at Gray who wore a knowing smile on his face.

Poor Tank drew the short straw and would have to guard the girls all night. His face pinched, and the line of his lips thinned as he took the news, but he offered up the news that he'd bring in a woman partner for that night to help. Shane thought he could handle the guys by himself and slapped Tank on the shoulder as he walked past him to answer his phone.

Jessie looked at Tank with a wink at Sam. "Tank, did you want to do a mani-pedi with us?"

Poor Tank turned about thirty shades of red and shook his head no.

After the meeting concluded and the room emptied, she and Gray threw away the containers and wrappers.

He wrapped his arms around her. "I can't wait until you're my wife. Just talking about this wedding makes me edgy and anxious."

Wrapping her arms around him, she sighed. "Really? I was thinking we were rushing into this wedding and maybe we should halt everything and rethink it all."

"We are NOT halting anything, and if you breathe a word of that again, I'll kidnap you and drag you to Vegas before you even know what's happening."

Laughing, she responded, "Aww, you're so sweet. No, I do worry that we're jumping into this quickly, but you seem so sure, and it helps me relax."

His lips covered her, softly but possessive. "How about you and I and Tank, go out to dinner tonight? I'm getting stir crazy, and I can tell you are, too!"

She smiled; he *did* know her well.

"I would love that. I promised I wouldn't complain, but I can't sit in that house another night without a break. Yes, please, let's go out."

He swatted her on the ass. "Behave and be ready to leave at five o'clock. You can work from Ethan's office this afternoon; he just left for a site visit."

"Yes, sir!"

Laughing she walked into the other room to log into the law office and get some work done.

At five, she logged off her computer and ran to the bathroom to freshen up. After all, they were going out after a week at home under protection. It was almost like a first date. She touched up her makeup and added a new layer of lip gloss before leaving the restroom. He grinned when she walked into his office.

"Ready, beautiful?"

"Well, when you call me beautiful, I am." She smiled. He stood and walked to her, took her hand in his and led them to the entrance of the building with Tank in tow.

Tank drove them to the Fox Harbor, where they'd had their first date. Gray asked for a table on the patio. The weather was warm and lovely, and being able to watch the river as they ate, added a sense of peace to their chaos.

They were seated, and luckily, it was early enough that Tank could get the table next to them. They ordered wine and perused their menus.

"Oh, my God, Gray, I'm so happy to see you. How are you?"

They looked up to see a woman walking toward them. She was about five-eight and had shoulder length, sandy-brown hair. Her slightly plump physique was squeezed into white slacks and a yellow tank top stretched tightly across her breasts. Gray glanced at Tank and slightly nodded. Her eyes darted between Tank and this woman.

Gray cleared his throat, "Cheryl, this is Sam, and this is Tank." Tank had moved to their table quietly and sat across from Gray.

Cheryl turned her attention to Gray. "Oh, so you haven't ordered yet. Good, I just got here myself. I'll join you."

Without waiting for a response, she sat down at their square table. Sam sat with her back to the fence that surrounded the patio, Gray to her right, and Tank to her left. That left Cheryl a spot directly across from her.

"So, Gray, how are the kids doing? I bet Lily and Lincoln are getting so big," Cheryl cooed.

"The kids and grandkids are fine, growing like weeds." His measured response stiffened her shoulders. He caught her eyes with his, a half-smile on his handsome face.

"I bet your mother's flower garden is absolutely fabulous. Oh, Sam, you must make it a point to go out into Mary's garden and see the lovely flowers she's planted. Or, maybe you have." Cheryl's familiarity with the family was beginning to grate on her nerves.

"Of course, I've seen it. It's the loveliest garden I've ever seen and one of my new favorite places in the world. It's where Gray proposed to me."

She smiled at him, and he reached for her hand.

"Proposed? I had no idea," Cheryl whined.

Sam held up her left hand and grinned. Cheryl's eyes darted from the ring to Gray. The waitress brought water for the group and stood silently by waiting for their orders.

"When ..." Cheryl cleared her throat. "When are you getting married?"

Tank spoke up. "Soon. They're getting married soon. We've been planning for a while now."

"Oh, well, how sweet to propose to you right in the garden. I suppose you were close to his roses; he just loves those purple roses."

"Actually, Cheryl, we were next to *our* roses. Mom and Dad planted roses for Sam this year right next to mine. I waited for them to be in full bloom so I could propose to her there."

Cheryl looked like she had been hit hard in the stomach. It served her right for barging in and just inviting herself to sit down—and constantly calling and stopping in at the office. She needed to hear this and know there was no hope for her and Gray to get back together. Sam was sick and tired of this little game Cheryl was playing.

She cleared her throat again and plastered on a fake smile. "Oh, well, congratulations. How exciting for you both. I hope you'll invite me to the wedding."

Sam looked at her with an eyebrow raised. Really?

Gray took a drink of his wine. The waitress asked, "Are you ready to order?"

Gray nodded and ordered for Sam and himself; Tank and Cheryl ordered their meals. The waitress nodded and finished writing. "Will this be separate or on one?"

Gray spoke up. "Put it on one, please." Once the waitress left, he squeezed her hand.

"Are you planning a large wedding?" Cheryl asked Gray.

He turned to look at Sam and squeezed her hand. "It will be as large as it can be on short notice. I don't want to wait." Turning to Cheryl, he continued, "I want Sam to be my wife right away. I would have married her the day I proposed, but she wanted the kids to be there. Even so, I'm not giving her much time."

Tank pulled his phone out and texted someone. Cheryl's eyes darted to his phone; she watched him tapping onto it.

"Work business?"

Tank looked up at her and nodded. "Hard to get away sometimes."

"Oh, what business are you in? How long have you known Gray?"

Tank leaned his arms on the table. "I've known Gray, and now Sam, for some time. We enjoy spending time together. I'm honored that they have included me in the planning of the wedding. Since I'm not married myself, it's an interesting process, and one I'm not ready to go through myself." He looked at Sam and smiled.

"How about you, Cheryl? Are you married?" he inquired.

If Cheryl noticed that Tank never answered her question about what he did for a living, she didn't say anything. She began fidgeting with her water glass.

"I'm widowed." The glare Cheryl swiped across to her was ever so brief, but it was enough to twist her stomach. Sam caught Gray's gaze and quickly looked to Tank. Just then a big hand slapped down on Gray's shoulder.

"Hey! Here you guys are. I went to the office thinking I'd catch you there. Sorry, I'm late."

David Haggerty walked around and kissed Sam on the cheek. He sat at the end of the bench Gray was on and pushed Gray toward Sam, putting himself between Gray and Cheryl.

"We thought you got caught up at work and weren't able to make it, so we came on ahead. Sorry, we just ordered; if we'd known you were going to make it, we would have waited." Gray's brows furrowed slightly, his lips thinned.

The waitress walked by with food for another table and David waved at her. "When you're finished, I'll order."

She nodded and kept walking.

"Tank, did they make you sit through wedding plans?"

David smiled, but it was tight—edgy.

Tank nodded. "Good Lord, who knew there was so much to think about. The whole family was at the office this afternoon. I don't mind telling you with all those women in the room talking about food, drink, music, cakes, and on and on, my head was spinning."

Tank gave a mock shudder; Sam and Gray laughed. But in truth, Sam worried her bottom lip between her teeth. Her appetite floated away and her nerves kicked up a notch. Her fingers shook slightly, perspiration gathered between her breasts and her shoulders stiffened beyond normal tension.

They made small talk, David engaging Cheryl in conversation as much as he could. She appeared to grow nervous, and as time passed, Sam became dizzy with worry.

Gray asked, "Are you living back in Harmony Lake, Cheryl, or are you just visiting?"

She licked her lips and lightly rubbed her neck. "I have an apartment here. I'm looking for a job right now, but have enough money saved up to live on for a while. Once I find work, I'll take my money from the sale of my house in Michigan and buy one here."

David turned toward Sam. "How are you doing, Sam? Have your headaches stopped?"

Surprise dropped her mouth open, but she quickly snapped it shut, her eyes sliding to Gray's. He nodded slightly which brought her to the question at hand.

"Just a little bit when I get tired. The doctor said it would go away in time. Gray takes care of me, though," she said as she caught his eyes.

"Gray, I heard Jamie has a girlfriend. How's that going?" Cheryl asked, a smirk on her face.

Gray looked at Cheryl, his brows raised and the surprise clear on his face. "This is new news to us all Cheryl; how on earth did you hear about that?"

She was quick to stammer, "I heard it at church ... just this morning."

Gray fidgeted and sat closer to Sam. He made a move to have Sam slide over so he could sit next to her on her bench. He looked at David. "Sorry pal, your ass touching mine on this bench is more than I care to deal with at the moment."

They laughed, and David shot back at him, "That was my plan, to get you to move. When my food gets here, it's no holds barred and I wanted the room."

Gray wrapped his left arm around Sam's waist and squeezed her.

The waitress brought their food, and Gray leaned down to Sam's ear and whispered, "Try and eat baby, so it doesn't look like you're nervous."

He kissed the side of her head. She looked at him, smiled, and nodded. She tried to eat a few bites, but they were sitting hard in her stomach. She settled for pushing her food around her plate.

Cheryl watched them like a hawk. Every move seemed as though it was under inspection. Her fascination with their life continued; it was almost as if she were torturing herself. She rubbed her neck a few times with the pads of her fingers, sat straight and arched her back to relieve tension. David and Tank continued to make small talk and Sam and Gray each joined in when they could.

"Gray, how are the honeymoon plans coming?" Cheryl asked.

Gray looked at David first, then to Cheryl. "Good, though I'm not divulging any information. It's going to be a surprise for Sam."

Sam looked at Gray and cocked her head to the side. "You aren't telling me where we're going?"

He shook his head no. "How will I pack?"

"I'll take care of it." His voice grew low and so darn sexy.

She furrowed her brows. When she packed, she really packed, leaving nothing to chance. Warm clothes, cold clothes, swimsuits, extra underwear and socks, extra everything. "I don't know how I feel about that!"

He chuckled. "You'll feel fine about it. You'll see. I'm a great packer."

Cheryl snorted and looked like she was going to say something but noticed everyone looking at her. Sam wondered if Gray and Cheryl had traveled somewhere together. That thought was the last straw during this dinner. The tension was tight enough without having to think that Gray and Cheryl had spent some romantic weekend away together, probably screwing each other's brains out.

The waitress came by and asked if they were ready for their bill. Gray nodded and she handed it to him; he, in turn, gave her his credit card and she was off.

Sam was ready to get the hell out of here, but she wondered how they were going to pull that off.

David saved the day. "You guys have plans tonight?"

Gray looked at him and shrugged. "It's been a long day, actually. We've been working since early this morning and right now Sam is working two jobs, trying to wrap up at the law office, so I think we'll just head home. How about you?"

David looked at Gray and Tank. "I know you guys are tired, but I wondered if I could follow you home and throw a couple business ideas your way. I would love your opinion on these as well, Sam. Do you guys mind? I promise not to overstay my welcome."

"No, we don't mind, David. Why don't you come on over? Tank's driving us today. He spent the night at our house last night and he's staying with us again tonight," Gray said past his tight jaw.

Cheryl looked between all of them; you could see the calculation in her eyes.

"Are you from out of town, Tank?"

He looked at Cheryl. "No, my apartment flooded and the repairs are still being completed. So, Gray and Sam were nice enough to offer me a spare room."

She looked at Gray and then her eyes slid to Sam. They narrowed, and Sam could tell she was having none of this conversation.

David stood quickly. "Cheryl, it was nice meeting you."

He looked at Gray, Sam, and Tank. "Should we get going?"

They all stood and began walking out, David first. Gray pushed Sam in front of him and behind David as they walked. Tank was right behind Gray, leaving Cheryl to follow. When they stepped out in front of the restaurant, Tank ran over to his SUV and opened the back door and ushered Sam inside. Gray climbed in the front so it wouldn't look suspicious and Tank climbed in and had the doors locked and the engine roaring so fast Sam was stunned a big guy like him could move so fast. They looked out the window and waved at David standing on the sidewalk with a very stunned Cheryl.

Once they lost sight of them, Gray looked at Tank. "What's going on?"

Tank looked at him and back at the road. "I texted David when Cheryl walked over. I could tell her behavior was off—stiff and controlled. Actually, too controlled. You both did great, baiting her a bit. It gave me the chance to watch her reaction. When David came to sit with you, I knew he had some information on Cheryl. I think when we get back to the house, he'll fill us in."

Gray looked back at Sam, who felt the blood drain from her face, a slight shiver tickled her spine, and the gooseflesh raised on her arms.

"It's okay, Sam We'll keep you safe, do you understand me?"

She nodded slightly. Her thoughts ran from one conversation to the next as she replayed dinner and Cheryl's comments and studious examination of the two of them.

When they closed the garage door, Gray jumped from the truck and opened the rear door for Sam. She scooted to the door and before she could step down, he scooped her up into a hug so tight she struggled to breathe.

"Sam, it'll be okay, understand?"

Sam nodded her head as much as she could.

"Did you travel with her? Go on an intimate weekend somewhere?" An inane question, but her stupid brain seemed to malfunction.

He pulled away just enough to look at her. "No, we never went on an intimate weekend anywhere. She snorted back there because she was constantly bitching about wanting to go somewhere for the weekend. I told you, I didn't have feelings for her. During our relationship, she was always the one pursuing me. I didn't ask her out, she just invited herself or made herself available. When weeks would go by, and I didn't take her to Mom and Dad's for Sunday dinner, she would invite herself. I just went with it. Yes, we had sex, but we never made love. I've only ever made love to you."

She stared into his beautiful chocolate eyes. The sincerity in them was a sight to behold, the slight creases at the corners seemed more pronounced now, the puffiness under them proving just how little he'd been sleeping these past few days.

"Thank you," she whispered.

He shook his head and squeezed her again.

"When will you get it, Sam? I've never been in love with anyone but you. Anything that ever happened in my past was me trying to get by until I found you."

The tears slipped from her eyes before she could blink them back. He used his thumb to swipe them away. David popped his head out into the garage. "It's all clear in here."

She smiled into her future husband's face as the smirk that lifted a corner of his lips mirrored her thoughts. He took her hand and led her to the house, into the kitchen and then the living room. He motioned to the sofa and gently nudged her to sit as he poured them each a glass of wine. "David, Tank, do either of you want anything?" Both shook their heads. They entered the living room and Gray sat next to her, while David and Tank each took a seat across from them. David set his laptop up on the coffee table and booted it up.

"Gray, what do you know about Cheryl's husband?"

Gray shook his head. "Nothing. I don't even know his name.

When she was getting married, she called me to tell me. I congratulated her and she invited me to the wedding. I told her I could make it and that was it. The day before the wedding, she emailed me the time and place in case my plans changed, but I had no intention of going. It didn't matter to me. I was happy she had found someone."

David nodded. "Okay, how long after you broke up with her did this happen?"

"I didn't break up with her, she broke up with me. She knew the relationship wasn't going anywhere. I didn't love her, never did. She wanted more; I couldn't give it to her. So, she broke up with me and about four months later, she called and told me she was getting married. About a week later, she got married and I heard they moved to Michigan."

"Did she ever tell you about seeing a psychiatrist or having any problems with anger or violence?"

His brows rose into his hairline, his eyes rounded in shock. "No, of course not. I wouldn't bring someone to my family if I thought they were going to bring problems. That may seem closed minded, but ..." He took a deep breath and let it out slowly.

"What did she tell you about why she was back here now?"

Gray inhaled. "She said she was recently widowed and came back to settle some real estate holdings her husband had here. I didn't care enough to ask anymore."

David let out a long breath. "You may care now. She married Jason McGinley. Do you know him?"

Gray shook his head no. Sam sucked in a breath. "Oh, my God." She raised her hands to press either side of her face. "Is it the same ... It can't be ... was he killed here in Harmony Lake?"

David nodded. "He's was an architect from Michigan. He was here in Harmony Lake visiting a local business, putting a bid in for a building. You bid on the same building, Gray. The Bank First National."

Gray's head snapped up. "I won that bid. I just finished designing that building when I met Sam." He looked at her; his brows furrowed creating deep grooves on his forehead.

David nodded. "Apparently, Cheryl met Jason while he was in town four years ago bidding on another job that you also bid on and won. She'd already broken up with you, but had been hanging around the hotel when she met Jason. Do you remember the timing of that? It was the shopping center in Wrightsville, and developers were meeting with architects over a two-day period. Everyone was filing in and out of that building one after the other."

Gray nodded. "I remember. I didn't see Cheryl there. I wasn't looking for her either. Bids were all placed in person at Harmony House."

"Right." David nodded. "She was hanging around, probably hoping to run into you and met him. They struck up conversation. When you won the bid, he was pissed and she used that anger and told him you had broken up with her, that you had been horrible to her. He married her quickly thinking he was getting back at you." He tapped a few keys on his computer. "We were doing research on Cheryl and Suzanne, and this came across my desk. I've been trying to find information about his death and it took me until about three this afternoon to find out. When Tank texted me, I ran right over. Jason was killed by Tim Powell."

David's eyes darted to her; she sat stone still, she'd recognized the name as soon as David mentioned it.

"Sam?" Gray asked, concern coloring his voice.

"Yes." Her voice cracked. She cleared it and started again. "I recognized the name as soon as David said it." She looked into David's eyes. "What are the odds?"

He nodded once more. "She's been in mental hospitals in the past, though it was a long time ago. Some of those records are sealed—juvie. Jason's sister told police that their relationship was volatile."

Slowly her head began to put thoughts together. "So, you think she came back here to confront me and found out that Gray and I were together and she snapped?"

He shrugged. "Either that or she came back because she is now widowed and thought she could get Gray back and then found him with you. Of all people, the widow of the man who'd killed her husband."

"So, you believe she's the person responsible for hitting Sam?" Gray's shoulders pulled back, his back ramrod straight.

David tapped a few more keys, and a picture popped up. "Is this the vehicle you saw, Sam?"

Her mouth dropped open as she stared at the picture on his computer. The navy-colored Tahoe looked like the vehicle she remembered. She closed her eyes and waited for the panic to pass. A shiver ran down her back; her stomach lurched remembering the pain she'd so recently suffered.

"Sam?"

Gray's deep voice brought her out of her own head. She opened her eyes to find his locked on her. "I'm okay." Her eyes darted to the computer screen again. She whispered, "Yes. That's it."

Gray handed her the glass of wine he'd poured for her. "Take a drink babe."

Her hands shook as she slowly brought the glass to her lips. Life seemed to be moving in slow motion. She sipped the delicious Moscato, breathed in deeply, and slowly let the breath leave her lungs.

Gray scooted to the edge of the sofa. "So, Cheryl is the person after Sam. And now she knows or may suspect that we know that. Is that good or bad?"

"Hard to say. My contacts at the police department are searching the Tahoe again; they still have it in impound. In the meantime, we're doubling up on security here. We're going to call in more security for your shopping trip. If she's watching, I think we should try and do as much as we can to look normal. We want you both safe, but we also want to draw her out so if she makes a move, the police can apprehend her. If we find evidence that it's her, we can have her picked up without her making a move."

Sam nodded. "I understand."

"Let's sit tight and wait to see what happens tonight. We'll be hawking the security system all night and I'm in constant contact with the police department—they know I'm here for security and why. They'll keep us informed of any new developments."

Sam took a deep breath, then another, waiting for the calm to descend. "So, you think she wants to kill me and not Gray? Gray's safe?"

"Sam, we don't know. My guess is that she would like you out of the way, but if she can't get to you, she may try to get to Gray so you can't have him. I was watching her today; she was glaring at you. Her vehemence, at least today, was directed at you."

"But I didn't kill her husband."

"No, but you stand in the way of her and Gray."

Gray jumped up. "No she doesn't—"

"We didn't say it was true, Gray."

David looked over at Tank. "What was your assessment of Cheryl today?"

Tank nodded. "I agree. The instant she came over she was sizing you up—checking out her competition. When you dropped the bomb that Gray had proposed, she was obviously shocked, her eyes narrowed and darkened when she watched you two. When Gray kissed you, she looked murderous. Her facial expression changed immediately when either of you looked at her—acting, unstable, plotting. I think she's definitely capable of killing you. You stand in her way and she's clearly not rational. Plus, if you hadn't dived out of the way when she hit you, she could very well have killed you."

David stood up. "Tank and I will be in the kitchen. I'm going to turn on the deck lights just outside the windows here, so if she would be able to get past the security system, we'll see her out there when it gets dark. If she lurks in the shadows, that's one thing, but she won't get close without us seeing her in the light. Just in case she has a gun, let's stay away from windows and keep a low profile. Do your best to try and give the appearance of life as usual, so if she is watching, she won't know we're onto her." Gray stood up and ran his hands through his hair.

"Let's go to a hotel or somewhere. I want Sam safe. I'm not comfortable here anymore."

Tank stood up and put his hand on Gray's shoulder.

"If we go to a hotel, we tip her off that we're onto her. Our goal here is to help the police get her if they find evidence, which we think they will. David's and my goal here is to keep you and Sam safe. Here we have a phenomenal security system. David and I are here, and we have people in place at the office monitoring the cameras, computers, everything. It's safer here than if she followed us to a hotel where we wouldn't have the added security. These smaller precautions are simply just in case."

Gray nodded. Tank and David walked into the kitchen. They were probably right. He sat back down on the edge of the sofa and Sam rubbed his back.

She leaned forward and whispered in his ear, "I love you. We're going to be fine. I'm going to make you put up with me for years and years."

He turned and wrapped his arms around her pulling her close.

"Now what? Do you want to take a shower?"

She nodded. He looked over to the kitchen where Tank and David sat at the table with their laptops open, monitoring the security cameras and messaging with the office.

"Sam and I are going to take a shower and change for bed." David and Tank nodded but didn't look up.

They walked to the bedroom, and she pulled yoga pants, a T-shirt, and underwear from her drawers. Gray grabbed pajama pants and a T-shirt, and they walked into the bathroom and locked the door. He turned the shower on to let the water warm up, turned to her, as she took her shirt off and was working on her pants. He walked over and hugged her.

"I told you, I'm going to make you put up with me for the rest of your life. Years and years, you're going to wake up in the morning and think, *What on earth have I done to myself?* We have security, protection, the police are looking for her, and we have each other. We're fine, Gray. We'll *be* fine."

After making love, he took her hand and brought her under the water to rinse her off. When they were finished, they stepped out of the shower and dried off, dressed in the clothes they'd brought in with them, then stepped out after she dried her hair.

They walked into the living room, a quick look at the clock told Sam it was eight-thirty. If she went to bed this early, she'd be up way too early in the morning. She grabbed her laptop from the case lying by the sofa and thought she'd check Facebook and see what's happening with friends and family.

"I'm going to go talk to David and Tank a little bit. I'll sit with you in a little while. Okay?"

Sam looked into his eyes. "Is there anything you're not telling me?"

"No, I just want to know if they have anything new and to reassure myself that everything is good."

She smiled and nodded.

31

SECOND CHANCES SERIES

G ray woke early in the morning to noise. He was on his side spooning Sam, holding her as close to him as possible. He lay there for a moment before hearing, "Jesus, she's bat shit crazy."

His heart hammered as his eyes scanned the horizon just outside the window, they must be talking about Cheryl. Sam stirred, and he pulled her tighter to his chest, loving the feel of her soft body against his. She rolled over so she was facing him and he quickly pulled her close again.

"Hey you, how did you sleep?"

Her soft sleepy smile was a sight to behold. Simply sexy. "Once I snuggled in next to you, I slept great. You?"

She nodded. "Pretty good. Did you just hear what Tank said?"

He took a breath. "Yeah, I was going to get up and see what they'd found, but I didn't want to wake you up. Do you want some coffee?"

"Yeah, I'll get up with you. I want to know, too."

They walked into the kitchen glancing at the clock on the stove—five o'clock a.m. They were used to getting up this early. Today was Saturday, and they would normally have gotten a cup of coffee and made love before getting up for the day. Having these guys in the house put a damper on that. He poured them all coffee while Sam pulled creamer and sugar from the cupboard. She set them on the kitchen table and sat in one of the wooden chairs. He brought the coffee and sat next to her casually laying an arm on the chair back behind her shoulders.

"What have you guys found out?"

David looked at Tank and back to him.

"It appears that Amanda and Cheryl have known each other for years. They worked together years ago at a bank, and they've been friends all along. Cheryl asked Amanda to apply for the job with you so she could keep her eye on you and report back to Cheryl. It seems as soon as you met Sam, Cheryl came back to town. She would have known that through Amanda."

"That is both disturbing and mind boggling! She's been spying on me all this time?"

Gray fell back against his chair like the breath had been knocked from his lungs. He felt betrayed and creeped out.

"The police visited Amanda this morning when they were able to get Cheryl's phone records. She'd been stabbed in the stomach, but she was alive. They'd been arguing, Cheryl said she had to do everything herself since she couldn't count on anyone else to do what they were told. Apparently, Amanda was supposed to bring her some information that would help her break you two up. Cheryl's been hanging out at the office, in the parking lot, watching when you come and go, following you. That's how she was at the restaurant last night."

"Oh. My. God. You've got to be kidding me!" Sam gasped.

Gray ran a hand through his hair. "How long has she been hanging out in the parking lot watching? I don't remember seeing any strange cars there. I would have noticed that. I know everyone's car."

Tank set his coffee cup down. "Since the night of Sam's accident."

Gray repeatedly shook his head back and forth in disbelief. He quickly stood and paced the kitchen.

"Where did they find Amanda?"

"At her apartment. Police went there to interview her, but when they arrived, they heard Amanda crying for help. When they busted in, she was lying on the kitchen floor in a pool of blood," Tank supplied.

David added, "Apparently, Amanda has been talking to the police. When Cheryl got married, she thought you would break up her wedding when you realized you didn't want her to be married to someone else. That's why she let you know when the wedding was."

Gray caught Sam's eyes with his; they locked for long moments. He hurried to her and put his hands on her shoulders.

"You guys have to keep her safe. Above all else, *she* has to be safe."

"Gray, we're doing everything we can, and we'll continue to do so. We'll keep both of you safe."

Her soft, sweet voice soothed his raw nerves. "Thank you. We know you're doing everything you can."

She reached up and placed her hand on top of his, still resting on her shoulders. She squeezed it, and he slowly released the breath he'd been holding in.

She stood. "Are you guys hungry? I could whip up some pancakes, sausage, and more coffee."

David grinned. "That sounds great, Sam, but we can eat later."

"Don't be ridiculous. We aren't going to cook and eat in front of you. Besides, I need something to do."

She busied herself in the kitchen pulling things from the pantry and fridge. He watched her graceful movements for a time, then padded to her, kissed the back of her head, and wrapped his arms around her.

"I love you."

She looked back at him, her shining green eyes a sight to behold, the fine lines at the corners defined a face that laughed often. "I love you, too." He could feel her take a deep breath and release it slowly. He kissed the top of her head and turned to grab the coffeepot, refilled everyone's mugs, and started making another pot. They worked in unison. Sam made the pancakes and he cooked sausage. They brought the food to the table along with plates and silverware, the butter, syrup, and whipped cream. The filled their plates and started eating.

David was the first to speak. "This is delicious. Thank you."

They both smiled. Tank nodded while shoveling more food into his mouth.

"You know, Gray, I have to say, watching you and Sam in the kitchen and over the past couple of days, you look peaceful and content. I'm happy for you."

He swallowed the bite of food in his mouth.

"I am content—beyond belief—except for this. The moment I saw Sam, I knew she was the one I was waiting for. You'll have to ask Jax about it; he just loves telling the story of when we met."

He looked at Sam, and she laughed. "That he does."

She turned to David. "I'm supposed to meet the girls at ten for shopping today. Is that still okay or do we need to make some changes? Do you think they're all safe? If I tell them to go ahead and shop for themselves, will they be okay?"

David glanced at Tank, and they both shrugged.

"You know, Sam, we're not sure what Cheryl is willing to do. So far, she hasn't approached anyone else in the family that we know of and after stabbing Amanda last night, I'd say she'll probably lay low. She's after you—and possibly Gray. We have two female security guards coming with you today, so they'll blend in and look like they're shopping with the rest of you. They'll hawk you like crazy. The others should be safe with them there. I doubt Cheryl would approach you to harm you in public. She would risk too much to do that, especially after stabbing Amanda. If she was watching her apartment at all, she'll know police found Amanda and that she may be talking. She could have left the area for all we know."

32

SECOND CHANCES SERIES

After cleaning up the dishes, Sam went to the bedroom to dress for her shopping trip with the girls. When she came back out to the kitchen, Gray stood and hugged her tight.

"I'm so sorry, baby. I wanted this wedding to be fun and exciting ... not like this."

She leaned into him and inhaled his fresh scent. She'd grown to associate the scent of him as home and that's the way she liked it. "I know you didn't plan on this, Gray, and I certainly don't blame you for it."

He exhaled. "Good, because I'm blaming myself enough here."

She tilted her head back to look into his handsome face. "Why in the hell would you blame yourself? You couldn't have known any of this was going to happen, Gray!"

He leaned forward. "It's because of me that she's after you."

"Actually, I think it's a combination of finding out that Tim killed her husband and then finding me with you. So, both of us are at fault." She rubbed his back.

David looked up. "Gray, hang tight with me, man. Hopefully, the police will find her soon. They're looking high and low. Thankfully, it's Saturday, and the office should be closed. If anyone was planning on going in, why don't you give them a call or email them to stay home today?"

There was a knock at the door, and she jumped. Gray turned and pulled her behind him in one swift move. David held his hand up and shook his head. "It's our relief. Tank and I need to get some sleep. We napped a little during the night, but we won't be any good to you without some shut-eye. Just in case, stay over by the fireplace."

Tank stood and put himself between them and the door.

"It's Shane and Nancy," David replied as he looked at the security screen on the wall. He opened the door and let them in. They'd previously met Shane, but not Nancy.

"This is Nancy Clemet, and I think you know Shane already." David manned the introductions.

Both Sam and Gray stepped forward and shook hands with Nancy. She looked like a tough chick, and she had sandy blonde hair and bright blue eyes. Her hair was pulled into a ponytail, and she wore black dress pants and a black, three-button placket polo type shirt with Haggerty Security on it. She had a gun strapped to her shoulder just like the men had, and she had one under her pant leg, by her ankle. She only noticed it because she had an ankle holster for her gun and knew where to look for the telltale bulge.

"I'm pleased to meet you both," Nancy replied.

David motioned them both over to the kitchen and prepped them for the day's watch. They'd received updates on the way over by phone and Shane knew the security system at the house, so they reviewed that. Once they were briefed, David came into the living room where both Gray and Sam sat on the sofa working on their laptops.

"Tank and I are taking off, but we'll be back in a few hours. You're in good hands here, and the office knows to contact me if anything new happens. Sam, in just a few minutes, your security detail for today will be here. Do you have any questions before I go?"

"No, I don't think so." They both shook their heads.

"Thank you, David, for being here all night; we really appreciate it. You as well, Tank."

Tank smiled at her and nodded—man of few words.

David said, "I'm happy to be able to help you and Gray out, Sam. But he'll be getting a huge bill when this is all over."

David grinned, and Gray rolled his eyes. They shook hands, and David and Tank slipped out of the house. Shane reset the security system and settled in. He told them that every hour one of them would be walking the perimeter of the house to look for any disturbances. If Cheryl was out there or had been, she would leave something behind—garbage, footprints, something out of place, a mark on a fence, or broken flowers. It could be anything.

Gray's phone rang.

"Hey, Dad, what's up?" His face fell, and he quickly walked into the kitchen where Shane and Nancy were sitting.

"Hold on, Dad, I want to put you on speaker."

He motioned for Sam to join them. Once they were all around the table, Gray set his phone down and put it on speaker.

"Okay, Dad, go ahead and say that again."

"Mary and I went out to the garden this morning to water and check on the flowers. She wanted to cut a couple of the purple roses to bring with her today. The roses are damaged. They've been cut from the stems and strewn around. Someone damaged the roses for your wedding, Gray. We don't know what happened. Who would do such a thing?"

Sam dropped into a chair—her hands shook, her breathing was erratic. She looked at Shane and Nancy; words wouldn't form in her head.

Shane spoke up first. "Mr. Kinkaide, this is Shane from Haggerty Security, are you and Mrs. Kinkaide all right?"

"Yes, we're fine."

"Are you in the house?"

"Yes, we're in the house."

Shane nodded. "Good, I want you to go and lock all the doors and make sure all the windows are closed. Do that now and keep your phone with you so we can hear you, okay?"

"Okay."

They could hear Harry get up and tell Mary to lock the front door. He would lock the back door, and once those were locked, they should check all the windows.

At the same time, Nancy got on her phone and called the office. She told them what was happening and that someone needed to head out to the Harrison Kinkaide house—right away. There was a good possibility that Cheryl had been there.

Shane whispered to Gray, "Don't mention Cheryl's name right now. We aren't sure she isn't listening. She may have done this knowing your parents would call you."

He nodded and looked at Sam. Her face paled, and her eyes grew big as saucers. Tears glistened in her eyes. She shouldn't have baited Cheryl about the wedding and the flowers. They didn't know she was that unstable, but still, they suspected she might have issues with them together. She felt terrible! Harry and Mary could have been hurt or worse.

When Harry finished with the doors and windows, he said, "We have the doors and windows all closed."

"Okay, good. Now listen to me, Mr. Kinkaide, I want you and Mrs. Kinkaide to go to a room with a window that faces the driveway and lock yourselves in that room. Will you do that for me, please?"

"Yes, we will. What is this all about? Gray, are you okay? Is Sam okay?"

Gray looked at Shane, and he nodded. "Yes, Dad, we're fine. It's just a precaution."

Shane spoke up. "Mr. Kinkaide, we have someone from our office stopping by your house to check it out. They'll be driving a black SUV, a Tahoe, and when they get out of the car, they'll have the black Haggerty Security shirt on. He'll knock on the door and will hold up ID so you can see it. Don't open the door for anyone who doesn't have the security ID, okay?"

"Yes, okay."

They could hear hustling and moving around. "Okay, we're in the den, and the door is locked."

"Okay, good. We'll stay on the phone with you until security gets there. The person coming to your house is ..."

Shane looked over at Nancy, and she said, "Kent Logan."

"Do you have a computer in the den, Mr. Kinkaide?"

Gray smiled at her. Mary loved her computer and her Internet. Gray had gotten her the laptop for her birthday this past year.

"Yes. Mary's computer is in here."

"Okay, Mrs. Kinkaide, I'm going to have our office email you a picture of Kent Logan, so you'll know it's him when he gets to your house. Don't open the door for anyone who doesn't look like him, okay?"

Gray wrote down Mary's email address, and Nancy relayed it to the office over the phone.

A couple of minutes later they heard Mary. "Oh, he's so handsome."

Sam had to bite her lip to keep from laughing. Gray did laugh, but only because Harry sniped at her.

"He isn't coming over to date you, Mary."

Mary gave it right back to him. "I'm not so old that I can't appreciate a handsome young man, Harry."

Even Shane and Nancy chuckled at them.

"I see a black SUV pulling into the driveway. It's probably that handsome Kent Logan," Harry bit out sarcastically.

Sam laughed. Gray did as well. She loved watching him laugh; he was impossibly handsome. He looked down, caught her staring at him, and he pulled her to him in a one-armed hug. He kissed the top of her head as they listened to Harry and Mary answer the door. They saw his ID and let him in. They introduced themselves, and Kent asked if he could have their phone for a moment.

"Kent Logan here, badge number 89256."

Shane responded, "Thanks, Kent. Why don't you bring the Kinkaides here? We can keep them safer here than over there. We're stretched pretty tight right now. Have them bring clothes in case they need to stay overnight."

"Will do. See you within the hour."

The house was filling up.

A while later, Nancy announced, "Your parents are here, Gray."

Sam and Gray walked into the living room toward the door.

Shane halted them. "Sorry folks, have to ask you to stand back."

They both nodded and stepped back. Shane opened the door for Harry and Mary.

"What the hell is going on, Gray?" Harry was flustered.

After his heart attack, they didn't want to get him riled up. They hugged the senior Kinkaides and motioned them into the living room.

"Why don't we sit and we can tell you all about it."

Gray got them both drinks, and they all sat. He proceeded to tell them everything.

"That bitch cut my flowers down! When I see her, I'm going to give her a piece of my mind."

Whoa! Mary said bitch!

Gray leaned forward. "If you see her, Mom, you are not to approach her, do you understand? She's dangerous."

Mary looked at Sam, tears shimmering in her eyes. "Sam, honey, the flowers for the wedding are ruined."

She mustered up a smile. "The important thing is that she didn't come into the house and hurt you and Harry. That's all that's important. Maybe there will be some flowers we can salvage; we'll see when it's safe to go and look."

Mary swiped at her tears and nodded.

About a half hour later, the second security detail arrived. She explained to Mary that they would have additional security on them today. Shane let them in and introduced them.

"Sam, Gray, Mary and Harry, this is Rachel Gerrity and Shauna Jackson."

They shook hands as the introductions were made. Both women were very pretty and on the small side. They didn't look like security at all, but Shane and Nancy reassured them that these gals were a force to be reckoned with. Oddly, she felt secure with these gals. The way they held themselves told her they meant business.

Sam glanced at Mary. "Are you ready to go?" Mary nodded and turned to hug Harry goodbye.

Sam hugged Gray to her, squeezing him tightly. "I love you, Gray. See you later."

He planted a kiss on her lips that threatened to melt her panties. When their lips parted, her face burned bright red.

"Get used to it. I love you, I love kissing you, and I don't care who sees it or what they think. Understand?"

She nodded, still embarrassed and not sure if she could turn around and face everyone after that kiss.

Mary grabbed Sam's hand. "Come on, Sam, or he'll hang onto you all day. We have some shopping to do, and we don't want to be late."

He kissed her nose as Mary pulled her away. "Make sure you two watch her and keep her safe—both of them," Gray said to Rachel and Shauna.

They both nodded and turned to follow Sam and Mary out the door.

Shauna was driving and motioned for Sam and Mary to get in the back. They were meeting the girls in downtown Harmony Lake at the New Beginnings Bridal Shop. When they arrived, everyone was there. After Rachel and Shauna had been introduced, Mary started telling the girls what happened with the flowers.

Then Mary asked her to tell them about Cheryl and what had transpired since yesterday. After relating everything to the girls—from dinner last night to the events of Amanda, Cheryl's husband, all of it—you could have heard a pin drop in that bridal shop. Finally, Jessie grabbed her in a bear hug and held her tight. After a long moment, she pulled away to look at Jessie. Tears ran down her cheeks.

"Sam, I don't want anything to happen to you."

She smiled at all the girls. "That's why Rachel and Shauna are here, to keep us safe. We need to listen to them, and if they think there's something amiss, we need to do exactly as they say. And, if any one of you feels it isn't safe being with me today, I completely under-stand if you don't want to stay. I won't be mad at any of you."

They all looked at Sam like she'd just sprouted an extra head.

Dani spoke first. "Sam, we wouldn't miss out on this because of Cheryl or anyone else. My brother is crazy in love with you, and I want to be a part of everything involved in this wedding."

They all nodded and wiped the few tears that had leaked from their eyes.

"Okay, let's find some awesome dresses. And, everyone, please keep a very close eye on Abby and Lily."

One of the bridal attendants walked over to their group and introduced herself as Debra.

"Which one of you is the bride?" She looked at Tracie and Sarah, the younger of the girls.

"I am." Sam grinned.

Debra looked surprised but quickly changed her expression.

"Okay, so do you have an idea of what you're looking for?"

"I would like a halter style dress or a tank style dress made mostly of lace. Oh, and in a champagne color. Last, but not least, we're getting married next weekend, so it will need to be something you have here or can get quickly."

Debra pursed her lips. "Not asking for much!"

Sarah spoke up. "My dad tends to be impatient with Sam. We're lucky we even got this week to plan and shop." She winked.

"Okay, well, tell you what. Why don't you all look around for dresses you would like to try on, and I'll pull a few dresses we have here that I think will be close to what Sam is looking for. Do you know what color the bridesmaids are wearing?"

"Purple!" Jessie squealed.

Mary sadly held up the purple rose she had plucked from the ground this morning.

"Okay, the purple dresses are all over in the corner toward the front of the store. I'll find you in the store when I have a few dresses for Sam to try on."

They dispersed throughout the store and looked through the racks of dresses for something that appealed to them. Mary thought she would like to wear a nice lavender dress. Dani wanted to coordinate and wanted to wear something in the purple family or maybe a bluish gray. Sarah thought that sounded pretty and wanted something like that as well. Eva with her blonde hair always went with softer colors and wanted something in a blue. For Abby and Lily, they hoped to find the dark purple dresses similar to the bridesmaids. Just then a loud squeal sounded throughout the store. Sam, a bit on edge, jumped. Mary did too. It turned out to be Jessie, who was running toward Sam with a purple dress in her hand.

"What do you think of this? It's the perfect color and style. Both Pam and I will look great in it. Do you like it? Can I try it on? What do you think?"

Sam laughed. Clearly, Jessie was excited.

"I think it's beautiful, and you're right, it'll look great on both of you."

She glanced at Pam who'd made her way over to them. "I agree, that's perfect," her bestie stated.

Debra came to tell them she had dressing room six set up with some dresses for Sam to try on. Dani and Mary joined her in the room. The other girls hovered around waiting for Sam to model each dress for them. The first dress was pretty, but not her style. The second dress, well, that was the one.

It was a beautiful lace dress with a V neckline and narrow straps that came to a low V in the back. It was a shimmery champagne color with a darker shade of champagne silk belt that tied in the back, then flowed all the way down to the end of the short train. The lace scalloped down both sides of the V-back, and scalloped down in the front to just between Sam's breasts, showing some cleavage, but not too much.

Dani piped up, "Gray is going to LOVE that dress!"

She had to agree; it was exactly what Gray would love. She remembered the open-back dress she'd worn to the Kinkaide wedding, where Gray had mentioned getting married for the first time. He loved that dress on her—partly because he could touch her bare back.

She was staring at it in the mirror when the other girls walked in to peek at it.

"Oh. My. God. That's the one. That's perfect." Sarah looked at her in awe. "My dad is going to love that one!"

The other girls talked at the same time, but the comments were the same. She had found her dress!

The seamstress came in to measure her, as the hem needed to be taken up and a little in at the waist, but she assured Sam that it would be ready for Friday afternoon. There was a little tweaking to do on Jessie's dress as well, and Mary needed hers hemmed, but that was it. Overall, it was a successful shopping trip. They decided to head over to the shoe store in town to see if they could find shoes to wear. She could wear the shoes she wore to the Downtown Harmony event. After all, she only had them on for a couple of hours, and they were the perfect shade of her dress. The other girls needed shoes, though, so they headed to the store.

She was now ready to take a nap. Something told her it was going to be a long night with the girls over for their slumber party. The clock said three-thirty, and everyone was due at her house around seven. She and Mary hugged everyone goodbye and climbed in the SUV driven by Shauna. They were drained.

"I don't know about you, but when we get home, I'm gonna need a nap," Mary stated. She laughed—great minds.

The rest of the ride was in silence; the peacefulness felt amazing.

When they got to the house, it was quiet. Shane and Nancy were in the kitchen working on their computers. They looked up and said hello when the women walked in.

"Where are Gray and Harry?"

Shane looked up from his computer. "Harry is taking a nap in the first bedroom, and Gray is in his office."

Mary headed toward the bedroom and Sam went in the other direction to where Gray was sitting in his office. When she walked in, he looked up at her and smiled.

"Hey there. Did you have a successful shopping day?"

She walked over and climbed on his lap.

"I did, actually we all did. We bought out the whole of Harmony."

Gray laughed. "I better get back to work then."

He hugged her tight. "I'm glad you're home. I missed you."

She smiled and looked into his tired eyes. "I missed you, too. You're going to love my dress. I'm excited for you to see it." She softly ran her fingers over his face, smoothing the tired lines she saw. If she could simply swipe away the worry, she'd happily do it.

He leaned back in his chair pulling her with him.

"I have no doubt. With you wearing it, anything would be beautiful."

She kissed him—a sweet, slow, wet kiss, sliding her lips over his.

"I need a nap. How about you?"

"That sounds great. Dad just went to lay down about a half hour ago. We had a nice talk this morning. It was nice spending the day with him, even though we were stuck in the house. We sat and shot the breeze and talked about so much. Were your ears ringing?"

She laughed. "Is that what that was? I thought it was from all the girls talking at the same time."

He hugged her close again.

"One more thing. We thought if you girls don't mind, that the guys would come here tonight. We'll stay in the basement. We're fully stocked down there, plenty of places for us to sleep, and we have a bathroom and food. So, if you don't mind, I thought it would be easier on David to have his security team in one place. I hate to spread his operation so thin."

"Oh, that's perfectly fine, Gray. We won't mind at all. Besides, if I need to see you, I can sneak down the stairs and grab a quick kiss and hug."

He laughed. "If you tempt me, it could be more than that!"

She giggled, and he squeezed her once more. He set her on her feet and stood. Taking her hand, he walked them to the bedroom. When the door closed, he turned, wrapped his arms around her waist and kissed her. His tongue slid into her mouth, and his hands roamed over her body. He put one hand behind her head holding her in place while his other hand kneaded her breast and pinched her nipple, rolling it to a tight pucker. Her breaths were labored, and her body was on fire.

She moaned. He moved his hand down her back and pulled her shirt from her jeans. His fingers nimbly unhooked her bra, and she thought again about how perfect this man was for her. Her shirt was pulled over her head and tossed to the floor. Her bra followed closely behind.

"This time next week, you'll be Samantha Kinkaide. You'll be my wife."

She smiled. "Yes."

Gray unbuttoned her jeans and slid the zipper down. He continued to kiss her and pinch her nipples. First one, then the other, keeping both straining tightly toward him. He leaned down and sucked one into his mouth, the warmth of his mouth caused a shiver to slide down her spine. He added more pressure to his sucking, and the moisture that rushed between her thighs brought her attention to that area and just how much she wanted him there.

"Gray that feels so good," she hummed.

He grinned against her breasts.

Pushing her jeans over her hips, he let them fall to the ground. His eyes were glazed and heavy. She reached over and rubbed her hand over his cock. Yes, he certainly *was* ready for her.

She massaged his hardness as he pushed himself into her hand. She unbuttoned his jeans and inched the zipper down. His erection bulged out of his pants as soon as the zipper slid down. He sucked in his breath but stood back slightly as she pushed the stiff material down his hips, lightly scraping her fingernails along his heated flesh as she brought her hands back to his cock, now only separated from her by a thin piece of material. She hooked her thumbs into the waistband of his boxer briefs and slid them down, releasing his cock from its confines. She quickly reached for it and marveled at the hardness covered in smooth, satiny, heated skin. The throbbing between her legs was almost unbearable as her hands brought him pleasure with their movement, up and slowly back down, swiping over the coarse hair at the base and slowly gliding to the tip. Swiping her thumb over the precum and smearing it across the tip, he huffed out a breath as he held her shoulders between his strong hands. When he finally spoke to her, his voice was husky and breathy. Sexy.

"Go over to the chair by the window and kneel on it, facing the back of the chair. Put that sweet little ass of yours in the air for me, Sam."

Sam stepped out of her jeans and slid her panties down and let them fall to the floor. She walked over to the chair, a crooked smile on her face as she thought about how he would feel sliding inside of her. Kneeling on the chair and facing the back of it, she braced herself and looked over her shoulder at him. He was watching her as he pleasured himself. Hot. His eyes didn't leave hers, and he stalked toward her very slowly, pumping his cock in his hand. As precum formed, he'd swipe it across the head and pump again.

"I love watching you, Sam. You're so sexy. I can't wait to slide myself into you. Are you wet for me?"

"Yes."

"Good. I love it when you're wet."

He lay his hand on her ass, rubbed, and squeezed both of her globes. He palmed her ass and used his thumbs to pull her cheeks apart. He bent down and licked her from the tip of her clit all the way to her anal opening and back down. Her knees shook as the moisture increased. Her breathing quickened, causing her to shudder.

Gray chuckled. "You like that, baby?"

Her throat was dry. She swallowed and nodded.

"No, I want to hear you, Sam. Tell me. Do you like that?"

Catching her breath, she moisturized her throat again. "Yes."

He chuckled and licked her again, giving more attention to her clit. He skillfully licked it and sucked it into his mouth, with an occasional flick of his warm tongue. She squirmed, and he increased the pressure on her ass to hold her in place.

He lapped at her opening, swiping his tongue over her sensitive clit forcing her breath to rush from her lungs. He stood, and she could feel the head of his cock at her entrance. He put his hands on her ass again and held her while he slowly slid inside of her. In and out he pushed and pulled until he was fully seated inside of her, his balls touching her pussy in the most erotic way.

He hissed out a breath. "I love the way you suck me into your wet, hungry pussy."

Pumping in and out—nice and slow at first—he let her feel every inch of him as he moved. Absolutely incredible! She felt so full when he was inside her.

His pace increased as he reached around and circled her clit with his fingers. He used the same tempo he set with his thrusts—circling and applying pressure in a beautiful rhythm.

Her climax built quickly; her skin wore a fine sheen of moisture, the heat radiating from her akin to the hot sun on a tin roof. "Gray, I'm close," she huffed.

He increased the pressure on her clit and pumped faster and harder into her. She could feel his balls smacking her pussy, his breathing labored.

"Gray," she gasped.

"Let go, baby, come for me." His voice was thick with emotion. "I'm right there with you."

She exhaled and let go crying out his name as they both crossed the bridge of satisfaction together. He tightly held her hips, thrusting into her a few more times. She could feel him squirt into her and the throb of his cock as he released himself.

He held her tight with a final push and leaned forward to lay his head on her back. She rested her head on her arms on the back of the chair. They stilled until their breathing calmed and returned to normal. He stood and placed loving kisses on her back and slowly pulled out of her.

"You okay, baby?"

Sam pushed herself up. "I'm great."

He chuckled. "Let's go clean up in the shower and take a nap."

She slowly stood up and let the blood flow into her legs again. He held her hand as they walked into the bathroom. He turned on the shower, then turned and hugged her while they waited for the water to warm up.

*****

After a short nap, they dressed and walked out to the kitchen to see if there was any news. Harry and Mary were in the living room watching television.

"Did you have a nice nap?"

"Yes, we did. How about you?"

Mary smiled. "Yes, it was lovely. I love all those girls with my whole heart, but I tell you, listening to them all talk at the same time gave me a headache."

She laughed. "God, I'm glad I wasn't the only one."

Gray addressed Shane. "Any news?"

Shane shook his head. "No sign of her anywhere. Her car was found at the airport. But that could be to throw us off. It's not very original, so we aren't banking on her having left. Her bank accounts have been frozen, so she'll need money soon. Amanda can't think of any friends that she could call for money or shelter or help her in any way.

"Amanda had surgery yesterday and is doing well. Police have a guard outside her hospital room. We don't know if she was more deeply involved than what she's already told us."

33

SECOND CHANCES SERIES

At seven o'clock the girls began arriving. The men floated in as well since most of the guys were coming with some of the women. It was fun, and the mood was light, despite discussing Cheryl and all that weirdness. They hoped the police would get her soon so no one else would be in danger. The support given to them was a testament to the solid family unit and close friends they had. He'd be forever grateful to David for coming to their aid.

As soon as all had arrived, he ushered the men downstairs to his man cave. It wasn't all that he wanted it to be, but there was time for that. He was beginning to feel more motivated to finish the projects he'd failed to finish before. Now, he wanted the perfect home to share with Sam, and he'd work night and day to make that happen.

"Can you still play cards, Gray, or have you forgotten how?" Jamie teased.

"I can play. Put your money on the table and start dealing."

Jax laughed. "Deal me in; I haven't played poker with the old man in years."

Ethan joined in, and so did Sam's sons. Harry opted to sit out and be the advisor.

Around eleven o'clock, Harry snuck upstairs to call it a night. Gray softly stepped up the stairs from the basement and into the kitchen. He felt relief that the women were all in the living room, then he spied Sam walking to the bedroom. He slowly followed behind her, and she stepped into the master bathroom and closed the door. He sat on the edge of the bed, facing the door, content to wait for her and steal a kiss and a squeeze.

He heard the water run and soon after the door opened. She jumped when she saw him staring at her. A slow smile slid across his lips. "Boo!"

He stood, walked toward her and pulled her in for a hug.

"I snuck up here to take a peek at you. We all heard the hoots and hollers downstairs, and I wanted to see what the commotion was about. As I got to the top of the stairs, I caught a glimpse of you walking back here. Sorry, I didn't mean to scare you."

Sam grinned. "We were watching *Magic Mike* and cheering for the sexy men on screen. Glad you came back here; I was missing you."

He kissed her and held her body to his for a few moments. The soft, clean fragrance in her hair soothed him and made him think of a warm, summer day.

"I have to get back downstairs before I'm missed. I'm winning in poker down there. The bathroom has been in constant use with all the drinking going on, so I decided to come up here and use this one."

She giggled. "I'll leave you to it, Mr. Kinkaide. Love you."

She swatted him on the ass, and he watched hers sway down the hall, then heard the girls whistle and coo when she entered. He chuckled and stepped into the bathroom.

As he entered the living room, Cole, Ethan, Nick, and Jamie had ventured upstairs. They turned toward him and laughed.

"Are you conceding that I'm the poker champion?"

Jamie gave him the finger and Ethan mumbled a "you wish."

Jessie told Jamie, "We're just getting ready to watch another movie. Want to join us?"

"Actually, I do want to snuggle up and watch a movie."

Jamie yelled down the stairs. "We're staying upstairs to watch a movie with the girls."

One by one, each of the guys ventured upstairs and settled in by their woman, and the movie was started. Jax, Caleb, and David Haggerty were the only single or unattached guys, but they found spots on the floor and settled in for movie time, too.

This wasn't a raucous bunch of people; these were people strong in family and relationships. He thought it was the best bachelor party ever.

*****

The next morning, one by one, people started waking up. They had all fallen asleep on the floor or sofa or wherever they had been sitting while watching movies last night. Sam smelled coffee and opened her eyes to look around. She smiled as she looked at the sea of people in their living room. They were lying wherever there was room. It was wall-to-wall bodies and drink glasses and bowls of left-over popcorn and snacks. It was going to take a while to clean everything up. She hadn't even seen the basement yet. But she was content and happy and didn't care. If they were still stuck at home, it would be something to do. Then it dawned on her that it was Sunday. What about the family lunch at Harry and Mary's?

She looked over at the kitchen to see who had made the coffee and saw Harry and Mary sitting at the table looking at their family, both wearing soft smiles. Mary winked at her, and she smiled. She twisted to sit up, and Gray's arms closed around her tighter.

"Where do you think you're going?" he whispered in her ear.

Sam turned her head to look at him. "I'm going to get a cup of coffee. Do you want one?"

He let out a sigh and hugged her tighter.

"Yes, I was going to get up and get you a cup when I heard Mom and Dad making it, but I wanted to lay here with you in my arms a while longer. Last night was nice, having everyone here, watching movies, laughing with each other. Thank you."

Sam turned in his arms to face him.

"Thank you. It was wonderful that all you guys came up here to watch movies with us. Sarah gave me the sweetest toast last night. She had us all in tears just before you all came upstairs."

He kissed her nose and her lips. "I heard about it. Cole told me last night."

Her brows furrowed. "When?"

He chuckled, and the rumbling in his chest sounded like the sweetest music. "You girls fell asleep before us men did. After the last movie, we just sat here talking and watching our women sleep."

She smirked and shook her head, kissed his sexy lips and stood to get coffee. She looked over the sea of bodies.

She whispered, "Wow, this is cool, isn't it?"

He nodded. "It's really cool."

They weaved their way through, making certain not to step on anyone. When they entered the kitchen, she bent and kissed Mary on the cheek, then Harry.

"Morning."

"Morning to you both. What time did all the men come upstairs?" Harry grinned at Gray.

"I guess around midnight. We watched movies and fell asleep."

Gray filled cups for himself and Sam and went around and refilled Harry and Mary's cups. She watched his backside as he made another pot, reminding herself once again how lucky she was.

Mary sighed. "I can't remember the last time all of my kids were sleeping under one roof, let alone my grandchildren, too. Except for Mori, everyone is here. We've been sitting here looking at you all and reflecting on how fortunate we are. It's a special moment for us this morning."

She turned to Gray, and they both nodded. "We were just saying the same thing, Mom. After the girls had fallen asleep last night, a couple of us were awake and talked about that same thing—Cole, Jamie, Josh, Jake, and I. We have women we love, everyone loves each other, no drama no bullshit. We enjoy spending time with each other. Last night for any other family would have been no men allowed and the women at the bar and vice versa, but with this group, we wanted to be together and laugh and talk and share. I don't think I've ever in my life had moments that make me feel like I do now."

They sat quietly and sipped their coffee and soon Jamie and Jessie came in and sat with them. Jessie hugged Sam and sat down next to her. Jamie got them each coffee and came and refilled everyone's mugs before sitting down.

He looked at Gray. "How will you know when the police apprehend Cheryl?"

Gray nodded toward David, who was just coming over to them.

"My office alerts me of any activity. Tank and Shauna are in the office right now. I'll go and check with them and see if there's any word."

David walked down the hall, and Mary asked, "Do you think we can have dinner at our house today or is it still too dangerous?"

Gray shrugged his shoulders. "When David comes back in we can ask him. Obviously, this isn't a good long-term solution. We don't know where Cheryl is and how long it will take to find her. Cheryl knew about the roses, and I told her that you and Dad had planted roses for Sam this year; I have no doubt that's why she cut them down. Other than the flowers, she didn't approach the house where you and Dad were, but I still wouldn't be comfortable with you two being there without security. We'll have to have someone from David's office stationed at your house until this is all over. But, still, we don't know her state of mind or how far she'll be willing to go. She knows we're getting married, but we didn't tell her when and we don't know how much she knows."

David walked back into the kitchen and went to the coffeepot to pour himself a cup. He looked over at everyone with the pot in his hand and raised it in question.

"The police haven't found her yet."

Gray asked David about dinner and suggestions for allowing Mary and Harry to go home and David said he would take care of it. Jessie leaned her head on Sam's shoulder.

Brushing Jessie's hair from her forehead, she whispered, "It'll be okay, you know."

Jessie nodded but didn't say anything. One by one, guests woke up and wandered into the kitchen. Mary, anxious for something to do, began pulling things from the refrigerator to make breakfast. Jessie jumped up to help her. When Sam started getting up, they both looked at her and told her to sit down.

"We told you, you wouldn't have to do anything, we have this. After all, it's still part of your bachelorette party."

She chuckled and sat back down. "Be my guest."

Mary and Jessie made a batch of fried potatoes, sausage, bacon, and scrambled eggs. As the food started cooking, the rest of the family wandered into the kitchen toward the aroma. Dani giggled and told the men Mary's dating stories of her and Harry and they all laughed. Even Harry, though his ears were tinted red. Breakfast was eaten, and everyone pitched in to clean up the messes from last night. Within an hour everything was clean, and people began leaving. David came in and said he had a security person coming to Gray and Sam's to take Mary and Harry to their house. There would be a security system installed, and that person would stay with them until this was all over. About an hour later, guess who walked in? Kent Logan was assigned to Mary and Harry. Harry rolled his eyes and Mary giggled.

David looked at Gray. "Is anything wrong with Kent?"

Sam giggled. "Mary thinks he's handsome and Harry's a little jealous."

David chuckled and nodded. "Oh."

Harry and Mary packed up and said they would see them in a few hours. They were excited to get home. They were going to need to learn how to use their new security system, and Mary just wanted to get home and check out her flowers. She hoped they would be able to save some of them.

Sam and Gray flopped on the sofa. Quiet was so wonderful after all that commotion. As nice as it was to have everyone around, it was a lot of activity. She leaned back and closed her eyes and let out a long sigh. Gray chuckled and did the same thing. They both fell asleep.

At eleven-thirty, they pulled into Harry and Mary's driveway. Tank was with them today and in good spirits. He was happy the way things worked out last night, and he wasn't stuck with the women like he was afraid he was going to be. He apologized to Sam; she laughed and said she completely understood his apprehension. As they walked into the house, Mary ran forward, excited.

"We have flowers; she didn't kill them all. You're going to have my flowers for your wedding."

She was talking excitedly, hands flailing, her breathing shallow. "Come on; I'll show you." Flanked by security, they walked to the gardens. Yes, there were a few roses Cheryl hadn't killed. Their bouquets wouldn't be as big as originally planned, but Sam would be able to carry them. The girls would each carry two, one champagne and one purple. Perfect. They would adopt the less-is-more attitude.

Mary said, "I'd like to sleep out in the garden in case that bitch comes back."

Whoa! Mary said bitch again. Sam pitied Cheryl if Mary found her before the police.

Dinner was a short affair. After last night, the family was tired, but in good spirits, especially since they knew Cheryl hadn't been able to take away the one thing Mary was so proud of for this wedding. Besides her son marrying the woman of his dreams, Mary wanted them to carry the flowers she lovingly grew for them. They ate, cleaned up, and went home.

She sighed. "I'm getting too old to stay awake till two in the morning and get up early and start again."

Gray chuckled. "It certainly has been a long few days—emotional and long—but nonetheless happy despite it all."

When they got home, Gray poured them each a glass of wine, and they went into the living room to sit on the sofa. Neither of them felt comfortable sitting out on the deck as they had gotten used to doing after coming home from Harry and Mary's. It was the first time they had been able to sit and just talk to each other.

The next day Sam conferenced with the office and got a lot of things taken care of. They had decided to promote one of the other paralegals, and she applauded their choice. They decided to Skype the following day for a mini training session. That left Sam able to go to the Kinkaide office with Gray.

He had some drafting to do, and she could spend time becoming familiar with the policies, procedures, employees, and the business-related things. They had licenses that needed to be renewed, basics on which vehicles the company owned and licensure. Then there was the demolition company. There was a little more involved with that because of some of the equipment involved. Heavier trucks meant DOT regulations and renewals. Jax could go over all of that with her.

The day flew by—she couldn't believe it when Gray told her it was time to go. She found a few things she needed to organize, dug through files and scanned in things that weren't scanned in for remote access. She was excited to get that much done. Tomorrow would be another day.

By Friday, she was tired. The week had been a whirlwind of meeting the employees, Skyping with the law office, learning how Gray ran the business and what he needed from her and where they were strong and where they were weak in the business. The fourth floor had gotten very little attention, but they'd gone up there a couple times over the week to eat lunch and look around to see where they left off. After they came back from their honeymoon, she wanted to get up there and finish some of the pieces for the new offices. They had one staff meeting this week with Ethan and two other architects in the office to discuss what was needed for the second and third floors. In addition, they'd need to come up with design ideas. Ethan said he'd take the lead with her ideas and when they return from their honeymoon they can see them. She was leaving at noon today to try on her dress and having lunch with Pam and Jessie. Gray insisted she take Tank along, even though there had been no word from Cheryl and no sightings. The police still hadn't found her and had no clue where she was. David was at the office with Gray, and they would meet back at the house.

Sam and the girls met at the Harmony House Inn for lunch. She wanted to treat them and spend some alone time with just the two of them. They'd had virtually no time together since Gray came into her life.

Jessie was madly in love with Jamie and told Sam and Pam all about their relationship. It was much different than Sam and Gray's. Jamie had loved Kathy very much and losing her had been incredibly hard. He wasn't sure he would ever get married again, or even have a one-on-one relationship. She said at first it was strained, but he had opened up with her these past few weeks, and she felt things were working out nicely. They were nowhere near getting married, but they both had fallen into a nice relationship. Jamie had finally told Jessie he loved her and she was very excited that he had taken that step.

Pam talked about Tom and their kids. They were remodeling parts of their house, and Pam was excited that she was finally going to be a first-time grandma.

"So, how do you feel about the whole Cheryl thing, Sam?"

She was waiting for that question. She figured Pam would get around to it sooner or later.

"Well, of course, it sucks. You know I have self-esteem issues anyway and knowing that Gray had a relationship with her for about a year bothered me, although I don't know why. He had a right to a life before me; I just have a hard time with stuff. I tend to compare myself to his past girlfriends and his ex-wife. They are both pretty women. I'm working on it, though. Anyway, the more we've learned about Cheryl, and the more crap she does makes it easier for me because I know without a doubt, he would never go back to her. The whole thing is crazy beyond belief."

Jessie stared at her for a long moment. "How many times have I told you that you are totally beautiful? You don't need to compare yourself to anyone."

She smiled. "I just have such a hard time feeling it in my heart."

Pam took Sam's hand and squeezed. "Let's not be morose on the day before Sam gets married to Gray."

"Agreed."

They finished their lunch and left for the bridal shop. Debra met them at the door. She looked Tank over a couple of times, and Sam smiled at her. "He's with me."

"Okay, well, I have your dress in dressing room number two."

Tank walked into the dressing room, looked around, and then came out to stand at the door. Jess and Pam were in other dressing rooms trying their dresses on.

Debra piped up, "It was as if that dress was made just for you, Sam. You're a beautiful bride."

"Thank you. I feel beautiful."

After undressing, Debra took Sam's dress and hung it and bagged it while she dressed. They paid for their purchases and walked out to get into the SUV.

"Do you guys have time to come back to the office with me and see the fourth floor?"

"Absolutely. I've heard so much about it. I'm dying to see it," Pam replied.

Entering Kinkaide & Associates, she lead them to Gray's office first. She opened the door to say hi and froze.

Suzanne sat in front of Gray's desk. He sat stone-faced and seemingly displeased. His eyes caught hers and his face completely transformed into the man she'd fallen in love with.

His voice was tight, "Sam, Suzanne came to congratulate us for tomorrow."

Sam stepped into the office, her friends in tow. Gray stood and met her halfway across the room. He kissed her tenderly, stepped back a half step and looked into her eyes. "How was lunch?"

As if remembering she was meeting friends, his eyes looked beyond her to the doorway. "Come on in, ladies. I hope you had a nice lunch."

She glanced at her friends, a soft smile on her lips. It was the first time she wasn't jealous when she was in a room with Suzanne. Not jealous at all.

Jessie's eyes darted between Suzanne and Gray. "It was wonderful. Of course, the company was fantastic." She bestowed a large smile on them both.

Pam stepped into the room, glanced at Suzanne then at Gray. "Sam's going to show us the fourth floor. Then, I've got to finish up a few things so tomorrow will be stress free."

Suzanne stood, the fake smile on her face looked as though her face would crack if she spoke, then she did. "I just came in to wish you both the best day tomorrow and congratulate you. The kids have kept me up to date on what has been going on and I'm very sorry for all you're going through. I also wanted to apologize for my prior behavior."

Sam raised a skeptical eyebrow. She wanted to apologize? What the hell was she up to?

She cleared her throat. "Thank you, Suzanne."

She wasn't going to go any further than that. She didn't know what Suzanne was up to, but she wasn't going to fall all over herself for her either.

"Okay then, I said what I came to say. I guess I'll go." She stepped forward as though she intended to hug Gray, but he stepped back. Suzanne stopped forward movement and gaped at him, which looked comical on her face. A slight shake of her head and she held her hand out to Sam. Gripping her hand in a firm handshake made Suzanne raise a brow. She smirked, and that was it. Suzanne turned and walked out the door.

Watching her walk out and close the door, Gray wrapped his arms around her waist from behind and laid his head on top of hers and rocked her back and forth.

"Are you okay?"

Sam took a deep breath. "Yes." She turned in his arms and looked deeply into his eyes. Long moments passed before she found the words. "How do you feel?"

His brows furrowed slightly. "Fine. Great." He leaned down and kissed her forehead. "I'm getting married tomorrow, so excellent."

His kissable lips parted in a smile and the breath caught in her throat. "I am too." She stepped back, but stopped and looked into his eyes. "I'm proud of you. You didn't let her manipulate you."

He winked and softly replied. "I'm proud of you too. You didn't let her get to you."

She stepped into his arms and wrapped hers around his waist. The close contact with him soothed the little bit of fraying her nerves had just suffered. Hearing Jessie clear her throat, she stepped back, a smirk on her face.

"Okay. Well, I brought Pam and Jess back to show them the fourth floor, so I'm going to take them up."

34

SECOND CHANCES SERIES

Gray peeked in on Sam. She'd fallen into bed as soon as they arrived home— poor baby was exhausted. She'd been running like crazy this past week trying to wrap up one job and get herself into a rhythm in her new job at Kinkaide & Associates. Not to mention bachelorette parties, wedding planning, and of course, Cheryl. She'd handled it all with grace and dignity. She just took it on the chin and kept moving forward. It was one of the things he loved so much about her—she just kept going. He'd fallen asleep with Sam in his arms thinking about how much he loved this woman. And he couldn't wait until tomorrow when she became his wife.

He sat on the edge of the bed, and gently brushed his fingers through her hair. "Hey baby, time to get up."

Her sweet eyes slowly opened and a sleepy smile stretched across her face. "Hey. What time is it?"

"Six-fifteen."

She sat up and scrambled to the edge of the bed. "Oh, my gosh, we're going to be late. Honey, you shouldn't have let me sleep so long."

"They can't rehearse without us—we're the bride and groom."

She nodded. "Yeah, but it doesn't look good that we ask everyone to be there and we show up late."

She trotted to the closet and pulled dress pants and a blouse from hangers. He chuckled as he stayed out of her way. He sat on the edge of the bathroom counter and watched her powder her face, add mascara, eyeliner, and lip gloss. She curled her hair and chatted with him while she got ready and his heart felt like it would burst from happiness. This is what he'd wanted his whole life. Just everyday things spent with a person he enjoyed talking to, sharing with, planning with.

They arrived at the church at five after seven. Not too bad. Pam and Jessie walked over to Sam and gave her a hug.

They continued walking into the church and up to the stage where they would stand while saying their vows. Mary and Harry were sitting in the front row. They each took a seat in a pew and waited as Caleb walked in with Pastor Jay. As soon as Pastor walked up to the stage, he turned and looked at their small group and smiled.

"Hello, everyone. Are you ready to rehearse tomorrow's nuptials?"

They nodded, and Pastor briefly explained how it would work. "Caleb, Jamie, and Gray will walk out in front of the stage and stand on the left of the stage facing the congregation. Once you are in place, Jessie, Pam, and then Sam and her boys will walk down the aisle. As the girls reach where the men are standing, the girls will grab their partner's arm and walk up on stage using the center steps," Pastor said, pointing along the path they would take.

"Once on stage, you will separate and walk to your respective sides of the stage." Pastor returned to stand in front of them.

"Now, shall we practice?"

They belonged to a community church which had a full-fledged band that usually played every Sunday. The band had agreed to come in for the weddings here tomorrow and play for each of them. Sam had sent the music over a couple days ago.

The girls and Sam's boys all walked to the back of the church. They were all walking her down the aisle. The groomsmen and Gray walked around to the side of the stage by the door leading out to the hallway where they would walk in. The pastor gave the signal and just then a door opened, and a man walked in with a guitar.

"Sorry, I'm a little late. I'll be here tomorrow with the band, but thought it would help a little to have the music to help you rehearse. If you don't mind, I thought I could play the guitar for you while you rehearse. My name is Jon Davis."

"That's very kind of you, Jon, and thank you very much. That will help a lot. I'm Sam."

Sam smiled at him, and he nodded his head at her and headed up to the stage. It only took him a couple of minutes to pull his guitar out and sit on a stool. He played the acoustic version of one of tomorrow's songs, Blake Shelton's "God Gave Me You." Gray picked it out for Sam for the processional. She'd never heard the song before, and he told her she would love it.

Jon started playing and singing the song.

Then Pam walked up the aisle.

Gage and Jake started walking up the aisle. Sam had worried that she wouldn't be able to walk down the aisle and not cry. The words of the song were the words Gray always said to her: "God made her for him."

Josh held out his arm to Sam, and they started walking down the aisle:

B ut I see you, before I ever knew you, before I ever knew you
I dreamed of you, I dreamed of you...

H e watched her walk toward him and tomorrow seemed so far away. The tears shining in her eyes gave away her emotion, the soft strains of the song with words he said to her often added to the moment.

When Josh and Sam stopped in front of him, he bent his head and looked into her eyes. "I knew you'd like this song. It's how I feel about you, Sam."

She swallowed in quick succession and only managed a nod. He held his arm out to her. She wrapped her arm through his, and they walked up on the stage.

G od gave me you, gave me you, He gave me you.

T hey stopped in front of Pastor Jay.
He reached into his pocket and handed Sam a tissue. He'd have to thank his mom for that tip. "Thought you might need this."

She chuckled and took the tissue, dabbing her eyes and nose.

"Thank you."

The pastor chuckled and leaned in to whisper, "Are you ready?"

Sam nodded and looked up at him.

"Okay."

Pastor Jay winked at her and took a step back. He ran through what he would say, when the next song would start, and when they would say their vows. They practiced their vows. They would give Gray's parents each two roses: one purple, one champagne. A final prayer would be said over the newly-married couple, and the recessional would play "A Better Life" by Keith Urban. Sam and Gray both thought it was the perfect song—happy, upbeat, and said so much about how they felt they'd have a better life! He knew it seemed corny, but if you can't be corny at your own wedding, when can you be?

They finished talking to Pastor Jay getting final instructions and when he wanted them at the church tomorrow. They thanked Jon for coming and playing for them, then headed to eat at Harmony House. David's team was there ahead of them, making sure everything was okay. Tank drove Sam and Gray. The poor man—he didn't get a lot of sleep. When they got there, a private room had been set up for their party. They sat and poured the wine that was on the table. As soon as everyone got a glass of wine, and non-alcoholic wine for the grand-kids and Ali, Harry stood.

"I want to make a toast to Gray and Sam."

He cleared his throat. "Gray, it goes without saying that your mother and I are so happy for you and Sam. We've watched you over the years, struggle with life, wanting something more, but not knowing what that was. We've worried about you, lost sleep over you, and prayed that the good Lord would hold you in his arms and bring you love and peace. And He did."

Harry turned to Sam. "Sam, when you walked into Gray's life, he changed ... his whole world changed. He was so excited when he told me he'd met you. His exact words were, 'I found her, Dad. I found the other half of my soul.'"

Harry's voice cracked. Sam's tears were flowing. Even Gray had tears in his eyes listening to his dad's toast.

"He knew the second he met you that you were his other half. He knew God made you for him, Sam. Mary and I couldn't be happier. I know I've told you this before, but welcome to the family. Josh, Gage, Jake, Tammy, Ali, Tracie, and of course, Abby and Dodge, welcome to the Kinkaide family. Cheers."

There were a few more toasts around the table. A lovely meal was served, and conversation flowed freely.

As the dessert dishes were cleared, Sam stood and cleared her throat. "You'll all need to bear with me while I try to say what I want to say."

Gray looked up at her and smiled and winked while he held her left hand.

"I don't know if there are words in the English language that can express how I feel about all of you. Of course, my children and grand-children, it goes without saying—I love you all so much. Pam and Jessie, without you ladies in my life, I would not have made it through my darkest days. Thank you; I love you both. The rest of you, Harry, Mary, Dani and Nick, Jamie, Ethan and Eva, Jax, Sarah and Cole, and Lily and Lincoln, Caleb, David, and Tank." Sam looked at Tank and winked.

Tank winked back and turned bright red.

"You all have been an amazing, loving, wonderful family and if I were to pick out of a catalog the family I would want to merge my family with, you are that family. I love you all and thank you for welcoming my family and me into your family. And Gray."

She looked into his eyes as he searched hers.

"Gray, when you walked into the office my world changed. The air I breathe is crisper, the colors I see are brighter, the sounds I hear are sharper, and the words I speak are more meaningful because I have you. You *are* the other half of me ... you make me whole. I love you."

He swallowed the lump that had formed and blinked back the tears that threatened. Standing he wrapped her tightly in his arms and breathed in the fresh scent of her hair. He prayed that this feeling that filled his heart—for the second time today—would never leave.

Soon the whistles and cheering interrupted their moment. He kissed her lips and they prepared to leave. Jessie teased, "Sam, you're going to come home with me tonight, right?"

Sam turned and looked at Jessie, a mischievous smile on her face. "The groom can't see the bride on the day of the wedding until she walks down the aisle."

Sam nodded her head. "Oh yeah, that's right. Well—"

"NO. You're sleeping with me. I don't care what the old wives' tales say."

The girls giggled.

When they got home, Sam set her purse down on the counter, and Gray swooped her up in his arms and carried her to the bedroom. Tank followed as far as the office while Gray and Sam continued to the bedroom.

"Gray, he's going to know what we're doing!" Sam whispered.

He laughed. "I've told you before. I don't care. If I want to make love to my wife, I'm going to make love to my wife."

Sam giggled. "I'm not your wife yet, you know."

"Close enough. Still can't wait for the paper, though."

He laid her on the bed and turned to close the door. He stared at her as he removed his tie. Laying it on the bed slowly his eyes raked over her body. He unbuttoned his shirt, pulling the bottom from his pants. Then he unfastened the button on his slacks and pulled the zipper down. Sam started to sit up and pull at the bottom of her blouse.

"No, lay there and wait for me."

She lay back down and turned, so she was lying on her side, with her head perched on her hand. He let his pants slide down his hips and hit the floor, hooked his thumbs in his boxer briefs and shimmied them down his hips and let them fall as well. A slow sexy smile spread across her face, and he marveled that she was settling in for what he wanted to do.

"Tonight, you get a show. Tomorrow night, I do."

"Really, what does that mean? I'm supposed to strip for you tomorrow night?"

He grinned. "I would love that. Would you strip for me tomorrow night?"

She hesitated for the briefest of moments. "I will do whatever you want me to do," she said breathily.

"Good to know. We'll see about the strip tease, I just might want to unwrap my wedding present myself, so maybe the strip tease will come later."

She chuckled. "You think I'm your wedding present?"

He leaned over her and pulled her up so she was sitting. He slowly unbuttoned her blouse to expose her pretty bra—light green with rhinestones and lace.

"Very pretty, Sam." He traced the lace line of her bra across her breasts enjoying the gooseflesh that rose in the wake of his finger. Dipping down between her breasts, he wiggled his finger under one heavy globe then swiped up over her nipple. He leaned down and kissed her lips softly. A moan escaped her as he nipped at her bottom lip.

He smiled. "You like that?"

"Yes," she sighed.

He repeated the action, then kissed his way down the side of her neck and gently nibbled at her shoulder. He reached around and unclasped her bra strap, pulled the bra from her shoulders, and threw it to the floor on top of his pants. He lowered her down to the bed and nipped his way from her jaw to her breasts. She sighed as he pinned her nipple between his teeth and flicked his tongue over the rigid tip.

He slid his arm under her lower back and lifted her just enough so he could pull her pants over her hips, then tossing them onto the growing pile of clothes on the floor.

As he reached for her panties, a sly smile formed her lips. "Don't you think we should do this tomorrow?"

"Nope. Tonight, I'm going to make love to you for the last time as a single man and you a single woman. Tomorrow night, I'll make love to you as my wife. You'll never again have sex as a single woman, Sam. I want you to remember this."

He slid her panties down her legs, slowly brushing his palms along her flesh as he did. After he tossed her panties on top of their clothing on the floor, he slowly slid his hands up her legs stopping at her hips. He pulled her to the edge of the bed and slid his fingers down to her ankles. He propped her heels on the edge of the bed, so her knees were bent and put his hands on the inside of her thighs and slowly pushed them open so she was fully exposed to him.

"So pretty, Sam. You have the prettiest pussy. I love it. I love tasting it. I love touching it. I love sliding into it."

He bent down and licked from her opening all the way up to her clit, swirled his tongue around a few times and sucked it into his mouth, flicking it with his tongue while holding it between his lips. She moaned loudly, so he repeated his actions loving the sound of her moans, dipping his tongue into her pussy and flicking it around he listened for her sexy voice.

He drove his tongue into her a few more times while circling her clit with his fingers. He licked back up to her clit and slid two fingers into her pussy at the same time.

"You're so wet for me baby ... I love how wet you get for me."

Her voice deepened. "Gray, I won't make it long like this."

He chuckled against her clit and licked her with the tip of his tongue then flattened his tongue as he applied pressure to her clit.

"Gray." She quivered at the continued onslaught of pleasure.

She reached down and dug her fingers into his hair. He pumped his fingers in and out of her and sucked on her clit until she exploded. She cried out his name as the spasms hit her. She hung onto his hair as he continued licking to extend her pleasure. As she began to relax from her orgasm, he stood and slipped his aching cock into her still-spasming pussy.

She moaned. "God Gray, you feel so good when you slide inside of me."

He closed his eyes. "Yes, I do feel good sliding inside of you. You fit me like a glove." A shiver skittered down his back as her warmth surrounded his cock. The sounds of their mating were the most beautiful piece of music he'd ever heard. Her moist pussy welcoming him inside was heaven. He opened his eyes and watched himself slide into her and then back out, and as if it were remotely possible, his cock hardened. He ground out, "Look at me, Sam." She opened her eyes. "Look at me slide into you."

She leaned up on her elbows and watched their mating. A breath escaped her lips as she watched, then she slowly looked into his eyes. "Beautiful." Her breathy exclamation stole his breath.

He rocked his hips forward, increasing the pace as his climax neared. He held her knees and intensified his thrusts. His skin was coated in perspiration as his movements stole his breath. She lay back and looked into his sexy eyes.

"Give it to me, Gray. Everything you've got, I want it."

He nearly lost consciousness; he was so stunned. Black dots floated in front of his eyes, his breathing came in staccato gusts, his fingers tightened on her knees, and he thrust into her with the power of a mad bull. His orgasm sped through him so powerfully he thought he'd pass out. The first spurt felt like fire, and he felt her clinch him as she cried out his name. He froze as he emptied himself into her, his heart trying to catch up. She shuddered, and he was frozen in place watching the emotions play across her face, her eyes glassy. Then she softly smiled up at him and whispered, "Holy hell."

35

S am woke up to the smell of coffee and light kisses on the back of her neck. She smiled and stretched before opening her eyes. As she stretched, she felt the bed dip and Gray's arms slide around her and pull her close. She wiggled her naked bottom against his rigidness. Mmm, that felt good. She wiggled again.

"If you keep doing that, I'm going to slide inside of you and have my way with you. I wasn't going to make love to you this morning. I was going to wait until tonight, but if you keep doing that, I won't be able to wait."

She giggled. "Sorry, I'll behave. You told me last night that it was the last time we would make love as single people. I don't want to make you a liar."

He chuckled in her ear. "Drink your coffee, baby; we have to get going soon. I want to talk to David and see if there's any word on Cheryl. If the police haven't found her, I want to run through the safety precautions for today."

He kissed the side of her head and rolled out of bed.

He leaned over and smacked her ass. "Don't make me wait, baby."

She sighed. "I hope you aren't going to be a bossy husband!"

She heard him chuckle as he left the bedroom.

At eight twenty-two, they walked into Tattoos by Ray to get their marks. Gray told her that he'd come in last week with the font his grandfather had made by an artist so they'd have the time to make up the marks for them. Harry kept the font in a safe at home and only brought it out when someone was ready to use it. She was amazed that he had been doing all this work to prepare for their wedding. He never said a word and never made a big deal out of it—he just quietly did what was needed.

She wrapped her arms around his waist and pulled him close. "Thank you for doing all the prep work. I didn't realize—I could have helped."

He chuckled against the top of her head. "Sam, this was such a pleasure for me. I've dreamed of this forever—about meeting my other half and being able to walk into a tattoo parlor to get marked with her. We're only breaking tradition a little. The tradition is you get marked on your honeymoon so you can show it off when you get home. But you mentioned something while making wedding plans about getting our marks this morning. I want pictures taken of us today with our wedding clothes on and our marks on our arms. I can't even begin to tell you how excited I've been for today—all my dreams coming true. And, it's because of you, Sam."

Her eyes filled with tears. He just crushed her with his capacity of love for her.

She choked back a sob. "Oh, Gray, I love you so much. You make my dreams come true, too. I didn't grow up like you did, knowing there was someone out there to complete me. But I *did* hope over the years that I would be with someone who would love me unconditionally, make me feel whole and beautiful. I found that in you."

His arms tightened around her.

"Okay, save it for later. You guys have tattoos to get." Dave, their tattoo artist, laughed.

"If you guys want to come in the back, we're ready for you. Darren and I are going to do your tattoos."

Gray shook Dave's hand and introduced Sam. She shook Dave's hand and followed him to the back where Darren was finishing the setup of their stations. They were directed to chairs that looked like padded chaise lounges. They sat facing each other, and the chairs were positioned so they could hold onto each other with their right hands. She was a little nervous, yet excited. Gray was just excited. He winked at her as he sat back into his chair; his fingers sought hers and held tight. The stencils were placed on their arms, and they were asked to look at them and make sure they were in the perfect spot. Both agreed they were perfect and the machines started. Tank watched from the corner, and occasionally, he would walk over and wink at her and nod at Gray.

At one o'clock, she was in the changing room at church with all the girls as they dressed for the wedding. The excitement in the room was palpable. Her hair was done—she'd done it herself. Her makeup was applied. Sarah had wanted to do it for her and did a beautiful job. It made her look ten years younger with smoky eyes and the green of her irises popped with the silver, gray, and champagne colors Sarah used. She wore fingerless gloves to hide her mark until they were pronounced man and wife. She didn't want to put her dress on until just a few minutes before she walked down the aisle, so she helped everyone else with their hair and dressing.

The photographer walked in and asked if he could take a few pictures. He took pictures of her helping the girls with their hair— pictures of each family member and the bridesmaids. So many she couldn't wait to see them.

At one-thirty Mary told her it was time to get her dress on. She removed her robe and stepped into her dress while Pam and Jessie held it for her. She slipped the straps onto her shoulders, and Jessie zipped the back. She turned to the mirror and had to blink fast to keep the tears at bay; she didn't want to cry her makeup off so soon. The room was quiet. She turned to look at everyone and saw the emotions on their faces.

Mary held her hands over her heart. "Sam, honey, you look so beautiful."

"Thank you, Mary."

Jessie bubbled with joy. "Oh. My. God. I can't wait to see the look on Gray's face when you walk down the aisle. Please wait until we get all the way down so I can watch him."

Then Jess turned to the photographer. "Make sure you have the camera on Gray's face when he sees Sam. It'll be priceless."

The women laughed. There was a knock on the door, and Jax stepped in.

He looked at her and froze. "Holy hell, you look amazing, Sam!"

She laughed. "Thanks, Jax."

He raised his brows and cleared his throat. "Um, it's time."

She nodded and smiled. "Thanks, we'll be right up."

He nodded and backed from the room.

Mary walked over to the long white box she had brought in earlier. As she opened the lid, the aroma of roses filled the room. She pulled the flowers carefully from their resting place, one grouping at a time. She and Dani had worked on the flowers last night after rehearsal. The gorgeous corsages were purple and champagne roses, mostly buds, but delicate and perfect. The baby's breath tucked into them allowed them more size and the purple ribbons trailing from them added color.

She walked to Mary. "May I pin your corsage on you?"

Mary sobbed. "Oh. Yes, please."

Carefully pinning the delicate flowers to her future mother-in-law, she swallowed the sob fighting for attention. "Thank you so much, Mary, for these beautiful flowers and for making all the flower arrangements for everyone today. They're beautiful."

Mary nodded, tears shining in her eyes. She reached into the box and pulled out her bridal bouquet. Her breath caught in her throat—it was stunning! There were seven champagne roses nestled together with baby's breath interspersed, and five purple roses tucked in between the champagne roses. The long stems were wrapped with a champagne-colored ribbon to hold them all together, and the ribbon trailed all the way to Sam's knees.

The only thing she could say was, "Oh ..."

Mary patted her shoulder and whispered, "Don't say anything. The look on your face is enough, and we don't want to cry off our makeup." She swiped under her eyes. "My friends came to the rescue when I called upon them. The grower who had the champagne roses in the first place overnighted me these for you. My gardening friends are so very special."

Mary kissed her cheek and turned to give Pam and Jessie their bouquets, consisting of three long-stemmed roses—two champagne and one purple—with baby's breath. They had purple ribbons wrapped around the long stems, and the ribbon trailed to the hems of their dresses.

They each hugged Sam and walked from the room leaving her with Jessie and Pam for a couple quiet moments, while they waited for the girls to take their seats.

She let out a long breath. "I'm getting married in a couple of minutes, you guys."

Jessie jumped up and down. A squeal pierced the air.

Pam hugged her tight. "You deserve to be happy, Sam. I love you, and I'm so damn happy for you. I'm happy for Gray, too. He's getting a fabulous woman."

She hugged Pam back, wrapping her arms tightly around her best friend, the woman who had been with her through thick and thin. "I love you, Pam. Thank you for being there for me all of these years. When I needed you, you were there. I'll always need you in my life, though hopefully, all the sad days are behind us. I'm so happy you're with me today when I marry the man of my dreams ... my true soul mate."

She turned to Jessie. "Jess, thank you for being here with me, for being my friend. Thank you for all of your advice and encouragement over the years. I love you."

Jessie took a deep breath. "Dammit, Sam, you're making me cry."

Jessie wiped her eyes the best she could without smearing her makeup. "I love you, too, Sam. Thank you for being my friend. Thank you for introducing me to Jamie, even though you didn't even know you did. Thank you for everything."

"Mom, you have to go get married." Josh stood in the doorway. "Wow, you look amazing, Mom! Gray's going to flip."

She laughed. "Okay, let's go get me married."

Standing in the front entrance to the church, she took a deep breath. The music started.

Jessie walked down the aisle, and she took another deep breath. She didn't want to cry; she wanted to smile. She was happy. She was marrying Gray.

Pam walked down the aisle next. From behind Gage and Jake, she snuck a peek at Gray. He was so handsome. He was perfect in his champagne tux, the purple shirt the same color as the girl's dresses and the purple tie. He looked like perfection. His hair was combed back with the length hitting the back of his collar and curling up. She loved how his hair curled up in the back. The front had a slight wave to it, and the little lock of hair that always fell forward on his forehead was there just calling to her to move it back. She grinned.

"Ready?" She looked up to see Gage and Jake looking back at her.

"Yeah, I'm *so* ready."

Gage and Jake began walking. She and Josh waited until they had walked several feet in front of them, then she and Josh began. When she walked into the church, she heard the audible sighs and gasps when people saw her. It made her smile that they thought she was beautiful. She looked at a few faces and smiled at the family members and friends who had gathered on such short notice to celebrate with them. Mr. and Mrs. Koepple had made the trip as well—how fitting.

Unable to resist any longer, she looked up at her future, the bewildered look on his face and the glistening in his eyes threatened to break her down, but she refused to cry today.

There's more here than what we're seeing, a divine conspiracy.

They stopped at the end of the aisle before Gray. Their eyes were locked on each other—it seemed no one else existed.

Josh nudged Gray. "Take care of her. We love her."

Gray glanced at Josh and shook his hand. "I promise you with everything I have in me; I'll take care of her, love her, and protect her."

Josh nodded at Gray, then turned and looked at Sam. "We love you, Mom."

She hugged her boys. "I love you all, too. Thank you."

Gray held out his arm, and she wrapped hers around it as they walked up the steps to the stage.

Pastor Jay cleared his throat. "Ladies and gentlemen, welcome ..."

The pastor read a prayer and spoke a few words, but she wasn't listening to the words, she was looking at Gray. Then the music started for the next song "All for Love," by Bryan Adams, Sting, and Rod Stewart. They each picked one song, and they chose their recessional together. This was her pick for him. She watched his face as the words floated over them, the gooseflesh on her arms created a slight shiver.

W hen it's love you give, I'll be a man of good faith, then in love you live...

S he smiled at him. "Do you like it, Gray?" she whispered.

His eyes watered. He swallowed and nodded. "I love it Sam ... it's perfect for us."

She grinned and nodded. She hadn't been sure she could keep the song a secret, but she did.

W hen it's love you make, I'll be the fire in your night,
        When it's love you take, I will defend, I will fight...
    That it's all for one and all for love, Let the one you hold be the one you want...

. . .

G ray turned to her and pulled her close, he swayed with her, then danced across the stage with her in his arms. She could feel his heartbeat against her chest as he held her close; his hand shook as he held hers. She blinked rapidly and swallowed. After taking a couple of deep breaths, she could calm herself. She looked into his eyes again and saw love. Perfect.

When the song ended, Gray, leaned down and kissed her very gently. She smiled and squeezed his hand.

The pastor cleared his throat, and they turned to face him.

"That's the first time a bride and groom danced during a song, but certainly a memorable moment."

They heard some chuckles, and she glanced over at Pam, who was wiping her eyes and grinned back at her.

They said their vows, exchanged rings and the pastor said, "You may kiss your bride ... again."

He reached over and put his hand on the back of Sam's head, his other hand went around her waist and pulled her close. She reached up and wrapped her arms around his neck. They kissed, tasting each other, loving the feel of the other, tongues searching and reaching. Neither of them cared they were in church in front of all their family and friends. They heard people cheering and more than a few whistles.

He lifted his head and grinned. "You're my wife, Sam."

She smiled back. "Yes, that sounds wonderful. You're my husband, Gray. That sounds even better."

Pastor Jay cleared his throat and introduced them. "Ladies and gentlemen, I am proud to introduce you to Mr. and Mrs. Grayson Kinkaide."

The congregation clapped and whistled again. Gray leaned down and kissed her once more.

Harry joined them on stage. He cleared his throat and smiled at them when they pulled away from each other. He kissed her on the cheek and shook Gray's hand.

"Congratulations, you two."

He winked at her and turned to face the congregation. They watched him, their brows furrowed—they hadn't rehearsed this. Gray just smiled and winked.

"It's tradition in the Kinkaide family to wear the mark of your soul mate, your spouse. The mark is your spouse's initials on your left forearm."

Harry rolled up his sleeve to show his mark. There were some sighs, and a few people clapped.

"Typically, the newly married couple ..." he turned and looked at Gray "... waits until they're on their honeymoon to get their marks. But Gray couldn't wait."

He smiled and everyone in the congregation who knew what they had just been through chuckled.

"So, I stand here to introduce you once again to Mr. and Mrs. Grayson Kinkaide and ask them to unveil their marks."

She glanced at the smile on Gray's face and shook her head. She handed Pam her flowers and began pulling off her fingerless gloves to show her mark to the congregation.

Gray glanced down at her arm and swallowed. "It looks perfect on you, baby."

She smiled. "I think so, too."

He shrugged out of his jacket and finished rolling up his sleeve showing his arm to the congregation. Loud cheers rose into the air.

After they had greeted their guests in the reception line, they went up front to take pictures. Gray wanted a special picture taken. He asked her, Dani and Nick, Harry and Mary, and Sarah and Cole to come up on stage. The photographer had Harry sit on a chair and Mary on his lap. He had she and Gray to their left and a little behind them. Dani and Nick were to the right and slightly behind Harry and Mary. Sarah and Cole were in the middle behind Harry and Mary. The photographer instructed them all in what he wanted.

The husband should put his left arm around his wife and hold her left hand, showing their marks. He wanted them to lean in so he could get a picture of the married couples with their marks. Then, he wanted just she and Gray, standing outside the church on the grounds, with the woods behind them. There was a slight breeze, so her dress billowed out perfectly. Gray stood behind her, took her left hand with his left hand and they showed their marks. They looked down at them when the picture was taken. It was sure to be another great picture—one that Gray said he wanted to have enlarged and hung above the fireplace in their living room.

The reception was a happy occasion. Sam had worried throughout the day that Cheryl would show up and ruin it, but so far, the security team hadn't seen hide nor hair of her. They were all dressed like guests and blended well, but always on the lookout. They had opted out of a Grand March and decided to have a dance for all the couples in the family instead. They danced with each other first.

"What a fabulous day, Gray. I couldn't be happier. I'm a married woman now." She glanced around and then whispered. "Rumor has it, my husband is going to ravage me later when we get home. I'm beyond excited."

He nodded. "Your source of information is correct. Your husband *is* going to ravage you."

He twirled her on the dance floor. "We're not going home tonight, Sam. We're leaving here in about an hour to get on a plane. We should start saying our goodbyes."

Her brows raised. "We're getting on a plane? I didn't pack anything, Gray. Where are we going? How long are we going to be gone?"

He laughed. "We're going to be gone for two weeks. I'm not telling you where we're going. You'll have to wait and see. And, I told you, I would pack for you. Everything is on the plane. I have a client who owns a private plane, and his wedding gift to us is the use of it."

"Wow. I don't know what to say."

Gray kissed her forehead. "Say goodbye to everyone so we can leave. I'll come with you. I need to be alone with you ... soon."

Tank drove them to the airport, pulling into a private hangar. Tank stepped out of the SUV first.

"Let me check with security on the plane and make sure we're good before you get out."

Tank walked to the plane, and the door opened to allow him to slip inside.

Gray whispered, "Are you happy, baby?"

She laughed. "I'm delirious. Of course, that could be all the wine I drank, but at any rate, I'm delirious." She laughed at the look on his face.

"Good. I like you delirious."

Tank opened the door, and they climbed out.

"All is good; we can take off."

They walked up the steps of the plane. The pilot and stewardess were there to greet them. She was surprised at the opulence of the plane. Cream-colored seats and dark wood tables and trim work. There was a sofa on one side and tables surrounded by chairs on the other side. Gray directed Sam to one of the chairs in front of a table, and he sat next to her.

"Until the pilot gives us the all clear, we need to sit here. Once we're up in the air, we'll head back to the bedroom where I intend to keep my promise and ravage you."

He winked and chuckled.

Her brows rose into her hair. "Holy cow! There's a bedroom on-board?"

He smiled. "Gregory invited me over this week to give me a tour of the plane and show me where everything was. He wanted us to enjoy this and asked me to extend his congratulations to you."

"Wow, what an amazing gift."

"He's a great client. I've designed several buildings for him over the years."

After takeoff, the stewardess came over and asked them if they wanted something to drink.

Gray nodded. "Yes, we would both like a glass of white wine."

Her brows furrowed.

Gray smiled. "We're taking our wine to the bedroom, where I intend to drink it off of you."

She giggled. "That sounds fun! When are you telling me where we're going?"

He leaned over and kissed her. "You'll find out later."

The stewardess brought them their wine, and Gray lifted his glass. "I want to make a toast. Samantha Kinkaide ..." His smiled was a sight to behold. "I love you beyond belief. I've been half a man my entire life, but today I'm whole. I'm so happy, for lack of a better word, that you are in my life. You are my life. Thank you, Sam, for making me whole."

She swiped at the pesky tear that slid down her cheek. She shook her head but couldn't say anything because of the lump in her throat. Gray looked over at Tank, who was sitting at the next table. "Tank, you're off duty while we're on the plane, so feel free to enjoy a drink or snack or just sleep. We'll be in the air for a while now."

Tank nodded and smiled. "Thank you, Gray. Congratulations to you and Mrs. Kinkaide." He grinned and winked at Sam.

A little while after takeoff, the pilot told them they could move around the cabin. Gray stood and reached for her hand.

"Bring your wine, baby, and come with me."

She stood and grabbed her glass of wine, following him to the bedroom, her cheeks tinted bright red.

He must have sensed her hesitation because he looked back and shook his head. "I've told you before; I don't care what anyone else thinks. I want you, and I've waited all day for this. Especially after this morning. I've been thinking about that all day."

She giggled. "Sorry."

The bedroom was equally as gorgeous as the rest of the plane. The bed had a cream-colored duvet with cream, gold, and light tan pillows were thrown about. The furniture was all dark cherry, making the contrast even more pronounced. She had never seen anything like it. He turned to her after closing the door, took the wineglass from her hand, and set it on the bedside table. He walked back to her and kissed her softly. He lifted her left arm and kissed her mark, never taking his eyes from hers.

"I love this. You'll never know how many times I dreamed about this or what it means to me that you're wearing my mark."

Gray kissed her again, tasting her, their tongues clashing and rolling together. She moaned loudly, and he deepened the kiss, sliding his arms around her and smoothing his hands across her back.

"This dress is absolutely perfect. I loved looking at your back all night. I loved touching it every time I put my arm around you—very, very sexy."

He ran his finger very slowly along the lace on each side of the back of her dress and up over her shoulders and back down the front. When his finger reached the V in the front of her dress, between her breasts, he stopped and looked into her eyes.

"I'm the luckiest man alive."

He slid his hand into her dress and massaged her breast.

"Actually, I'm the luckiest woman alive. Gray, you have surpassed any fantasy I've ever had about romance and love."

She reached up and unbuttoned his shirt. When they were unbuttoned to his waistband, she opened his shirt and kissed his chest. She heard him inhale deeply and she smiled against his chest and kissed him again. The coarse hairs tickled her lips, but she continued showering him with kisses until she reached a nipple. She sucked his nipple into her mouth and flicked it with her tongue. He groaned and held her shoulders.

"I'm supposed to be seducing you."

She laughed. "You did—you do, every day. You are as much my present as I am yours, Mr. Kinkaide."

"Turn around, Sam, and let me take this beautiful dress off. I want what's under it."

She turned, giggling. Gray unzipped the short zipper and slid his hands up her back to her shoulders. He slid his fingers under the straps of the dress at her shoulders and pulled them off, letting the dress fall to the floor in a pool of lace at her feet. His breathing quickened when he saw her lingerie. She wore a champagne lace thong with a tiny little bow at the top of her butt, thigh-high stockings with little bows at the back and front, and the sparkly, sexy shoes she'd purchased for the Downtown Harmony event.

He walked around her, the admiration on his face apparent. He softly ran his fingers around the lacy champagne colored bra with the deep V in the front, which pushed her breasts up, showing them off like prized jewels.

"God, you're sexy," he husked.

He ran the back of his fingers across the swell of her breasts. He looked lower and saw the front of her panties were a light lace, see-through with the same tiny little bow at the top. He ran his hand down her flat stomach and touched the little bow and saw something sparkle and move when he touched it. He touched it again and saw the heart-shaped charm dangling from the little bow. His eyes sought hers, a brow arched. She smirked as he reached down and held the charm between his thumb and forefinger. He dropped to his knees and read the inscription: *I love you, Gray.*

He looked into her eyes and swallowed. "I love you, Sam."

He placed both hands on her hips and pulled her forward and kissed her stomach, her navel, and trailed kisses down to the top of her panties. Slowly, he slid her panties over her hips and let them fall into the pile of lace at her feet. He slid his hands forward just enough that his thumbs touched her clit. He rubbed a few circles over her button, then he parted her folds with his thumbs and licked.

She reached down and slid her fingers into his hair; the soft silky strands felt good between her fingers.

"Gray." It came out breathless and whisper light.

He held one of his hands up. "Step out of your dress, baby."

Sam took his hand in hers and stepped to the side.

Once she had cleared the pile of lace on the floor, he wrapped his fingers around one of her ankles and held it. "Spread your legs for me, Sam."

She moved her other leg, so she was spread open for him. She still wore her stockings and heels. He sat back just a little and assessed her.

"Look at yourself, Sam. So sexy ... open and waiting for me."

He leaned forward again and sucked her clit into his mouth and flicked it with his tongue, making her gasp.

He slid two fingers into her pussy and let out a breath. "God, I can feel you quivering with my fingers. That is so damn hot!"

He pulled his fingers out and pushed them back in a few times, and each time, she thought she'd explode. She pushed against his fingers and tightened the grip in his hair. "Gray, please."

He pumped his fingers faster, increased the pressure of his sucking, and she exploded. He pulled out his fingers and continued to suck her creamy sweetness as he plunged his tongue deeper inside.

"You taste so fucking good." He lapped at her furiously.

Kissing his way up her body, he tightened his hold on her. She was grateful as her knees had begun to shake. He kissed her stomach, kissed up to each breast, the tops of each mound and ran his tongue over each. He kissed his way to her mouth by way of her neck. His mouth claimed hers and their tongues danced and mated.

When they needed air, he pulled away just a little. "See how good you taste ... delicious."

She hung onto his shoulders and watched his lips as his tongue swiped across her breasts in one fluid motion.

"Walk over to the bed and bend over it so that sweet little pussy is open for me. We're just getting started."

She walked the few steps to the bed and slowly bent over it. Excitement bubbled in her chest, desire making her extremities tingle.

His deep, sexy voice slid over her, "Slide your legs open wide, sweetheart, and put your hands behind your back."

She eagerly did as she was told, loving the new adventures he took her on when they ventured into this sexual play. He removed his tie and wrapped it around her wrists. She tested the tightness; it wasn't bad. The soft silk felt cool on her skin.

"You're so beautiful, Sam. Look at you bent over with your legs spread with your heels on and my tie binding your hands. Perfect."

She felt his palms slide up her legs to her ass. He squeezed each full globe with his hands, massaging them. His thumbs pulled her open, and she felt his tongue, hot and firm, sliding into her pussy. A loud groan escaped her. He slid his tongue further into her pussy, in and out, fucking her with his tongue. He slid one palm between her and the bed and found her clit rubbing circles over it while continuing to tongue her entrance. It was so erotic that she began to tremble. The heat built fast and she exploded in his mouth.

Her ragged voice sounded foreign to her, "Gray, that feels incredible."

Then she felt him lick all the way up and over her anal entrance. "Oh."

She heard a zipper, and his pants hit the floor. She could hear clothes rustling and more clothing dropping. She heard a drawer open and close and something squirt. She felt pressure at her anal opening as Gray rubbed around it.

"Open up for me baby, let me in."

Sam tried to relax as she felt Gray push his thumb into her ass.

"So pretty."

Then she felt his cock slide into her pussy with one push.

"Oh, Gray," she huffed out. The emotions running rampant through her were dizzying. Her skin felt like she was on fire, the multiple sensations from her husband pleasuring them both almost overwhelming.

"Gray ... baby ..."

He sucked in a breath. "Let go, baby ... come for me again."

She moaned out her pleasure, and he thrust harder and faster. She closed her eyes as the fire roared through her, her climax racing toward its end. She cried out. It hit so fast she heard his ragged voice in exclamation—though unintelligible—then his long groan as he pushed into her and froze, spilling himself into her.

36

"Wake up baby; we're about to land." He kissed the top of her head, resting sweetly on his shoulder.

She lifted her head, her sleepy eyes locked on his. "You need to buckle up again, sweetheart."

She sighed and nodded.

"Everything all right?" he asked.

She leaned her head against the back of the seat. "Yes, I just can't believe it's over so soon."

They'd spent two amazing weeks in Tuscany, Italy on the outskirts of town in a private villa with a housekeeper/cook named Bianca, and her husband Tony, who was the caretaker of the villa. Tony and Bianca had a little house on the property. They were in their early sixties and had lived at the villa and worked there for forty years. Their children had grown and gone. They had eight grandchildren and were expecting another.

Bianca was an amazing cook, and Sam had learned to make some great meals. Bianca sent her home with the recipes and plenty of tips. They had spent one full day cooking with Bianca at the villa because it was raining and they were tired from running around every day. Needing a restful day, Sam had asked Bianca during breakfast if she would share a few recipes. Bianca smiled and agreed to show them a few tricks. They spent the day cooking, and they had a fabulous day. They drank wine the whole day, sipping as they cooked. By the end of the day, they both had plenty of wine and food and were exhausted. They went to bed early, made love, and fell asleep. Probably one of his favorite days on their honeymoon.

After Bianca made breakfast each day, she left the house until he and Sam left. If they didn't leave, she would come into the villa through the kitchen and make lunch and leave again until it was time to make supper.

The villa was spectacular, boasting a library with floor-to-ceiling bookshelves containing any book you'd ever want to read. The den was very warm and inviting—the old wooden desk faced the doorway to the room. There was plenty of space on the desk for spreading out work as well as a credenza with equal space. Across the room sat a smaller table and chairs for meetings or work.

The living room was old-world Italian furnished with beautiful overstuffed furniture and an antique armoire hiding a modern television set. Three spacious bedrooms, with ornate pieces of wooden furniture and two bathrooms, each had showers to die for and top-of-the-line fixtures. The kitchen was massive and was filled with the best quality appliances and modern fixtures. They bought several cases of wine and had it sent home, as well as souvenirs for the entire family and a few pieces of art for the house.

Tank made himself scarce, though Gray spoke with him each day, checking to see if the police had found Cheryl. It had already been five weeks, and Cheryl was nowhere to be seen.

He glanced over at his new wife and smiled as she watched with rapt attention as their plane descended to the runway in Harmony. "Where are you, Sam?"

She chuckled and turned to lock eyes with him. "Still on our honeymoon. It was absolutely the best trip I've ever been on, Gray. I loved having you to myself and spending every day with you. Thank you again for such a wonderful surprise."

He laughed. "You'll be with me every day for the rest of your life,

Sam, count on it. But, it's you that should be thanked. That was the best trip I've ever been on. In all of my dreams of finding my soul mate and honeymooning with her, I never could have dreamed what we just experienced. It was beyond wonderful."

A couple hours later, Tank pulled into the driveway of their home. It was Sunday morning, and they had about three hours until they were expected at Gray's parents' for lunch to see everyone and tell them about their honeymoon.

David was there when they walked in and greeted them both with smiles and hugs. David asked them to sit at the kitchen table so he could update them on the activity since they'd been gone. He watched Sam bustle around the kitchen, making drinks for everyone —iced tea and water—and settle at the table next to him to hear what David had to say.

Basically, the police had frozen Cheryl's accounts, so she had no money. Amanda was singing like a bird to save her own hide, and she knew the names of a couple of friends that police had spoken to and were also watching to see if they might be helping Cheryl.

Right now, things kept working as they had been before the wedding. They would have security always, and the family members now had security systems in place at all their homes. Tammy and Sarah were to be very careful when taking the kids anywhere, and preferably, not alone. Either Josh or Cole needed to be with them when they went with the kids, or they were to call one of David's people to come with them until the threat of Cheryl was over. Harry and Mary had the security system and still had someone on the premises staying with them since Cheryl had already proven she wasn't afraid to go there. It was unlikely she would return after destroying the roses, knowing they were likely onto her. But, given her state of mind and possibly feeling as though she had nothing to lose, anything was possible, so they wanted to be vigilant always.

Sam was tired and headed to the bedroom to take a nap. He smiled as he watched her little ass round the corner and down the hall. Unable to control himself, he rose from the table to join her. He closed the door behind him and sat on the edge of the bed to slip his shoes off. He turned to lie down next to her and saw she was smiling.

"What are you smiling at?"

Sam sighed. "You. I was just thinking it's too bad we can't have children together—they would be beautiful."

He turned onto his side and rested his head in one hand brushing his fingers along her cheek with the other.

"I've thought about that so many times, Sam. I've been mad at God for not allowing us to meet when we were younger. I would love to see you swollen with my child. It's one of the things that makes me sad to think about."

"Aww, Gray, thank you for that, but please don't be sad. God did allow us to meet and we're good. We can't be angry at what could have been. Let's just enjoy what is now and look forward to our future together."

She kissed Gray softly and sighed.

He pulled her tightly to him and closed his weary eyes.

A couple hours later, they were driven into his mom and dad's driveway. He looked over at her, a grin on his face. "Ready?"

She giggled. "Ready!"

They walked hand in hand into the house and were the first family there. He enjoyed that—he liked being first and having his mom and dad to himself for just a few minutes before the craziness started. Once Lily, Lincoln, Abby, and Dodge arrived, it was hard to carry on a conversation. They hugged his parents and took seats at the counter to regale them with tales of Italy. Mom pulled out wineglasses from the cupboard and held one up to him; he nodded. Harry shook his head no, so she pulled out three glasses. She poured them each a glass and handed them over and began cutting up vegetables for lunch.

Mom furrowed her brows when Sam offered to help cut vegetables. Gray chuckled and kissed the side of his wife's face. She always offered.

"So, tell us about your honeymoon, kids. Where did you go? What did you do? The PG version, please," Mom teased.

He laughed, and Sam blushed a bright red. He began telling his parents all about Italy, the villa they stayed in, and the wineries they toured. Sam interjected where appropriate, but mostly she listened. He was so happy to be sharing this with them after all they'd all been through.

Soon, the other Kinkaides arrived. Sam's boys and their families were considered honorary Kinkaides now, so they were all there as well. So many hugs, kisses, and much excitement. They handed out the gifts they'd purchased in Italy. It was fun to watch family members receive their gift and hear the story of why he and Sam thought it would be perfect for them.

After an hour or so, Harry, Gray, and the men went out on the deck—with Tank in tow—to grill the chicken and enjoy some "man" talk. The girls stayed inside to set the table and talk.

The weather was perfect this time of year. August in Harmony, Wisconsin could sometimes be sweltering, but today it was a balmy eighty-three. He leaned on the rail of the deck next to Jamie, looking over the gardens when something caught his attention from the side of the house. He glanced over and saw Sam walking toward the SUV. He straightened as he watched her open the door and then close it, a small bag in her hand—the necklaces they'd purchased for Lily and Abby.

A phone rang. He recognized it as Tank's, but he only half listened as he watched Sam peek into the little blue bag, a soft smile on her face. She looped her fingers through the blue loop on the bag and began walking toward the house.

"When. How long?" Tank brusquely walked to the deck rail alongside him. He quickly ended his call and ran toward the edge of the garden.

Jamie yelled, "No. Stop her."

Gray spun his head and saw Cheryl running from the back of the gardens toward Sam. He took off running toward Sam, his heart racing, the blood rushing from his head as the glint of metal in Cheryl's hand caught his attention. Sam turned toward him, almost as if in slow motion, the smile slipping from her serene face then her eyes rounded a split second before he heard the loud bang.

He jumped and tackled Sam, and the two of them fell to the ground, a burning sensation in his chest as more banging rang out. He heard something crack and the breath whoosh from her lungs. The commotion behind him faded to the background as he realized Sam was struggling to breath. He rolled to his side, so he wasn't crushing her, and he groaned at the pain that shot through his body and took his breath away. He heard Sam yelling at him, calling his name.

She tugged his shirt and shook him—his mind was foggy. Sam began crying, and he saw blood on her hand as she brushed a tear from her eye. He looked into her eyes, but he couldn't say anything. He felt confused and suddenly very cold. Then, he felt nothing at all.

****

Oh no, no, no, no. What on earth happened? It felt like they laid there for a week. Gray wasn't moving. No one was coming to help him get up, what was happening? She shook Gray and tried talking to him. Her ribs hurt and she struggled to breathe and pain shot through her when she moved.

She shook him. "Gray, baby, wake up. Please, please wake up."

She felt something sticky on her hands and looked at her fingers over Gray's head. Blood! Oh, God, no ... Those were gunshots she'd heard! Panic seized her.

"Gray, please, please stay with me. Please don't make me live without you."

Sobbing Gray's name over and over, she begged him to wake up, to stay with her.

Finally, Tank was there taking Gray's pulse. Sam watched, horrified, as tears streamed down her face, praying that Gray would live. She begged God to keep him with her.

Shane slowly pulled her away from Gray so they could help him. She cried in pain as he moved her. Shane lifted her shirt and examined her, but she couldn't take her eyes from Gray's pale face. Tank pulled a first aid kit from the back of the SUV and was barking out orders to someone.

She heard crying from a distance but didn't know who it was. Soon sirens wailed and came close, then shut off. There were people all over the place—David was there, the police, the ambulance. Gray was surrounded by paramedics and she was pulled away and put on a stretcher, crying that she needed to be with Gray.

"Hey, I need you to calm down." She looked into Jamie's sad face. He brushed her hair away from her forehead and cooed softly to her.

"They're taking you both to the hospital. As soon as you're both checked over, you'll be together. Stay calm, Sam, so they can focus on Gray."

She nodded her head slightly; it was the only thing that didn't hurt. She turned her head to look over at Gray. They were running with him on a gurney toward the ambulance. Oh, my God, it must be bad. She began crying again, wincing in pain, but she couldn't help it. She could hear people talking to her, but she couldn't process what they were saying or who was saying it. Finally, she felt a kiss on her forehead.

"Mom, please calm down. They're taking you to the hospital with Gray. We're all right behind you, okay? We'll see you after you get checked out. Please stay calm so they can examine you."

37

SECOND CHANCES SERIES

"**M**rs. Kinkaide?"

She looked up and tried to stand, but the man shook his head no and held his hand up for her to stay sitting.

"I'm Dr. Dickson—Mr. Kinkaide's surgeon."

She smiled weakly. "How is he, Dr. Dickson?"

She had two broken ribs from Gray falling on her. It hurt to take a deep breath or to move, so she was trying to stay still and calm, but this waiting was killing her. She needed to see Gray and to know he was going to be okay.

"He's fine. The bullet hit him in the upper shoulder, glancing off his shoulder blade. It didn't travel past that point. Fortunately, the shot was from far enough away that as it hit his shoulder blade, it was already slowing down. Good thing it was dropping in height too; it could have hit him in the head."

Sam sucked in a sharp breath and was instantly sorry she did —ouch.

"No repairs were needed to his shoulder blade, but it will be sore for a few weeks. Tissue damage to the muscle around the shoulder blade was minimal, but enough that repairs were needed. He'll be able to move his shoulder normally after healing and therapy. We'll be doing some light therapy in a couple of days to keep his muscles from atrophy. His lung was pierced by a broken rib. That was repaired and he will be very sore for a while, but he's breathing on his own. Do you have any questions, Mrs. Kinkaide?"

She nodded. "When can I see him?"

Dr. Dickson leaned forward and smiled at her.

He patted her knee. "When he wakes up in recovery, he'll be taken to a private room. A nurse will come and get you at that time and take you to his room. I would say about forty-five minutes or so."

Mary sat to her left and rubbed her left shoulder as the doctor spoke with them. She was sure it served as a distraction for Mary and gave her something to do. She was grateful for the contact. They'd been separately whisked away by ambulance to the hospital, put through x-rays, and bandaged tightly. She insisted on waiting with the rest of the family and not being admitted to the hospital. The emergency doctor only agreed because she would be in the hospital waiting for Gray to come out of surgery, and if she needed anything at all, there was an ample supply of nurses and doctors to help her.

Jessie came to stand behind her and touched her other shoulder. The others in the room stood close to hear the doctor. Sam heard low voices and looked around to see all the family members there waiting for her. She was so grateful for these people.

The door opened, and David Haggerty walked through it. He was ashen and looked weary. He knelt in front of her. "I'm so damn sorry, Sam ... I failed you and Gray."

Her brows knit together. "David, you didn't fail us. Please don't feel that way. Thanks to Tank and Shane, Gray is alive."

David shook his head. "We knew it was a possibility that Cheryl would feel like she had nothing to lose. If we'd had more security at Harry and Mary's, we'd have seen her sooner. I'm so damn sorry, Sam. Have you heard anything? How is Gray?"

She nodded. "He's out of surgery and in recovery. He had a punctured lung, and the bullet hit his shoulder blade but didn't do serious damage. The doctor said he was lucky it was slowing down by the time it hit him. We can see him in a few minutes."

David nodded and stood. He kissed Sam on the temple and silently walked to the corner of the room to wait.

Soon the nurse walked in and told them they could go in and see Gray. She scooted to the edge of the chair and slowly stood with the assistance of Gage. She was afraid of what she might see; she felt weak and light headed. Mary and Harry walked with her, and Mary held and squeezed Sam's hand as they walked. When they entered Gray's room, tears streamed down her cheeks. He was so still and pale. Tubes and IVs ran from his strong arms. His heart beat was steady, and that was a plus.

She slowly made her way to the bed and touched his hand. He was lying on his back, but he was propped up by a foam, wedge-shaped pillow. The nurse explained that the pillow had a hole cut in it, like a donut, and his incision was laying inside the hole, so there wasn't any pressure on it. They needed to keep him elevated a bit for his lungs, and they didn't want him on his side, which would be more painful and not allow him to breathe properly. The nurse explained that they could visit for a bit, but he would be in and out of consciousness. They would also be getting him up and moving in a little while.

The nurse got her settled in a chair next to Gray's bed, with pillows behind her for support. She held his hand waiting for him to wake up. Mary and Harry walked around the other side of the bed and Mary held his other hand. The kids, Jamie, Dani, and others all gathered around and fit in where they could. Sam leaned her head back and closed her eyes for just a minute. The day was finally starting to catch up to her. All the adrenaline had left her body.

******

The soft murmur of voices was soothing. He could tell there was love in this room by the tone of the soft murmuring. He tried opening his eyes, but they felt like something was holding them closed. He tried to bring one of his hands up to rub his eyes, but they were held in place. He squeezed his hands just a little, and someone squeezed back.

"Gray, honey, we're all here for you."

His mom. Why was she here now? He couldn't remember what happened. Where was he anyway?

"Gray, baby, can you wake up? I need to look into your eyes and see you."

Sam! My God—Sam! Gray's heart began racing. Jesus! Cheryl was trying to kill Sam ... she had a gun. It was coming back to him. He opened his eyes, and there she was.

"Sam." His voice sounded like a frog, scratchy and hoarse.

"Hey, you need to calm down, baby. Your heart's racing. You're okay now. We're all here for you."

Gray studied the green eyes he loved so much. "You're okay?"

She smiled, and a tear raced down her cheek. "If I would have known marrying you would make you jump in front of a bullet, I wouldn't have married you. You scared the crap out of me, Gray. What the hell were you thinking?"

"I needed to save you. She was going to kill you. Come here and hug me."

She stood, slowly, trying hard not to wince or show any signs of discomfort.

"I can't lean down and hug you, but I can sit next to you."

She watched his face show concern—his brows furrowed and his mouth turned down.

"What happened?"

She shook her head and gave up trying to perch on the bed. "I'm okay. Just a couple of bruised ribs."

"Sam!" Mary admonished.

She sighed. "I have two broken ribs Gray, but I'm going to be just fine."

"I did that when I fell on you." He frowned. "I'm so sorry, Sam. I'm sorry I hurt you."

She let some breath out of her lungs. "Geez, Gray, you saved my life. I'm fine. You're the one who almost got himself killed."

Mary leaned in. "Gray, honey, how are you feeling?"

He looked over at his parents and the worry on their faces. "Not sure, a little groggy."

His mom nodded. He scanned the room, and his eyes landed on David standing in the back.

"Did you get her?"

David nodded. "Shane shot her. She's dead and won't bother either of you ever again."

Gray pressed, "Tell me what happened. I don't remember much."

David took in a deep breath. "Gray, I'm so damn sorry. We should have done more to protect you and Sam." His eyes were full of worry and remorse.

"We were standing on the deck, and you saw Sam walk out past the side of the house toward the SUV. Then you saw Cheryl run toward Sam. You took off at a run to get Sam. Cheryl must have realized her opportunity to shoot was closing up, and she shot at Sam just as you got to her. She shot you instead. I feel so bad about all of this. Please accept my apology."

He looked at Sam. She squeezed his hand.

"All that matters is that she's safe and we don't have to worry about Cheryl ever again. You did everything you could do, and we're so damned grateful." His voice sounded foreign to him. He licked his lips and tried clearing his throat. That sent a sharp pain searing through his body, and he gasped.

"Do you need something? All you can have is ice chips, but do you want some of those?"

He nodded. Mary took the bed control and raised his bed a fraction. She grabbed the cup with the ice chips and spoon in it and handed it to Gray. He winced when he tried to grab it with his left hand, but he did it anyway.

He slowly spooned a few ice chips into his mouth and lay back as he swirled them around wetting every surface he could. He looked at Sam and winked, wanting the worried look on her face to go away. Everything would be okay from this point forward.

38

S he settled Gray on the sofa with his laptop and the remote while she made lunch. He was stronger today than yesterday, but he still tired easily, which was normal after surgery. The anesthesia took a while to leave the body and even though he was in great shape at fifty-five years old, it just takes the body a bit longer to recover. Much to his frustration, he thought he should have been able to go to the office today. The shooting was just six days ago.

Sam looked over at Gray to see he'd fallen asleep with his laptop open and the remote in his hand. Poor thing, it hit him fast and— boom—he was out. She smiled as she watched him. They'd had quite the scare. She loved him beyond words. It was hard to believe how he had completely consumed her whole life in such a short time.

She admired his beautiful features in sleep—relaxed and resting. His hair was combed back, but a lock always fell forward on his fore-head. There was a dusting of gray at the temples, just enough to be sexy as hell and make him look distinguished. His full lips, a strong jaw, and a beautiful nose added to the list of all things beautiful about him. Her attention turned to his steady, deep breathing He didn't get much rest in the hospital because there were always people coming and going.

She continued cutting up some fruit to make Gray a fruit salad. She was keeping it light today—ham sandwiches. The kids said they would be stopping by sometime, so if they were all here, she would come up with something for dinner. She had been at the hospital with Gray for the past six days, so she hadn't been shopping. After finishing the fruit salad, she walked into the living room and sat at the other end of the sofa and gingerly laid down in a way that didn't hurt her ribs. She covered up with a blanket and fell asleep.

*****

Gray woke and glanced at Sam sleeping at the other end of the sofa. He smiled as he watched her. Thank God, he was able to keep her safe—he couldn't live without her. All these years he managed, but now that he knew what he'd been missing, he couldn't ever let her go. He moved to get up when the doorbell rang. Sam woke up and scooted to the edge of the sofa.

"No, baby, I've got it. I'm awake anyway."

He slowly stood and gently stretched before walking toward the door, a nervous twisting in his stomach as he neared. It was the first time they didn't have security there to check the visitors before opening the door. He looked at the computer screen on the wall and smiled as he swung the door open for Jake and Ali.

"Hello, come on in. We just woke from a nap," he greeted.

Jake and Ali walked in, hugged him then strolled over to Sam, as she stood.

She hugged them both. "Thank you for coming over."

"Mom, we wanted to see for ourselves that you guys were doing well. We also brought food. Everyone is coming and bringing something, so you don't have to cook." Jake set the bags of items they'd brought on the counter.

It wasn't long, and all the kids were there. They each brought something and sat around in the living room—on the sofa, the floor, the fireplace hearth—anywhere there was room. It was a fabulous afternoon and evening with their newly-blended family. They had blended quite well.

Of course, it was easier that they were all older and out of the house and didn't have to share their toys and rooms. Jax and Jake bonded together quickly. They had a bit in common, and at one point during the day, Jax asked Jake if he would like to come and work with him at the demolition company. Cole had recently joined the company, and they still needed one more. Jake and Ali looked at each other and smiled. Jake said he would stop in the office on Monday and talk to Jax about specifics and they'd go from there.

Around nine in the evening the kids began packing things up to leave. By nine-thirty, the door closed on the last kid. They both leaned against the door with smiles on their faces. Sam looked at him and smiled.

"Wow, that was really nice. Tiring, but nice."

He turned to her and wrapped his right arm around her. "This was meant to be. We both have great kids, and they can see it in each other as well. It doesn't mean it will always be smooth like it was tonight, but it should be reasonably peaceful."

He leaned down and kissed her. "Now, Mrs. Kinkaide, I need to make love to you."

"Gray, are you kidding? You don't want to hurt yourself."

He chuckled. "Sam, we can take it slow. I don't want to hurt *you* either, but I need to touch you. At least we can get naked and hold each other."

******

Monday brought their first day back at the office at Kinkaide & Associates. They were greeted by all the staff and told how happy they were that both were safe. Word traveled around the building quickly that they were there. The first hour didn't allow them to get much accomplished because of the warm greetings. Ethan walked in about an hour later wearing a huge grin. "Do you two have a minute? I'd like to show you something."

He nodded and glanced at Sam; she shrugged and stood. "Can you join me on the second floor?"

Ethan was unusually quiet as they followed him upstairs. He glanced at Sam once and shrugged.

When they arrived on the second-floor landing, Ethan looked back at them and smiled. "We've been working on this for a little while."

He opened the door, and they walked in. There were easels set up around the big open space, which only had the bookcases installed where the conference room would be. On the easels were drawings—beautiful drawings of a gorgeous office space. Ethan watched them walk around and study the drawings.

"Well?"

Sam looked over at Ethan. "Is this what this office will look like?"

Ethan smiled. "Of course, we can make any changes either of you wants, but we knew how hard you guys had been working on wedding plans, the fourth floor, getting the furniture refinished, and then the shooting. Anyway, we finished up the drawings without consulting you, as a surprise. What do you think?"

The pride he held in his son was not unlike any father's pride, but right now, he was so proud of Ethan he thought he'd burst. He stood unable to answer until he could control his emotions.

Sam walked toward Ethan, her smile bright. "These are great, Ethan. Wow, you've captured the furniture from upstairs, too. This will be a beautiful office space."

Ethan was proud. "Did you notice your offices?"

He pointed to an easel across the room by the windows. They walked over and inspected the drawing. It depicted a set of office suites next to each other with a doorway in each office opening to an adjoining bathroom they would share. The bathroom had a shower and separate toilet and sink area. There was also a small closet in the bathroom for hanging clothes. It was extravagant and beautiful.

"Wow, Ethan, this is fabulous, but why the shower and closet?"

Gray chuckled. "You mentioned that you wanted a work-out facility on the third floor, remember? You said you wanted everyone in the building to be able to work out whenever they had the chance. You thought it would lower our health insurance rates and we could bring in trainers to help employees with their specific needs and wants."

Ethan nodded. "We all thought it would be awesome to have that facility available to us. Most of us are in and out and visiting work sites and aren't able to make it to a traditional gym but want to stay in shape. The more we talked about your ideas, the more excited everyone got. We had a meeting while you guys were out and we networked and threw ideas out there on what we would like. The gym drawings are over in that corner."

He pointed to another easel with drawings on it. They walked over to the drawings of the gym and perused them.

"Oh Ethan, these are phenomenal. You did an impressive job with all of this. I'm speechless." Sam hugged Ethan. "Thank you so much for listening to what we said and working with it. I'm pleasantly stunned and awed."

Gray hugged Ethan as well. "I couldn't agree more, Ethan. Thank you so much for incorporating everything we've talked about. You're a remarkable architect, and I'm so proud of you. You're a great son as well as a great man."

Ethan's face filled with a huge smile. His chest puffed out a bit, and he grew just a bit taller.

They stayed at the office for a couple more hours before heading home to take a nap. They had plenty of time to work. Ethan and the others had taken care of his clients, and the remodeling on the second floor would start next week. Then they would tackle the third floor.

He had the wife he'd always dreamed of. They had a grandchild on the way from Jake and Ali. Sam often spoke about how she hoped Jessie and Jamie would end up marrying, but only time would tell.

Securing Kiera's Love, Book 2 of the Second Chances Series, is David Haggerty's love story with the one who got away, Kiera Donnelly. Find out why Kiera got away and if David can forgive her... Now available.

Get book #2 Securing Kiera's Love now.

ALSO BY PJ FIALA

Click here to see a list of all of my books with the blurbs.

Contemporary Romance

Rolling Thunder Series

Moving to Love, Book 1

Moving to Hope, Book 2

Moving to Forever, Book 3

Moving to Desire, Book 4

Moving to You, Book 5

Moving Home, Book 6

Moving On, Book 7

Rolling Thunder Boxset, Books 1-4

Military Romantic Suspense

Second Chances Series

Designing Samantha's Love, Book 1

Securing Kiera's Love, Book 2

Second Chances Boxset - Duet

Bluegrass Security Series

Heart Thief, Book One

Finish Line, Book Two

Lethal Love, Book Three

Bluegrass Security Boxset, Books 1-3

Big 3 Security

Ford: Finding His Fire Book One

Lincoln: Finding His Mark Book Two

Dodge: Finding His Jewel Book Three

Rory: Finding His Match Book Four

Big 3 Security Boxset, Books 1-4

GHOST

Defending Keirnan, GHOST Book One

Defending Sophie, GHOST Book Two

Defending Roxanne, GHOST Book Three

Defending Yvette, GHOST Book Four

Defending Bridget, GHOST Book Five

Defending Isabella, GHOST Book Six

RAPTOR

Saving Shelby, RAPTOR Book One

Holding Hadleigh, RAPTOR Book Two

ENJOY THIS BOOK? YOU CAN MAKE A BIG DIFFERENCE

Reviews are the most powerful tools in my arsenal when it comes to getting attention for my books. As much as I'd like to, I don't have the financial muscle of a New York publisher. I can't take out full page ads in the newspaper or put posters on the subway.

(Not yet, anyway.)

But I do have something much more powerful and effective than that, and it's something that those big publishers would die to get their hands on.

A committed and loyal bunch of readers.

Honest reviews of my books help bring them to the attention of other readers.

If you've enjoyed this book I would be so grateful to you if you could spend just five minutes leaving a review (it can be as short as you like) on the book's vendor page. You can jump right to the page of your choice by clicking below.

Thank you so very much.

FOLLOW PJ

Follow me!
Website
PJ on Facebook
Instagram
Bookbub
See inspiration photos on Pinterest

MEET PJ

Writing has been a desire my whole life. Once I found the courage to write, life changed for me in the most profound way. Bringing stories to readers that I'd enjoy reading and creating characters that are flawed, but lovable is such a joy.

When not writing, I'm with my family doing something fun. My husband, Gene, and I are bikers and enjoy riding to new locations, meeting new people and generally enjoying this fabulous country we live in.

I come from a family of veterans. My grandfather, father, brother, two sons, and one daughter-in-law are all veterans. Needless to say, I am proud to be an American and proud of the service my amazing family has given.

My online home is https://www.pjfiala.com.
You can connect with me on Facebook at https://www.facebook.com/PJFialaı,
and

Instagram at https://www.Instagram.com/PJFiala.
If you prefer to email, go ahead, I'll respond - pjfiala@pjfiala.com.